THE NECROMANCER'S END

THE NECROMANCER'S END

BOOK 1

Jack Pembroke

Podium

Podium

THE
NECROMANCER'S
END

CHAPTER ONE

We Got Ourselves a Mage!

Jeremiah gazed into a dark tunnel and imagined how it would feel to descend the slick steps into its depths. He could feel the air growing cooler and damper, wrapping him in the fertile scent of earth, his torch revealing stairs one by one as he crept toward the first landing of the dungeon. The very thought made the hairs on his arms stand up. Pain, terror, and even death could be lurking just past the twilight of the torch's influence.

He had explored several of the dungeon's tunnels already and had mapped as much as he could, but Jeremiah had not actually entered the dungeon at all. He had sent others to do the exploring for him, learning all that he could from each foray before his servants met their grisly ends. But he never spared any of them a single thought, never shed a tear, never contemplated their passing. For Jeremiah was a necromancer, and his servants had long since left their suffering behind.

It was a warm day, despite remnants of snow still clinging to shaded hollows underneath trees. Jeremiah had abandoned his heavy traveling cloak as the sun climbed. He leaned back on his rock and stretched, enjoying the afternoon rays on his face. The solitude of the clearing was picturesque—and he didn't have to worry about hiding his magic when he was alone.

Well, almost alone. Jeremiah turned to a fat gray toad sitting on a rock beside him. "Okay, Gus, whatever is down there has defenses of some kind. They're all getting killed at the same spot." He peered into his bag of dead rats, waving off the spring flies. He was running low. "I could try to find some larger animals to send down there. Or see if there's a graveyard nearby. What do you think?"

Gus, Jeremiah's familiar, didn't respond. He only lifted his head. Jeremiah obliged him by stroking his chin.

Jeremiah scanned the clearing. It was sizable, meant to accommodate the structure that had long since deteriorated to a few scattered flagstones. The reinforced door of the dungeon itself was set in the clearing's center like a cellar hatch. The forest encroached on all sides, the trees just beginning to bud with new growth.

He recalled the words of his old master: "Necromancy in practice is resource management. Do the absolute most with the absolute least." What resources did he have? A dwindling bag of dead rats, good for scouts and little else. The forest itself, filled with game that was out of reach, given Jeremiah's lackluster hunting ability. And his secret weapon, carefully packed away in his backpack. "Not yet. I still don't know what we're dealing with."

Jeremiah perked up at the crunch of underbrush. He leapt to his feet and unsheathed a dagger. The clearing was still. His hearing and vision sharpened, and he became aware of the silence that surrounded him. If he was lucky, it might be an animal he could kill and use. If he was unlucky, it could be any of the countless things in the world that would eat him alive.

A minute passed, and Jeremiah's worry grew. An animal would have moved by now. Whatever was out there was holding still because he was looking for it, and that realization made him tremble.

"Who's there?" Jeremiah shouted into the obfuscating greenery. "I warn you, I'm a mage! I just want to be left alone!"

The silence was oppressive. His eyes darted around, looking for an ambush. It felt like the trees were moving closer, every twitching leaf a potential attack. The icy claw of terror began to grip his heart.

A voice from the trees. "Stop panicking and look exactly where I tell you."

Jeremiah froze, his muscles so tight they hurt. He awaited further instruction, even while part of him felt shame at his obedience.

The voice spoke again. "Look a little to the right of where you're looking now . . . Higher, a little more . . . Stop! Now to the right. I'm going to move. Remember, do not panic."

Jeremiah was now staring into the dark upper reaches of a nearby tree. He saw nothing at first. Then a slow wave of motion revealed a figure aiming a bow at him.

"Don't panic!" the figure said. "I'm not going to hurt you if you just stand there and relax. But I promise, and listen now, I promise I *will* kill you if you do something stupid. You understand?"

Jeremiah tried to quell his fear by reminding himself that if the archer wanted him dead, he'd already be dead. It didn't work.

"Tell me you understand, or I'm going to shoot you through the leg."

"Yes!" said Jeremiah. "Yes, I understand! I'm not going to do anything."

"Two people are about to step out of the woods. They're my friends. Either of them could kill you as soon as look at you, so don't. You. Move.

A woman's voice said, "For fuck's sake, Bruno, he's got the idea."

The archer, Bruno, shouted back, "He said he was a mage! You want to take chances, be my guest, but don't expect any sympathy when your skin gets melted."

Jeremiah caught a glimmer of steel amid the trees, then a woman entered the clearing. She was tall and clad in full armor. In a moment, she crossed the distance to Jeremiah, twisted the dagger from his grip, and replaced the weapon with a firm handshake, smiling all the while. Her other hand gripped his shoulder. "Allison Allday, pleased to meet you."

"Jeremiah Thorn," said Jeremiah on reflex. She had disarmed him, introduced herself, and placed him in a controlling hold in the blink of an eye. *Oh dear*, he thought. *This woman is obscenely dangerous.*

A second woman appeared by Allison's side. Whereas Allison's very presence demanded attention, this woman seemed to disappear among the vials, jars, and pouches that adorned her, as if she were more shelf than person. Jeremiah spotted a slightly pointed ear under her hair—a half elf? She extended a hand. "Delilah Fortune."

Allison transferred Jeremiah's hand to Delilah's and stepped to his side. Her grip on his shoulder never slackened.

"Sorry for the theatrics," Allison said, nearly in his ear. "Bruno didn't think much of you till you said you were a mage. Can't be too careful where mages are concerned, can we?" She emphasized her point with a squeeze of his shoulder.

"No, no," said Jeremiah, turning his head to smile awkwardly at her. "I'm just glad you're not thieves."

Delilah's smile warmed, inching closer to genuine. She gave Allison's hand two quick taps, and the vise-like grip loosened. "Can I ask what brings you out here?"

Jeremiah looked back and forth between the two women. The tension and air of threat from Allison had diminished, though her hand still rested on his shoulder. "To be honest, I . . ." Jeremiah trailed off. If he told them about the dungeon, they might want whatever treasure was within for themselves. But then, if they were out this far, they were likely here for that very reason. "I heard there was an unexplored dungeon and came to make a go of it."

Allison finally released his shoulder and clapped him on the back. "Attaboy! That's why we're here too. Good on you for not trying to lie about it."

Jeremiah was stunned by her directness and struggled to find a response. He was saved by Bruno's arrival.

Everything about Bruno spoke of a hard, cutthroat life. His eyes were suspicious and cold, his bare arms covered in tattoos ranging from artistic to vulgar, and he moved with a tension like he was ready to sprint away at any moment. He stopped at a distance that would make a handshake awkward and instead nodded a greeting. "Bruno of Dock Road Two."

Jeremiah cocked a brow at the surname. Bruno gave him a look that said, "your assumptions are right, and you're not smart for figuring it out."

Bruno crossed his arms. "So! We have a problem. You're here for the dungeon, and so are we. How are we going to handle this, young man?"

Before Jeremiah could answer, Allison said, "No problem at all! We'd be foolish not to ask a mage to join us, wouldn't we?"

Delilah gave Jeremiah a studious look, then nodded. Bruno sighed but also gave a curt jerk of his chin.

Delilah began to speak quickly. "Jeremiah Thorn, will you join our party for this endeavor? We operate on an equal shares basis, with one share awarded to party treasury."

Jeremiah opened his mouth to speak, but Delilah continued.

"Upon the endeavor's completion, one quarter of the party treasury will be additionally awarded to you if we go our separate ways. Any member may purchase a found item from the party at its market cost, the amount paid to be divided among other party members. A caveat pertains to items that specifically and uniquely benefit one member at the sole discretion of the party. Agreed?"

They all stared at Jeremiah.

"Umm . . ." Jeremiah tried to remember everything she had said, then thought about what they might decide to do to him if they thought he was competition. "Okay, that sounds fair."

Allison whooped. "Hell yeah! We got ourselves a mage! Tents up, everyone! Bruno, give us a three-sixty scout. Delilah, get a trap on that dungeon entrance. Jay, get a fire going."

Allison's voice had such innate authority that Jeremiah barely noticed the shortening of his name. Coming from her, it sounded like it had always been his nickname.

Jeremiah watched them go. He turned to his familiar, who hadn't moved an inch in all the commotion. "This is bad, Gus," he said, bending to scoop up the toad. "It's good, yes. But it's very, very bad."

It was nearly dark by the time the campsite had been set up. Jeremiah busied himself with the fire as he tried to surreptitiously learn about his new companions.

Delilah poured a vial of thick amber liquid down the dungeon steps, which spread to leave a barely perceptible sheen. The handful of glass beads she scattered onto the stairs stuck immediately, as if they had been tossed into syrup. The layers of her robes clearly hid plenty of fascinating admixtures, but Jeremiah's eyes kept being drawn to the formidable longspear piled with her gear.

Bruno had disappeared into the forest to scout the perimeter. Jeremiah knew he wouldn't be spotted again until he decided to be.

Allison, for her part, had erected the tents with what Jeremiah could only describe as military efficiency. She used the rest of the time to inspect her equipment. The plate armor took most of her attention, but she also performed basic upkeep on her longsword, steel shield, and battle-axe. Jeremiah couldn't help but notice that these tasks were routine enough to allow her to maintain a watchful eye on him.

The group gathered around the fire just as Jeremiah finished building it. "We're clear," said Bruno, tossing his shortbow aside. He unhooked the pair of shortswords from his belt and carefully lay them to either side of his sleeping bag. "Our escape route is east. If east is cutoff, we go north."

Delilah rolled her eyes as she shed layer after layer of stiff leather strips. "What if they come at us from all directions?" she asked with a knowing smile.

"We say that you're a princess and offer you as a hostage," Bruno said, without a hint of humor.

"What? I can't be the princess?" Allison said.

"I've never seen a princess with calluses like yours, so no," Bruno said. He still sounded completely serious.

"I think Bruno should be the princess," said Delilah. "He's daintier than either of us."

Jeremiah chewed his own day's ration slowly as he listened to their effortless banter. He felt more isolated in the presence of their camaraderie than he did when he was alone. He recognized the urge to try to participate in their friendly jesting and quashed it. *I'll join them for the dungeon, earn whatever treasure I can, and then get as far away as possible.* He knew from experience just how friendly they would be if he let slip that he was a necromancer.

"Jay, tell us what you know about the dungeon so far," said Allison, startling Jeremiah back to the present.

Jeremiah fished a single scrap of parchment from his bag. "It's not great, but it gives you an idea of the layout."

Allison's face flickered with a hint of a frown as she looked at the map. Only a few lines were drawn, showing two dead ends and a third continuing into the unknown. "Why only this far?" she asked.

Jeremiah had thought of only one good answer to this question. "I got scared."

Bruno hung his head and laughed. "Oh, that's adorable."

"It's smart." Allison took a swig from her waterskin. "Fear is an instinct to be heeded. There's no such thing as an 'easy dungeon.' Always be prepared to fight for your life. More than a few adventurers should have 'They're just kobolds' written on their tombstones."

Jeremiah nodded sagely, grateful that his timidity had been labeled as wisdom.

"What sort of magic do you practice?" asked Delilah.

Jeremiah's pulse quickened as he prepared to lie again. "Conjuration, but I'm not very good yet." Necromancy and conjuration had similar effects at low levels. Any mage worth their salt could perform a handful of simple universal spells, and this group looked competent enough that he hoped those would be all he needed.

"Is there anything else about your abilities we should know?" asked Allison. Jeremiah fought the urge to squirm under her penetrating gaze.

"Hmm . . . Oh! I forgot to introduce Gus." Jeremiah pulled the toad from his robes and lifted him for the others to see. "This is Gus. As my familiar, he is magical, more intelligent than a normal toad, and very important to me. Please be careful around him."

Bruno studied the creature as though memorizing its features, then locked eyes with Jeremiah and nodded once.

Delilah's eyes lit up. She leaned close and inspected Gus with intense curiosity. "That's a blue-spined swamp toad! Mind if I take a venom sample? They're so rare; I'd love to have a look at its properties."

Jeremiah allowed himself to feel flattered by her excited bounce. This was the most interest anyone had ever shown in Gus. "Sure! Be careful, though; being a familiar strengthens his venom's potency."

Delilah's expression shifted to awe. "A dose of blue-spine venom is already strong enough to paralyze three men!" With utmost care, she produced a metal loop and pressed down on Gus's back, exposing a blue-tinted spine. She coaxed several drops of a clear, viscous liquid into a glass vial. She swirled the vial and peered at it in the firelight. Then she thanked Gus with a stroke under the chin.

Jeremiah withdrew into his thoughts while the others chatted among themselves. He hoped the dungeon would yield enough wealth to get him a few nights at the local inn. It was safer in the wilderness, away from people, but he was becoming desperate for a real meal and bath.

Allison soon declared it was time to sleep. Jeremiah, wanting to be helpful, offered to take the first watch.

Bruno barked a terse laugh. "No offense, but I would rather take a full night's watch myself than have us all asleep around a mage we just met."

Jay couldn't argue with that. Then he wondered whether he was being too trusting himself but decided that if they wanted to kill him, it wouldn't much matter if he were awake for it or not.

As he settled back into his sack, he allowed himself to feel a little excited. Tomorrow he'd be delving a dungeon alongside powerful adventurers. He had dreamed of this since he was a boy! What child didn't? But he was also afraid, and not just of what dangers might be lurking underground. If they learned what he could do . . .

Jeremiah pushed the thought aside. All he had to do was not perform any necromancy. He'd make a few silver and be on his way to Barad Celegald. Or maybe River's Run? Or even the great city of Dramir . . . On the wings of imagined riches, Jeremiah drifted to sleep.

The next morning, the party prepared in near silence. Jeremiah suspected there was a graveness with which one should approach a dungeon delve. After stretching routines and a light breakfast, Allison and Bruno worked together to assemble her armor. Delilah layered herself in leather and fabric. Jeremiah donned a billowing black robe. It offered a modicum of protection, but its real purpose was to allow him to perform complex gestures, hide various components, and provide a safe place for Gus.

He hoisted his pack and felt the secret cargo inside shift. Allison paused in her armor assembly to address him. "Ask yourself right now—'Do I *need* what's in this bag?'"

"Yes," said Jeremiah, with solid conviction.

Allison nodded. "All right, I trust you."

They gathered at the dungeon entrance and Delilah used the butt of her spear to break one of the glass beads. The stairs burst into a blazing white fire so bright, Jeremiah had to turn his head, the intense heat shocking him as much as the flash.

Allison slapped a leather cap onto Jeremiah's head, buckling it in place. "Keep Bruno and me in front of you, Delilah behind you. I don't know your magic, so I'm trusting you to act as you see best. Stay in formation unless I say otherwise. Warn us if you're about to do something that could affect us. Focus on magic and keeping your eyes and ears open." Then she wrapped her hand around the back of his head with a reassuring grip. She leaned forward and touched her forehead to his, holding his gaze. "I can tell you haven't done this before," she whispered. "We'll protect you, but be safe. No heroics."

Jeremiah swallowed at the intensity of her proximity, but he appreciated her words. He nodded and she released him.

Allison moved to the head of the party and turned to face them. Suddenly, that dangerous woman from the day before was back. The sun broached the tops of the trees, washing his companions with a golden glow. They glanced back toward Jeremiah.

They look . . . heroic. Jeremiah took a deep breath, reminding himself of the helmet Allison had put on him to protect his skull. That thought sobered him up. He nodded to the three of them and drew his dagger.

"Good?" asked Allison.

"Good," said Bruno and Delilah.

Jeremiah's stomach swooped. "Good," he managed.

"Let's delve this dungeon," Allison growled, and led them into the depths Jeremiah had only dreamed of.

CHAPTER TWO

First Contact

Allison moved down the long hallway behind her shield. As the light from the entrance dimmed, Bruno whispered from behind Allison, "Hold. Delilah, eyes."

Delilah produced two tiny flasks and reached forward, past Jeremiah, to hand them to Bruno. Jeremiah saw they had forgotten there was an extra body between them now. He resolved to make himself worth bringing along.

Bruno shared one flask with Allison, then upended the flask's contents directly into his eyes. He sucked air through his teeth and got back into his ready position.

"Clear ahead," he said. "Good to move."

As they began to move again, Delilah whispered to Jeremiah, "Night Eye tonic, helps see in the dark. Don't shine a light in their eyes."

Jeremiah whispered, "Why not just make a light? I can do that if you want."

Allison answered from the front, "A light means anyone can see us coming a mile away. Delilah watches the back; Bruno watches the front."

"Oh," said Jeremiah. "What about me?"

Without hesitation, Allison said, "Delilah, eyes Jay."

A firm hand pulled Jeremiah's head back till he was looking at the ceiling, then a cold liquid poured into his eyes. He gritted his teeth against the sting and tried to stay quiet as the hand released him. He bent over and rubbed his eyes. When he blinked again, he marveled at the effect: what had been pitch black moments before was now bright as day, though colors were muted.

His rat scouts had relayed only the most basic of information—scurry, turn right, death. Now he saw the dungeon with his own eyes. The cobble under their feet had been worn smooth over the centuries, and the halls were wide enough that Jeremiah could imagine small carts being wheeled up and down the sloping floor. The air was cool and musty, undisturbed by the years, although Jeremiah thought he could sense a rancid edge emanating from farther down. The stone-brick walls exaggerated the smallest sound, making up for an age of silence.

Jeremiah shivered. They were really doing this.

They crept deeper and deeper, hearing only their own footsteps. Soon, Bruno called a halt and inched ahead of Allison to inspect something on the ground.

"Rat skeleton," he said. "Picked clean and smashed."

He looked up and farther down the hall.

"Couple of them. Weird."

Jeremiah knew these rat skeletons well. His pulse quickened as they approached the defenses that had destroyed so many of his scouts.

They heard soft footsteps a moment before a small form appeared around the corner ahead—a goblin! It clutched a crudely made sword, standing only as tall as Jeremiah's waist. Its large eyes widened as it pointed a clawed hand toward the party and screeched an alarm.

The goblin died mid-screech with Bruno's arrow in its skull, but the damage was done. The staccato of multiple pairs of feet emanated from the hall ahead, accompanied by a growing hiss.

The goblins shrieked as they charged around the corner—three, five, eight, soon more than Jeremiah could count. They swung their swords overhead and launched at the party with reckless abandon.

Bruno's arrows flew with deadly accuracy, dropping the lead goblins to the floor. The rest of the goblin pack trampled their bodies without slowing.

"*Siege!*" shouted Allison. She knelt and planted her shield against the ground, angling it toward herself to direct blows upward.

Delilah pushed Jeremiah aside to make room for her spear, reaching past Allison. She braced to meet the charging swarm.

The goblins crashed against Allison's shield, attempting to spill around it to reach the blood they were craving. Delilah's spear impaled two with a powerful thrust. Bruno dropped his bow in favor of twin shortswords and began hacking at goblins spilling around Allison's other flank.

Jeremiah gaped at the efficiency of the bloodbath. There seemed to be nothing for him to do.

More goblins poured around the corner to meet their end on the party's formation. They crawled over each other to try to breach Allison's defenses. Small dull hatchets and swords hacked at her armored legs before they were cut down by Bruno or Delilah.

"*Sallying out!*" roared Allison. She shoved against her shield, toppling the goblins piling onto it, then brought her sword around in a wide sweep. Her blade never slowed as it passed through goblin after goblin.

The goblin offensive stalled while they struggled to time their attacks in between Allison's swings, only to find her vulnerable moments were covered by Bruno and Delilah. A few blows landed on Allison's legs and feet, and she swore at the more solid hits, but her armor held . . . for the most part.

Jeremiah's reverie at the carnage was broken when a goblin hatchet connected with Allison's leg. He heard her cry out, saw the blade come back slick and red, and snapped into action.

His master had forced him to drill relentlessly, casting the same spells over and over again until he was at risk of casting them in his sleep. All for a moment like this. Without hesitation, Jeremiah spoke ancient words that, with the proper will, could alter reality itself. He gestured his hand forward, angled toward the ceiling beyond Allison, and from his outstretched palm flew a congealed ball of deep green acid.

The acid splashed against the ceiling and rained down on the goblin horde. The goblins screamed as the acid sizzled through their flesh.

"*Oh, hell yes!*" Allison said, and pressed ahead. Those goblins not killed by the acid rain were cleaved down in moments as she pressed forward in strong, controlled steps.

Delilah shouted into Jeremiah's ear over the screeches of the goblins, "Again on three!"

"*One!*" Something flew past Jeremiah's head far back down the hall, into the crowd of goblins.

"*Two!*" There was a flash, a bang, and a rush of air as fire erupted into the hallway, immolating a group of goblins. Those beyond the fire backed away, but those closer to the party crammed tightly together, their fear of the flames driving them to clamber over one another.

Jeremiah cast his spell just as Delilah shouted "*Three!*" and once again, it rained acid, this time into the densely packed goblin mass. Their screams were deafening. Jeremiah reeled at the stench of so much melting flesh. The farthest goblins fled, while any who survived the acid were cut down by Allison. Bruno kicked his bow up into his hands and began loosing arrows after the retreating goblins, dropping one after the other until they had all disappeared.

The entire fight lasted only moments. Allison finished off the last few and stood atop her conquered foes, drenched from head to toe in blood and drawing deep, controlled breaths. There was silence but for the sound of their panting.

"Heh." Bruno gave an uneasy laugh. "Hehe! Hahaha!"

The break in tension was contagious, and soon all four of them were whooping and hollering in their victory. "That," shouted Bruno, "was fucking spectacular! Raining acid? That was the most heinous thing I've ever seen!"

Jeremiah took it as a compliment, heady with giddiness at his first combat victory. Then he remembered the event that had inspired his attack. "Allison! Are you all right? I saw you take an axe to the leg!"

Allison raised her visor and grinned. "Psh, flesh wound. Let me show you my scar collection sometime. I've got some that put Bruno's nicest tattoos to shame."

They laughed, but Delilah insisted on inspecting the wound. The axe had left a shallow gouge between the armor plates on Allison's thigh.

"Superficial, but it's likely to get infected," said Delilah. "We're better off taking care of it now." She wiggled a small unguent bottle at Allison.

Allison nodded and showed only the smallest of tics as Delilah used her fingers to push the milky white unguent into the wound. Jeremiah noticed Bruno turn away and pretend to keep watch. When she was done, Allison shifted her weight onto the wounded leg and grunted. "It's better. Thanks, Delilah."

Jeremiah's relief was cut short by the echoes of more goblin screeches from up ahead.

"All right," said Allison with grim authority, "we're moving on. These goblins don't have anything we want."

Jeremiah gazed at the exposed skull of a dead goblin, its flesh melted off by the acid. "No," he sighed, "I guess they don't."

Jeremiah marveled as they continued on. The party had just endured a potentially deadly ordeal, and now they were carrying on like nothing had happened. A smile bloomed on his lips as he thought of the praise he had received from companions. In his first life-or-death fight, not only did he survive, but he did a damn good job! Maybe he really could be a useful ally, even without undead.

The hallway began to curve downward, the air chilling further as they descended. Spatters of blood on the ground marked the goblins' retreat, alongside a few goblins that had succumbed to their wounds.

The hallway leveled off into a wide corridor with large alcoves left and right. "Ah, storage," said Bruno. "Was wondering what this place used to be."

Jeremiah peered into one of the hollows and imagined it loaded with crates of dried food, hogshead barrels of wine, and stacks upon stacks of cheese.

"They used to hang salted meats down here," said Delilah, pointing to long metal runners in the ceiling. "Must have been a real fancy place upstairs."

"Hey, Al," Bruno said, "this place might be bigger than we thought."

"Could be," said Allison, focused on her slow march forward.

There was a pregnant pause before Bruno spoke again. "That was an awful lot of goblins for a front guard. Should we consider whether this place is a Warren?"

"It's crossed my mind," said Allison without looking up. "If anyone wants to make the call that this is a Warren, say so and we bail right now."

There was a bit of nervous shifting, but no one explained. Jeremiah felt compelled to ask, "What's a Warren? How is it different from . . . whatever it's normally not?"

Bruno answered, "Goblins normally live in Hollows. They're led by a chieftain or whoever can keep them in line. They breed like rabbits, and they go from infant to dangerous in less than a year."

"If left unchecked," continued Delilah, "the population will continue to grow, assuming enough space and resources. After the Hollow reaches a certain size, one of the females will transform into what's called a Matriarch. Massive, powerful, and, worst of all, she exerts a kind of mental control over the other goblins. They become meaner, more organized. She can also breed even faster than normal females. That's when a goblin problem really gets out of hand—you can get hundreds, or even thousands, of them. That's why it's important to take care of Hollows quickly, before they can develop into Warrens."

"So if this *is* a Warren . . ." Jeremiah said, guessing he knew the answer.

"If this turns out to be a Warren," said Allison, "you turn, you run, you don't stop running till you're miles away and in a fortress."

Delilah shuddered. "My teacher's sister's husband was part of the Red Ridge Mountain group."

Bruno glanced back. "Seriously?" Seeing Jeremiah's confusion, he explained. "Bunch of damn-near-legendary adventurers delved the Red Ridge Mountain Warren. They had mages, healers, warriors, specialist spelunkers, the whole lot. The only guy who came back was one of the porters. He said it was some kind of *super* Warren that had hundreds of thousands of goblins. That place is still active, isn't it, Allison?"

Allison frowned. "Technically, in that no one has cleared it out and killed the Matriarch. But it's been years since anyone has encountered more than a couple of goblins out there. Some people say a plague must have wiped them out, but these things live in absolute squalor and almost never get sick, so I doubt it."

"I think there was a catastrophic collapse," said Delilah. "See, the Red Ridge Mountain geological zone is notori—"

"Quiet," said Allison, raising her hand. She cocked her head, listening to the depths.

Jeremiah strained his hearing. After a few moments, he became aware of a low grinding emanating from the darkness below them. Was it growing louder?

"Let's go," Allison said, checking each alcove they passed for lurking goblin ambushes.

They left the storage corridor behind to continue their descent through the cool stone passages. Allison's wariness ratcheted ever higher as the grinding grew louder. Jeremiah found his eyes fixating on every shadow as though it were a goblin sneaking up on them in the low din.

Allison stopped so suddenly that Jeremiah ran into Bruno in front of him. "Get ready," Allison growled, setting her sword and shield.

Ready for what? Jeremiah didn't dare ask as the grinding echoed up the stonework, now unmistakably moving toward them.

Out of the darkness beyond the range of Jeremiah's Night Eyes materialized an enormous wooden wall, advancing inexorably on their position. It filled the square corridor completely. There wasn't even space for Delilah's spear to poke around the top or sides. Jeremiah's jaw dropped as the wall rumbled toward them, seemingly heedless of the adventuring party in its path. Then he realized the wall's surface was bristling with crossbows. As the wall closed on their position, crossbow bolts began to pelt Allison.

The party ducked as Allison angled her shield to protect them from the volley. She exchanged her sword for the battle-axe at her side. "I'll breach. *Cover me!*"

Allison launched herself the last dozen feet toward the wall, Bruno and Delilah falling into step to cover her flanks. Jeremiah stared after them for a split second before urging his feet to follow. He wasn't sure how he could help, but he did not want to be left behind.

Allison reared back as she neared the wall and swung her axe against the wood with a battle cry. Several small windows opened as her blade rebounded, and a riposte of spears and daggers thrust at her armor. Allison spun away and Delilah drove her spear into an open window, withdrawing it covered in blood. Bruno loosed a few arrows, but the windows closed as soon as Allison was beyond reach.

Jeremiah shouted, "Acid!" and launched an acid ball over the party's head to splatter against the wall. Allison raised her shield against the splash, but the ball of acid merely slid off the wood without so much as marring its engraved surface.

"It's been alchemically treated!" shouted Delilah.

Allison swung her axe again and again but was barely able to cut splinters from the wood. Each attack left her open to the stabs of the wall's defenders. Jeremiah could hear the goblins behind the wall chittering with excitement and cheering with each successful breach of Allison's armor.

A daring set of hands waited for Allison's swing and seized her shield, pulling her against the door. As Allison braced her foot on the wall to yank it free, a cruel blade sank deep into the underside of her knee. Allison screamed as the blade twisted, then brought her axe down and severed the attacking arm. With a final wrench she was able to free her shield, but as she tried to adopt her stance, her leg gave way. She dropped to a knee with a grunt.

A triumphant shriek from behind the party filled Jeremiah's heart with dread. He turned in seemingly slow motion to see a single goblin (*How did we miss him?*) plunge a lit torch into a small barrel. An instant later, an explosion immolated the goblin and spread toward them, flaming oil engulfing their only avenue of retreat. The goblins behind the wall cheered, and it began closing in on the party again.

"Ideas?" shouted Bruno. His continuous stream of arrows helped dissuade the small windows from opening but did nothing against the advance of the wall.

Allison raised her shield and slammed against the wall, trying to brace her good leg against the smooth cobble floor. Immediately, knives and spears appeared, looking to punish any gap in her armor. Delilah thrust her spear toward the attackers' windows, only to have them snap shut and reopen again like a macabre festival game.

Jeremiah began to cough as the oily smoke filled the hallway. Delilah had abandoned her spear and was frantically combining vials. Bruno was pressed against Allison's back to help her push against the wall. But it was gaining on them, shoving them back toward the flames an inch at a time. Jeremiah shied away from the heat of the flames, trying to breathe through the sleeve of his robe as he began to cough harder. They were all beginning to choke on the smoke, which stirred something in Jeremiah's memory.

He hurried through the words of power in between coughing fits, puffed out his cheeks, and blew. A cloud of yellow gas emanated from his mouth and settled on the floor.

Jeremiah shouted, "Hold your breath!" He blew again and again, willing more of the yellow gas into existence. It billowed across the floor, seeping past the edges of the wall. The victorious shrieks from behind the wall turned to coughing and became strangled and wet. Jeremiah continued casting.

Finally, the goblins' coughs gave way to chokes of pain. The pressure on the wall relented. Jeremiah quickly conjured a counterspell, his lungs crying out for oxygen. The yellow gas around their knees began to dispel slowly, far too slowly. Jeremiah resisted as long as he could before collapsing to his knees, gasping for air.

Jeremiah blinked, realizing he must have blacked out for a moment. His throat burned from the residual gas, but it had not reached his lungs. He continued gulping down air, relishing the relief it brought. Behind him, the *whoosh* of a mini windstorm snuffed out the remains of the fire as Delilah finished her admixture and tossed it onto the flames.

There was no laughter with this victory. Jeremiah rolled onto his back, still panting, barely aware of the rest of the party taking stock of their wounds and equipment. Eventually, Bruno appeared overhead, offering a hand. He pulled Jeremiah to his feet.

"Brilliant," Bruno said, slapping him on the shoulder. "Even better than the last one. Can't wait to see what you pull out next."

Jeremiah gave a weak grin. "I'm just glad it turned out that gas wasn't flammable."

Bruno's hand fell away. "Me too."

"We should just have you fill the rest of the dungeon with gas," said Allison. "Would save us a hell of a lot of work."

Jeremiah shook his head. "Can't. That would take way too much focus."

"Focus?" asked Allison. "Like, you'll get bored?"

"Not quite. Casting takes a massive amount of directed willpower. After a big spell or too many small ones, it gets harder to will things to happen. Like reading a very boring book—eventually you just can't force yourself to concentrate on it anymore. Or on anything, really. Once your focus burns out, it becomes tough to differentiate what's important from anything that just catches your attention."

"As someone who has read a lot of boring books," said Delilah, "I now fully understand magic and am ready to begin my training."

"I'm terrified to think of this party with two mages," said Bruno with a mock shudder. Jeremiah laughed but at the same time felt touched at Bruno's wording including him in the party. "How's our girl?" Bruno asked, turning to Allison.

"She's all right," said Delilah. "It could have been a lot worse if a ligament had been cut. I put a healing accelerant on it for now and numbed the area. It'll be okay by tomorrow, but don't overexert yourself." She spoke the last words with a touch of sternness.

Allison shifted weight onto the leg with the merest of grimaces and nodded. "Fuck, that hurt. That was actually a new place to get stabbed for me." She began moving gingerly through a series of combat stances. "More importantly, though, what the hell is alchemically treated wood?"

Delilah's eyes widened. She darted over to the wall where it still blocked the corridor and began inspecting it. She scratched it, smelled it, listened as she tapped on it, touched her tongue to it, even produced a metal file and, with effort, managed to scrape off some shavings.

"This," she said, turning toward them, her face bright, "is Ironwood! Strong enough normally but has received further alchemical resistance treatments as well! *And* it's over four inches thick!" This conclusion she announced with a flourish.

Bruno crossed his arms. "I know Ironwood is rare, and alchemically treated sounds interesting, but how do we get past this thing?"

"Get past it? Oh, no, no, no!" Delilah gestured toward the wall as if revealing a work of art. "This is a custom-built fortress door! These little windows are for repelling attackers, as we saw. The workmanship is excellent, and the treatment is top notch. Lady and gentlemen, this thing is worth a lot of money! Especially to whoever had it commissioned!"

Jeremiah felt Delilah's enthusiasm tug at the corners of his own mouth. "How much are we talking?"

"No way to know for sure until we get it appraised and see if we can find the original client. But if we manage to take it back to Dramir, we could be looking at *quite* a bit."

Bruno clapped his hands together and rubbed them. "Now you're talking! Grab some rope and let's get it out of our way for now. Then we'll just push it back out the entrance when we leave!"

The other three gave Allison a break and spent quite a while rotating the door flush against the wall. Despite being on small wheels, the immense door had required several dozens of goblins to move it, and Jeremiah felt nearly as exhausted after the effort as he had immediately after casting the gas.

Delilah continued to run her fingers over the Ironwood's surface, admiring different aspects until Allison barked at her to get back into marching order. Energized by their victory and the promise of future wealth, the party delved deeper into the dungeon.

CHAPTER THREE

Desperate Times

Allison led them farther, prepared at every turn for an attack that did not come. Jeremiah's anxiety had been sharpened to an edge of excitement. He and his companions had faced death twice and had overcome the challenge. He had contributed. He was part of the team. A small seed of trust was starting to germinate, the roots tickling inside his chest. Then he stepped over another dead goblin and remembered that such friendships were impossible for a necromancer. He pressed on.

The corridor ended in a large stone door, hewn from the rock itself. Allison gestured with her sword, and Bruno, crouched low to the ground, moved like a shadow toward the door, pausing frequently to listen or inspect the floor. Upon reaching the door, he spent several long moments scrutinizing it, its handles, hinges, and edges, before reaching into a pouch and producing a small metal cone. He touched the mouth of the cone against the door, his ear close to the hole at the narrow end.

The group waited in total silence. Jeremiah's heartbeat thudded in his ears. He became all too aware of the metallic scent of blood covering Allison's armor. He checked on Gus and found him in good health, nestled deep in the most protected pocket of his robes.

At last, Bruno returned, this time rather more like a man than a shadow. "Quiet as a tomb in there, and the door isn't trapped or locked. I can feel airflow, though, so I think the room on the other side is sizable. But, goddamn, does it stink."

Allison nodded and Bruno began the painstaking process of opening the door, one inch at a time, scanning for any sign of trap or alarm. Then it was fully open.

The room was enormous, stretching beyond the range of their Night Eyes in all directions. The smell was pervasive and thick, a carrion stench that coated Jeremiah's tongue and seeped down his throat.

Allison peered into the darkness. "Can one of you make more light?"

Jeremiah and Delilah nodded together. Jeremiah conjured a ball of white light that hovered near his shoulder, casting a soft glow around the party. Delilah pulled out a thin glass tube and twisted it, cracking a seam in the middle. It flared almost blindingly bright, illuminating the space for at least a hundred feet in all directions.

The light revealed row after row of massive stone columns. Piles of refuse towered like sentinels all around them—bones, broken furniture, rags, animal carcasses, weather-beaten tools and weapons. The detritus was punctuated by wooden beams and large stones that must have crumbled from the ceiling high above.

After the claustrophobic press of the hallways, stepping into this space should have been liberating. Instead, it squeezed them tighter. Angular, alien shadows swarmed around them as they swung their lights, seemingly waiting for the chance to leap upon them.

"What is this place?" asked Jeremiah.

"No clue," said Delilah. "I can't imagine the purpose of a room this big, so deep underground. The fact that it exists at all is a marvel of engineering."

They ventured farther into the room, heads on a swivel. The stench grew stronger, adopting an acidic tinge that stung their nostrils.

Bruno's expression turned to disappointment as he took a closer look at some of the refuse. "I'm not seeing anything that looks like treasure. There can't be much more to this place, can there?"

Allison scanned the room, but before she could answer, a sound like rocks being crushed reverberated around the room. She whirled, ready to sprint for the exit. "Cave in?!"

They spun, looking for signs of falling debris. A movement caught Jeremiah's eye.

One of the massive boulders heaved and rolled across the floor, great wooden timbers caught in its wake, and shuddered to a stop. The boulder began to rise, and Jeremiah finally recognized it for what it was.

Towering over them was a titanic creature, nearly eighteen feet tall. It had hands the breadth of wagon wheels at the end of long, flabby arms. In its wicked nails, it clutched a decomposing body in crushed armor, still clinging to a sword and shield. The creature's gray, blubbery flesh oozed with boils and sores. But the sight that struck terror into Jeremiah's heart was its head—a grotesque version of a goblin's face, stretched to fit red bulbous eyes and teeth as long as daggers.

Jeremiah stammered as those horrible eyes bulged down at him. He stumbled backward, unable to look away, and managed only a strangled whimper to alert the others.

"A Matriarch," whispered Delilah, her voice filled with terror and awe.

"Get to the door, *now*!" Allison shouted.

They ran for the exit. The entire room shook as the Matriarch gave chase on elephantine legs, triggering avalanches of refuse. The party darted around protrusions of timbers and tangles of rotted rope that attacked their ankles. The Matriarch bellowed, so close that Jeremiah felt the wind and the heat of her rancid breath. The roar rang through his thoughts, driving any sense from them.

"She's summoning the Warren!" yelled Delilah.

The ancient door still hung ajar. As they hurtled toward it, lights began to appear beyond it. The tunnel flickered and danced with the silhouettes of hundreds of tiny forms rushing toward them, their wrathful screeches like steel scraping against steel.

Bruno suddenly planted a foot and rammed his shoulder into Jeremiah. Jeremiah stumbled against a pile of splintered boards, then felt a *whoosh* as the Matriarch's decayed warrior flew past and smashed into the stone wall beside the door.

"*Delilah!*" shouted Allison. "Burn that hallway! Give it everything you've got! When we reach the door, we turn and kill this thing!"

Allison's orders were suicide, but the authority of her voice was a comfort. At the wall, Bruno and Jeremiah turned, seeing that Allison had stopped earlier to interpose herself between them and the Matriarch as the massive creature plowed through the debris in her path. Delilah continued through the doorway and began heaving bottle after flask after box as fast as she could down the hall. Then she darted back into the room and slammed the door shut, just as a roar of flame drowned out the shrieks of pain. A bright white glow shone through the gaps in the door, but beyond it, the furious screeching soon rose again.

The Matriarch let out another roar as she lumbered toward Allison. Jeremiah recognized the large wooden square suspended from her neck like an oversized necklace to cover her chest. "It's more Ironwood! She's made armor out of it!"

Bruno began loosing arrows at the Matriarch, aiming for her face and neck. They stuck into her skin like needles, but she didn't seem to notice. Then a shot connected with her bulbous eye. The Matriarch clutched her hand over it and roared. Her advance staggered. Blood and other fluids ran down her face, and her screams of pain turned to rage.

"Listen." The stoic calm in Allison's voice cut through Jeremiah's panic. "She dies before those fires go out, or we're done. Fight like a wolf pack: surround her and attack when she's not focused on you. We can do this!"

Jeremiah willed his feet to follow Allison's orders, but it was as though he were rooted to the floor. He watched as Bruno and Delilah fanned out to either side, and to his horror, Allison raised her shield and countercharged the Matriarch.

When they met, the Matriarch swung her fist so hard that the blow exploded stones from the floor. Allison, however, had already twirled to avoid the blow and close the remaining distance. She slashed her sword up the Matriarch's arm before plunging it hilt-deep into her prodigious belly.

Delilah rushed in at an angle to thrust her spear into the Matriarch's stumpy leg, driving her down to a knee. Bruno continued his barrage of arrows, searching for the second eye.

The Matriarch was stunned for only a moment. She stood, dragging Delilah across the stone floor as she clung to the spear. The Matriarch yanked the weapon from her leg and from Delilah's grasp with a growl and a spray of thick dark blood and swung it at Delilah like a switch, snapping the shaft.

Allison used the distraction to thrust her sword into the Matriarch's hip, penetrating the outermost layers of fat. Bruno abandoned his empty quiver to leap onto the Matriarch's back, digging a shortsword into her side for grip. The Matriarch howled and swatted at him. Bruno dodged the massive hand, pulling himself up farther to hack at the heavy ropes around her neck.

The Matriarch spun with surprising speed, causing Bruno to lose his grip on his sword, and threw him unceremoniously from her back to land in a heap of rotting meat some distance away. In the same motion, she caught Allison with a backhand that sent her sprawling. Jeremiah's cheer at Bruno's success died in his throat as he watched his friends tossed aside like rag dolls.

Still clutching the broken spear, the Matriarch turned her attention back toward Delilah. With a swing like a whip crack, she drove Delilah into the ground. Jeremiah heard breaking glass. The delicate sound seemed so out of place that it finally broke his paralysis.

As the Matriarch raised the spear to impale Delilah like a sausage on a stick, Jeremiah launched an orb of acid directly into her long, pointed ear. The Matriarch screamed and reeled back, dropping the spear to frantically wipe off the acid, and some skin with it. To Jeremiah's dismay, though, only the skin was blistering. Painful but not nearly as debilitating as the spell had been on her smaller kin.

The Matriarch turned from her closer meal and leapt toward Jeremiah, closing the distance in an instant. Jeremiah scrambled, trying to flee in two directions at once. A massive hand drove him into the ground. His head bounced off the stone, his leather cap cushioning the deadly blow to be merely dizzying.

As the world spun, Jeremiah felt those elongated fingers closing around him. He couldn't bring his limbs to move. Instead, he struggled to focus his swimming vision on a figure fast approaching from behind the Matriarch.

The armored form of Allison charged into clarity. She slashed at the back of the Matriarch's ankles, looking for any part of the creature unprotected by thick blubber.

The Matriarch released Jeremiah and turned toward Allison, seeming to take account of the situation for the first time. Allison was battered but uninjured, sword and shield raised defensively. Bruno had pulled himself to his feet, a single sword still in hand. Delilah was stirring, shaking her head to clear it, and rummaging through her robes. The Matriarch's dinner was proving an annoyance.

From his vantage point on the floor, Jeremiah realized that the once-bright glow from under the door was dimming rapidly. Countless goblins squabbled beyond the fading light. The Matriarch seemed to reach the same conclusions as he did. She began to laugh, a cold, cruel laugh that froze the blood in Jeremiah's veins.

"*Kill her!*" bellowed Allison, banging her sword against her shield to draw the Matriarch's attention. The beast lumbered toward her, swinging her arms in wide, sweeping haymakers. Allison caught some blows on her shield, but even those sent her reeling. She was being battered like a cat's toy, fighting for footing as she backpedaled through rubble, her shield beginning to crumple. A particularly vicious series of strikes ripped her helmet off and she counterattacked, hacking at the Matriarch's knuckles and wrists, but the creature didn't seem to mind, splattering blood in great arcs as she continued the onslaught.

Bruno jumped in to slash at the Matriarch's injured knee, trying to give Allison a moment to breathe. The Matriarch punished his interference by snatching his legs with lightning quickness and swinging him at Allison like a club, slamming him into her shield and then tossing his limp form aside.

Delilah launched a ceramic pot against the Matriarch's back. It exploded with a sharp bang and sent slivers of pottery digging shallow wounds into her flesh. It seemed only to further enrage her attacks on Allison, who had been backed against a boulder and was now fighting fully defensively under the cascade of blows.

Jeremiah tried to summon the focus to cast another acid ball, but his head swam as he said the words and the force of will needed to shape reality eluded him. Behind him, the goblin's frenzied shrieks reached a fever pitch. He glanced back to see that the glow of the fire was gone.

Delilah appeared at his side. "I'll hold them. You have to help Allison. Go!" She tossed two jars of gelatinous goo against the threshold of the door and braced her back against it. The door jumped open an inch as countless tiny bodies began slamming it from the other side, but she threw all her weight back into it to keep it closed. "Go!"

Jeremiah ran toward the melee as the Matriarch rained blows upon Allison. She had discarded her battered shield and was ducking and twisting to avoid the attacks. For every few attacks she managed to evade, however, she would take another on the armor, crushing the steel plates in lieu of her bones.

Jeremiah knew Allison wouldn't be able to hold out much longer. He forced himself to ignore the ringing in his head, to draw upon his battle training and summon the focus that should still be within him. This time, the acid ball materialized, and when it splashed against the Matriarch's back, she howled in pain and fury.

The Matriarchs next punch was wild, granting Allison a rare opportunity to counter. She rammed her sword deep through the Matriarch's wrist and twisted the blade. Jeremiah launched another acid ball into the beast's shoulder, willing her to break off the attack, to come for him, anything to spare Allison her fury.

Instead, the Matriarch's eyes gleamed with cold cunning. In a flash, she snapped the rope holding her armor, then swung the Ironwood door at Allison as if swatting a fly with a book. Allison shouted in pain as the blow connected. She was slammed back against the boulder, and in a surprisingly graceful motion, the Matriarch thrust the edge of the massive door into Allison's shoulder, crushing the armor as well as the bones inside.

Allison let out a bloodcurdling scream. The Matriarch grinned, ignoring the sword still piercing her wrist. A thick tongue parted the Matriarch's purple lips and wetted them with slime as she savored Allison's helplessness.

Allison kicked and swore, clawing uselessly at the improvised weapon with her free hand. When she met Jeremiah's eyes and saw him preparing to throw another acid ball, she screamed directly at him, "*Kill her!*"

The world moved in slow motion for Jeremiah. He saw Allison moments from a grisly death. He saw blades reaching through the growing gap in the door as Delilah strained to hold it shut. The fog in his mind gave way to clarity—he had no choice. Kill the Matriarch. No matter the cost.

The bag slung over Jeremiah's shoulder was a gift. His teacher's warning echoed in his ears: *"I don't give this lightly. This is your 'no-win scenario' solution. Understand this: it will kill anything and everything it can. You will, at best, be able to suggest what it goes after first."*

Jeremiah upended the bag, his heart pounding. Human remains clattered onto the floor. Tendons formed neatly folded joints, connecting skull, spine, torso, limbs—a complete skeleton. The bones were blood red and looked slick and wet. The tips of its fingers, toes, and teeth were sharpened to needle points, and its skull was deformed into a crown of bony spines. Jeremiah's throat was dry, but he spoke the practiced words and focused his willpower into the skeleton. He found it already brimming with necromantic energy; reanimating it was as easy as firing a crossbow.

Jeremiah struggled to maintain his mental connection with the skeleton. It seethed at his control, accepting instruction only with the promise of violence. Like a picket fence on either side of a raging bull, Jeremiah could only offer the suggestion of direction and pointed it directly at the Matriarch.

The red skeleton exploded into motion, moving so fast toward the Matriarch that dust lifted in its wake. A small part of Jeremiah's mind was stunned at the speed, but the rest was devoted to imbuing the skeleton with an all-encompassing drive to kill the Matriarch. *Kill her.*

The skeleton leapt onto the Matriarch's back, who was leaning over Allison, jaws wide. The sharpened bones on the skeleton's toes dug into her skin, and it slashed with its claws with such speed and ferocity that they were a blur, tearing out gobs of flesh and fat, digging into the Matriarch's body as if it were made of sand. The Matriarch spasmed in pain, her good eye rolling and her face distorting in agony. She released Allison and the door and flailed with frantic desperation to dislodge the source of torment.

The skeleton sank its teeth in the Matriarch's back and tore out great mouthfuls with superhuman strength. It leaned back and opened its jaw wide, rib cage expanding as though breathing deep into nonexistent lungs. Instead of drawing air, however, the blood began gushing from the Matriarch's wounds like a geyser, spraying into the skeleton's mouth with such force that it dug in its claws to keep from being blown off her back. The blood exploded out the back of the skeleton's skull like a waterfall against rocks, coating everything nearby in a thick layer of blood.

The Matriarch staggered, her blood pressure suddenly dropping. What would have instantly exsanguinated a human only weakened the Matriarch. The skeleton leaned forward again as if exhaling, allowing the blood geyser to cease. Then it "inhaled" again, streaming blood from every scratch and cut into the skeleton's mouth.

Jeremiah's focus was already being taxed with controlling the skeleton. He knew that losing it would mean the death of everyone, including him and his friends. But there was more to be done.

He dug deep into reserves of strength he didn't know he had. He extended a hand toward the rotting corpse the Matriarch had thrown. The body stirred and pulled itself up, hands still clutching the shield and sword in its rigor mortis grip. At Jeremiah's will, the zombie heaved itself toward the door, stabbing its sword into the gap to impale goblins on the other side. Delilah recoiled in horror but did not question a source of aid. With the zombie's help, the door began to inch closed again.

Jeremiah extended his will into the corridor beyond to those goblins who had just fallen under the zombie's blade. The fresh corpses sprang to life and began slashing and biting at their former companions. The pressure on the door ceased as bloodlust gave way to confusion and pain, and Delilah and the zombie heaved the door closed.

Jeremiah was nearing his limit. He collapsed to his hands and knees. Controlling the red skeleton was like trying to hold a hurricane in his mind.

The Matriarch had finally conceived a plan to deal with her attacker. She threw her back against a stone column, forcing it to move lest it be crushed by her bulk.

The skeleton crawled around her body like a spider. In a moment, it was perched on her face where it immediately dug claws into her upper lip. It pulled away two huge bloody chunks, then inhaled blood straight from the ruined eyeball. The Matriarch bellowed in pain and fear. She swung wildly and managed to bash the skeleton off her face. It clattered along the ground, then dug its claws into the stone and sprang back toward her.

Allison was struggling to her feet, looking on in shock. Her mouth worked wordlessly and her broken arm hung at her side. Jeremiah noticed her dazed expression and a small part of him was glad that he wasn't the only one to get battle-shocked. "Allison!" he called. "Give it a weapon!"

Her expression settled into one of grim comprehension at his words. She unhooked the axe from her belt and tossed it toward the skeleton as it sprinted toward the Matriarch. The skeleton caught the weapon without even a glance, then leapt over the Matriarch's grasping hand and latched onto her arm, whipping the axe into her elbow. The axe rose and fell, a blur of metal removing hunks of flesh and bone in moments.

The Matriarch howled as her arm was shredded. She turned and shoulder charged a boulder, crushing the skeleton between her massive body and the stone. The skeleton disappeared under her girth. The Matriarch screamed as geysers of blood erupted from her wounds again, streaming toward the skeleton pinned against the rock. She slammed against it again and again even as its claws reached for her, scrabbling for purchase.

At last, the skeleton dropped to the ground. The matriarch raised her elephantine foot and stomped, exploding the lower half of the skeleton in a splintery crunch of blood-soaked bones. The upper half had not yet been dissuaded and dug both claws deep into the flesh of the Matriarch's foot. The Matriarch yowled and brought her foot down again with a mighty crunch. The hurricane in Jeremiah's mind blew out like a candle.

The Matriarch had no time to recover from her battle with the skeleton before Allison recommenced her attack. In a single motion, Allison scooped Delilah's broken spear off the floor and hurled it into the Matriarch's fleshy neck. Then she kicked up the axe the skeleton had dropped into her open hand and charged the Matriarch, screaming a desperate battle cry.

The Matriarch grunted as Allison's axe sank into her knee, finally severing something critical. She pitched and fell forward, where Allison was already waiting.

Allison caught the spear lodged in the Matriarch's neck as the creature fell and pushed it with all her remaining strength. The Matriarch's body followed the direction of her twisting neck and rolling onto her side. Allison yanked the spear free and thrust it deep into the Matriarch's wounded eye socket.

The Matriarch's body went rigid. She seized Allison, trying to crush her armor in her grasp. Allison unleashed a litany of curses and wrenched the spear, slicing it through whatever it had punctured deep inside the Matriarch's head. The Matriarch's body went limp and silent.

Every goblin beyond the door began to scream. The corridor erupted in the sounds of battle, of feral violence, of fleeing feet back up the hallway and into the distance.

There was quiet once more. But Jeremiah saw the darkness on Allison's face as she pulled herself free from the dead Matriarch's grasp. For him, the danger was graver than ever.

CHAPTER FOUR

Disgust

Allison stalked toward Jeremiah, who was still dazed from the effort of commanding the red skeleton. He scrambled to his feet as she approached but needn't have bothered. Allison kicked him square in the stomach, knocking him breathless to the ground.

"You're a necromancer." It wasn't a question.

"Yes," Jeremiah gasped. He searched Allison's eyes for mercy but found only anger and exhaustion. She raised the tip of her sword to his throat.

Bruno limped toward them. He stopped a dozen feet away, staring at Jeremiah with disgust. Jeremiah didn't have to ask if he'd seen what happened.

Delilah gave the now-still zombie warrior a wide berth and began inspecting Allison's wounds, avoiding Jeremiah's gaze. "You need a healing potion. I know they're expensive, but there's a good chance you'll get blood poisoning soon otherwise."

Allison nodded without taking her eyes off Jeremiah, and Delilah delved into her robes for a bottle of oily red liquid. Allison swallowed the contents. The fingers of her shattered arm wiggled, but the arm still hung limp.

Jeremiah wanted to plead his case, but he was terrified that any movement would spur Allison to finish the job. So, he remained silent, hoping against hope that she had had her fill of killing for the day.

Bruno and Delilah looked at him, then looked at each other. Allison continued staring at Jeremiah.

"We need to get out of here," she said at last. "We'll deal with him when we get topside, assuming we don't need to sooner." Her sword fell away.

The immediacy of the danger faded, leaving Jeremiah feeling numb. To have come all this way, to have battled and clawed his way to an impossible victory (saving all their lives in the process), only to be cast aside, treated like a problem to be solved . . .

Rage and despair sparked within him. His fists clenched, nails biting into his palms, but he hardly noticed. It had been the same thing every time, starting with his family. He was sick of hiding away, of being treated like a monster. These people didn't understand the first thing about necromancy, but they were still willing to kill him over it. Just because they feared it. Just because necromancy made practical use of death, when most people would rather pretend it didn't exist.

Yet, ignorant though they were, he was at their mercy. Allison no longer held a blade to his throat, but injured or not, her control over the situation was indisputable. Jeremiah gritted his teeth as she relieved him of his dagger and bound his wrists with a length of leather but was careful not to give her any reason to recant her temporary reprieve.

Delilah was busy with the Matriarch's corpse. "What the hell are you doing?" asked Bruno. "Don't think it was wearing any jewels."

"Do you know the leading cause of death for Matriarchs?" asked Delilah. "Armies. Only a few people in history have credibly killed a Matriarch as part of an adventuring party. If we want anyone to believe we did it, we need a trophy!" She carved off the Matriarch's undamaged ear with surgical precision and tucked it inside her robes.

"What about these Ironwood doors?" asked Bruno. "We've got two now, counting the one upstairs." He tugged on the rope tied to the Matriarch's former breastplate. The door didn't budge.

Delilah frowned. "It'd be a shame to leave one behind. But I don't see how—"

"I can get it upstairs," said Jeremiah. Allison whirled on him, eyes blazing, but he didn't care. "You want your payoff for this place? I can get that door outside, no problem." At his silent command, the zombie warrior raised its head and began shambling toward them.

Allison jumped, apparently not having realized the zombie was still a potential threat. She seized the front of Jeremiah's robes. "Another step and you're dead!"

"Fine!" Jeremiah shouted back. "Let the Ironwood rot, then, if you're so scared. Never mind that that zombie saved your lives. Never mind that if I had wanted to kill you, all I had to do was nothing!"

"You were just saving your own skin," growled Allison. But her eyes flicked back to Bruno struggling to shift the door and then to the zombie standing stock-still, waiting for orders.

Delilah spoke, her voice suddenly small in the cavernous space. "Having both doors will almost certainly be worth more than double. If they were commissioned as a set, as I suspect, then being able to fulfill the original order will be even more valuable than the material and craftsmanship alone."

Jeremiah blinked. Was Delilah standing up for him? No, of course not—she was just stating the facts. No doubt she'd be more than happy to dispose of him once he'd outlived his usefulness.

Allison's jaw worked as she weighed the decision. Then she released his robes, letting him settle back onto his heels. "It follows behind us," she said. "Far behind. Bruno, you take point. Delilah, cover him. Necromancer, you're with me. You slow us down or do anything I don't like, and I'll hamstring you for the goblins to find. Now move."

The group fell into formation. If it weren't for the tension of the silence, their return journey would have been nearly peaceful. Narrow tunnels had been revealed in the walls and ceiling, explaining how so many goblins had remained concealed. Now they echoed with the sounds of distant battle. Jeremiah guessed that the loss of the Matriarch's psychic bond had fractured whatever cohesion had bonded the Warren. Bruno dispatched the scant resistance they encountered without difficulty.

When they reached the wheeled door, Allison removed Jeremiah's bonds and ordered him to push the door with Bruno. It was slow going. The wheels were crudely made, and the hallway was a narrow fit. As they struggled, Jeremiah mentally checked that the zombie warrior was still progressing with its burden. A zombie was more than twice as strong as a normal man, but its door lacked wheels. It was thanks only to the tirelessness of the undead that the door moved through the dungeon, inch by inch.

Jeremiah relished their first taste of outside air. Although he was not looking forward to whatever fate awaited him on the surface, he was more than ready to leave the dungeon behind. If he was going to die, he preferred to do so with a fresh breeze on his face.

They heaved the door up the entrance stairs with considerable effort, then they were out. The sun was beginning to dip below the tops of the trees, casting the clearing in shadow. Jeremiah glanced around the familiar landscape. It felt like a decade since he had last stood here.

"We have to keep moving," said Delilah. "After losing the Matriarch, some of the goblins are likely to split off to look for new territory."

Allison nodded. "Grab your gear. We're heading north, to White Rock River. We'll float the doors while we walk and see if we can catch a boat to Dramir."

They were setting off again within minutes. As they reached the edge of the clearing, the zombie warrior emerged from the tunnel with the second door in tow. Its sinewy remains flexed with unnatural strength to maneuver its burden. Allison cast it a wary look but didn't comment.

Moving the door through the dense forest was difficult and Jeremiah was nearing exhaustion, but at least he hadn't been killed yet. He and Bruno communicated only when necessary to navigate the uneven terrain. His zombie followed dutifully at a considerable distance, thankfully requiring little focus to maintain the task. Jeremiah noticed that Allison seemed tolerant enough of the undead when it was benefiting her.

They reached White Rock River as the last vestiges of light settled on the horizon. The river was wide and lazy. Nothing disturbed its placid surface as Jeremiah and Bruno finally let their burden rest. Jeremiah rolled the ache out of his shoulders and glanced back toward Allison. Had he outlived his usefulness?

Allison paid him no mind, however. "Set partial camp," she said. "No lights. Keep your armor on. We'll take watch in pairs, so make the most of the sleep you get."

Jeremiah quietly unrolled his sleeping sack and arranged it under the emerging stars. It seemed that his reprieve was to extend until morning. None of the others seemed eager to address the issue, and he was grateful for the chance to get some rest.

A low, continuous grind announced the arrival of the zombie warrior at the camp with the other door in tow. Jeremiah commanded it to stop.

"Right, we don't need this anymore," said Allison. She drew her sword, strode over to the zombie and plunged the blade into its chest. The zombie remained utterly unfazed. Jeremiah knew it would take more than that to stop the creature but held his tongue. He didn't want to attract Allison's attention while she had weapons drawn.

Allison swung the sword with a pained grunt, wedging it in the zombie's neck. The zombie did not seem to notice. She began to hack at it, swinging the sword over and over, her strikes losing their usual finesse, until the blade finally worked through the magically reinforced remains. Jeremiah's mental connection with his minion severed as the decapitated zombie collapsed. Now he really was helpless.

Allison panted, sword loose in her good hand. She gestured toward Jeremiah without looking at him. "Delilah, put him out. I don't feel like being throttled in my sleep by some ghoul."

Jeremiah balked at the vial Delilah presented him with. "I'm not just going to drink poison! If you want to kill me, you'll have to do it yourself."

Delilah scowled. "Don't insult me, *necromancer*. None of us would have any problem killing you on your feet. This will put you to sleep and keep you asleep until morning. Now, you can choose to drink up like a good boy, or I can make the choice for you." She glared at him.

Jeremiah glared back and quaffed the vial, daring her to be a liar about the contents. But her face softened just a little when he drank it.

Satisfied, Allison crawled into her sleeping bag, careful not to jostle her bad arm. She was asleep almost at once.

Jeremiah wavered on his feet. He groped for his own bag and pulled himself into it, fighting for lucidity.

"We're not waking her up, right?" Delilah's voice drifted across the camp.

"We're not waking you up, either," came Bruno's reply. "I'll take full watch tonight. If I can't keep my eyes open, I'll get you. No arguing."

"Take this. It'll will help you stay awake, but you might be a little twitchy."

A rustling sound, and then Delilah's voice was much closer. "Jeremiah?"

Jeremiah managed a grunt in response.

"I'm sorry I don't trust you."

A wave of guilt and sadness washed through his exhausted mind. Why did things have to be this way? What else could he have done? Gus emerged from his hidden pocket and nestled by Jeremiah's cheek. Jeremiah took comfort in his familiar's unconditional approval.

It was impossible to keep his eyes open any longer. As the potion and his own fatigue carried him to sleep, it wasn't with anger in his heart but with longing for the friendship that could have been.

Jeremiah awoke to birdsong. His body felt stiff, and the ground spun like he was drunk. He groaned, and the world began to slow down.

The midday sun reflected off the peaceful river. The water lapped gently against the shore, hardly disturbing the tall cattails lining the bank. It would have been a lovely spot had Jeremiah been able to think about such luxuries.

Instead, his hands were bound again, his stomach was empty and cramped, his head pounded like a punishment, and his bladder was full to bursting. Worst of all, though, was his burning thirst. He squirmed out of his sack and staggered to the water's edge.

Jeremiah dropped to his knees and gulped down long pulls of cool, refreshing water, more delicious than anything he'd ever tasted. The water spread through his body like a salve, easing the ache in his joints and the pain in his skull.

Feeling considerably more human, Jeremiah turned back toward the camp and jumped—Allison was seated on a rock barely five feet away. Her left arm had been bound in a sling and her eyes were fixed on him with cold fury.

"Look how alive you are," she said. "That's a gift—you're welcome. We decided, barely, that we're not *yet* going to do the world a favor and kill you. We decided to give you the opportunity to explain yourself, on the remote chance that you have anything to say to convince us you deserve to live. Take care of your business in the woods. Bruno is watching. Do anything he doesn't like, he kills you."

Jeremiah did as he was told. The woods were dappled and lovely, fresh with life after the chill of winter. He wished he could linger here forever, but he was wary of Bruno's surveillance. What could he say to convince them not to kill him? He had imagined countless conversations over the years, helping people to see the error of their prejudice, dazzling them with flawless logic, winning them to his side. Yet these were real people, people he had lied to, and they wielded very real weapons. With great reluctance, Jeremiah returned to the camp.

Allison pointed to a log that had been placed facing three others. It seemed this was the stand from which he would defend himself. The log wobbled slightly as he sat.

Allison chose the log directly in front of him. Her hard gaze never wavered as they waited.

Delilah soon emerged from the woods with a basket of herbs, flowers, and roots. She took her spot beside Allison and regarded Jeremiah, her expression deliberately neutral.

Bruno arrived next. "Oh, he's awake? We can get started, then." He gave Jeremiah a sarcastic smile. "How ya feelin', Jay?"

Allison can lie, thought Jeremiah. *Good to know.* "Hungry. Where's Gus? Is he okay?"

Delilah said, "Gus is fine." No one responded to him being hungry.

Allison set her jaw. "We're listening."

Jeremiah swallowed. His eyes darted to the sword at Allison's hip. His mind blanked; his tongue felt thick in his mouth.

The three accusers looked at one another. Then Delilah said, "Why don't you tell us about how you became a necromancer in the first place?"

Jeremiah seized the prompt like a lifeline. "Okay. I can do that." He took a deep breath, ordered his thoughts, and began.

CHAPTER FIVE

Capital "E" Evil

Jeremiah was on his fourth day of slogging through the nastiest swath of swampland he had ever seen. His boots had long since soaked through as he trudged through fetid pools filled with crocodiles, venomous snakes, and quicksand. The cloud of mosquitos was so constant that he had given up swatting them. His shoulders throbbed under the straps of his pack, which held as much fresh water as he could carry, in addition to his normal supplies, and each step sank that much deeper into the muck because of it. But Jeremiah's face was plastered with an unassailable grin through every boot-sucking step, for his goal was finally in sight.

Out of the swamp rose a wide, dark mesa. A massive castle squatted atop it. The black stone structure was slick with slime, and chunks of the stone architecture had fallen away, leaving the impression of a rotting, worm-eaten fruit.

A footpath rose from the muck, creating a narrow avenue of dry land that sloped upward to meet the castle's gate. Sheer cliffs on either side of the path dropped away into a moat of sorts, a sea of smooth black water, bereft of trees, amid the vibrant life of the surrounding swamp.

Jeremiah stepped onto the footpath gratefully, the only dry land he had seen in days. It was time to learn if his miserable journey had been worth it. After so many failures under the tutelage of mages renowned and obscure, this derelict castle in the heart of the Throatlock Swamp was his last hope.

It was only his last teacher's pity that gave him this chance. "Your focus is too fractured," the wiry transmutation master had told him. "You'll never wield more than the most rudimentary of spells." Jeremiah had thrown himself onto his knees in a shameless display, begging for another chance, another hope. The decision to follow this dream had cost him his home and family; if he couldn't become a mage, it would have all been for naught.

Jeremiah centered himself on the memory of the night he left home. It had been a provincial life, but a safe one, and his parents had never understood why he was so desperate to escape it. When he explained his desire to make a difference, to help people, they had scoffed and accused him of self-aggrandizing heroics. The discussion had become heated, as it always had. But this time, as he was finally of age, his father had defied him to leave. Jeremiah had thrown himself out, his parents wishing him a suitably humbling return, and that had been that.

As the footpath began its ascent toward the castle gates, Jeremiah happened to glance into the moat. From a distance, the dark water had seemed fathomless, but now Jeremiah spotted something just beneath the surface. He crouched lower to take a closer look.

Grinning up at him was a human skull, picked clean to a pristine white. Jeremiah recoiled in shock and stepped off the opposite edge of the walkway. He fell backward into the moat, flailing for purchase as his pack dragged him beneath the surface. His fingers grasped a series of smooth, slender curves—a rib cage. With a cry smothered by water, he shoved the bones away. He kicked off against something hard below him—he did not dare wonder what—and fought his way back to the surface.

Jeremiah pulled himself back onto the path. His heart was pounding, but he couldn't hear it over the voice in his head screaming at him to run, to flee this place while he still could. Instead, Jeremiah forced himself to take a deep breath, then another. He had one final chance to find a teacher, and he damn well wasn't about to waste it on being scared.

Jeremiah stood and stared straight at the front gate of the castle, not letting his eyes or mind wander to what filled the lagoon around him. *One step at a time,* he told himself. *Behind those doors is the key to becoming a mage.* He only needed to be brave enough to reach it.

The gate loomed before him, its jet-black wood studded with iron rivets. It was in pristine condition, standing in stark contrast to the decaying mortar that ran through the castle walls. The gate was adorned with two life-size bronze skulls, each with a large iron ring piercing the bone between their empty orbits. As strange as it felt to follow common courtesy in a place like this, there was a comfort in it as well. Jeremiah raised one of the iron rings and struck once it against the wood.

There was a single muted thud. It sounded no louder than if Jeremiah had pounded on the gate with his fist. But he waited, imagining a servant or guard lurking just within the entryway, and a few moments later the gate cracked open, projecting a spike of sunlight into the castle. Hidden hinges groaned ominously as the gate swung to admit him. As the sound echoed through the entrance hall, it occurred to Jeremiah that this all seemed a tad overdramatic. He stepped into the hall cautiously, looking for whoever had opened the door for him.

As outside light flooded the entryway, it revealed a room that had once been a sight to behold. A wide staircase flowed like a waterfall from an ornate set of bronze doors set high against the back wall. Tall windows of stained glass had been darkened by ages of dirt and dust, and a fireplace large enough to roast an ox stood cold against one wall. Distant ceilings disappeared in darkness, and countless empty torch sconces lined the walls. Jeremiah could imagine this place as a warm and inviting refuge to travelers through the Throatlock Swamp, but the room was cold now. Dark and dry, like a tomb.

There was nobody else in the entryway. "Hello?" Jeremiah called. "My name is Jeremiah Thorn. I came here because I'm looking for a teacher of magic. I want to be a mage." His own words echoing back to him was the only response.

"I-I've already learned some of the basics, and I . . . Hello? Is someone there?"

A chill rolled across his skin like a wind had blown through the room, but the air was still. He knew he was being watched from somewhere, judged from somewhere. This was it. He stood up tall and spoke with conviction.

"I am prepared to work hard and be a student you can be proud of! I am smart and capable, and I'm willing to work off any debt for the privilege of accepting you as my master!" He stood stiff, waiting for a response.

A hissing whisper emanated from the shadows far above, like how he imagined a spider would talk. "You are a special kind of stupid, aren't you, kid?"

Jeremiah gasped. That wasn't the response he was expecting. Well, he expected to be tested or mocked, just not . . . in that tone.

The voice continued, moving above him from shadow to shadow. "We haven't even met and you're willing to accept me as your master to 'work off any debt.' That's how people get stuck in slave contracts."

Jeremiah drew himself taller and delivered his planned reply. "I am *that* serious about becoming a mage. I want you to kn—"

"You'd think living in a swamp with a moat of bones would be enough of a 'No Trespassing' sign," the voice said. "Yet here you are. How did you even hear about this place?"

This wasn't going the way Jeremiah had envisioned. "The mage who taught me the basics of magic told me to come here. He said there was a teacher here who could make use of my talents."

The room was quiet again. Jeremiah waited for the response from above, goose bumps still prickling his skin.

"Did . . . did he tell you anything about me?" the voice asked.

"No, sir," said Jeremiah.

Another long silence. Then, "Did you mouth off to him or something? Did he hate you? He actually told you *nothing*? No teensy little details you might just be forgetting?"

Jeremiah's pulse quickened. He racked his brain for some detail that he could have missed, some hint he could extrapolate, but he found nothing. "No, sir?"

The front gate behind Jeremiah started to swing closed, drawing out that same ominous groan until it slammed shut with a frightening finality. Jeremiah was plunged into darkness, save for the dim glow from the blackened windows. As his eyes adjusted, Jeremiah became aware that a figure stood at the top of the stairs. It was human-sized, but he couldn't make out any details. Jeremiah continued to stand at attention as the figure began descending the stairs.

"You afraid to die, kid?" asked the voice.

"No, sir!" Jeremiah lied.

Jeremiah became aware of a feeling he couldn't identify yet felt innately familiar. It felt like fear, but on an entirely different level. It was as if a sense he never knew he had was stirring to warn him of a danger he didn't understand. The feeling started growing stronger, but he held his ground and tried not to tremble.

"Weird answer," said the figure growing closer. "Most people are afraid to die. The ones that aren't are usually psychos. You a psycho, kid?"

"No, sir!" The strange new feeling kept growing in his chest, threatening to overwhelm him. Jeremiah's eyes darted about in the darkness, his heart threatening to explode from his chest.

"Something wrong?" asked the voice knowingly. "You're sweating and shivering."

"I . . . I don't . . . Yes," said Jeremiah. "Something feels . . . wrong."

"Oooh, something *is* wrong, child," the voice said with sick delight. "What you're feeling now is your soul. It senses a predator."

It was oblivion. That was the source of this primal panic building in him. It was a threat to more than just his body—his immortal existence was crying out in terror. Whatever eternity that awaited him beyond death was in jeopardy.

Jeremiah wavered on his feet as the figure continued its approach. The horror in his heart was rising to a fever pitch. He felt sick, unable to hear what was being said to him. He gripped the sides of his pants with tightly balled fists to keep from fleeing. "I—I want to learn magic."

"Why?!" The figure suddenly swooped toward him. "To strike down your enemies? Do you seek revenge against those that have wronged you? Do you desire power? Riches? The secrets of the universe?"

The figure was now directly in front of him, still shrouded in darkness. Jeremiah couldn't bring himself to look at it. He panted, his mouth dry as dust, his bladder threatened to release. "No . . . Yes . . . I—I just want to be important!"

His voice rang out in the austere hall, the stark truth echoing his own selfishness back to him somehow worse than everything that came before.

The figure remained inches from Jeremiah's nose. When it spoke again, it was in a more inquisitive tone. "Still here, huh? Good for you. Figured you would have run for your life by now. Well, no worries. We'll get you figured out. But first, let's grab some dinner . . ."

The figure reached toward him. Jeremiah's heart pounded so hard, he was sure he was about to die. In the dim light, he watched the figure raise a skeletal finger, felt it press against his forehead, then everything went truly black.

Jeremiah awoke in a room that was the polar opposite of the last. He was lying in a large, soft bed atop sheets with an old, but clean, smell. Torches lined the walls and a few logs burned in a small fireplace. Warm light filled every corner of the room.

Jeremiah sat up to recollect his thoughts. He was wearing the same clothes, but they were dry and clean. His pack was propped in a corner and similarly cleaned. Jeremiah remembered what had happened in the castle entryway like a fading dream. He recalled the fear he'd felt, but couldn't quite place where inside him it had come from.

He had a sinking feeling that he had squandered his chance with this teacher by panicking. It must have been some sort of test, to see if he could handle some minor magical stress, and he had obviously failed. His mood continued to sour as he imagined all the things he should have done, all the confident words he could have said. He fell back onto the bed and pressed his hands into his eyes with a groan, then proceeded to torture himself with hindsight for several minutes.

After a while, he decided that despairing wasn't going to help. He took several deep breaths and tried to clear his mind. *I'm still here. He didn't kick me out or kill me. There's still a chance. I just need to prove I'm still serious,* Jeremiah thought.

There was a trio of knocks at the door. A chillingly familiar voice called to him, but softly, like a parent waking a child, or rather someone mocking that situation. "Heeey, you awake in there? You feelin' okay, buddy?"

Jeremiah leapt off the bed, and marched to the door, his face growing stern with determination. The first meeting could have gone better, but now he was rested and prepared to make a good impression. He threw open the door and immediately began talking. "Sir! I apo—"

Standing before him, Jeremiah saw the most horrid thing he had ever seen in his life. Terror welled up inside him as his mind took in every detail of what he was looking at.

It was a skeleton wearing an ornate red tunic that revealed bony arms and shoulders. Every individual bone was wrapped in human skin from several different people, complete with freckles, moles, and scars. The only bare bones were the sharp, skeletal fingers and the teeth set in the skull. But worst of all were the eyes—two human eyeballs were suspended in the skull's empty sockets with cord, which threaded through the eyeballs before looping back through the skin of the sockets. The effect amounted to a skeleton made of flesh, with floating eyes that were somehow conveying surprise.

Jeremiah screamed.

"Nooope!" the horror said, and in a flash touched a bony finger to Jeremiah's forehead yet again. Everything went black.

Jeremiah woke up in the same bed in the same room, but this time with a start, sitting up quickly and panting in fear.

"A nightmare!" he said. "Just some horrid nightmare, thank the gods."

There was a trio of knocks at the door. A chillingly familiar voice called to him, but softly, like a parent waking a child, or rather someone mocking that situation. "Heeey, you awake in there? You feelin' okay, buddy?"

Jeremiah froze. It was too similar, the memory was too strong. Jeremiah rose slowly and went to the door. He swallowed and reluctantly pulled it open.

Standing on the far side of a hallway was the same figure wearing the same ornate robe, but now with long baggy sleeves and leather gloves. On its face, it wore a plaster mask fashioned after a smiling cherubim with rosy cheeks and wide innocent eyes. The effect unsteadied Jeremiah. He thought he knew what was behind that mask and under those robes, but he prayed that had just been a dream.

"There we are!" it said, voice still dripping with sweet sarcasm. "Feeling better?"

Jeremiah paused before answering. "Yes, I'm feeling fine. Thank you."

"Oh, good!" the thing said, popping up on one foot and raising its hands like an excited child. "Why don't you join me for dinner, then? You must be starving, and I haven't had dinner guests in quite some time! Right this way!"

Jeremiah followed, acutely aware that his host made no noise as it walked.

They arrived at a warm and inviting dining room. A great fire crackled softly along one side. Thin rugs covered the floor, extending into the hallway. A long table occupied the center of the room, bare except for two places set at either end. Each had a jug, glass, and silver-domed serving dish. A spicy aroma stirred Jeremiah's hunger, despite his reservations.

His host pulled out Jeremiah's chair for him and then pranced to its own place at the far end, sitting delicately.

"Now then," it said in the same sweet tone, "ask anything you like!"

There was only one question on Jeremiah's mind right now. "Was what I saw before real? Are you a . . . a skeleton?"

The thing folded its gloved hands. "Something like one. I normally try to ease people into my appearance, but I didn't expect you to open the door. Now that I'm a good distance away and you know what to expect, I'd like to take off this mask. Are you going to shriek like a child again?"

Jeremiah's blood chilled at the thought, but something told him it was necessary if he was to become a student of his host. He gripped the sides of his chair to steady himself. "You can take it off. I won't scream."

"Finally! I hate this thing." The thing whipped the mask off unceremoniously, revealing the same grotesque face.

Jeremiah's adrenaline surged, and his grip tightened at seeing the horror again, but the second viewing from farther away wasn't as intense.

The skeleton waited a moment to see if Jeremiah would react, those floating eyes on flesh-colored bones twitching back and forth on its cords. "All right! We're getting somewhere." It gestured to the silver-domed platter in front of it. "Don't be shy. Get to eating. There's wine in the jug. Help yourself."

Jeremiah lifted the cover, half expecting to reveal some new monstrosity beneath. To his relief, he found a small roasted fowl. It was surrounded by boiled potatoes and carrots and smelled delicious. He began eating with gusto. The warmth and flavor of the food made him feel almost normal.

"Not bad, eh?" asked the skeleton, shattering the illusion. "Took me three tries to get it right. Haven't cooked in ages."

Jeremiah noticed the skeleton was also eating the meal in front of it. The question spilled out before he could wonder if it was rude. "Do you actually need to eat?"

The skeleton took a drink of wine, pouring it toward the back of his throat before responding, "Nope."

"Then why are you doing it now?"

"'Cause it would be weird to just sit here and stare at you while you eat."

Jeremiah had to agree, though it would have been far down on his tally of the evening's weirdness.

As Jeremiah finished his food, he felt an urge to somehow return the kindness of the meal. He took another deep breath and forced himself to look directly at his host, doing his best to quiet the alarm in his mind. "What's your name?"

The skeleton straightened up a bit under his direct gaze. "Lookit you! Color me impressed; I thought that would take longer. You can call me Flusoh."

"I'm Jeremiah."

"Indeed you are, and word is you're looking for a teacher in magic."

"Yes. But to be honest, I don't know what sort of magic you do, or even, forgive me, what you are. Are you an undead?"

"I"—Flusoh stood and gave a little bow—"am a lich, and the magic I do is necromancy. I used to be a human and learned enough necromancy to transfer my consciousness into the vessel you see before you."

Jeremiah had never met a necromancer before. All the stories he had heard involved zombies devouring innocent people, undead abominations wreaking havoc, and monsters rising from ancient crypts. But this one had just washed his clothes and fed him dinner.

"I take it you didn't come here wanting to *be* a necromancer," said Flusoh. "You just want someone to teach you magic, any kind at all. Am I right?"

Jeremiah's cheeks reddened. "I just haven't found the school of magic that suits me yet, sir."

Flusoh pushed food around his plate absentmindedly. "The person that sent you here, did they say why you should come see me? Assuming it wasn't to have you killed."

Jeremiah thought back on his previous teacher's criticism. "He said I have a fractured focus. 'Strong but fractured,' he said."

Flusoh stopped pushing food around. "Reeeaaally! That's a rare quality. Usually you either have a strong singular focus or a weak fractured focus. But a strong fractured focus . . . You might indeed make a good necromancer."

Elation rushed through Jeremiah. He'd never been told he was good at any-thing, even hypothetically. The feeling was quickly overcome by dread. "Mr. Flusoh, I don't mean to offend, but I don't know if that's true. I'm not evil."

Flusoh's eyes rolled and Jeremiah's stomach churned. "'Evil' is such an abused word. Look, bones and bodies are bones and bodies—not people. I know it's creepy, but that doesn't change the facts. There's no one in there."

Jeremiah thought hard, trying to remember everything he had heard about nec-romancy. "What about . . . souls? Necromancers do something with souls, right?"

Flusoh shook his head. "Hell no! We don't mess with people's souls. Souls, in a vague cosmological sense, belong to gods. Any god, from the most righteous, stick up their ass, holy avenger to the most scheming small-minded evil cretin"—Jeremiah noted the disdain with which Flusoh spoke of gods—"won't tolerate you taking their stuff. Messing with souls is how you get crusades on your door-step, 'cause they followed a star that appeared over your lair!"

Jeremiah found Flusoh's explanation somewhat reassuring, but he couldn't shake the stories he'd heard. "Okay, so no souls. But necromancy is still unnatu-ral magic, isn't it? Making the dead walk and all that?"

"Psh, unnatural! Anything shaped by the hands of mortals is unnatural. You think fighters pluck their swords from trees? Or this table"—Flusoh rapped a bony knuckle against the wood—"you think this table would just spontane-ously slap itself together of its own accord? People make up words like 'evil' and 'unnatural' to beat you into submission, to control you."

"Wait, so you're saying evil isn't real?"

Flusoh tilted his head noncommittally. "Eeeh, didn't say that. Look, 'Evil,' with a capital *E*, is a natural force of the universe. Demons, devils—there's all sorts of things out there that are actually Evil. But mortals? It takes a special kind of mortal to actually reach Evil and not just be stuck at conniving, greedy prick. Most that manage it are being helped by those actual Evil things. I promise, Jebediah, Evil works on a whole different mindset."

"It's Jeremiah. So, you're not . . . Evil?"

"I could hear the big *E*, good job." Flusoh drew himself up taller. "I am a moral relativist. Some people may see me as evil, others may not. I submit to you that evil exists from the standpoint of the observer only. When dealing with things that aren't Evil, anyway."

Jeremiah considered this claim. It seemed too convenient, but it was still exciting to be discussing it with a lich. And he wanted it to be true, that he could learn necromancy without becoming the villain in a bedtime story.

Flusoh clacked his finger bones on the table. "I'll admit, necromancers haven't done a great job from a public perception angle. They tend to be a misanthropic, power-hungry bunch, and the whole dead bodies thing doesn't help. But, like anything, it's what you decide to make of it. Necromancy is no different than any other school of magic, except that you might actually be good at it."

Jeremiah turned this new perspective over in his mind. "So, I could use necromancy to help people?"

"Sure! Why not? Defend the innocent, fight the good fight, dig a damn ditch for all I care." He tented his fingers and looked Jeremiah in the eye. "You wanna learn some magic? It's gonna be hard, and I'm gonna make you redo your basics. We start with fundamental biology, and we stay on that for a long time!"

"You're really willing to be my master?" Jeremiah was both shocked and elated.

"Nope! Your teacher. I want a pupil, not a pet. I also reserve the right to revoke that status and kill you for my own entertainment." He added at a whisper, "Almost never happens."

Jeremiah's relief and excitement threatened to overwhelm him. He could make this work. He would be different from those dark and sinister mages who lurked in the shadows. He would show the world what he was capable of.

Jeremiah's face broke into a grin, his first smile in quite a long time. "All right. I'll be your student. Teach me to be a necromancer!"

CHAPTER SIX

Rise

"Are you *fucking kidding me*!" Allison shouted while Delilah stared in shock and Bruno dropped his face into his hands. "A lich? Your teacher was a gods-damned *lich*?!"

"Come on, you didn't need to tell us that part," Bruno said. "Work with us here. We're trying to find reasons *not* to kill you."

"For the record," said Delilah, "moral relativism is all well and good for a philosophical discussion, but when someone says they live by it, it just means they're evil and they like philosophy."

Jeremiah held up his hands. "No, I know! I knew it then, too, but believing him meant I had a teacher. Though, when I was with him, at least, he didn't do anything that struck me as evil. Kept to himself, mostly."

"How about all those bodies in the moat? You're telling me they came voluntarily?" Allison spat.

"Actually, those were deliveries," said Jeremiah. "Every two months, we got a visit from some folks with a caravan loaded with the recently deceased. Now, I know what you're thinking, but I sorted a lot of those bodies, and they all looked like they passed from natural causes. Sick or elderly types."

Bruno eyes flashed. "That's what the Gray Market is doing?" At his friends' confusion, he explained. "It's a real hush-hush thing. Someone dies, and the family's too poor to give him a proper burial. These Gray Market guys pay a good price to take bodies off your hands. They give final rites as well. They're a standup group. At least, that's what I thought before I knew they were being funded by a lich."

"He was picky, too," said Jeremiah. "Once, a different group showed up with hundreds of skeletons. It looked like they pilfered a whole necropolis. Flusoh listened to their pitch, and next thing I knew, every one of the skeletons jumped out of the carts. Killed all the men in about two seconds. I got the feeling he didn't like the idea of grave robbers. Maybe hit too close to home."

"Clearly he's a paragon of virtue," Allison said. "Now, are you finished with your story? Because for your sake, I hope you're not."

Jeremiah continued.

True to his word, they began with biology. Jeremiah was forbidden from summoning even a spark of magic. Flusoh proved to be a demanding but patient teacher. Jeremiah was always challenged but never out of his depth.

He dissected humans, dwarves, elves, orcs, gnomes, and a whole assortment of other creatures. Once he overcame his aversion toward seeing a once-living being disassembled on a table like a puzzle, Jeremiah realized how similarly humanoids were built—adjusting for size, the bones, musculature, and organs were near identical between the races. Animals, on the other hand, threatened to overwhelm him with their variety.

He studied the function these structures served in life from dusty books with remarkably detailed illustrations, some stuffed into the pages by Flusoh himself. As the months stretched beyond his first year, Jeremiah learned more about the construction of a body than he'd ever imagined there was to know.

Time not spent studying saw Jeremiah performing chores to earn his keep about the castle. Aside from the standard servant chores of sweeping, polishing and dusting (Jeremiah suspected Flusoh made him do these simply because he thought that's what a student ought to do—the castle didn't look like it had ever been cleaned before Jeremiah's arrival), he was also tasked with sorting and cleaning corpses, retrieving components from the swamps, and researching esoteric information in the vast library.

Jeremiah had one day to himself each week. Distractions were sparse in the castle, but he made the most of them. He discovered a small collection of fiction in the library. Classic stories of underdogs overcoming great evil through acts of heroism. He read them over and over again, their presence was a conundrum Jeremiah never solved.

He also spent considerable free time in the armory, where there was always a zombie to practice against, though it was docile enough to present more of a target than a sparring partner. Jeremiah had quite a bit of fun acting out dramatic adventures and climactic battles, once he got past his discomfort of hacking into a humanoid body.

"All right!" Flusoh burst into Jeremiah's room in the darkest hours of the night, a year and a half into his tutelage.

Jeremiah sat bolt upright in bed with a shout, but Flusoh kept talking. "Tomorrow we're gonna start the magic stuff. Get ready to learn some fundamentals!"

Jeremiah, brain addled from sleep, was slow to respond. "But I already know the fundamentals."

"You don't know anything, kid! We're gonna drill those fundamentals till you couldn't do them wrong if you tried. Without strong fundamentals, even the most powerful arch-mage in the land is useless unless conditions are perfect. Ever hear warriors talk about balance? Fundamentals are your balance—if you're off balance, you're dead!"

And as suddenly as he had arrived, Flusoh left, slamming the door shut behind him.

When Jeremiah mentioned fundamentals and balance, he noticed Allison absently nodding along. He decided to skip past the hours of meditation and making coins spin and candles flicker to talk about something she might relate to. "So, Flusoh decided that I should undergo something called pain training."

Delilah looked at him with shock and pity. "He tortured you?"

Jeremiah hesitated. He couldn't keep characterizing Flusoh as evil without reflecting poorly on himself.

To his relief, Allison came to his defense. "Pain training isn't torture," she said. "It's a valuable conditioning exercise!"

"Exactly," Jeremiah said. "The ability to act even when you're uncomfortable is how you survive real world situations. I had to wear a briar shirt so th—"

"Oh, that thing is awful," said Allison. "I couldn't sleep a minute in the briars."

Bruno glanced between them. "Did you two go through the exact same thing?"

"Warlord Uuba's Torment," said Jeremiah. "It's a brutal protocol, but it really does work."

Allison nodded. "Actually, you and Delilah could do with some pain training yourselves. It's great for your fundamentals."

"Pass," Bruno said. "Can we get on with it before Allison starts drawing up a training schedule?"

Allison reassumed her rigid posture. "Continue," she said, but Jeremiah thought her furrowed brow looked forced. The sharp edge of her anger had been blunted against the armor of camaraderie.

He continued.

For a long time, Jeremiah performed no magic he could call necromancy. He did learn a number of utility and minor combat spells, and he learned to channel his focus under so many levels of duress that he was convinced he could cast while unconscious.

Finally, it was time to turn his attention to the signature technique of the necromancer: reanimation.

Flusoh met Jeremiah in an open-air courtyard. In the middle of the over-grown floor lay the corpse of an old human man, still dressed in bedclothes.

"This is going to feel pretty strange when you get it," said Flusoh. "It's no use trying to describe it, so just give it a try."

Jeremiah paused to absorb the magnitude of the situation. After months of rehearsing the words and gestures in preparation for this moment, he was about to animate a man . . . No, not a man. The man was at rest. He was about to attempt to animate a body and attach it to his will.

Jeremiah began speaking the words of reanimation, his fingers and hands moving deftly. He finished the spell by laying his hands on the corpse's icy chest.

Something was trying to invade his mind with nonsense. Concepts flooded his consciousness: lying down, hardness, sky. He winced and stumbled backward.

Flusoh steadied him with a hand on his shoulder. "Easy now! What you're feeling is a piece of your consciousness attaching to the zombie."

Jeremiah was struggling. It was like he kept remembering something impor-tant he had to do, then forgot it again, then remembered it again.

"Don't fight it, just let it run. Now, I want you to try and move the zombie. Just impose your will toward that sensation in your head. It'll pull everything it needs to know to follow your commands without you even noticing."

Trying not to fight the sensation was like trying to ignore a song stuck in his head. With difficulty, Jeremiah isolated the sensation into a distinct section of his mind, where it persisted like a little bubble. That was better. He then focused on the bubble and urged his will to be done.

Rise.

Slowly, the zombie stirred. First just a twitch, then a spasm, but then it jerked on the ground and pushed itself into a sitting position. It clambered to its feet, and Jeremiah noticed how natural the movement seemed. The zombie's eyes were still clouded, its skin still pale, but it moved for all the world like an able-bodied man getting up from a nap.

"Well done!" said Flusoh, clapping Jeremiah on the back. "First try, too."

"It moved so smoothly!" said Jeremiah. "Did I make it do that?"

"Eh, yes and no. The body remembers what it often did in life. It's called muscle memory. Keep that in mind: fighters make great zombies!"

Jeremiah was elated. His first real spell! He turned to Flusoh, grinning so wide his cheeks hurt, and saw from the corner of his eye that the zombie had copied his movement exactly. When he turned back to it, it resumed its normal stance.

"Oop!" said Flusoh. "Looks like you've got a one-to-one connection there. Totally normal for a novice necromancer. We'll work on it until the minion enacts your will without direct input."

Jeremiah found the creature fascinating. He embraced the one-to-one controls to experiment. He made the zombie touch its nose, wave its arms around, and step forward. He tried jumping, but the zombie just bounced.

"Yeah," said Flusoh, "zombies aren't great for running or jumping. Bit too dead for that, even fresh. Wait till you control a skeleton, though. Those things can jump five feet straight up!"

"Even though they don't have muscles?" asked Jeremiah.

"Yup! Skeleton strength comes from magic, but their frames are so light that they move like the wind. Zombie strength is from their musculature, so while they're actually stronger, they don't move as quick. One day I'll tell you all about enhanced skeletons and zombies, ghouls, wraiths, ghasts, abominations, vexons, all sorts. This fella is just the beginning! So, what are you gonna name him?"

Jeremiah considered this odd question for a minute before Flusoh laughed. "I'm kidding, I'm kidding! Never name your minions. That time of their existence is over."

Jeremiah continued playing with the zombie. It was already becoming less strenuous and more fun. He decided to push himself and focused his will to instruct the zombie to walk without walking himself.

After a moment or two of concerted effort, the zombie took a couple of shambling steps. Flusoh looked on silently, but started moving his jaw back and forth a little, which Jeremiah knew meant he was thinking.

"Interesting. That's very interesting," said Flusoh, uncharacteristically subdued. Then, with his usual exuberance, "All right! Go ahead and sever that connection. I don't need you getting ahead of yourself before you've got the basics down. This part's easy. Just pop that little bubble in your head."

Jeremiah did, and the zombie collapsed, completely limp.

"Great, now chuck that body in the moat."

Jeremiah began dragging the corpse toward the front hall. "Can't we reuse it later?"

"Nope!" said Flusoh. "Necromantic energy burns out a corpse. Once you cut the connection, you can't pick it back up. But I'll teach you how to maintain it in a minimal state. Uses less head space, you'll see."

As Jeremiah practiced, the knack of reanimation became second nature. Within a few weeks, he could separate his minion's movements from his own, and began to command them while carrying out his own increasingly complex tasks. He learned to raise a body from a distance, as long as he could see the target, although this technique required proportionally more focus. When he managed to use a zombie to chop a cord of wood while he, Jeremiah, dissected a dwarf half a castle away, Flusoh deemed him ready for the next step.

"Two undead at once!" Flusoh said, indicating two lifeless bodies on the ground. "This will feel just as weird as the first time, maybe weirder. It's like having several of those bubbles in your head, and the more bubbles there are, the less room there is for you."

They stood in the same courtyard as his first ever reanimation. Jeremiah was buzzing with excitement. After a lifetime of mediocrity, necromancy was something he was actually good at, something that just made sense. The visions of himself as a powerful mage were more concrete than ever. He imagined his army of minions defending against wave after wave of monsters, a village of grateful citizens cheering his name. After today, he would be one step closer to that reality.

Jeremiah cast the reanimation spell and the first zombie stood.

"All right, I want you to make a skeleton out of the second one," Flusoh said.

Jeremiah had never animated a skeleton out of an entire corpse before, only bones. He looked to Flusoh for guidance.

"It's the same thing, but animate just the bones when you touch him. Give it a little more energy too. Things are gonna get gross."

Jeremiah did as instructed, focusing his will into only the bones of the corpse. The body spasmed, its flesh warping, then the skin split and turned runny. Muscle fell away, and the skeleton burst forth, sloughing off its previous mortal husk and emerging wet and red, like a newborn baby. Jeremiah had dissected every humanoid there was, but the sight made him feel sick.

"Aw yeah, it's just awful," said Flusoh. "I never get over how gross that is. The extra energy melts away the—"

"I get it," Jeremiah croaked. He averted his eyes as he directed the skeleton to step away from the puddle of its excess. He then started, realizing he had two bubbles in his head at the same time, and had issued orders to one without affecting the other.

"Flusoh! Did you see that?! I controlled one at a time!" He immediately began trying to issue distinct orders to his undead, but now they only seemed able to follow the same command.

Flusoh laughed. "Distracted you, didn't it? I love that trick! All right, relax, you're turning all red for some reason. This is the trickiest part, but your fractured focus will help."

Jeremiah gazed dejectedly at the bloody skeleton. Then he had a thought, but Flusoh interrupted him.

"No, you can't animate someone's skeleton out of their body while they're still alive. Their natural life force prevents it. To answer your next question, life force is derived from the soul. It's very powerful natural magic, like medusas turning people to stone or dragons breathing fire. You can't overpower it. Believe me, I've tried."

Jeremiah's mouth snapped shut in surprise.

"No, I'm not reading your mind," said Flusoh. "You're just not the first student I've ever had, and you all ask the same things."

Jeremiah swallowed his surprise. Flusoh had never mentioned any previous students. He never really talked about himself at all. "Have you had a lot of students before me?" Jeremiah asked, hoping to take advantage of Flusoh's sharing mood.

"Not too many, no. Keep in mind I've been around for a very long time."

Jeremiah inspected his boots. "Sooo, if you were to rank me, you know just for fun, you'd put me, like, in the middle? Maybe a little better?" Jeremiah side-eyed his teacher.

Flusoh imitated a sigh. "Look, if you get caught up in shit like that, you'll never stop. You'll always be worried about how you compare, and it'll mess up your training. The only person you should compare yourself to is the you from yesterday. Do you know more? Are you stronger? Smarter? Better rested? More determined? That's all that matters."

"Right, of course, of course," said Jeremiah. "But . . . you know, if you *were* to rank me . . ."

"You are the worst student I've ever had."

Jeremiah's stomach dropped. Tears welled in his eyes as Flusoh continued.

"*Because* all my other students were much older and more experienced than you. See how useless it is to compare yourself? Now, that's the most you're going to get out of me. Ask again, and I'll animate the layer of dead skin over your body and command it to fight you."

The threat didn't land quite as intended. "You can *do* that?!" Jeremiah exclaimed.

Flusoh chuckled. "Kid, if you knew the things I could do, you'd kill yourself just to not be in the same world as me."

Jeremiah held his tongue, but only briefly. He was too curious. "Can I get a demonstration? A little one? I think it would be motivating for me to see what I could be capable of in the future."

Flusoh rolled his eyes, a motion Jeremiah never quite got used to. "C'mon, kid. I know what you're doing; I want that on the record. But what the hell. Come on, let's do a demo."

CHAPTER SEVEN

Visions of Power

Jeremiah's anticipation threatened to bubble over. He had never seen Flusoh perform any but the most basic of spells. The floodgates were now open for additional questions as his teacher led him to the upper floors of the castle.

"Are you superstrong?"

"Yes."

"Are you super fast?"

"Yes."

"Why do you have those eyes?"

"To see."

"Do you need them?"

"No."

"Whose were they?"

"A prophet's."

"Can you see the future with them?"

"Sadly, no."

"Sounds like you thought you'd be able to."

"Yup."

"Was there any benefit at all?"

"Prophet seemed a lot more legitimate without eyes."

"He was *alive* when you took them?!"

Flusoh stopped and glared at Jeremiah. Jeremiah stared back into Flusoh's eyes and had a sudden insight.

"Were you lying?" Jeremiah asked.

"I lied about half the questions you asked me, including this one. Now shut it. We're almost there."

Jeremiah followed Flusoh to the parapet of the highest tower. The noonday sun illuminated the world through a sheet of gray haze, casting the swamp into monotone. Jeremiah spotted the path he had once followed to come to the castle and reminisced about how he had had no idea what he was getting into.

"You want a demo? You sure?" Flusoh asked.

Jeremiah nodded, unable to suppress a boyish grin.

Flusoh stood astride the battlement and shouted across the swamp. "By show of hands, who thinks this is the most obnoxious student ever to curse my castle halls?"

The swamp exploded in activity as countless—truly countless—skeletal hands erupted out of the water in every direction. Jeremiah's eyes grew wide at the field of white wheat stretching to the horizon. There were humanoid limbs, tail bones, an arm at least ten feet long ending in three-foot-long claws, and innumerable others that even his extensive knowledge of anatomy could not begin to identify.

Just as Jeremiah was starting to comprehend the number of bodies that had to be in the swamp, the bony appendages receded back below the surface of the swamp. He stared after them with awe, then turned to his teacher. "Why did you do that? Why did you answer my questions?"

"'Cause you've been here for three years, you've done everything I said, and you've never pried. I respect and appreciate that, so I had to indulge you a little." Flusoh patted Jeremiah's shoulder. "But the hands have spoken. You're obnoxious. Now go practice."

With the vision of incredible power fixed in his mind, Jeremiah set to his work with renewed vigor. Soon he was able to manage the two undead as easily as one. From there, he advanced quickly to reanimating three undead at a time, then four, then five.

With each additional minion, another bubble would appear in Jeremiah's mind, but the more bubbles there were, the less room there was for him. With five undead, he had to move slowly and methodically in order to do anything, and once he reached six he felt there was no room left for him at all in his own head. He sat on the floor of the room they were working in. He couldn't bring himself to move, cast, or even think straight.

Flusoh stood by, observing, then ordered Jeremiah to minimize his connections.

All six bubbles shrank considerably, and the zombies collapsed to the floor. In low focus mode, the undead could not be commanded but some mind space was returned to the necromancer. When needed, the bubbles could be reinflated back to their normal state for full control. Jeremiah sighed with relief as he began to feel more himself again.

Flusoh looked thoughtful. "Your headspace will increase with practice, but I'm thinking it's time we got you a familiar. Let's go outside."

Jeremiah knew from his reading that familiars were bonded creatures meant to enhance a mage's power through mental delegation. The specific effects varied depending on the creature and caster, but Jeremiah was intrigued by the possibilities. He reactivated two zombies to follow as he and Flusoh made their way to the castle gates.

The gates creaked open as they approached. Flusoh pointed to the swamp beyond. "Step one. Go get yourself an animal."

"Just . . . any old animal?" asked Jeremiah. "Whatever I want?"

"Smaller tends to be better. Getting your familiar killed is a serious problem, so you want to be able to hide them. But it's up to you, so by all means feel free to pick an alligator or a timber wolf or whatever."

Jeremiah descended the muddy path, his zombies following like bodyguards. He'd never stopped to consider the variety of life teeming in the swamp, but as he slogged deeper into the mire, he found himself paralyzed with options. Jeremiah sat on a stump to ponder the flaws and virtues of each.

"Snakes are cool, but maybe too obvious? Fish are less obvious, probably for a reason, though. Rats are smart, that's good, but they get fleas. Crows are smart too, and they can hide by flying. But a bird of prey would be more useful for hunting small animals for corpses. Maybe an owl?" The permanence of the decision weighed on him.

The shadows were growing longer. His zombie companions maintained their vigil in silence. Jeremiah was beginning to consider the advantages of the bats flitting overhead when a fat gray lump hopped out of a nearby puddle and began dragging itself across the mud.

Jeremiah considered it. "A blue-spined swamp toad. You don't come from much, do you? Just crawling across the mud, trying to get where you're going. But you've got a secret talent . . . I like it."

One of the zombies stooped and picked up the toad. Its blue spines sprang out to puncture the zombie's indifferent hands as it struggled to escape, and Jeremiah returned to the castle with his prize.

"A blue spine, huh?" said Flusoh. "Good choice! Suits you, and that poison is no joke. Glad you didn't come back with a crow. That's just *so* predictable. Well, let's get you two bonded."

Flusoh brought them to the ritual room. Jeremiah had never been allowed in here, and looked around with interest. The room stood in stark contrast to the spartan spaces that made up most of the castle. Instead of dark stone bricks, the walls, floor, and ceiling were solid sheets of smooth gray marble. A towering wooden shelf displayed hundreds of meticulously organized components.

A chalk diagram took up most of the floor, its complexity staggering.

Jeremiah struggled to make sense of the designs with his sparse knowledge of ritualism. Hundreds of geometric shapes and symbols were interwoven, precisely connected by long thin lines, which seemed to never overlap. He recognized small metal amplifiers on certain junctures, as well as dams of powdered copper distributed around the diagram in precise patterns, designed to control the levels of resistance for magical energy. The design was so intricate, however, that Jeremiah couldn't begin to comprehend the layers of effect involved.

The diagram featured two empty circles, a large one for Jeremiah and a small one for the toad. Jeremiah took his place. The zombie placed the toad in the other circle, where it sat contentedly.

"Shouldn't I be learning how to do this?" asked Jeremiah.

"Hell no! Ritualism is a whole different mess you're not ready to handle. Just accept that I'm doing a nice thing for you." He stood at the end chalk line extending toward the diagram. "Ready?"

"Wha—"

"Too late!" Flusoh slammed his hand down on the line.

The chalk glowed blue. In a flash, the entire floor transformed into a riot of modulating hues of blues and purples, the color changing as magic coursed through the diagram. Jeremiah's hair stood on end as he cried out in surprise at the energy's intensity. He felt his mind absorbing something, changing into a whole new place. He looked toward the toad and saw himself sitting in the circle instead, a perfect mirror image.

There was a flash and, quick as it came, the magical chaos was gone. The toad was back, sitting in its circle as though nothing had happened. Jeremiah smiled at it. He couldn't describe how, but he knew that this toad was very important to him, and that it adored him unconditionally. The toad gave a happy wiggle and crawled toward him across the diagram with haste. Jeremiah picked up and cradled the creature.

"Aww, ain't that cute!" said Flusoh. "Now, reestablish control over your minions. Feel any different?"

Jeremiah turned his attention to the small bubbles in his mind. He gasped as he reflated all of them with room to spare. "There's so much more space than before!"

Flusoh nodded. "Familiars take some of the burden. Just don't get it killed, or your limits will snap back, and if you're controlling too many undead, you'll end up comatose. Also I won't be there to help you get a new one, 'cause you got to *go*!"

Jeremiah did a double take. "I—w-what? I have to go?"

Flusoh nodded with enthusiasm. "Yup! Can't stay here forever, right?"

Jeremiah was stunned. "I know, but I thought there was a lot more for me to learn!"

"Oh, tons! I could write books about what you don't know. In fact, I have! But you're not gonna learn it here. You need experience outside these walls. So, out you go!"

Jeremiah found himself being herded back toward the exit, dazed, toad still cradled in his hands. His pack was already waiting for him by the gates as they swung open once again.

"Ah, one small thing," Flusoh said as he thrust the pack toward Jeremiah. "I've included a little gift for you. I don't give this lightly. It is your 'no-win scenario' solution. Understand this: it will kill anything and everything it can, and you will, at best, be able to suggest what it goes after first."

"Um," said Jeremiah. "Thanks." He shrugged on the pack, taking some comfort in sensing his own confusion and apprehension reflected in his new amphibian companion. "Any advice?"

Flusoh leaned forward like he was about to say something cutting, then seemed to reconsider. A long moment passed as Flusoh worked his jaw and looked out over the swamp. "Look, Jeremiah," he said finally, "you're a good kid. That's a rare thing in our line of work. Might be worth seeing where that leads."

He jabbed Jeremiah with a bony finger. "Now get out."

Jeremiah nodded and smiled and set off down the dirt path away from the castle that had become his home. He was about halfway down when he heard Flusoh call to him. "Hey, kid . . ."

Jeremiah turned to see Flusoh leaning casually against the door. The lich flashed a skeletal grin. "Run like hell."

The waters on either side of the path erupted as hundreds of undead clambered over each other in a mad effort to reach Jeremiah, who screamed and fled into the night.

CHAPTER EIGHT

You Deserve to Die

Jeremiah could feel Allison's eyes on him as he concluded his story. "I looked for opportunities to practice my craft, but people weren't exactly advertising. I did a few odd jobs, but that was just labor work for food. And the few times someone did find out what I was, well, it just became easier to keep to myself. Then I heard about that dungeon, and . . . I guess you were all there for that."

Jeremiah felt his words hanging awkwardly in the air. He wished there was more he could say, some grand conclusion that would leave no doubt in anyone's mind that he deserved to live. He forced himself to raise his gaze to see his audience.

Bruno, Delilah, and Allison remained motionless, still watching him. They seemed to be coming to conclusions for themselves.

"So . . ." Jeremiah said, trying to sound cheerful in the silence. "No one has jumped up to murder me yet."

Continued silence. Then Bruno then set his jaw and clapped his hands on his knees. "I don't wanna kill him," he said. "He saved our lives, he hasn't tried to escape, and he doesn't sound like the evil type. There, that's my couple coppers."

"He seems like a nice enough guy," said Allison slowly, "but there's only one thing to be done with necromancers." Allison stood and drew her sword, her demeanor grim.

"Al, come on," said Bruno. "He ca—"

"No!" Allison said. "We agreed, if even one of us thinks he needs to go, then he needs to go. No questions, no voting, no arguments. On your knees, necromancer. I promise it won't hurt."

Jeremiah's fear and rage surged. He had nothing left to lose.

He leapt to his feet, startling Allison and the others, and even himself. "Tell me what I did! Tell me who I hurt! You let me tell that whole gods-damned story just to kill me anyway? I was a necromancer the whole time. There wasn't some revelation waiting at the end that I'm not! So why did you wait? Just feeling dramatic?"

Allison's face darkened. "How the hell should I know who you hurt? Everything you said could've been one big lie! All I know is you raise the dead, and I've never, *ever* heard of a necromancer that didn't murder people eventually! I've got every reason to believe killing you is saving lives down the line!"

Delilah stood as well, biting her lip, but she seemed unable to speak.

Jeremiah stepped toward Allison. "Look me in the eyes and tell me I deserve to die. I want to hear you say my name when you do it. My name isn't *necromancer*. It's Jeremiah Thorn. Look me in the eyes and say 'Jeremiah Thorn, you deserve to die'!"

Allison's arm shot out of her sling as quick as a snake and seized him beneath the jaw, her broken bones audibly grinding. She lifted his chin and pressed the edge of her sword against his exposed throat. A trickle of blood ran underneath Jeremiah's shirt. She leaned close, oblivious to any pain in her arm. Teeth bared, she locked eyes with him, and spoke with ugly hatred.

"Jeremiah Thorn. You deserve to die."

Jeremiah gagged and gripped the forearm of the hand that was choking him. Tears ran down his cheeks and over Allison's fingers as he waited for cold steel to cross his throat and bleed the life from him. So much learning, so much potential, all about to run out onto the grass.

A mournful croaking came from Delilah. She clutched Gus as the toad struggled to free himself and come to his master's rescue.

Moments passed. Jeremiah became increasingly aware that he was still alive. He opened his eyes and saw Allison frozen, eyes still blazing, teeth still bared. But she hadn't killed him.

"I'm so sorry." He choked the words out. He didn't even know why he said it.

He felt Allison's arm shaking. Delilah placed a tentative hand on Allison's shoulder. "It's okay not to kill him," she said, her voice near a whisper. "You won't be doing anything wrong by being merciful."

Allison's body jerked at Delilah's words. She gave a low growl that grew into a shout of frustration. Her grip tightened around his throat. His vision swam, his feet kicked desperately in the air. He was being lifted higher, higher.

Then all at once he slammed into the ground, air leaving his lungs in a rush. He gasped for breath as he heard heavy stomping growing fainter. Then he was being helped to sit up by Delilah and Bruno. "You're all right. You're all right," Bruno murmured, brushing dust off him.

Jeremiah's body ached from the slam and he was struggling to breathe, but

Bruno was right. Delilah carefully deposited Gus on Jeremiah's lap. He wriggled and croaked in relief while Jeremiah scratched his chin.

Jeremiah could still feel tears spilling down his cheeks. The residual fear and adrenaline combined with the relief of survival into a nauseatingly sweet cocktail. He looked up at Bruno and Delilah, who couldn't quite bring themselves to meet his gaze.

"Thank you both," he rasped. "I know that must not have been easy, but it was the right decision. I promise you, it was."

"What are you going to do now?" Delilah asked.

Jeremiah looked between them. "I'm going to the city with you to collect my share of money from those doors, of course. As per our contract."

Delilah's eyes widened ever so slightly. "Ah. I was afraid you'd say that. Are you sure we can't interest you in taking some money to leave? I wouldn't exactly say you're safe from Allison at this point."

Jeremiah shook his head. He had earned his share and lost a very powerful skeleton in the process. From what Delilah had said about the doors, they were worth more than a cursory payoff. "I'm sure. I won't get in the way. I'll just take my cut and be off."

Bruno ran a hand through his hair. "Told you he'd want to get paid if he lived."

Delilah sighed. "Let me talk to Allison about it. Fair's fair, and I won't go breaking an agreement just because I can. I guess you can . . . well, I guess you can do whatever you want now. Your stuff is over there. We went through it a bit, but we didn't take anything." She picked up her longspear and followed Allison's trail into the woods, muttering, "Going to have to reset that shoulder anyway."

With a weary groan, Bruno rubbed the heels of his hands against his eyes. He managed a wan smile at Jeremiah, then retrieved his swords. Jeremiah stiffened, but Bruno merely sat some distance away. He wiped them clean and applied a mixture of oils, then settled into sharpening the blades.

Jeremiah found his own dagger among his things and joined Bruno, who offered him a spare whetstone. Bruno slowed his sharpening, allowing Jeremiah to imitate his technique. They sat together, absorbed in the ritual of maintenance. After so much fear, the rhythmic scraping of steel soothed Jeremiah's nerves.

Finally, Bruno set his swords aside. "So, it's clearly not a death wish, assuming you don't consider what happened a missed opportunity. So why'd you do it?"

"Do what?" asked Jeremiah. The question could've been about anything at this point.

"Become a mage. Learn necromancy. Try to adventure."

Jeremiah tested the edge of his dagger with his thumb. Sharp as a butterknife. "Well, the home life never felt quite right to me. I didn't want to be a jeweler like my dad or a launderer like my mom."

"But why a mage? You could have been a farmer or a carpenter or any number of things. Learning necromancy was an awful lot of time spent ruining your own life."

"I didn't want to while my days away in a nothing little town doing nothing little jobs, living a nothing little life. Necromancy was the one thing I was good at. I really thought it'd be different for me." He gave a hollow laugh. "You can see how that turned out."

"Was it worth it?"

The question caught Jeremiah off guard. He remembered fleeing for his life from angry, axe-wielding villagers. Being spit on by people that didn't know his name. He reflected on the long nights of loneliness he'd accepted as his life, and on the very real possibility that he could've been killed this very afternoon. Then he remembered his mother's bleached white hands, thin nails jagged from the washboard. He remembered his father's strained eyes and the belligerent chastising of ungrateful customers. He remembered that without him, Allison, Delilah, and Bruno would have all been the Matriarch's dinner. "Yes. Definitely."

Bruno cast him an appraising look. "Hope it holds. Not sure you've got the instinct to live a vagabond's life."

"Well, what about you?" asked Jeremiah, suddenly feeling defensive. "Why do you bother risking your life adventuring?"

"No idea! I grew up on less than dirt and have been taking care of myself since before I could walk. I know I want the wealth, just not sure what will be different when I get it. Delilah thinks it's about the security I never had. Allison says it's about having control of my life. They might both be right. But I adventure for the same reason fish swim." Bruno slid a piece of grass along his blade, shaving it in half. "It's what I do."

Delilah and Allison returned then. Delilah gave Jeremiah a weak smile, but Allison did not even look at him as she kicked his pack slightly farther away, then sat on the opposite side of the camp. He supposed it was still an improvement over their previous interaction.

A shrill whistle interrupted the uncomfortable silence.

"Boat!" said Bruno. He jumped up and ran to the river's edge. Sure enough, a wide, flat-bottomed vessel soon drifted into view.

"Looks like a river barge," said Bruno, squinting. "They're bound to take us, anything to make a run more profitable." He pulled out a small silver whistle, cupped his hands around it, and blew a sequence of short and long notes. Moments later, a different sequence came back from the boat.

Bruno sighed. "It's a bit steep for four people, but with cargo as large as ours, it's hardly unreasonable. Gonna need six silver from the treasury."

Allison handed him six silver coins. Jeremiah was grateful—he had all of two silvers and four coppers to his name. Bruno blew out a series of staccato whistles and the barge slowly began making its way toward the bank.

It was a sturdy-looking vessel, weathered wood with little in the way of decoration, save for the words *The Happy Hippo* in faded letters on the side. As it approached the bank, Jeremiah and Bruno moved the Ironwood doors into position to load onto the boat.

A narrow gangplank splashed into the shallow water. It took the aid of several sailors to maneuver the doors along it, their weight tipping the barge's knuckle into the muddy riverbed until they were fully aboard. Delilah followed to supervise the doors' journey to the storage hold while the others acquainted themselves with their new surroundings.

CHAPTER NINE

Don't Name It

The barge had not been designed with comfort in mind even at the best of times, which these were not. The passageways were crammed with armed and armored men and women, adorned with scars, tattoos, and permanent scowls. There had to be twice as many passengers as the barge was meant to transport, and then some. They shouted at each other, bantered, and squabbled as they shoved past Jeremiah, who shrank and tried to disappear into the woodwork.

Bruno seized Jeremiah's arm and whispered, "Quit darting your eyes around like a scared rabbit. These are some real cutthroats, and I don't want to have to rescue you from some thug's bit of fun." He hauled Jeremiah upright to follow Allison, who had adopted an air of bravado, exuding strength and authority as she moved through the crowd.

Jeremiah tried to imitate Bruno's intimidating scowl as they descended the stairs to the lower deck, then decided he must look ridiculous and simply raised his hood to obscure his face. Hopefully it made him seem mysterious and dangerous. He reassured himself that if it came to it, a display of magic would probably dissuade anyone from a fight. Probably.

The air on the passenger deck was thick with the smell of tobacco smoke, booze, and unwashed bodies. Jeremiah could make out the strumming of a lyre from some corner, its whimsical melody nearly drowned out by the oppressive din of boisterous voices. By the time his eyes adjusted to the dark, Bruno and Allison had disappeared.

Jeremiah swore under his breath. The low-ceilinged room was packed with narrow tables and benches. He couldn't tell where the ale was coming from, but it was flowing freely. He started making his way through the room, looking for his companions.

After being shoved one time too many and drawing a growl from a burly dwarf who had nearly spilled his tankard, Jeremiah decided to continue his search from a stationary position. He ducked into a narrow spot at a nearby table. The elf he sat beside paid him no mind, already embroiled in conversation.

"And I keep telling you, you're mad if you think we're headed all the way to Nosirin!" The slender elf was playing with a nasty-looking dagger, twirling it between his fingers to catch the lantern light. The pointed tip of his ear was notched with an ancient scar. "Dramir will post us on the wall and keep us plump and happy without a barbarian in sight."

A human with an eye patch turned and spat in a corner. "What a waste of money! Who would hire an entire company of mercs to sit on their asses and do nuttin'?"

"Scared rich folk, that's who," said the elf. "Dramir doesn't give a shit if Nosirin falls to a Barbie horde, but they wouldn't want to risk their guardsmen's shiny armor, so they fatten our purses for months on end, just in case the horde looks southward."

Jeremiah's ears perked up at the topic of Nosirin falling to barbarians. Nosirin was the closest thing he had to a home city, although he'd actually grown up several day's journey away and had only visited once.

"Nah, no one'd be daft enough to move on Dramir, barbarian or not. Even if you could take it, which you can't, then you're surrounded! And even if Nosirin did fall, ain't no one can stand against Barad Celegald, Elminia, Shabad, *and* Tempest City all fightin' together, wall or no wall. The king knows all that, so he must be sendin' us all the way north." The human sat back, satisfied.

Jeremiah nodded in agreement inside his hood. By all accounts, the central city of Dramir was a formidable fortress in its own right. However, what truly ensured its security was the fact that if any one of the five surrounding cities disrupted the power balance by conquering Dramir, they would immediately face a united enemy from four directions. It simply wasn't worth it. Thus, while the other cities warred among themselves, Dramir had been allowed to flourish, growing from a humble merchants' station to the kingdom's seat of power. Several centuries ago, an allied rebellion between Shabad and Elminia had failed to overthrow Dramir, but did bring about an agreement in which the royal families of each city would pay tithes to Dramir in return for the right to appoint Dramir's ruler. This arrangement ensured a relative peace still enjoyed to this day.

A halfling piped up, moving to sit on the table for greater visibility. "I think you're right, Jasko, but for the wrong reason." The human rolled his eyes, but the halfling continued. "We're going to Nosirin, but it's because King Hector is scared." She paused for dramatic effect. "He's scared because these Barbies really could take Dramir *and* hold it against everyone else. He's scared because *these barbarians don't die.*"

She spoke the last at a hiss that Jeremiah had to strain to hear, which meant he was nearly deafened by the uproar of laughter from the others around the table. "You can't be bloody serious!" said the elf, when he had regained control of himself.

"She's serious," sighed Jasko. "Got a letter from a cousin or something up in Nosirin last week and hasn't shut up about it since."

"You calling my kin liars?" The halfling stood on the table now, eye to eye with the seated human.

"Seems a lot more likely than the alternative," said Jasko. He tucked another wad of tobacco into his lip and chewed it ostentatiously.

Jeremiah realized what was about to happen only an instant before it did. The halfling sucker punched Jasko and the table erupted into motion. The bench he was sitting on was knocked backward, and Jeremiah sprawled on the floor, narrowly avoiding a thrown tankard. He scrambled away from the rapidly expanding brawl, ducking past mercenaries rushing toward the scene, and raced up the stairs to the promise of fresh air and sunlight above.

Bruno, Allison, and Delilah were gathered by the gunwale on the upper deck. Delilah looked up as Jeremiah hurried over. "There you are," she said. "Bruno was worried you'd been tossed overboard."

"Sorry, no such luck," said Jeremiah.

"I was just telling Bruno and Allison that it might take a little while to collect payment for the doors in Dramir," said Delilah. "You're welcome to stay with us at my apartment until it's resolved."

Allison looked like she wanted to scream but instead just glared at the trees passing slowly on the bank.

"My house, my invitation," Delilah said to the unspoken objection.

"What are you gonna do with the big ear?" asked Bruno.

"Ah! That will be our 'Proof of Meritorious Service' to the kingdom. No one wants a Warren near their borders, so we can get a reward for presenting evidence of having destroyed one. Or better yet, attention!"

"Attention?" asked Jeremiah.

Delilah clasped her hands with enthusiasm. "Oh yes! The right attention from the right people can open a lot of doors for us! Maybe even"—Delilah's eyes were gleaming now, and she bounced ever so slightly—"*introductions!*"

Bruno turned dramatically to Jeremiah. "Mr. Thorn, may I please present to you Madam Delilah Fortune. Madam Fortune, please make the acquaintance of Mr. Thorn."

Jeremiah adopted a pompous, blustering voice. "Madam Fortune, the honor is all mine, I assure you!"

"Yeah, okay," said Delilah, deflating a bit. "Now imagine I'm a duke looking for someone to manage my six-thousand-acre land holdings, and you, being *so* upstanding and with *such* a prestigious introduction, would be just perfect for the job. But for tax reasons you need to be a baron, so I intercede with the crown and from one sentence to the next, you go from tattooed adventurer bumming in his friend's apartment to landed noble dwelling in your own estate with servants and a cycle of wealth."

There was a long pause. Delilah smiled sweetly.

"Oh," said Jeremiah.

"Damn right."

Allison slammed her fist against the gunwale. "Stop getting cozy! I won't have you naming this whelp before we toss him out!"

There was another long pause, but this time the awkwardness was palpable.

Bruno drummed his fingers on the gunwale. "Well, I should go carouse a bit and see what sort of group we've got aboard, rumors and such."

"I need to catalogue some chemicals," said Delilah.

"Ugh!" Allison stomped away, leaving Jeremiah alone to watch the water lap against the hull of the barge. It was splinters all the way down.

Jeremiah stayed by the gunwale with only Gus for company as the wooded shore glided past. He wondered whether he was still in danger from his traveling companions. Bruno and Delilah seemed amicable enough, but Allison's anger scared him.

"As far as I know, they're going to turn me in to the authorities once we hit Dramir," he said to Gus. "But that doesn't seem like something they'd do, does it? Maybe Allison would, although it doesn't seem her style to have me killed secondhand."

The toad blinked, first one eye and then the other.

Jeremiah gazed at the shore. He could swim. Maybe he should just jump ship and disappear out of their lives. He'd be right back where he started, broke and alone, and minus the red skeleton. The very idea was exhausting. And besides, terrifying as Allison was, she hadn't killed him when she had the chance. Part of him insisted on the hope that they could still become friends.

Feeling listless, Jeremiah turned away from the gunwale. The crowd had thinned somewhat as mercenaries crammed below deck for an evening of revelry. The sun kissed the horizon behind the barge, washing the placid river in gold.

He wandered around the deck, giving a wide berth to the clusters of merce-naries crouching in circles to drink and throw dice. He spotted Delilah kneeling beside one of the deck cabins, surrounded by bottles and jars, peering into some and rattling others. She glanced at him as he approached, expressionless, and went right back to her inventory.

"Do you mind if I sit?" asked Jeremiah.

"By all means," Delilah said without looking up.

Jeremiah sat back against the cabin, watching her work. There was something reassuring about her methodical movements, the sureness with which she evaluated her stock. Like it somehow added weight to the fact that she had heard his story and had judged him deserving of mercy.

Delilah rattled the final bottle, then tucked her entire arsenal among the folds of her layered robes and turned to him. "So. Are you doing okay?"

Jeremiah was startled by the question. He hadn't expected his state of mind to be of concern to her. "I think so? I'm not angry or anything. In fact, I'm grateful to be alive. I just wish things didn't feel so . . . temporary. I enjoyed delving that dungeon with you guys."

Delilah nodded. "Things took a pretty abrupt turn for you. I hope you at least understand our concerns. Even Allison's."

Jeremiah returned the nod. "Yeah, I get it. Necromancers aren't exactly known for anything other than atrocities."

"Is there a reason for that?" asked Delilah. "Why are necromancers such evil people?" At Jeremiah's hurt expression, she added, "Sorry. Mostly such evil people."

Jeremiah shrugged. "They thrive on death. In a way, death is their source of power. Most people reject that level of morbidity, so the person that would seek that power is going to tend to be the kind of person who doesn't value life . . . or community."

"But not you?" she asked. "It seems like you value life and community. Why are you different?"

"I've spent a lot of time thinking about that. I think it's because I never set out to be a necromancer. I just wanted to be a mage. I took the only opportunity I could. Also, I'm pretty sure that if I turned down Flusoh's offer, I would have ended up as another body in that swamp."

Delilah gave a half smile. "You know he's most likely evil, right? Regardless of the philosophy he wraps it in?"

"I know it seems that way. But does it make sense if I said I thought Flusoh was just selfish beyond morality? Good or evil was irrelevant to him; it was just whatever he wanted to do."

Delilah cocked an eyebrow. "Oh, I understand. But my understanding of that is also called evil."

Jeremiah frowned and looked away. "You may be right. But I don't think I'm ready to admit that about my teacher yet."

Delilah face turned sympathetic. "Hey, I could be wrong. Maybe your teacher was the one good lich out there and you're the one good necromancer."

"Yeah, maybe." Jeremiah smiled.

Bruno reappeared then, making Jeremiah jump. "Not too much in the way of news. A new gang of brigands called the White Light have started marauding in the area. The charmers downstairs were hired by Dramir, but they don't know for what. Someone said it's to put down some uprising in the far north, but no one knows anything for sure. We'll have to camp on the deck and keep watches. I don't trust anyone on this boat."

"Did you tell Allison?" asked Delilah.

"Not yet. I think she's downstairs somewhere, hopefully not causing trouble. Why don't you claim a spot, and I'll go let her know the plan." Bruno started to leave, then spun around. "Hey, Jeremiah, do you know how to play cards?"

"Sure I do. Why?"

"'Cause I've got an idea to make some money, but I need a second set of hands."

"Is it by cheating?" asked Jeremiah.

"Oh yes!" Bruno grinned wickedly and slipped away.

CHAPTER TEN

Silver Tongue

Jeremiah and Delilah set up their campsite near the anchors, away from most of the foot traffic. Allison soon joined them and tossed her bag among theirs. She didn't mention her previous outburst, but there was an undeniable tension in the air as Delilah retied her sling.

Bruno reappeared once it was fully dark, practically vibrating with excitement. "Come on, Jeremiah, we're gonna play some cards!"

Delilah and Allison exchanged a look, but Jeremiah stood at once to join him. The thrill of cheating at cards with a bunch of cutthroats sounded like exactly what he needed. A bit of fun and mischief to lift his spirits would be a relief, and he was curious to see how they were going to cheat.

At the top of the stairs, Bruno handed him two silver coins. "This is the buy-in. We'll be betting mostly in coppers, though." Bruno showed him a small silver metal tin, similar to something that would hold makeup, and revealed a strange clear paste inside. "All I need you to do is play and, as you come across them, touch any aces, faces, or tens on the upper right corner with"—he took Jeremiah's hand and lightly dipped a finger into the paste—"this finger. If it's a seven, eight, or nine, mark the upper left corner."

"That's it?" Jeremiah asked. The sheen of the clear paste on the corners of cards would be pretty hard to spot.

"That's it! Play conservatively at first, you need to encounter as many cards as possible to get the deck marked up properly. But if you've got a good hand, don't be afraid to go for blood."

"Are you marking them too?"

Bruno shook his head. "Nah. They'd expect it from a guy like me. I'm gonna be watched like a hawk. But you? No offense, but you don't exactly look like a card shark. Just someone trying to have a little fun."

"Any code words we should use if something starts to go wrong?" Jeremiah asked. "I could still get caught."

Bruno considered him for a moment. "You don't have to do this if you don't want to. I hope you already know that. But if you start to think something bad is about to go down, I'll be two steps ahead of you. If things start getting out of hand, we leave our money and go. No need to spill blood over two silver. If things actually get violent, well, you know what to do."

Jeremiah nodded. "Raise zombies."

Bruno stared. "No. Don't do that, just do the acid thing. That'll be fine."

"Maybe. But if it comes to it, being revealed as a necromancer is still better than being dead."

Bruno groaned and rubbed a hand over his face. "Fine." He gestured toward the deck below. "All right. Now you go and find a game. I'll join up in a minute."

Once again, Jeremiah descended the dark stairs. He navigated the crowded bowels of the ship, trying to act casual, until he spotted a group of nasty looking men and women around a makeshift card table in a small side room. A dwarf with thick iron piercings through the bridge of his nose nodded when Jeremiah flashed the silver coins Bruno had given him.

"You lookin' to play cards?" the dwarf growled. His dark gray beard was wet with the bottle of wine he was drinking, and Jeremiah noticed one of his eyes had been replaced with a sphere of gold metal.

"Yes, indeed!" Jeremiah smiled broadly in what he hoped was a convincing facade of someone with more money than sense. "I love a good game of cards. Heard there was a two-silver game and had to come give my luck a go. Great way to pass the time."

The other players were all too ready to believe him. They included a brute of an orc with fully grown tusks jutting from his pronounced jaw, a gnome that kept packing more and more tobacco into his cheek, a human man with no teeth, and a human woman whose expression was a permanent sneer. They all had hard eyes and at least one obvious weapon. Jeremiah kept up his cheerful demeanor despite his nervousness. Only the orc and woman accepted an introductory handshake.

Jeremiah made small talk while they waited for any other takers. The orc's name was Gagthu'k, and he was a mercenary who sent most of his money back home to his family in Invictus. The dwarf was Ballathu; he was partial owner of *The Happy Hippo*. The two humans and gnome weren't very talkative.

Bruno sauntered up to the table, his hardened scowl making him indistinguishable from the other cutthroats. He threw down his coins without a word and scanned the table. He indicated no recognition of Jeremiah. Jeremiah kept up his side of the act by attempting small talk with Bruno and offering his hand, which Bruno refused.

Ballathu cleared his throat speaking with professionalism. "Ladies and gentlemen, I run a fast game. One copper minimum per hand. No hemmin' or hawin'. I deal the whole game. If you don' like it, you can leave." He placed a deck of thin wooden playing cards on the table. "Anyone who wants can inspect the deck now."

Bruno, Jeremiah, and the gnome all inspected the deck. Jeremiah commented on the impressive quality of the cards and meant it. Bruno tossed the cards back and forth, testing their weight. He smelled them and ran his fingers along their edges, he stared intently at their backs, searching for imperfections or markings, and finding none. But he did succeed in making everyone at the table suspicious of him and his apparent knowledge of card cheating techniques. All players satisfied, the first coppers were tossed to the middle and the game began.

As planned, Jeremiah played conservatively and marked as many cards as he could with the thin layer of paste on his finger. Even knowing exactly what to look for, he was unable to see the marks himself.

The human man and gnome were knocked out in two rounds after being goaded into all-or-nothing bets against Ballathu. After about seven hands, Jeremiah began to see the same cards again, and assumed that the deck was now fully marked, his task complete. Jeremiah's role was to eventually be knocked out of the game by Bruno, who had all the information to win. But what was the harm in a little more fun?

Jeremiah started playing just aggressively enough to win a couple hands and stay above his two silver entry fee, taking his cues from Bruno's bets. Soon the orc and the woman were knocked out, leaving Ballathu and Bruno far and away the coin leaders. Jeremiah managed to siphon off some of Bruno's winnings, while Ballathu languished and bled coppers, much to his frustration. Eventually, Bruno caught him out, and Ballathu was broke. To his credit, he accepted his loss peaceably and continued to deal.

Now that it was down to him and Bruno, Jeremiah enacted his plan. In the first round, he allowed his stoney face to slip and frowned, fiddling with his cards. His fidgeting marked them all on the upper right corner. He then folded. Over the next five hands, Jeremiah's coins dwindled as he marked every single card as high and then folded.

"I'm not here for a fucking tea party," Bruno growled. "Bet or quit."

With his next hand, Jeremiah stacked his cards and viewed them by sliding them down, concealing the top corners from Bruno. Bruno didn't seem to notice and started building the pot to force Jeremiah out of the game. After the third raise on Bruno's part, the pot was substantial and Jeremiah had almost nothing left. Jeremiah casually flared his cards, exposing the marked corners, then raised the remainder of his coins. Bruno scowled and folded.

Jeremiah repeated the feat on the next round. His pile of coins had grown substantially. Near the end of the third round, he saw a flash of confusion in Bruno's eyes, followed by insight.

Bruno laid his cards face down on the table as if contemplating a bet, and his eyes flicked to the backs of his own cards. Then he glared daggers at Jeremiah, but only for a moment.

With a sickly sweet smile, Bruno leaned forward. "Look, I don't have all night. How about this—you quit, and I'll give you a silver for a good game."

Jeremiah adopted an air of bewilderment. "Why would I do that? I'm winning!" Bruno's smile remained plastered on his face as he compared their piles and saw that Jeremiah was right, if only by a little. Jeremiah was nearly giddy with excitement. The seven silver and two copper on his side of the table was more money then he'd ever had.

"So you are," said Bruno. "Let's fix that, shall we?"

The next few hands were an absolute massacre. Jeremiah couldn't draw Bruno into anything that Bruno didn't eventually win. Jeremiah's excitement turned to cold sweat as his reserves dwindled; losing so much money so fast was fraying his nerves, even if he was in cahoots with his opponent.

As he circled the drain, Jeremiah noticed Bruno start to shift uncomfortably. His gaze kept returning to the door behind Jeremiah. Jeremiah turned without a hint of subtlety. The two humans and the gnome from before were blocking the door, arms crossed and staring Bruno down.

Ballathu noticed as well. "There a problem, gentlemen?" he asked as he stood from his chair. One of his hands rested on a small war hammer on his belt.

The human man spat on the floor. "These two know each other. My boy here saw 'em getting on together. They're pretending like they don't."

Ballathu shrugged. "Ain't nothin' against the rules about that."

"They're cheating!" said the man.

"I've been keeping an eye, and there's been no cheatin'. There's nothin' that would get past me. I know every trick there is and invented a few myself. Now quit bein' sore and get lost."

A ripple of indignation swept over the man's face, but before he could answer Bruno stood, hands raised in a placating gesture.

"Relax, I don't want any trouble. Here." He reached down and pulled out six silver worth of copper and slid it across the table toward them.

The gnome and woman moved to grab the money, but the man stopped them.

"Sorry, friend, but in the time you've been holding our money, it's accrued interest. Skin interest."

At the words "skin interest," Jeremiah saw Bruno tense like a ballista ready to fire.

You're going to make wonderful zombies, Jeremiah thought as he prepared to dive under the table.

The man drew a sharp curved knife and pointed it at Jeremiah. "I think I'll take a lip from you." He pointed at Bruno. "And from you? Hmm . . . one of them tattoos would make a mighty fine patch."

A crowd had been gathering outside the door in anticipation of a fight. As the man spoke, however, the on-lookers seemed to evaporate. Behind the three aggressors, Jeremiah spotted Delilah in the doorway, brandishing the business end of her broken spear toward anyone who looked in.

The knife-wielding man finally realized something was wrong. He started to turn as Allison entered the room, her eyes steely and full of malice. Without taking even a second to analyze the situation, she punched the man in the kidney so hard he collapsed across the poker table.

Jeremiah ducked out of the way just in time, scurrying under the table to the opposite side. When he emerged, the man was lying face up on the table as Allison straddled him and rained punches down on his face.

Coins rattled onto the floor with each blow. The man raised his knife, but Allison disarmed him and slammed it hilt-deep into his leg before returning to her reconstruction of his face. The man's struggles got weaker and more defensive, and the eagerness of his comrades turned to dismay at the savagery.

Jeremiah climbed to his feet beside Bruno. Delilah held the crowd at bay with her spear. Ballathu, who had retreated into a corner, looked on in horror.

Allison's face was red with effort, her hair whipping around her head. She let out a long warlike roar and shouted at the man while she bludgeoned him, every blow coming with a new accusation. "Bastard! Coward! Liar! Fucking monster!"

Allison's fist came back with a fragment of tooth lodged in the knuckle. The sight seemed to break her berserker rage. She looked at the unconscious man beneath her, then directly at Jeremiah. But her face wasn't the mask of rage he expected. Well, not *just* rage—he also saw hurt, sadness, and disappointment. Without another word, she rose to her feet and left.

The only sounds in the room were the gurgling wheezes of the beaten man, his face pummeled beyond recognition. As Jeremiah started to follow Allison, Bruno grabbed his shoulder, shaking his head in warning.

Jeremiah shrugged Bruno off and continued past Delilah and out the door. Allison had already vanished up the stairs to the top deck.

The chill of the night air was a relief. Stars twinkled between the clouds overhead as Jeremiah looked for Allison. He walked nearly the entire way around the deck before he spotted her.

She was slumped against the gunwale, looking out over the water, chin resting on her good hand. She seemed diminished. That attention-grabbing energy was nowhere to be found. Jeremiah realized he had no idea what he was going to say.

He leaned against the gunwale, leaving a fair amount of space between them for both of their benefits. Tears ran tracks down her face, but her expression was placid and disinterested.

"Please tell me one of them tried to stop you from coming up here," said Allison in a flat monotone.

"Bruno did, yeah," Jeremiah said.

Allison didn't reply right away. Jeremiah gazed out over the water and wondered if coming up here had been a mistake.

"I'm tired," she finally said. "I've been so angry. I don't think I have the energy to keep it up."

Jeremiah was tempted to reach over and touch her shoulder, but Allison probably didn't need a lot of energy to break his hand. He tried to think of something comforting to say instead. "I'll be out of your hair soon. Couple more days, then I'm gone."

More silence followed. After a minute or so, Allison asked, "That guy dead?"

"No. At least not yet."

"His friends cause any trouble?"

"Also not yet."

"If they didn't yet, they won't." Allison wiped her eyes on her sleeve.

She hadn't lashed out at him yet. Jeremiah decided to take a chance and try a show of compassion. He reached out his hand and placed it on Allison's shoulder.

"Ow," she said.

Jeremiah yanked his hand back, realizing he had touched her injured arm. "Oh gods! I'm so sorry!"

To his relief, she laughed a little. She sniffed and once more wiped her face on her sleeve.

"I'm sorry," she said, to Jeremiah's astonishment. "I've been treating you like shit. If I'm not going to kill you, and apparently I'm not, I can at least be civil until you're gone."

"I'd appreciate that," Jeremiah said.

Allison sighed, then straightened and faced him without any of the disgust or hatred that had been in her eyes. "Don't get any ideas. I want you gone. I'm pretty sure what you do is evil, even if you might not be. But you can join us at Delilah's place until we get your money sorted."

Jeremiah smiled. "Thanks."

"Can you go find Bruno and Delilah? We need to move our camp spot. Thanks to Bruno, we'll be doing another round of double shifts and sleeping in armor."

Jeremiah nodded and left. The peace with Allison was as fragile as platinum filigree, and the longer he hung around, the greater the chance he'd destroy it by saying something stupid.

He ran into Bruno and Delilah hurrying up the stairs. "Oh, thank the gods you didn't find her yet!" Delilah said, smiling with relief.

"I did, actually," said Jeremiah. "I think maybe we're going to be okay."

Bruno barked a laugh. "Who *is* this silver-tongued devil that we've got following us?" He pulled Jeremiah into a headlock. "You thought you were so clever, didn't you? Trying to pull one over on The Shadow of Dock Road Two! And now you've got the gall to talk to Allison and return without a single broken bone!"

Jeremiah laughed and slipped the headlock. "I almost had you! One or two more hands and I would have cleaned you out."

Bruno grinned. "Yeah, except you lick your lip if you've got something good, and you look at your hand twice as long if it's a straight, cause you're a typical double-checker."

"Were you looking for us?" Delilah asked.

"Oh yeah. Allison says to move camp, and that we're doing double shifts in armor again because of what happened downstairs."

Bruno's face fell. Delilah said, "You took care of the whole watch last night. I can cover you this one."

Bruno waved her off. "Nah, just lemme sleep till third shift and I'll be okay. We'll be home in a few days. I'll live till then."

Jeremiah noticed the assumption that he still wasn't allowed to pull any watches. *Still not trustworthy*, he thought.

Allison had already set up the campsite. Jeremiah bedded down and gazed at the stars as the others discussed the watch schedule, and despite his earlier misgivings, he was grateful for a full night's rest. It had been a long, long day.

As Jeremiah began drifting toward sleep, he heard a metallic clink. A silver coin had landed next to his bag.

"For a good game," came Bruno's voice from the dark.

CHAPTER ELEVEN

Tourist

Allison had been right about the lack of trouble—they were left alone for the rest of the journey. But another two nights with double shifts in armor didn't do anyone any favors. Jeremiah felt guilty as the bags under his companion's eyes deepened, but there was little he could do.

On the morning of the third day, Jeremiah awoke to a sailor shouting, "One hour till port! One hour till port! Left belongings will become property of *The Happy Hippo* and Happy Hippo Enterprises!"

The barge buzzed with activity as people started to pack up. Jeremiah and the others hurried to gather their gear and join the crowd waiting near the gangplank to disembark.

Soon enough, the barge rounded a bend in the river to reveal a small dock town. Jeremiah craned his neck for a glimpse of Dramir's legendary wall, but beyond the town was acres of rolling pasture, scenery reminiscent of where he grew up.

Messages whistled through the morning haze as the *Hippo* neared the dock. The river port was already swollen with activity as harbor hands tended to boats, sailors scrambled over their vessels, and merchants hawked their goods to departing and arriving passengers. A long line of carts and carriages unloaded travelers and picked up new ones before trundling back along a long dusty road. Jeremiah decided they must be heading toward Dramir.

The Happy Hippo dropped her anchor and was lashed to the dock. Once the gangplank went down, Jeremiah and the others joined the claustrophobic press of passengers. A sizable chunk of the hull of the *Hippo* opened to give access to the cargo hold. Jeremiah, Bruno, and Allison found an out-of-the-way spot to wait as the Ironwood doors were unloaded, while Delilah secured transport to Dramir.

Presently, Delilah returned with a wide cart drawn by a pair of powerful-looking oxen. It took the help of five dock porters and the driver to wrestle the doors aboard. Delilah tipped them a copper apiece, then clambered after the others onto the simple bench seating. The oxen strained against the load, and the cart peeled away from the dock.

Jeremiah tried to contain his excitement as they passed the outlying farms. His companions were silent, gazing into the distance as the wagon rattled along, but Jeremiah was restless with anticipation. He squinted at the horizon, wishing the oxen would plod just a bit faster.

They traveled for well over an hour through farmland and sheep fields. Buildings grew more frequent, and they passed more travelers on the road. Finally, they crested one last hill and the sight Jeremiah had been waiting for came into view.

Jeremiah dropped all pretense and leapt out of his seat to see better. His jaw dropped as the famous wall of Dramir rose over the horizon, and dwarfed the pastoral buildings surrounding it. Only the spires of the palace towers surpassed the height of the wall, revealing that a city may indeed be hidden within. Huge slabs of polished gray limestone had been affixed to the wall's outside surface, removing all texture and transforming the wall into an enormous monolith of smooth, reflective stone. Ballistae and scorpions lined the battlements, and round towers stood like sentries at regular intervals. It was easy to see why Dramir had never been tested in siege. The wall was more than imposing—it was awe-inspiring.

"You're the worst kind of tourist." Bruno laughed. "You have no idea how hard it is to not rob you right now."

Jeremiah sat back with a bashful grin. "Sorry. I've only ever been to Nosirin before." Nosirin wasn't nearly as big as Dramir and was much uglier.

"There's a lot to see!" said Delilah. "The markets are some of the best. You can buy anything there."

He watched, enthralled, as the wall somehow grew larger and larger. Closer, he spotted suspended wooden platforms, supporting tiny figures washing the wall's surface. It looked like a hopeless chore, like trying to clean a mountain.

Allison said, "You get in any kind of trouble here and the first thing they do is assign you to a wall-cleaning crew."

Bruno shuddered. Jeremiah wondered if he had memories of that very thing.

The road led right to the base of the wall, where a queue of travelers was ushered one by one through a massive gatehouse. Soon they passed into the shadow of the wall itself. The high sun disappeared behind the gigantic barbican, and the echoes of dozens of slow-moving wheels filled the air. The wheels of their cart rumbled as they crossed a wooden drawbridge over the swift-moving river moat below.

Jeremiah did his best to contain his excitement. The ceiling of the barbican featured murder holes so broad a pair of horses could fit through them side by side. Countless arrow slits lined the walls, some large enough to hide ballistae or worse.

This is a killing zone, he thought. *Imagine what they could do with a necromancer on their side!* He imagined hordes of orcish warriors being torn to shreds, only to rise as the new undead defenders of the city, turning on the terrified and hapless attackers . . .

Jeremiah came out of his fantasy to realize their turn for inspection had arrived. A guard in leather brigandine armor greeted the driver and began looking over their cart. Jeremiah noticed Bruno had stiffened and seemed to be holding his breath. Allison gave his shoulder a reassuring squeeze, but he didn't relax until the guard motioned them forward, seemingly satisfied.

They finally passed through the barbican and into an explosion of sound. The cart rolled through a wide market plaza swarming with people and carts and wagons. Jeremiah's head reeled at the sheer number of brightly colored market stalls, displaying everything you could imagine. Barkers hollered advertisements for their goods, frugal shoppers haggled with miserly store owners, and children holding aloft meals, snacks, and drinks swarmed the carts that entered the city. They shouted and touted their offerings as the best in the city, the best there's ever been, the best there ever could be, everything so cheap it was practically free, of course.

Jeremiah's senses fixated on the aromas emanating from freshly cooked slabs of meat, spiced kebabs, and still-bubbling iced cinnamon rolls. Though he wasn't hungry, the compulsion to eat was overwhelming.

"It's your money, tourist," said Bruno. But he joined Jeremiah by the side of the cart. Jeremiah fished in his pockets for a handful of coppers and let his eyes do the ordering. Once he had replaced the coins with an armful of food, Bruno shouted something in a language Jeremiah had never heard, and all but two of the children vanished. One of the children shook his head no and ran off, but the other handed Bruno a rolled piece of parchment. Bruno tossed this child a silver coin and she disappeared.

Jeremiah couldn't help but marvel at the scale of it all while he savored his treats (which his comrades declined to share). Delilah directed the driver through the cobble streets until they stopped along a residential road. Two identical rows of well-appointed houses with white walls of daub and bare wooden beams lined the street.

"Home sweet home!" Delilah said. She gave additional instructions to the driver regarding the doors, then paid the fee and ushered everyone inside.

Delilah's home was beautiful. The front door opened onto a refined receiving room connected to a small kitchen. An ornate oak table straddled the transition between kitchen and receiving room, etched with intricate geometric designs. An elegant sofa faced a cold fireplace from the center of the receiving room. It was flanked by a pair of stately upholstered chairs. This was by far the fanciest house Jeremiah had ever set foot in.

The others dropped their bags with groans of relief and kicked off their shoes to enjoy the lush carpet. Jeremiah followed suit, although he wasn't sure he could ever be comfortable in such a lavish space. Three more rooms were accessible down a hall from the receiving room. The nearest door was ajar, revealing a tidy bedroom bereft of decoration save for a panoply of weapons, arranged neatly on the wall. A narrow staircase off the kitchen led to an upper floor. For Jeremiah, whose childhood home had consisted of two rooms for his whole family, the house might as well have been a palace, albeit one that had been accumulating an air of abandonment.

A pleasant spring breeze filled the room as Delilah threw the windows open, disturbing the thin layer of dust over everything. Bruno yawned, which was soon imitated by everyone else. He hastily removed his armor, letting it fall unceremoniously to the ground. He collapsed on the sofa wearing only his trousers.

"Oh, that is so much better," said Delilah. She sat beside Bruno and began unwrapping layer after armored layer.

"No, don't get comfy yet," said Allison. "Help me get my armor off, then you can sit." Bruno groaned, but climbed to his feet. He and Allison tugged at the straps of her armor until she was down to a padded doublet. This too she threw aside, leaving only her smallclothes. Her skin was crisscrossed with innumerable raised white scars. She and Bruno sank heavily into the sofa next to the delayered Delilah.

Allison, Bruno, and Delilah stared blankly at the empty fireplace. Jeremiah lowered himself into one of the chairs, acutely aware of how exhausted the three of them were, and how rested he was.

Minutes slipped by. The peaceful room was a thousand miles from the bustle of the city Jeremiah yearned to explore. He drummed his fingers on the arm of his chair. A cart rattled past outside. Somebody nearby sang a pleasant melody as they performed their chores. He was finally here, in the great city of Dramir! But on the list of things he wanted to see and do here, sit quietly in a room was quite low.

Several more minutes passed before Jeremiah dared disturb the quietude. "What do we do now?" he asked.

Nobody answered at first. Finally, Delilah closed her eyes. "We need to . . ." She trailed off, then took a slow breath. "We need to get some rest. Allison, Bruno, get up. No sleeping on the sofa."

Bruno stirred a little, but the rhythmic rise and fall of Allison's chest remained undisturbed.

"Allison!" Delilah said. Allison started awake. Delilah slowly rose to her feet. "Jeremiah, get some water from the well pump outside, please."

Jeremiah did as he was asked. Delilah made everyone drink two full cups of water. Allison disappeared into the first bedroom the moment she finished.

"Jay, your room is up the stairs on the right," Delilah said. "Might be musty, but it's furnished. My lab is upstairs on the left. Stay out." With that, she went to her own room down the hall.

Bruno paused before heading to his own room. "If you go out today, be back here by dark. No gambling. No dark alleys. No looking for trouble. If trouble finds you, you say my name until the trouble goes away."

"Yes, Mom," said Jeremiah, rolling his eyes.

"That's m'boy." Bruno patted him on the head, then staggered down the hall and closed the door behind him.

And with that, Jeremiah was alone for the first time in days. Just him and Gus, like it always should have been. Alone was safe, and there was a certain freedom in that. His excitement swelled as he stepped out the front door. In a couple of days he'd have a few extra silver to his name, but for now he had a roof to sleep under and a city to explore.

Jeremiah started toward the center of the city, a short distance from Delilah's house. There were so many different kinds of people here! Elves, dwarves, halflings, gnomes, half elves, half orcs, and even orcs mingled among humans, dealing with shopkeepers or rushing past on business. Jeremiah, whose home village had whispered for a week about a single dwarf visitor, was caught gawking more than once, much to his embarrassment. He even saw a troll in chain armor escorting some sort of rich merchant. The troll returned his curious stare with a snarl and flex of his enormous clawed fingers.

Dramir's center was dominated by the palace, its massive peaked towers visible from anywhere. Four spires stretched skyward, arrayed around a tremendous fifth. The area was full of other visitors taking in the sights, and Jeremiah joined them in craning his neck to marvel at the golden creeping vines that grew along the palace's white stone walls, which were as smooth as marble. Statues became more and more frequent as he neared the palace, and he found himself stopping frequently to gaze up at the bronze-cast features of some renowned hero, beloved nobleman, or brilliant scientist from the city's long history.

Jeremiah passed through the gate to the palace grounds, noting that the guards were armed to the teeth. He had to shield his eyes against the sun glinting off their plate armor and full-faced helms. He gave them a wide berth, but still felt their scrutiny as he hurried by.

The palace proper was closed to the public, but access to one of the ornate towers was granted for just two copper. Jeremiah scaled the seemingly endless tower steps, his lungs and legs burning and his robes soon drenched with sweat. He kept his eyes on his feet as he climbed, glancing up only to squeeze past other visitors stopping to catch their breath or to manage a strained smile at those lucky enough to be descending.

At last, he rounded the last few steps and emerged at the top of the tower. With shaking legs, he leaned against the battlement, gulping down the fresh air. After a few minutes, his breath returned, and he was able to appreciate the dizzying distance to the plaza below. The tower afforded a view of the entire city, revealing rings of the city's expansion like the growth of a tree.

"Nice view, eh?' said a voice at his elbow.

Jeremiah turned to see a gnomish couple standing on tiptoe to peer over the embrasure of the battlement. The male gnome was grinning at him. "Absolutely!" said Jeremiah. "Worth climbing all those stairs to see."

"First time in Dramir?" asked the female gnome.

"Yeah. First day, actually," said Jeremiah.

"Oh, you picked a wonderful place to start! My husband and I come every year, and we always make sure to climb the tower. Works up an appetite so we can eat plenty of treats later!"

Jeremiah's stomach rumbled in agreement. "You come every year? You must know all about the city, then!"

The husband puffed out his chest. "You could say so! I'm something of an amateur historian myself. I can tell you stories about every street and alley in Dramir. For example, right down there is where they executed Gillian Folds for treason after she sold state secrets to Barad Celegald. Drawn and quartered she was, exceptionally brutal by all accounts!"

The gnomes introduced themselves as Goshwick and Mathilde. Jeremiah spent an enjoyable half hour listening to their stories and entertaining their curiosities about him, though always mindful to not let slip anything incriminating.

Goshwick explained that besides the imposing wall, Dramir enjoyed the protection of a river that had been diverted around either side of the city to form a running moat. A channel of the river entered the city itself to transport goods within the walls. Jeremiah squinted at those dingy roofs, packed together around the docks as tight as snake scales, suspecting they may have been where Bruno grew up.

Once Jeremiah's stomach rumbling became too obvious for even the politest gnome to ignore, Mathilde tugged her husband's hand.

"Goshy! The boy is skin and bones, and you're boring him with your stories. Come, Jeremiah, Red Coals Tavern is just nearby and we're having lunch there. I insist you join us! It's the best in the city."

Mathilde was right—Jeremiah was famished by the time they reached the bottom of the tower. At Red Coals, they enjoyed splendid (if overpriced) skewers of veal steaks charred over an open hickory and peachwood fire, in what Jeremiah was assured was the most authentic Dramian tradition.

Jeremiah tried to surreptitiously count his coins, but Mathilde spotted him and slapped his hands. "You put those away this very moment! We invited you, so it's our treat."

"Ooh, you've done it now, lad," said Goshwick. "You'll sooner stop the rain than convince Milly to let you pay!"

Jeremiah put up as much protest as seemed appropriate, but he was grateful. He was beginning to realize that tourism in Dramir was awfully pricey, and his pockets were already running light. Nevertheless, Jeremiah's discomfort at the gnomes' generosity led him to bid them farewell after the meal. He reminded himself he'd be getting paid soon, but that fact didn't lessen the sting of his lack today.

Escaping the gravity of the crowds, he began heading toward the tucked away corners of the city, where visitors rarely roamed. Buildings became less ostentatious and more practical, the streets became dustier, and the residents were no longer dressed to impress. Here, it felt like he was discovering the city for himself, not as it was presented to him.

Jeremiah wandered, as entranced by the densely packed urban dwellings as he had been by the grand architecture of the center. He soon found himself meandering neighborhoods cast into semidarkness by the shadow of the great wall as it stretched in the afternoon light. He felt eyes sticking to him while he walked.

Jeremiah heard a charismatic voice speaking with authority and turned to spot a small crowd gathering in a grimy plaza. He took a step toward it, curious, and froze. Something about the area was unfriendly. The houses on either side glared down at him.

These aren't your streets, he thought in Bruno's voice. *Don't butt into people's lives.*

But he was free and alive and eager for new experiences.

Jeremiah joined the dun-colored crowd. Before them, a halfling stood on a barrel. Two men of prodigious size flanked him, wearing breastplates dented with a thousand heroic stories. Their service to the halfling made him seem all the louder as he gesticulated toward the gathered crowd. "My friends, your chance has finally come! Adventure, prestige, hearty meals, generous pay, and the skills to make you a person of value! I see strong arms and barrel chests in this crowd, the glimmer of keen eyes and minds too, oh yes."

The halfling pointed at a young half-orc boy, lanky and underfed, his skin yellowish green. "You there, young man! Orc blood earns you a place of pride in the Keepsmen Mercenary Company. Would you like to be proud of your heritage and come to share in the brotherly love of camaraderie?"

The young half orc stammered as the crowd turned toward him, "I—I s'pose I would?"

"Of course you would! Gallas, take the young lad aside and fit him for a suit of his very own armor. A weapon as well! I think I see the makings of a great spearman in that one."

One of the big men pushed the crowd aside and put an arm around the boy. "Make way for a warrior!" he said, pulling the boy toward a table that had been set up beside an alley.

"A good local boy has just decided to become a hero. I hope he won't have to go it alone! Who else would like to receive five silver as a signing bonus as soon as next month? On *top* of your pay?"

Jeremiah found himself slowly nodding along with the boisterous halfling. His manner of speaking was infectious. Jeremiah could imagine himself charging into glorious battle alongside his brothers in arms.

I do need a plan for after I get my money, don't I? Mercenary work might be just the thing. Might be the perfect thing, actually, he thought.

Jeremiah snapped out of his reverie as the halfling's unrelenting charisma focused on him.

"Aha! There's another strong soul, I think. Tell me, boy, what sort of labor do you toil at day after day? Hmm?"

"I, um, I actually, I don't yet have—"

"I can't you hear you, son, speak up!"

The crowd turned to stare at him as one. Gus wriggled in his robes.

"I-I'm not . . . I do magic."

The halfling squinted and tilted an ear toward him. "Wassat, boy?"

"I'm a mage," Jeremiah finally said with confidence.

There was a collective murmur and Jeremiah felt the heat of bodies around him abate. The halfling's jovial nature transformed into intense inspection.

"That true, boy? You're not having a laugh?" The halfling's voice dropped to a conspiratorial pitch.

Jeremiah took a breath, bringing his focus to bear. He was numb to the pressure of performance, at least where magic was concerned. A sphere of light ignited in his hand. He let it float and oscillate gently. The crowd gasped, and the halfling's eyes gleamed.

"Two gold. Son, you come sign up for the Keepsmen, and I'll hand you two gold coins right this minute." He produced a pair of golden coins with a flick of his wrist, a magic trick that pulled more awe from the crowd than Jeremiah's paltry ball of light. The coins danced across his knuckles in a lustrous waltz, glinting and whispering to each other in metallic clicks.

Jeremiah was hypnotized by them. Just his name on a dotted line was worth two gold?

The halfling, taking his silence for indecision, upped the ante. "And I'll promote you right now. You'll come on as a sergeant. You know what that is, eh? An officer. Better pay, better meals, and authority. We won't have a mage shoveling shit in the Keepsmen, no sir."

The crowd was silent with anticipation now. Jeremiah was right along with them. A future stretched out before him, a place where a mage like him would be lauded and respected . . .

We'd be foolish not to ask a mage to join us. He remembered Allison had said that mere hours before he was begging for his life. They'd want to see what he could do, want to know how best to use him. And Jeremiah, in turn, would raise the dead.

"What say you, boy?" The halfling licked his lips.

"I—I think I should go," said Jeremiah. "Thank you." He turned and hurried away, pulling his hood up over his head.

"Lieutenant! I'll make you a lieutenant! You come back to me, boy. I'll be waiting!"

CHAPTER TWELVE

Payday

Jeremiah woke up late the next day. The house had been silent when he'd returned the evening before, and he'd collapsed into bed with the accumulated exhaustion of weeks of sleeping rough. He slept like the dead. It was with great reluctance that he forced himself to leave the comfort of the bed in the morning, convinced finally by the aroma of breakfast wafting up the stairs.

Delilah was practically dancing about the kitchen, humming to herself as she cooked, wearing a smart dress and bodice in the fashion that Jeremiah had seen near the palace yesterday. There was no sign of the weariness or fatigue that had so recently plagued her. She beamed as Jeremiah came in. "Good morning! Did you sleep well? I stopped by the market earlier so we have fresh food for a change! Would you like milk in your tea?"

Jeremiah thanked her, his grogginess banished by her energy. He busied himself finding plates and utensils and set four places at the table.

Delilah deposited a serving of ham, eggs, tomatoes, and toast in front of Jeremiah, then darted into the hallway and rap sharply at the doors. "Up, up! Breakfast is ready, and we've got things to do!"

Bruno and Allison emerged, looking rested but groggy. The difference between their appearance now and while adventuring was striking. Bruno was any day laborer, overworked and underfed, with a fondness for tattoos, while Allison wore a simple belted tunic that suggested her muscular frame may have been acquired by toiling in a field. They joined Jeremiah and Delilah at the table.

Breakfast was delicious, doing almost as much to restore their strength as the night's rest. As they ate, Delilah issued instructions. "Allison, go see a healer about that arm today. Get it fixed. Add it to your debt if you need to. Bruno, check the Hall of Records for anything about fortress doors that were ordered and never delivered. Name drop me if they give you any difficulty. If the Hall doesn't have anything, we'll need to browse your usual contacts, but I'm hoping we'll have payment in hand by the end of the day."

"Good," said Allison. Her eyes flicked to Jeremiah, then away.

Jeremiah hadn't realized he could be out on his own again so soon. He poked at his eggs. "Your arm seems a lot better, Allison. Do you still think you need a healer?"

Allison wiggled the fingers her injured arm. "I really depend on my shield arm. Delilah's a great doctor, but there's always a chance it'll heal wrong and cost me strength or mobility. Magical healing is expensive, but it removes that chance and gets me back out there faster."

Jeremiah turned to Delilah. "You're a doctor *and* an alchemist?"

Delilah blushed and smiled. "And a legal counselor. Not to boast, but I'm one of those prodigy types. If I'm not working toward some lofty goal or another, I go stir crazy."

"She's fixing to be queen one day," said Bruno with a wink.

"Not necessarily queen!" said Delilah. "I just want to make the jump into politics. I think I can do a lot of good for a lot of people, and . . . okay, yes. I want to be queen. One step at a time, though."

Bruno and Allison laughed, but Jeremiah detected a distinct sense of pride in their friend.

"Anything I should do?" Jeremiah asked Delilah, who had begun sorting through the pile of mail that had accumulated in her absence.

Delilah stared off for a moment. "Umm . . . you're welcome to explore the city, if you like."

"I spent quite a while wandering yesterday. Actually ran into some recruiters for a mercenary company, The Keepsmen." The two gold coins still glittered in Jeremiah's mind.

Allison shuddered. "Nowhere is a boy's life more disposable than in the Keepsmen."

Jeremiah remembered the young half orc. All at once, those two gold seemed less lustrous. He scrambled for a less distressing thought. "Delilah, do you actually own this house?"

"I do, yes. Actually, my family owned all of these houses at one time." She gestured toward the identical houses along the street.

"One time? What happened? If you don't mind my asking."

"I sold them all. I didn't want to be a property-manager type. Needed the money to pay for law school, medical school, and alchemy training." She paused, reading a letter. "Speaking of which, I've apparently got a symposium to get to.

I'll see you later tonight!" Delilah leapt out of her chair and sprinted out the door. Bruno and Allison finished their breakfast soon after and headed out as well.

Jeremiah found himself alone once again. He decided to be at least a little useful and cleaned up the plates from breakfast. The mundanity of the task stood in contrast to the enormity of the unknown before him. What was he going to do? He'd never even considered mercenary work before yesterday (although Allison's reaction did sour the idea). But what other opportunities were out there? He didn't even know what he didn't know. He buried himself in chores to keep from having to think of it.

By the time Delilah returned several hours later, the house was pristine. Jeremiah had banished the dust and cobwebs in the corners, vanquished the layer of grease in the kitchen, and even obliterated the forgotten dirt nestled in neglected crevices around the house. "Hi, Jay," said Delilah as she entered. "Have you been cleaning this whole time?"

Jeremiah emerged from under the sofa with his dust rag. "Just started tidying up a few things . . . Guess I got carried away. I hope you don't mind."

"Of course not. Thank you very much! I've been meaning to get to it." Delilah dropped a stack of papers on the kitchen table with a thud. She began signing and stamping them at a rapid pace. "So, how do you like Dramir?"

"Oh, it's incredible!" said Jeremiah. "All the people and the history and the things to do and see—though I'll be able to enjoy more of it once I get a few more silver from selling those doors."

Delilah glanced up when he said this, the steady rhythm of her stamp pausing. She studied him for a moment, then returned to her work. "Mm-hmm" was all she said.

The front door opened again and Bruno poked his head in. "Hey, Delilah, we might have a problem. The doors were ordered by the city of Dramir, but over sixty years ago. There's a record, but they're saying they can't make a payment on it."

"Incorrect," Delilah said. "Tell them that pursuant to Article fifty-"—she squinted at the ceiling—"four? Actually, tell them that pursuant to the Commerce and Trade Declaration of King Kuro the Unstoppable, procurements of kingdom security, which the doors certainly are, maintain a protected status of—"

"Delilah?" interrupted Bruno, eyebrow raised.

"Right, I'll just come with you," said Delilah. "Jay, can you give me a hand with something?"

"Sure," Jeremiah said. "How can I help?"

She sat him down in her chair and stamped the back of his right hand. "You are hereby authorized to sign in my name for twenty-four hours. Please sign all of these documents in my name, Delilah Fortune, or initial as appropriate, and stamp after each signature." She placed a quill, stamp, ink pad, and two copper coins in front of him. "Some of these papers are confidential, classified, or sworn to attorney-client or doctor-client privilege, so please don't read them. Thanks!"

She and Bruno were out the door before Jeremiah could ask for clarification. He shrugged and began slogging his way through the stack of papers.

Allison returned an hour later. Jeremiah smiled a greeting. "How's the shoulder?" he asked.

"Like new," she said. "Healing magic is powerful stuff." She rotated her arm to demonstrate, then frowned as she watched him stamping Delilah's paperwork. "Should you be doing that?"

Jeremiah held up his stamped hand. "Delilah authorized me to work on this while she and Bruno deal with the door payment."

Allison hesitated a beat longer, then grunted, turned on her heel, and retreated to her room. She did not emerge. Jeremiah sighed and resumed signing and stamping. If she wanted to be moody about his being here, that was her problem, he decided. He'd be gone soon enough.

The sun was beginning to set by the time Delilah and Bruno returned. Jeremiah offered his handiwork to Delilah for inspection, but she merely thanked him and set the stack of papers aside.

Bruno set a plain but sturdy-looking chest onto the table. "Ladies and gentlemen," he said, "may I have your attention! Please be seated, as we're about to begin that most delightful of chores: the splitting of the take."

Allison and Delilah took their places around the table. Jeremiah suddenly remembered something. "Hey, wait a minute! You never gave me my share from the card game!"

Bruno looked a bit taken aback at having his dramatization interrupted. "Your share? It was my money you went in with, and I gave you a silver anyway."

"Right, but I helped. I should get a share of the whole take."

"Bruno, be fair. You almost got the kid killed," said Allison.

Bruno looked at her with surprise. "Well then! I suppose fair is, indeed, fair." He gave Jeremiah a sarcastic smile, reached into a pouch and pulled out two silvers and ten coppers. "I hope a total of three silver in payment is amenable to you, given the distribution of expertise in the matter."

Jeremiah was thrilled to have the extra three silver. Combined with the split from the take he might even have a gold or more! More than enough to enjoy the city to its fullest, and to secure safe passage to wherever he decided to go next. He scooped up the coins and jingled them in his hand. "Three silver is fine. Thank you, Bruno." He tried to return the sarcastic smile, but his was all too genuine.

"But of course! Three silver is nothing to sneeze at, is it?"

"Umm, no. Certainly not." Jeremiah was confused. What was Bruno doing? Was he making fun of Jeremiah for being poor? That didn't seem right.

"Now then. If there are no other points to discuss, shall we continue?" Bruno looked pointedly around the table. "No? Are we sure? Are we absolutely, positively certain—"

"Get on with it," said Allison, rolling her eyes while Delilah snickered.

Bruno unlatched the chest and lifted the lid. Jeremiah's anticipation mounted. It was a sizable chest and would hold quite a lot of copper!

Bruno wiggled his fingers in delight, reached into the chest, and dropped a small golden bar in front of Jeremiah. It landed with a dull metallic thud. Jeremiah stared at it as a chill ran down his spine. The bar was as long as Jeremiah's palm and covered in intricate stamps and numbers.

Then a second gold bar appeared next to the first. Jeremiah was hypnotized by their gleam, their hue, their size . . . and they were his.

A third bar appeared, then a fourth and a fifth. Jeremiah broke out in a sweat. His heart pounded in his chest. He was dimly aware of movement around him. Gold. He had gold. He tried to think, but his thoughts were gone.

A sixth bar layered on top of the neat row of five. Seven, eight. Jeremiah was starting to feel nauseous as his excitement corroded into shock. Nine, ten. Bruno was building a pyramid of gold in front of him. Time slowed down and disbelief left him a passive observer to more money than he had ever seen in his life accumulating before him. The bars kept coming, building the pyramid higher and higher, until, with a touch of exaggerated finality, Bruno placed a final bar on top of the pyramid with a soft *clink*.

Fifteen bars in total. Jeremiah slowly looked up and saw the other three had pyramids of their own, and another was set aside. They grinned at his obvious shock.

"Fifteen," he managed to say. "I have fifteen gold?" He expected to be informed he was having a hallucination.

Delilah cleared her throat. "Actually," she said gently, "those are Dramir Crown Reserve Ingots. Used for more official transactions and payments. Each of those is worth five gold."

"Five . . . five times . . ." Jeremiah felt numb. "I have seventy-five gold?"

"Well, no," said Delilah. "You'll also receive a quarter share from the party fund, as you're leaving. That's an additional fifteen gold, seven silver, five copper. I'll make change o—"

Jeremiah was looking at the ceiling. He was lying on the floor, Delilah looming over him and tapping his cheek. He vaguely remembered a jolt to his body when he fell out of his chair.

Allison and Bruno made no effort to hide their laughter as Delilah helped Jeremiah back into his seat. He didn't mind, he lacked the ability to feel self-conscious right now. Carefully, as though it were made of glass, he lifted the bar of gold off the top of his pyramid and hefted it in his palm. "I-I've never seen . . . Is this normal? For adventuring?"

Bruno waved his hands over the table. "Not exactly. It's nothing shocking, but I wouldn't say it's typical. We're adventurers; we don't risk our lives for coppers. Big risk, big reward."

Jeremiah couldn't believe he was so calm. "But you're rich now! We all are! I don't even know what to *do* with this much money!"

Allison shifted in her seat. "You know my armor? It's custom-made. My weapons are the best money can buy. I spend a lot on personal training, supplies, and better equipment. To succeed in this lifestyle, you're never good enough—you've always got to be improving, and that costs gold. A lot of gold. And all that's before I get to my healer debt, which is why I'm doing any of this in the first place."

Bruno nodded. "I've got a whole network of contacts to pay—informants, fences, engineers to keep me up-to-date on lock and trap advances. My arrows are expensive, and my tool kit always needs updating."

"And I'm always restocking the lab," said Delilah. "The medical, legal, and alchemical guilds all have membership fees, and new alchemical recipes can be very expensive. If you want to pursue adventuring, you need to always be pushing yourself to gain every possible advantage you can. Adventurers aren't rare, but, well . . ."

"They die in *droves*," Allison said.

Jeremiah listened without comment, still staring at his pyramid.

"But maybe . . ." said Allison, plucking three bars from the group pile and sliding them toward Jeremiah, "you should think of retiring. You got damn lucky—hell, we all did—but I bet if you take that home, you can have yourself quite a comfortable life."

Delilah slid the three bars back to where they started. "Don't touch the pile," she said curtly.

Bruno tutted them. "Now, now, ladies. He's a man with three more silver than he started the day with, and we must take him out to make some impulsive big-city choices before we send him on his way!" Bruno slammed his palm on the table. "Jay, change into your finest clothes! We're going to Corbyn's!"

Jeremiah hesitated, but Allison and Delilah stood as well. Delilah stopped him as he started to collect his gold. "I'll take care of that," she said. "We've got a safe spot to store money."

In his room, Jeremiah realized there wasn't exactly anything fancy to change into. His bag held a few simple shirts, trousers, and braces. At least the black robes he was already wearing were a little mysterious, he decided. He cinched a belt around his waist and thought briefly about the clothes he could buy now. The word "retirement" echoed in his head. He shook it off and reminded himself to focus on enjoying the evening. After all, he was alive and wealthy in the greatest city in the land!

He returned downstairs to find Bruno fastening a black fur-trimmed cape to his collar. He wore a white low-cut shirt that showed off his tattoos. Allison emerged from her room in a blood-red tunic, black breeches, and high leather boots. She looked lethal. They both regarded Jeremiah with a look of mild disappointment.

"Looking . . . classic?" said Bruno.

Jeremiah just shrugged. The knowledge that he could now afford to dress any way he pleased blunted the sting of embarrassment.

Delilah made them wait quite a while longer, but she emerged from her room a completely different person. Her floor-length midnight-blue dress matched her eye shadow, and her normally tied-back hair was styled down across half of her face with a lazy twisting curl. The look was nothing short of glamorous. Jeremiah's eyes went wide.

"Well, now I feel like a heap of rags," Jeremiah said.

Allison sighed. "How come I can't look like that?"

"You *can* look like this," Delilah said, "but every time I offer, you get too impatient. Also you cry when I try to brush out your hair."

Bruno clapped his hands. "All right! Now that we've all seen Delilah in husband-hunting mode, let's get out of this house and into a bottle!"

CHAPTER THIRTEEN

Outed

Corbyn's turned out to be an upscale stone building. Music escaped into the night air through glowing windows. A barrel-chested dwarf and fearsome orc chatted in the doorway. The guards greeted Bruno, Delilah, and Allison by name and welcomed the group inside.

The music picked up as they entered a world separate from the cool, silent night outside. The tavern was warm and lively. Jeremiah felt immediately out of place. A sleek mahogany bar lined one wall, with mirrored shelves filled with liquors in elaborate crystal bottles. A raised stage in the center of the room supported a trio of performers: an elf played a melodic brass pipe that effused clouds of sweet-scented smoke, a singing gnome pounded a hardy rhythm on a kettle drum, and a beautiful half-elven girl danced in kaleidoscopic silks like a living rainbow. The rest of the space was filled with couches around sturdy tables and armchairs conspiring in the corners.

Jeremiah gaped in the entrance before getting nudged by Bruno.

"C'mon, tourist, let's grab a seat and a drink."

From the back of the room, a huge bearded man stood and bellowed across the bar. "Allison Allday, you rotten liar! People are saying that your no-talent self took down a gods-damned Matriarch!" Almost every patron in the bar stole a glance toward her, and a few openly stared.

Allison puffed out her chest and marched toward the man's table with exaggerated swagger. "Not only did I *kill* a Matriarch, I slaughtered her guards"—she stepped onto a chair at the man's table—"plundered her Warren"—she continued her march to stand on his table—"didn't lose a single man"—she stepped up one foot on the man's shoulder and leaned down over him—"and *I looked damn good doing it!*"

A cheer erupted from the tavern. The man and his friends lifted the table with Allison on it, hands on her hips and looking over her admirers imperiously as they cheered.

"Such a ham," said Bruno, pulling Jeremiah over to a fireside couch that Delilah had selected.

Allison sat with the group of men, who appeared to be other warriors and soldiers, trading insults and laughs. A waitress appeared beside Bruno, Delilah, and Jeremiah to take their orders.

"Three shots of rum, two whiskey," said Bruno.

"Martini. Dry," said Delilah.

Jeremiah started to check his pockets, but Delilah stopped him. "You're on our tab tonight." She nodded to the waitress.

"Fortified wine," Jeremiah said. "A double, actually!"

Bruno clapped him on the back. "Attaboy! Let's have some fun!"

Their drinks came and they toasted to a good night. Before long, Delilah spotted someone at the bar. Jeremiah followed her gaze to see a pair of distinguished looking gentlemen engaged in intense conversation. She excused herself and sashayed her way toward the two men, who seemed to recognize her and greeted her respectfully. Jeremiah felt a painful flick to his ear.

"I know, but quit staring," said Bruno. "I've got a man to see about a medusa. Go sit with Allison and make some friends. Oh, and make sure you have fun." Bruno made his way to one of the pairs of whispering chairs in a dark corner. There was no one in the adjoining chair, or at least there didn't appear to be.

Jeremiah followed Bruno's advice and went to join Allison. She waved him over, her cheeks already flushed from the ale she was drinking. She kicked the person next to her out of their seat and pulled Jeremiah down beside her.

"This is the lost little mage we found outside the Warren!" she said a little too loudly. "A conjurer hoping to do it all alone! Brave lad, eh?"

The men around the table cheered and their raised glasses. Jeremiah smiled and raised his glass as well. He found the bravado of their boisterous celebration came easily to his lips. "You should have seen this woman! Brought down that beast with axe and spear like a hero of legend!"

The men cheered again and begged Allison and Jeremiah to tell them the story. He followed Allison's lead, trading the tale back and forth with her as they recounted their descent into the Warren. Jeremiah allowed himself to be swept up in the excitement. It was thrilling, to be lauded as a hero, and any fear Jeremiah would have had of speaking in front of a crowd was soon swept away by his drink and their audience's adulation.

Jeremiah and Allison rebounded details off each other and built on embellishments, building in volume until they were shouting to the whole tavern. Even the performers paused to listen. As they reached the climax of their tale, Jeremiah allowed Allison to take the lead, and listened to a version of events that edited him out completely. He stepped away from the table amid roaring cheers. There was a sour feeling in his heart now; his smile grew more and more forced. He excused himself back to his own table.

Jeremiah sat by himself, watching as Allison cheered another adventurer's boasts. Bruno shared a pipe with whoever occupied his opposite chair while Delilah held court with a group of aristocrats, discussing something about taxation law and river commerce. His mood spiraled ever downward. Much as he wanted to be a part of this band, he never could be. He was a necromancer. They might act like his friends, but they'd be glad to be rid of him.

He sneered at the bottom of his cup. *No wonder necromancers end up living alone. Suddenly the magic you know is more important than your actions.*

The couch cushion rolled under him like an ocean wave. Allison had sat beside him, her breath thick with alcohol. "What's wrong? Why you over here sulking like a preacher in the rain?" Her speech was slightly slurred.

Jeremiah contemplated pretending things were fine. But hell, it was his last night. Might as well be honest. "I know why you did it, but it sucked being cut out of the story. It just reminds me that I have to leave soon. And not even because of anything I did, but because you all are afraid of what I know."

He watched with some satisfaction as Allison's cheeriness clouded over. Then she surprised him by leaning her head on his shoulder. "Can't you just not be a . . . a what-you-are?" she asked with a heavy sadness. "If you didn't do it, there wouldn't be a problem. We wouldn't care if you only *knew* how."

"I'm not interested in being a burden or a butler." He put a little venom in his voice. "How would you feel if you weren't allowed to carry a shield anymore because someone else decided they were evil?"

Allison tensed at his accusatory tone. She sat up. "That's not a fair comparison."

"It is to me."

Allison's mouth twisted. "Try to have fun, Jay." Then she returned to her friends, leaving him all alone again.

As Jeremiah continued to stew, his anger eroded to sadness. His self-pity disgusted him, but he couldn't escape it. *Like I could ever be a real adventurer anyway. I'm pathetic.*

The waitress brought another cup of wine, which he accepted against his better judgment. The music grew oppressively loud. The fire burned too hot. Soon, even the wine tasted sour. Jeremiah emptied his cup and made for the door. He didn't want to bother any of the others by telling them he was leaving, although he felt Bruno's eyes on him on his way out.

The chilled night embraced him. Jeremiah wandered the dark streets, eager to leave the tavern behind. Distant bells echoed through the alleys, and Jeremiah let his feet carry him, paying no mind where they went. He wished he could recapture the frustration he felt before, could wash away his misery with righteous anger. But he just felt painfully alone.

Jeremiah wandered for the sake of wandering, hoping that maybe if he got lost enough, tomorrow wouldn't come. The bells that had stalked him had become very close, and they tolled with frantic rapidity. A bright orange glow illuminated the sky a few streets over. A distraction would be more than welcome. He made for it at once.

Jeremiah rounded the corner to see a tall residence building engulfed in flames. People scrambled on the street, shouting and pushing past each other, and more people poured out of their homes. The clanging bells echoed up and down the streets, each bell seeming to awaken another.

Jeremiah turned to an old man watching the commotion. "Is someone coming?"

"Aye," the man replied. "Fire brigade should be here any minute. Meantime everyone tries to keep things under control."

Lines of people formed between the burning building and the public wells. Jeremiah wanted to help, but feared he'd only be in the way as people began heaving buckets of water onto the fire. The inferno raged on, unconcerned by their efforts.

Then the screams started, screams that froze everyone in their tracks. A person burst through a window of the second floor of the burning building, shattering the glass, and fell to the street below, engulfed in flames.

The screams stopped. Bystanders rushed to the fallen body, but it lay utterly still.

Several onlookers cried out in horror. Air rushed through the broken window and the flames surged. Moments later, half of the upper floor shuddered and collapsed. The bucket line scattered as an avalanche of burning timber crashed to the ground.

Jeremiah shielded his face as a wave of heat prickled his skin. The bucket line reformed quickly and doused the rubble. This time, Jeremiah moved to help. He joined several others in kicking aside the newly fallen debris, looking for survivors. The only people they managed to pull from the smoldering pile were burned black from head to toe. They gathered the unfortunate souls to one side of the scene as they kept looking.

A crowd of onlookers was forming. The bucket lines continued to douse the nearest flames, but the main fire was beyond their reach. Jeremiah was looking for some other way to help when a dozen men in heavy leather coats and full body coverings arrived.

The fire brigade scoured the perimeter, searching for a safe way into the building. Two, then three of them gathered around the same spot, then one man removed his mask and shouted louder then Jeremiah had ever heard someone shout before.

"QUIET!!!"

All bucket movement and chatter on the street ceased, leaving only the roar of the fire. The three fire brigadiers leaned close and listened again, before waving their fellows over and ordering bucket lines to extend to the same spot.

"WE'RE COMING! STAY WHERE YOU ARE! LIE DOWN ON THE GROUND!" the loud man bellowed into the building. The bucket lines worked at an invigorated pace, hurling water at the entrance to douse the flames. The fire raged back, though, and their efforts were barely enough to hold it at bay.

The building groaned. Jeremiah heard timbers crumbling inside. The fire brigade began shoving the bucket line away from the building. "MOVE! MOVE! IT'S COMING DOWN!"

There were anguished cries from the crowd. The fire seemed to roar in victory, the flames devouring the building like a starved beast.

Oh, you've got to be kidding me, Jeremiah thought. *Don't make me do this . . .*

He approached the building, right up to the line enforced by the brigade. He saw their rage and frustration. One of them was arguing with his superior, begging. Jeremiah couldn't hear everything, but he heard enough to understand—people were still alive in there.

There was no time for subtlety. Jeremiah turned and moved to kneel beside the bodies he'd helped pull out of the rubble. He spoke, gestured, and silently apologized to the mass of people for the horror they were about to witness.

The blackened bodies cracked as he animated them, including a little extra necromantic energy to break out of their rigid shells. People saw him—he knew they did—but he tuned out their screams to concentrate on his task. The blackened husks split as liquified flesh poured through the widening gaps like cracked eggs. Red-stained bony fingers tore through the bodies as one dwarven and three human skeletons rose. The skeletons' slick bones reflected firelight as they stood at attention before Jeremiah. People fainted and ran.

Jeremiah willed the skeletons toward the burning building, to seek life and protect it. The dwarven skeleton charged into the inferno, smashing through a wall as the three humans leapt eight feet into the air right into the heart of the flames. Jeremiah sat down in the dirt and focused. He knew he wouldn't have much time. His orders were complicated (*seek, protect, remove obstacles*), and he could afford no distractions. He closed his eyes to concentrate on his minions.

Heat. Fire. Light. Sound. Voice. Voice! Get closer, closer, closer. Climb. Crawl. Lift. Closer. Loud voice! Screaming. Fear.

Jeremiah muttered a curse. The people inside were already terrified for their lives, and now the undead were emerging from the flames. Nevertheless, he had to keep trying.

Beckon. Clear. Beckon. Protect. Sooth. Screaming. Fear. Grab. Lift. Drag.

His focus was shaken only slightly when something knocked into him. He was aware of shouting, of bodies moving around him, but pushed it away. It didn't matter.

It was a mess in there! It was impossible to tell if he was leading them toward safety or further into the fire. He gritted his teeth and concentrated as hard as he could, letting his consciousness delve into the bubbles and struggling to interpret the streams of information from his minions. Slowly, the internal layout of the building became clearer in his mind.

Jeremiah ordered the dwarven skeleton to lead, lifting and clearing a path through the debris. The other skeletons followed the new path, dragging the survivors behind them. He prayed the building would withstand the additional damage long enough for them to escape.

There were several raised voices beside Jeremiah now. A heavy thud as something landed in front of him. He risked opening his eyes and saw the face of an angry man, his lip and nose bleeding and his face pressed hard into the dirt by a black boot. He followed the man's twisted arm to see Allison, backlit by the inferno and looking just as powerful. She yelled something at the crowd. Two other people stood near him, and he guessed who they were.

The building groaned again and the rest of the second floor collapsed. A plume of fire lit up the night sky.

Air! Faster! Pull. Push. Blocked. Heat. Smash. Smash! SMASH!!

A wall exploded outward as the dwarven skeleton pounded its way through the weakened construction. Behind it, the other skeletons dragged two elven adults and two elven children through the hole. Jeremiah leapt to his feet to see. They were all injured, and three of the four were unconscious. But he knew they were alive. He didn't know how he knew, but he knew.

The skeletons dragged the bodies toward the fire brigade, who raised their axes in defense. Jeremiah immediately severed the connection and the four skeletons clattered to the ground, motionless. As the fire brigade tended to the rescued elves, Jeremiah turned toward the gathered crowd, hoping to at least address them before he was lynched. Instead, he saw a furious pair of eyes, tinted with midnight blue, then a cloth clamped over his face, and everything went dark.

CHAPTER FOURTEEN

Irresponsible Forgiveness

Jeremiah awoke, which was a pleasant surprise. He shook off the heaviness of a drugged sleep and sat up.

He was in a dank prison cell, small enough that his outspread arms could reach across its width. Except his hands were bound by steel gauntlets, fixed into clenched fists and wrapped together by a chain. Mage's manacles.

His cell contained a cot with a thin blanket and a bucket in the corner. The other cells of the prison stood empty. Jeremiah recalled Allison saying most crimes earned assignment to a wall cleaning crew and decided this place must be for special prisoners. He called out from his cell and banged his manacles against the bars till his ears rang, but only his echo answered him. He resigned himself to a corner of his cot, flagellating himself with the memory of every action that brought him here, and the clarity that only hindsight could bring. Hours passed in total silence.

A door swung open and a squat dwarven guard entered. "Yer counselor's here to see you."

Delilah entered, straight-backed in fine formal robes, her hair pulled back in a sleek bun. Her immaculate appearance stood in stark contrast to the filth of the dungeon and the two guards who tailed her.

Jeremiah met her eyes, hoping for a sign of friendship, but saw only professionalism and weariness. "Jeremiah Thorn," she recited, "you are currently being tried by the highest court of Dramir. As your legal aide, I implore you to be forthright with me and not to answer questions posed to you by anyone else without my explicit permission. *Anyone.*"

"What's the charge?" Jeremiah asked.

Delilah sighed. "They're drafting the law that you would be accused of violating. By stroke of luck, *being* a necromancer isn't illegal. Yet. Right now, you're being detained on counts of corpse tampering, but I expect the new law will get passed within the next few days so they can find you guilty of the practice of necromancy."

Jeremiah was stunned. "They're creating new laws to prosecute me?"

"Yes," said Delilah. "These are unprecedented circumstances, to be sure. The last few days of your trial have been—"

"Wait, 'few days'? How long have I been out?"

"A few days," Delilah said matter-of-factly. "I've only recently been given permission to end your medical sedation."

"There's a trial going on? Shouldn't I be there? Shouldn't I be . . . giving testimony or something?"

Delilah glared at the ceiling. "Normally yes, but . . . it's a mess up there. The prosecution is running rampant, and the judges are letting them get away with it. Suddenly everything is a matter of kingdom security. The entire charade is frankly disgraceful."

"So we're all just killing time until I'm sentenced to death," Jeremiah said. It was the outcome he'd expected, but to drag it out like this was just cruel.

Delilah scowled. "Jay, I'm a damn fine legal counselor and I'm working my ass off to make sure that doesn't happen." She turned to the guards. "I'd like some time alone with my client."

One of the guards grinned. "Make it worth our while, and maybe you'll get it."

Delilah's eyes turned stone cold. "I can make your lives very difficult for a *very* long time. Can you afford a good attorney? Because if I have to, I'll make the two of you my pet project for years to come. If you want to avoid that, and I can assure you that you do, all you have to do is walk out the door." She didn't even look at them as she spoke.

"C'mon," muttered the other guard. "Leave 'em to it." They left, and Delilah's demeanor relaxed just a little.

"Dammit, Jay," she said. "Why do you have to make things so difficult? Would it have been so hard for you to just walk away from that fire?"

"Sorry this is so inconvenient for you," Jeremiah spat.

Delilah glared. "I thought you'd try and be a little more grateful to the person trying to save you from the consequences of your own actions."

"My actions?" Jeremiah wanted to scream. "All I did was help people! Would I be here if I had made it rain on the fire? If I had teleported them outside? If I had jumped through a window and carried them out with my bare hands? I'd be a hero. But I made skeletons drag them out, so here I am! Because even saving lives when no one else can isn't enough for you people!"

"'You people'? We're on your side, Jay! Allison's already taken the stand in your defense. Now everyone knows she conspires with necromancers. She could end up in jail herself! Meanwhile, I'm risking everything I've worked for since before you were even *born*, just to stick my neck out for you. The easiest solution for all of us would have been to let that mob do what mobs do best!"

Tiny flecks of spittle fell on his face as she shouted, and the tips of her pointed ears reddened. Jeremiah held her furious gaze for a beat after she'd finished, but his anger crumbled before hers. The news that Allison had publicly defended him shook him to his core. "Sorry," he mumbled.

Delilah closed her eyes and recomposed herself. "It's fine. We're all under a lot of stress right now. All I need you to do is be patient and don't talk to anyone else. I might be able to get you a chance to testify, let you humanize yourself a little bit. Right now, the rumor mill is working overtime—people are swearing you started the fire with a fire-breathing zombie dragon."

Jeremiah sank onto his cot and rested his chin on his manacled fists. "Thanks for doing this, Delilah. Tell the others thanks too."

"I will. Right now, I need to get back to the archives to look for any historical precedent of positive outcomes for necromancers. Are you going to be okay?"

"I'll be fine. Is Gus with you?"

Delilah's face softened as she nodded. "Yes, Gus is staying with me right now. I can tell he's worried, but he's a great reading companion." She offered Jeremiah a weak smile. "I'll be back as soon as I have news, okay? Just hang in there until then."

She left and took all the light with her. Jeremiah was back to being alone. He lay in bed for hours, trying to plan what he'd say if only given the chance and an audience. Thoughts blurred into his imagination and soon became dreams.

"Now what in the world is a straight-laced townie like you doing here?"

Jeremiah bolted upright on his cot. A figure in the cell across from his was watching him through the bars. A dream of footfalls and clanging metal suddenly made more sense.

"I'm being—oh! Umm." His voice faltered. The woman was gorgeous. She had aristocratic features and shining metallic hair, like countless threads of copper, tossed casually over her shoulders. A scar cut across the right side of her mouth and the tip of one of her elven ears stopped short in a flat plateau, but these imperfections only enhanced her exoticness. Her dark eyes seemed to pierce right through him, and he felt terribly exposed.

Her mouth twisted into a sardonic smile, as if she knew exactly what he was thinking.

"I, uh, committed a crime." Jeremiah winced at his recovery.

"No, you didn't."

"What?"

"No, you didn't. You don't think so anyway. But you didn't say 'nothing,' so you still know you did *something* wrong. You're wondering if it was worth it. Tell me what you did."

"I probably shouldn't, my counselor said—"

"Tell me what you did."

Jeremiah snapped his mouth shut. He wondered what the consequences would be of telling her. Could she be a spy? Was she trying to pump him for a confession? He should lie back down and ignore her. Instead, he asked, "Why don't you tell me about what you did first?"

"Theft, and we're moving on. Tell me what you did."

He wanted to tell her. He had been over it in his mind a hundred times, and he ached to talk about it. Under the woman's expectant gaze, he shoved Delilah's disapproving face from his mind and told his story. He had intended to dance around the details of how he had participated in the rescue, but he found himself eager to reveal his secret to this stranger, to shake her unflappable demeanor. She didn't even flinch at his admission.

By the time he finished, the intensity of her stare had grown even stronger. "Pretty stupid move, showing your hand like that."

"No, it wasn't," he said firmly.

She bristled, leaning closer to the bars. "Obviously it was. You're in jail now."

"That doesn't make it stupid. Those people needed help, and I was the only one who could help them."

"By the time you're on the headsman's block, you'll wish you'd let the whole city burn."

"No, I won't!" Jeremiah sprang to his feet. "I did the right thing! They can't change that by killing me."

Those dark eyes bored into his. Jeremiah resisted the urge to look away, but it was like staring into the sun. When he glanced back, the corners of her lips had twisted up just a little, which did nothing to soften her gaze.

"Tell me your name," she said.

"No."

"I'm Vivica."

"Jeremiah Thorn." Why did he say that? He had just said he wouldn't.

"You didn't do anything wrong, Thorn. You're a victim of a system obsessed with control. They didn't own you, so they jailed you. A necromancer that saves lives? People in tall towers are working you into their schemes at this very moment. They won't let you out until they can control you or kill you."

"Thanks, I think. You seem nice, too." *Why the hell did I say that?*

Vivica's face fractured into a genuine laugh, the touch-and-go smile finally reaching her eyes. Jeremiah wanted very much for that to happen again. "I'm about as far from nice as it gets, but thanks. So, Thorn, how is it you became so eager to do the right thing that you're willing to die for it?"

"I . . . don't know? People usually want to do the right thing, don't they?"

Vivica slammed her fist into the bars, making Jeremiah jump. The snap of bones could be heard over the ring of steel. "That's naive *bullshit!*" She radiated with a fury that prickled his skin, glaring at him with something akin to hatred. Then it passed like a summer squall.

"I didn't mean to scare you," she said, calm as ever. "I just don't agree. That doesn't fit my experience. Or yours, for that matter. Why would people trying to do the right thing put you in here?"

"I guess . . . it's complicated. People make mistakes. They don't understand what I do, so they're afraid of me. I knew this was a possibility when I saved that family. I don't blame anyone."

"Your forgiveness is irresponsible." She ran a hand through her hair and flicked it outward. It was longer than Jeremiah had thought. Little spots in her hair reflected torchlight like embers. "You think, deep down, they know the right thing to do, and yet you forgive them anyway. The people who will likely have you killed."

"I never said I forgave them. What they're doing is horrible." But the words felt weak in his throat. Did he forgive them? No, he just understood them. But maybe that was close enough.

She ignored his objection. "Can you fight them? Can you kill them? They won't permit you to be what you are. If you want to live, you need to hate them."

"It doesn't make sense to hate them. I'm a necromancer; they're afraid of me. But maybe I can show them—"

"They'll never learn from mercy! You have the power to punish them, to protect others like you, but you refuse to hold them responsible. All you'll get for your trouble is death."

"Vivica, I don't want to punish anybody. I just want them to understand me, just like I understand them. Hating them will be a waste if I've got an opportunity to show them."

"You're really serious," said Vivica in a tone somewhere between curiosity and awe. "I didn't think people like you really existed."

Jeremiah shifted uncomfortably. "I'm not sure if you mean that as a compliment or not."

"Maybe I don't know either. It was nice meeting you, Thorn." She slipped back onto her cot and turned her back toward Jeremiah.

"Wait, your hand is broken. You should wrap it or something."

"I'm fine. Go to sleep."

Jeremiah listened for signs of pain, but all was silent. He slipped back into the timeless darkness of imprisonment.

* * *

Jeremiah woke to the sound of fabric tearing. With nothing else to do, he was becoming an expert napper. Now, his stomach told him it was nearing dinner. He heard the tearing sound again. It was coming from Vivica's cell.

"What are you doing?" He could just barely see her gnawing at the short edge of her blanket.

"Tearing up my sheets." She spoke around a mouthful of cloth as she managed to create a split in the threadbare fabric that passed for a blanket.

"Why?"

"For fun. Now, don't talk until I ask you to."

The rebuff stung, but he couldn't find the strength to answer it. He sat in the dim light, listening to her work the fabric to some mysterious purpose. The lack of stimulation in the prison had sharpened his hearing. A soft wooden scrape from the room outside was particularly interesting, as it meant the guard was fetching dinner.

Meals were as monotonous as they were cheap—a bowl of water and a half loaf of bread that Jeremiah had to soak before his teeth could tear it apart. Eating without the use of his hands was complicated and devoid of dignity. His mouth watered in anticipation.

The lever on the prison door squeaked as the dwarven guard entered, balancing a pair of meager dinners atop splintery wooden planks.

"Get yer slop!" the dwarf said. As he approached Jeremiah's cell, Vivica leaned against the bars of her cell.

"Jailer, we need better food," she said.

"Wha?" The guard set Jeremiah's plank in front of his cell.

"We need something substantial. We can't live on just bread and water. Get us some cheap cheese or some watered-down milk. Something to keep us above starving."

The guard whirled on her and stared like she had just thrown ice water in his face. He was an open sore of a dwarf, dirty, ugly, and rotten. His beard was matted and thick, with dreadlocked clumps of greasy hair. Whatever he'd eaten last always left traces.

"Cheese?! You 'spect me to get you *cheese*?!" He stamped toward her as he spoke. "Oh, I'd likey love me some cheese, miss! A nice runny cheese for me, thank you! A lager as well! But I don't gets no cheese, and I don't gets no lager! So till I does, I'll have no *prisoner* eatin' better than me!"

He picked up her ration of bread and bit off a large chunk. It sounded like a stone cracking apart. Then he dropped the loaf, which bounced away as he roughly set the bowl of water in front of Vivica's cell, a few precious drops sloshing over the edge.

"Wantin' cheese! Elf nonsense, prisoner cheese is. 'Spects a bunch of . . . of those little. . . round fruit things next she doe—*HURK!*"

The moment his back was turned, Vivica had flicked out a rope of woven blanket strips, wound together tight. It was now cinched shut at the guard's neck. Vivica yanked him back against the bars and braced her feet against them, using his weight to hold herself up.

Jeremiah's jaw dropped. The guard sputtered and clawed at the rope digging into his throat with one hand, while the other reached toward his boot. Seeing this, Vivica bent backward almost completely in half, head to heels, maintaining the pressure at the guard's throat. She snaked a hand between the bars, yanked up his pant leg, and snatched the boot knife hidden there.

The jailer's eyelids were fluttering, his face turning purple. Vivica pressed the knife to his eye and allowed the rope to slacken just a little.

"This is mine now. Try to shout, and I strangle you. Try to move, and I take your eye. Tap your right hand against the bars if you understand."

The guard was laboring to breathe. He looked to Jeremiah with watering eyes as if the necromancer had some way to help. But he tapped his hand against the bars.

"Good. I'm going to give you a little more air for cooperating. If you disobey, I take your air away. Tap if you understand."

The rope slackened just a bit more and the jailer took a heaving gasp. He tapped the bars again.

"Good. You won't let a prisoner eat better than yourself, is that what you said?"

The guard nodded carefully. His knees were shaking and he flinched with every tiny adjustment of the rope.

"Good. Thorn, I think the dwarf has a point. Prisoners shouldn't eat better than their jailers, should they?" Her intense stare now burned a hole in Jeremiah. He glanced toward the door, waiting for another guard to investigate the commotion, but none came. "Thorn. I asked you a question."

"N-no," Jeremiah said. The dwarf's pleading eyes told him that Jeremiah was as much a part of this now as Vivica was.

"No, I don't think so either." With a flick of her wrist, she replaced the stolen knife with a golden coin. The gold danced over her fingers in front of the dwarf's face. He trembled as his eyes followed its gleam.

"Maybe we need to make sure you eat better, then, huh? That way we can eat better too. Would you like to eat better, Mr. Jailer? Would you like that runny cheese and lager? Maybe some nice roasted apples and cinnamon? Or a slug custard? Those are my favorite. Would you like those things, Mr. Jailer?"

The guard nodded.

"I thought you might! Sounds much better than being strangled, doesn't it?" He nodded. "Sounds better than lying to me and having to explain what happened to your boss, too. Won't make you look too good, getting jumped by a prisoner, will it?" He shook his head. "So why don't we keep this our little secret. Thorn, can you keep a secret?"

"I won't tell anyone. Sounds like they don't pay their jailers enough."

"Clearly not, clearly not. Tell me your name, Mr. Jailer."

"Borstonnis," the guard choked out.

"Well, Borstonnis, I think we can be friends, can't we? Friends that keep each other's secrets?"

Borstonnis was getting the measure of things now. His trembling subsided and he watched the coin dance more eagerly. "Aye," he croaked. "Friends."

"Wonderful. So, you'll go buy us some cheap cheese, cheap as it comes, and you can keep all the money that's left over. Sound good?"

"Aye."

The rope released and Borstonnis fell forward. He huddled on his knees and drew in coughing, drooling breaths. He stood and turned toward her, his shoulders hunched and his gaze lowered. Vivica dropped the gold coin. It bounced with a metallic *tink* and settled on her side of the bars. Timid as a kitten, Borstonnis reached through the bars and picked it up. Then he retrieved Vivica's bread and placed it carefully on her plank before hurrying from the prison.

An hour later Borstonnis returned. Jeremiah had sat in silence after eating his bread, unsure whether he was now culpable by association if the guard chose to seek revenge. But Borstonnis merely slunk to Jeremiah's cell and placed a new plank holding a hunk of pale yellow cheese. He set another before Vivica's cell. Borstonnis sidled away as quickly as he had entered.

The cheese was indeed the cheapest of the cheap. It was too soft and was almost tasteless but for a sour tang, but Jeremiah relished it. When he finished, he gathered up his blanket and wadded it as best he could with his bound hands. Then he tossed it toward Vivica's cell. "You might get cold with your blanket all torn up."

She grabbed the corner and hesitated, her fingers rubbing the fabric, then pulled it inside. "Thanks."

The next day passed slowly. Jeremiah's hopes for Delilah's return faded as the day wore on. His attempts to coax Vivica into conversation became shallow monologues, his questions going unanswered. Borstonnis brought them cheese at both meals, always nudging Vivica's plate toward her cell like he were feeding a caged beast.

In the evening, Jeremiah's thoughts turned dismal. What if Delilah had been forbidden from visiting him? Would he be woken the next morning by an executioner? Or maybe his sentence was being carried out at this very moment and would continue to be until he went mad in isolation. Lost in dark imaginings of the cruel punishments that awaited him, Jeremiah started when Vivica spoke as if no time had passed at all.

"What good comes of your forgiveness?" she said. "You absolve them of their sins and free them of consequence."

"Huh?" asked Jeremiah.

"In a way, Thorn, I think you're right." She rolled her shoulders and cracked her neck. "People *do* know what's right and what's just self-serving greed."

Jeremiah didn't remember saying that last part, but his response was interrupted by the shriek of metal grinding on stone as Vivica rotated her cot away from the wall. She wedged it instead between the bars and the back wall, where it held fast.

"Well-educated people whose decisions create a systematic unending source of pain, depravity, and desperation," Vivica continued. She braced her feet against the bed and pressed her head against the bars.

"Vivica, what are you doing?"

"Since we're dealing with people who know the right thing to do, yet choose to do the wrong thing time and time again, such people must be nothing short of monsters!"

"Vivica, stop!"

Vivica pressed her face against the bars. Then she pushed harder, her features deforming as her skin was squeezed between bar and bone. Her arms bulged with taut, powerful muscle. She began pushing with her legs, hissing with effort as tiny pops from her skull gave way to the crunch of bone breaking.

Jeremiah looked on in silent horror as the flesh on Vivica's face tore. Her eyes bulged out obscenely as their sockets were squeezed and broken. She made no utterance of pain, even when her skull finally caved from the pressure against its sides. A moment later her head hung limp on the other side of the bars.

There was a groan of relief. Vivica raised her face to Jeremiah's and smiled. Aside from the rivulets of blood dripping off her chin, she was completely intact.

Jeremiah retreated to the back of his cell, unable to look away. Vivica began pushing again, dislocating her shoulders with two audible pops. Her arms snapped back into position the moment her shoulders were through, and she pushed again. Her ribs broke one after the other, till she was stopped by her hips. She braced her hands against the bars and wrenched her lower body violently. Finally, something in her pelvis gave way, and she was out.

Vivica climbed to her feet, apparently no worse for wear.

Jeremiah's mouth opened and closed a few times. "Are you okay?" was all he could think to say.

"Never better."

"What just happened?" He had seen no magic, but what else could it be? Vivica just crushed her own skull and emerged totally unscathed.

"You should come with me," Vivica said.

"With you?"

"I can get you out the same way I did. Come with me. I have people up north. I can give you a better chance than the tyrants here ever will. A necromancer would be welcome with us."

"Through the bars . . ." Jeremiah couldn't even imagine imitating what he had just witnessed.

She nodded sympathetically. "It hurts, but it's over fast."

"I . . . can't. Delilah needs me here. If I run, I'm a fugitive. I need to face this."

"Thorn, they're going to kill you. Not right away—they'll want to use you first—but eventually, when they've gotten what they want from you, they'll kill you. You're a necromancer."

"Maybe, but I think I can fight this. I think with my friends' help, I can be okay."

Vivica took a long look at him. "If you get out, I want you to come find us."

"Us?"

"My people and me. We're headed this way. You'll know us when you see us."

"Why are you here, really?" Jeremiah asked.

Vivica tried to give him a hard look, but it broke into a laugh. Despite everything, Jeremiah was happy to hear it. "I told you. Theft."

She motioned him closer to the bars. She had a wicked smile as he leaned toward her and he felt his pulse quicken. She touched his chin and for a thrilling, terrifying moment Jeremiah thought she was going to kiss him. But she turned his head and whispered in his ear, the warmth of her breath making his hair stand on end.

"Keep what you saw a secret for me? Promise?"

"I promise," he said.

She walked toward the exit, glancing back at him once before stepping through the door like she was the warden.

Jeremiah waited for shouts of alarm or the sound of a scuffle, but none came. Hours passed in silence, and his fear of a tragic resolution to Vivica's escape dwindled. He even dozed, waking to the arrival of the morning meal.

The guard who wasn't Borstonnis bore two planks of wood with bread and cheese. He set Jeremiah's food outside his cell, then turned and stared at the emptiness of Vivica's cell. He glanced around the rest of the cells, then returned to Vivica's as though staring hard enough would conjure a copper-haired elf, previously hidden by some trick of the light.

The guard turned to Jeremiah. "Oi, where's the girl what was in there?"

"Don't know. Woke up and she wasn't there. Thought you took her."

The jailer yanked on the empty cell's door and found it locked. He hunkered down to check that Vivica wasn't clinging from the ceiling, waiting to ambush him. Jeremiah nibbled at his cheese and tried to act disinterested. The jailer set the spare meal on the ground and stepped outside, returning with Borstonnis, who approached the cell cautiously to help stare at it.

"She was there, right? Elf girl?" the first guard asked.

"Pretty sure she was," said Jeremiah.

The guards huddled together and whispered for a minute, then faced Jeremiah. Borstonnis picked up Vivica's food and held it toward Jeremiah. "Ain't no girl was in that cell. Not ever. Right?"

"What girl?" Jeremiah asked, turning his head like he might spot her.

"Good lad." Borstonnis set the plank beside the first and the prison door slammed shut.

The supply of cheap cheese continued even after Vivica's departure. Jeremiah noticed Borstonnis glancing nervously around with each meal delivery, as though he expected the elf's imminent return. Jeremiah himself awoke several times thinking he could hear her voice in the dark, a whisper at the edge of his hearing, but these were his imagination. Loneliness began to squeeze him as he lost days. Puzzling over his memories of Vivica anchored his mind, keeping him from straying into dark oceans of possibility.

Delilah returned late one evening, and Jeremiah nearly wept with relief. Her eyes were bloodshot from lack of sleep, but she exuded energy.

"I've got good news and bad news," Delilah said. "The bad news is you've been found guilty of performing necromancy."

"Found guilty?" Jeremiah's heart sank. He realized he'd been harboring hope after all.

"There was no avoiding that one, unfortunately, as you did raise the dead in front of dozens of witnesses. However, we've got a chance to make something of this! I've convinced them to let us present testimony from circumstantial witnesses, including yourself."

"Circumstantial witnesses?"

"They can do things like vouch for your character or talk about the events surrounding the crime in general. This testimony won't overturn a guilty verdict, but it can lessen your sentence."

"What kind of sentence are you expecting?" asked Jeremiah. He wondered if she would consider a less gruesome execution a victory at this point.

Delilah rubbed the back of her neck. "I really can't say. There's a lot going on here that's without precedent. But Bruno has been pulling every string he has to find witnesses on your behalf, and this is your chance to take the stand and speak for yourself. The judges will listen."

Jeremiah took in her disheveled appearance, a far cry from the last time he had seen her, and tried to imagine the tireless work she must have put in to achieve even this opportunity. He forced himself to smile. "Thanks, Delilah. No matter what happens, thank you."

Delilah returned the smile. "The final trial is in two days. I'll be right there with you. We're going to get you through this, Jay."

Jeremiah looked into her eyes and wished he could believe her.

Nights in the prison were inky black stretches of the imagination. Once the torches were extinguished, the rats made their customary rounds, their clawed feet clicking softly across the stone floor. Close, and always seeming to draw nearer. Jeremiah shivered underneath his ragged blanket, just thin enough that he was still uncomfortable against the damp air. His hearing played tricks on him, his own thoughts echoing off the cell walls startling him awake. He scanned the dark for signs of life, unsure if he wanted to find them.

It was during one such search, wrenched from a shallow sleep on the night before his trial, that Jeremiah heard a voice in the dark.

"I've been thinking about what you've decided to do. I don't understand it. You're putting your neck in the noose. They've proven where they stand. What mystery are you trying to solve?"

Jeremiah froze, unsure if it was his own sleep-sick mind that had spoken out of a dream. He waited, searching in vain for a shape among the shadows deeper than the rest.

"Hello? Is someone there?" he asked.

The voice had moved, closer now.

"They'll burn you out. Lead you along with hope on a string till you can't even crawl. Then they'll profit from every last dying gasp they can whip from you."

Jeremiah knew that voice. "Vivica?" He crossed his cell, arms outstretched, until he felt the bars and tilted his head to listen. Was she back in her cell?

"You want to give them a chance, is that it? Yet another chance to do the right thing? You don't owe them that."

"Wait, how did you get out before? Where are you going?" He had so many questions for her, but as they jostled for priority, he scattered them.

He leapt away from the bars as Vivica's voice shouted at him from the dark. The bars of his cell rattled.

"They've already failed, Thorn! They've devoured a thousand people just like you, and they're always hungry for more. How many more chances do we give them? How many more people do we throw in the grinder in the hopes that it will sate their appetite?"

"I don't know! I can't control what anyone else does; I just know what I have to do. And I trust my friends. They're my best chance to get out of this."

"I don't understand you, Thorn. But for your sake, I hope you're right."

The prison door's hinges screeched, admitting a dim ray of light. Jeremiah winced, anticipating the earsplitting slam of the heavy door. But the sound never came.

CHAPTER FIFTEEN

Sentencing

Jeremiah's stomach churned from the moment he awoke the next morning and realized what day it was. He picked at his bread and cheese until Delilah arrived to collect him. She tried to display an air of confidence, but he noticed her expression settled into grim determination as they left the prison.

It was raining, slightly heavier than a drizzle. Delilah and Jeremiah were escorted through the street by a dozen heavily armed guards. At first Jeremiah assumed the guards were meant to contain him, but as they approached the austere courthouse, he realized they were just as likely meant to dissuade rash actions by the public. The street near the courthouse was packed with onlookers, jostling for a chance to glimpse the evil wizard on his condemned march. Some performed superstitious gestures meant to ward off evil; a few shouted obscenities as he passed. Most just watched.

One woman shoved her way through the crowd. "Necromancer!" she cried. "My husband, necromancer! I need you to bring him back! Necromancer, please!" She was restrained by a pair of guards as Jeremiah climbed the courthouse steps.

Even under the circumstances, the Hall of Justice was impressive. Composed almost entirely of marble, the courtroom was cold and unyielding. A massive statue of a man with severe features and hopeful eyes dominated the space of the huge entry hall. He wielded an axe in one hand and a scepter in the other. Jeremiah recognized the statue as the god Jalus, with dominion over contracts, order, and justice. Jeremiah bowed his head in silent prayer as they passed.

A low murmur rose from the hundreds of well-dressed people crowded onto the courtroom's benches as Jeremiah made his way toward the front. There, seven podiums towered over a pulpit. Delilah directed Jeremiah to a closed-in area beside the pulpit, and he turned to face the crowd. His breath caught as he scanned the further hundreds of people who filled the balconies lining the upper level, less distinguished than those on the lower floor but no less eager for the trial to begin. All these people, just to see him sentenced. Then he spotted Bruno and Allison, seated on the bottom floor. They smiled when they saw him looking, and Bruno flashed him a thumbs-up. Jeremiah felt a mite braver.

"All rise for the Seven Judges!" said the bailiff. The shuffling of a thousand standing feet accompanied the entrance of five men and two women through seven different doors, each one positioned behind a podium. The judges simultaneously approached their podiums, their black robes billowing out as they ascended the narrow spiral steps. They took their seats as one, and all seven banged gold-capped wooden rods on their podiums three times.

"Justice. Order. Law," they declared in unison. The people of the courtroom sat down. One of the judges, an elf with thin golden tattoos stenciled around his eyes, spoke with practiced authority.

"Jeremiah Thorn. We have heard the testimony of your counsel, your friends, witnesses, and experts. We have found you guilty of the following charges: performing acts of necromancy, corpse tampering, public endangerment through use of magic, and destruction of property through use of magic. You have been afforded a chance to have others speak on your behalf so that we might know the measure of the man we are sentencing." The judge looked toward Delilah. "Counselor Fortune, you may proceed."

Delilah rose from her seat. "Thank you, Judge Lannis. I invoke the rights of Allison Allday." Her voice carried across the crowded courtroom with crystal clarity.

Allison marched to the pulpit like she had just been challenged to a duel. She glared up at the judges.

"Ms. Allday," said the judge on the end, a wizened gnome, "I hope we can expect proper decorum today, as befitting this house of law."

Allison continued to glare. "Yup."

Delilah made her way before the pulpit. "Ms. Allday, you served in the army of Dramir, did you not?"

"I did."

"Was it a particularly exemplary service?"

"That's not for me to decide."

"Let me rephrase. Would you tell us of any awards, honorifics, or titles you received during you time?"

Allison recited, "I earned the rank of Master of Arms, I was awarded the

Medal of Valorous Action, three Commendations for Exemplary Service, six Blood Chevrons, and the Golden Spearhead."

"Ms. Allday, can you describe what you are able to assume about Mr. Thorn, given your observations of him on the night of the fire?"

"I certainly can!" said Allison fiercely. "I saw a man who knew he'd get jail or worse if he did what he had to do to save those people. I also saw him act without hesitation or regard for his own safety. I saw a man, who I previously considered to be a misguided but otherwise good person, make the hard choice to sacrifice himself to protect the innocent from a grisly death. Then I saw that good man—no, that *hero*—get his name dragged through the mud—"

"Thank you, Ms. Allday," Delilah interrupted, but it was like trying to stop the tide.

"—and laws created just to punish him! For stopping people from burning to death! Have any of you ever been burned so bad you thought the pain would never stop?!" Allison pointed toward the judges' podiums, ignoring Delilah waving for her attention. "*I have!* If you had, you'd be honoring this man for saving children from a grisly death!"

"Ms. Allday!" shouted one of the judges. "Your opinion of the process of law is not something we are—"

"FUCK YOU!" Allison said. She was red in the face and clutching the rails of the pulpit. "I will *not* stand idly by while a good man is persecuted. They were already dead! No one suffered from their creation! I swear by Jalus, if you—"

"Allison!" Delilah reached across the pulpit rail to grab Allison's shoulder and forcibly turn her away from the judges. "*Thank you*, Ms. Allday, for your commendable service and for your time here today."

Allison growled, but stomped off the pulpit. Bruno, for his part, was in hysterics in all but sound. He gnawed at his fist while he rolled in his seat, tears in his eyes. Allison dropped back into the seat beside him, stone-faced.

The courtroom was dead quiet. Jeremiah realized his jaw was hanging open. To have heard from Delilah that Allison spoke in his defense was one thing, to watch her berate the judges to their faces was entirely another. If he was executed, part of him could die happy knowing Allison Allday was angry about it.

Delilah rubbed her eyes for a moment, muttering to herself, then took a breath to regain her composure. "I invoke the rights of Professor Gortanan."

A scholarly dwarf made his way toward the pulpit. He was old, but his movements were smooth and measured, a dwarf who would not be hurried by anyone else's schedule. It took several minutes for him to cross the room, climb the steps of the pulpit, and turn toward Delilah expectantly.

"Professor Gortanan," said Delilah, "would you please describe to the court your area of expertise?"

Professor Gortanan bowed his head. "My specialties are the studies of law and philosophy. I have been a teacher for ninety-eight years, and in this room I count four judges and one counselor among former students of mine."

Delilah betrayed a small smile at being included by him. "Professor Gortanan, my client, Mr. Thorn, has been charged with performing acts of necromancy. Can you provide the legal definition of necromancy?"

"I'm afraid I cannot, Counselor Fortune. There is no legal definition of necromancy."

One of the judges stood. "Counselor Fortune, this trial is an opportunity for you to provide accounts regarding the nature of your client, not to attack the laws your client is being tried under!"

"I understand, Judge Morton," said Delilah, "but I assure you I'm leading toward something important, if you will allow me to proceed."

The judge sat, frowning, but waved his hand to continue.

Delilah turned back to the dwarf. "Professor Gortanan, would you know necromantic magic if you saw it?"

"I certainly would not."

"Do you believe that any non-expert would recognize necromancy if they saw it?"

"I certainly do not."

"Interesting!" Delilah raised her voice, although it already reached every corner of the courtroom. "If, hypothetically, a law required an expert's assessment at the very moment the law was broken in order to be sure it had, in fact, been broken, such a law would be very difficult to enforce, wouldn't it?"

"Sounds like a tricky one, to be sure," said Professor Gortanan, his eyes twinkling.

Judge Morton stood, but Delilah raised her voice so that it rang off the walls. "That is particularly interesting! Professor Gortanan, you would think a law so circumstantial and so complex that only an expert could testify to it ever having been broken would not only be nearly unenforceable, but would be considered ridiculous and irresponsible?" she practically shouted.

Judge Morton interrupted. "Counselor Fortune! You will not disgrace the court wi—"

"It is my opinion that you are correct, Counselor Fortune. However, Hubert is correct—this line of questioning is not relevant to the character of the accused," said Professor Gortanan. He did not raise his voice, but the very act of him speaking silenced Judge Morton.

"I now see that you are correct, Professor! Thank you for enlightening me. My apologies to the judges. It's certainly not up to me or anyone else here to determine whether the law influencing my client's sentencing makes no sense at all. You may return to your seat." Delilah turned toward the crowd. "I now invoke the rights of Mrs. Calis Jarraka."

As the aged Professor Gortanan plodded back to his seat, he was passed by a dwarven woman wearing a black dress and a somber onyx tiara. As the woman reached the pulpit, Jeremiah noticed her eyes were watery. She looked bedraggled and sickly thin.

Delilah's tone became gentle. "Mrs. Jarraka, please share with the court how your late husband was involved with the events of this trial."

Mrs. Jarraka sniffed and produced a handkerchief, dabbing at her eyes. "My husband was Natgrik Jarraka, and he"—she choked a little—"he died in the fire."

Delilah nodded solemnly. "Was he involved in any other way?" Mrs. Jarraka shuddered a little and looked at Jeremiah, but he couldn't understand what he saw on her face. Revulsion? Pity? Anger? It looked like a mix of all three.

"Natgrik was one of the people that was . . . changed."

Delilah continued to nod with sympathy. "Mrs. Jarraka, I understand this is hard for you, but I have to ask you something. Do you think your late husband would have been upset by what happened to him after he had passed? If we could ask him now?"

Mrs. Jarraka's head whipped toward Jeremiah, and she looked at him with wide, hopeful eyes. "C-can you do that? Can you ask him questions? Can you speak with the dead?"

Jeremiah shook his head. It was a common misconception of necromancy, but he hated seeing the light of her hope fade.

"I'm afraid we'll need you to speak on behalf of those who cannot, Mrs. Jarraka," said Delilah.

Mrs. Jarraka was quiet for a few moments. Jeremiah could see his own nervousness reflected in Delilah as the woman considered her answer.

At last, Mrs. Jarraka spoke. "Yes, I'm sure he would have been greatly upset! His body can't be viewed by the family anymore. He's only bones now!" There was a gasp in the courtroom and the blood drained from Delilah's face.

"But . . ." Mrs. Jarraka continued, "he would have said it was for the best, to save those people. He knew the boy of the family—Aloomus, I think his name is—and was quite fond of him. Yes, I'm very sure my Natgrik would have been proud to serve his friends, even in death. I'm proud as well! A dwarf that is able to be useful even in death? That's indeed a noble thing!" There was a murmur from the crowd as many other dwarves nodded.

The color returned to Delilah's face and she thanked Mrs. Jarraka before ushering her down and calling the next witness. "I now invoke the rights of Harwick Featherfall."

A tall elven man limped to the pulpit. His neck and hands were covered in recent burns. Jeremiah realized the man was one of the people his skeletons had saved from the fire. Harwick looked up at the elven judge, Lannis, and said something in Elvish that Jeremiah couldn't understand. The judge repeated the same phrase back to Harwick.

"Mr. Featherfall," asked Delilah, "can you please tell the court about your feelings toward Mr. Thorn?"

Harwick nodded and spoke confidently. "Mr. Thorn saved the lives of my family and me. That's worth everything to me." He then spoke directly to Jeremiah. "Thank you, Mr. Thorn."

"Do you have any reservations about the method with which my client saved your family?" asked Delilah.

"I don't care how he did it," said Harwick. "I was scared when I saw the, uh . . ." He glanced at Delilah, who nodded for him to continue. "When the, uh, recently departed entered the room we were trapped in, but I knew they were trying to help us. Well, I knew after a minute."

"Would you consider the actions of Mr. Thorn to be evil?" asked Delilah.

"No, of course not! The man saved my children! I'm in his debt from this day forward. Mr. Thorn, if you ever have need of a cartographer, you need only say the word!"

"Thank you, Mr. Featherfall," said Delilah. "You may return to your seat." She waited a moment as the court digested the most recent testimony, then turned toward Jeremiah and mouthed, *Ready?*

Jeremiah nodded. Seeing a person he'd saved and hearing his gratitude had kindled a special glow in his chest. It filled him with confidence.

"I now invoke the rights of the accused! Jeremiah Thorn!"

Jeremiah felt brave as he approached the steps of the pulpit. All of those people had spoken in his defense. He felt righteous. Despite the pounding in his chest, he walked as tall as he could, showing the judges and crowd that he would face his sentencing without cowardice.

Delilah had no questions for him; she only invited him to speak. Straight backed and staring at the podiums with what he hoped was righteous indignation, he did.

"Judges of the high court," Jeremiah said, "I want you to know one simple thing: I do not regret what I did. I knew what would happen to me, but I will not sit by while people die if I can save them. If my sentence were to permit me to walk free from this courtroom, provided that I never use necromancy again, and I saw someone I could save on the very steps of this building, I would not hesitate. I will never hesitate. I will protect the safety and well-being of my fellows with every power at my disposal, whether or not people are scared of it. If that decision is to be punished, I accept."

There were rumbles of approval from the people of the courtroom, but a few hisses and soft jeers as well. He signaled he was done, and Delilah gestured him back to his seat.

"Not bad," she whispered. "Concise, admitted no fault, framed it around helping people. Good job." Jeremiah smiled and thanked her, though he was glad to sit again. He thought his knees would soon give way beneath him.

"I've been practicing for days," Jeremiah whispered back.

Judge Lannis banged his rod of office on the wood. "Justice. Order. Law. The Seven Judges will now retire to discuss a fitting punishment for the accused, taking into account all that has been said during the trial. The accused and counsel are to remain here until we have reached an accord. All others may leave should they so choose."

"All rise!" announced the bailiff. The Seven Judges descended from their podiums and exited through the doors from which they entered.

Time slipped by. Most of the crowd had remained, eager to hear the sentencing. They chattered excitedly. Jeremiah was growing anxious. What was taking so long?

Delilah, noticing his fidgeting, squeezed his shoulder. "This is a good thing," she said. "If they had decided in advance what your sentence would be, they'd be done by now. It means they're seriously considering what to do."

Jeremiah nodded. Her reassurance made sense, but did little to assuage his sense of foreboding as the minutes grew into hours.

Enough time passed for his adrenaline to subside, only to surge again when the bailiff strode to the front of the room. "All rise!"

The doors of the courtroom reopened, and the Seven Judges returned, settling in their seats on the raised podiums. "Justice. Order. Law." Three bangs of the rod silenced the room. The sound lingered on in Jeremiah's ears. The large room seemed to be closing in on him.

"Please come to the pulpit to hear your sentence," said Judge Lannis. Jeremiah walked to the focal point of the room. His legs felt like jelly and seemed to take an eon to carry him to the pulpit, but his head was clear and focused on the words of the judges.

"Counselor Fortune, please join Mr. Thorn at the pulpit."

Delilah recoiled at the request. She seemed tiny as she approached, and Jeremiah thought she looked more nervous than he did. She stood beside him meekly, with none of the presence that she'd carried during the entire trial.

"Jeremiah Thorn. We have discussed your crimes and the circumstances surrounding them. We are forced to admit that your situation is without precedent in our halls, and without the wisdom of precedence to guide us, we are obligated to make our own. You have performed a noble deed, but in doing so have brought a corruption into our city that flies in the face of the natural order. That you are guilty of necromancy is without question. However, the law falls short of suggesting the appropriate punishment for your actions in their entirety.

"It is therefore, after considerable deliberation, that we pass down the follow-ing sentence: Jeremiah Thorn, we are providing you with a period of one year and one day with which to prove to this court that you and your magic are of benefit to the city of Dramir. What you do with your magic is up to you, but you are to receive no payment for services your magic provides. Your abilities are at the service of the people of Dramir. It is at the sole discretion of the court which activities will constitute proof of your benevolence. If you are unable to con-vince the court by the end of the period provided"—Lannis paused for dramatic effect—"you will be executed."

Pandemonium erupted in the courtroom. Jeers and hisses rained down from the balconies as people called for Jeremiah's blood *now*. Even the gentry cried out their outrage. The phrases "corruption," "unholy magic," "mockery of justice," and "you've doomed us all" rang out among the uproar. The guards who had escorted them to the courthouse stepped forward to reinforce the bailiff's control over the room.

Jeremiah himself was filled with a hurricane of emotions. Being executed *later* was not among the infinite scenarios he'd imagined. But today he was safe, for a year and a day he was safe, and there was a chance still to save himself. He could even continue to practice magic, an outcome he had not dared hope for.

The judge turned to Delilah, who shrunk under his gaze. "Counselor Fortune, you are well respected by the courts of Dramir. As such, the court is entrusting you with the safety of the city by requesting your oversight of Jeremiah Thorn's housing and care. He will reside with you until the end of the described period. You will provide the courts with reports on his activities to inform our decision at the end of one year and one day." The judge looked to his contemporaries, as if trying to see if they were still in agreement.

"Counselor Fortune, you have of your own volition chosen to stand in defense of your client. You have attested and fought to restrain the hand of jus-tice. Despite having prior knowledge of the particular magic of your client, you brought him into our city and into your own home, at inexcusable risk to the safety of our people. You had hoped he would escape the eye of justice, but he has not. It is for this reason that, if after a year and one day, Mr. Thorn has failed to prove himself to be a benevolence unto the city, you will be stripped of your Counselor status and be prohibited from future practice of law."

"What." Delilah's mouth opened and closed like a displaced fish, but no more words came out.

"From this moment, Mr. Thorn is under house arrest. He is confined to the Fortune residence unless on business pertaining specifically to his sentence. He is forbidden from leaving the city without express written permission from this court."

The Seven Judges together raised their gold-capped rods and declared in unison, "Our justice is passed! Justice! Order! Law!" The final strike echoed around the room, triggering another volley of jeers.

The bailiff removed Jeremiah's manacles. "Given the circumstances," he said under his breath, "you probably want to exit out the back."

CHAPTER SIXTEEN

Work for Good

Jeremiah and Delilah avoided the bloodthirsty crowds on the way home from the trial via a complicated route of back streets and alleys. Delilah was uncharacteristically somber during the walk, and Jeremiah kept his own silence to avoid disturbing her thoughts.

The moment they entered the front door, Allison welcomed them with literal open arms, pulling Jeremiah into a powerful bear hug that crushed the air from his lungs. "He lives! By the grace of Talus, he lives!" She swung him around once before setting him on his feet. "That was ballsy as hell, making skeletons save people from a fire!"

Jeremiah grinned at her exuberance. "Thanks. Sorry it means I might not be out of your hair for another year."

"Are you kidding? You saved innocent lives by risking your own life and freedom. In my book that makes you a hero. The least we can do is put you up for a while!"

Bruno pried Jeremiah from the grip of Allison's adoration. "If you'll come this way, hero, I've taken the liberty of preparing some culinary options. I know the stuff they give you in that prison is pretty dire."

"Actually, I—" Jeremiah stopped himself. He had almost mentioned the additional cheese Vivica had procured for them, but he had a feeling she wouldn't have wanted him telling his friends, although he wasn't sure why that mattered. "I'm starving!"

A banquet of meats, cheeses, pickled vegetables, and breads was arranged on the table, and Jeremiah fell upon it like a starved wolf. "Fanks, Bruno," he said around a mouthful of roasted meat and cheese. "Vat's so much bebber." He chased the food with a rich, satisfying mead, savoring the medley of flavors.

"Gotta say," said Bruno, "I was impressed with how you and Delilah handled those judges. Whenever I've been in that room, all the big chairs and echoing made me fumble my words."

"It was all Delilah," said Jeremiah. "Her and the witnesses, anyway. Without everyone saying so much nice stuff on my behalf, I would've been shaking in my boots. I owe all of you. Really."

"Don't worry, you're going to make it up to us by working your ass off!" burst out Delilah. She thrust a finger toward Jeremiah. "You're going to take the jobs I find for you, and you're going to do them perfectly. You're not going to cause trouble, you're not going to cut corners, and you're not going to slack off just because you're stuck here. Got it!?"

Jeremiah stared at her, the latest bite of bread forgotten between his teeth. "Mm-hmm?"

"They're screwing me with this verdict," Delilah continued, eyes blazing, drawing so close to Jeremiah, the heat of her rage was palpable. "No counselor has ever, *ever* shared a sentence with their client. It's obscene and it's wrong, but it's the hand we're playing with, and I'm sure as hell not going to fold just because the whole game is bullshit. We are going to destroy this little geas and prove to everyone that *you* are a good person and that *I* am not to be *fucked* with!"

Jeremiah swallowed. "Uh, yeah. Definitely."

"Good! You can have Gus back tomorrow. I need him to help me think tonight." With that, Delilah turned on her heel and disappeared into her room, slamming the door behind her.

Delilah's determined fervor only intensified over the next few weeks, but Jeremiah began to doubt the feasibility of achieving a stay of execution. Delilah had wasted no time in reaching out to her vast network of professional contacts about work for a necromancer, only to discover that many refused to even accept her communications. She even made inquiries with several of Bruno's connections, where there was slightly more promise. However, once the discussions turned to official court reports, interest vanished faster than a tipsy tourist's purse.

Meanwhile, a cadre of protesters had formed outside the house. Jeremiah awoke each morning to chants calling for his exile, torture, or death. As he wasn't allowed to leave the house except on official business, and Delilah had been unable to drum up any official business, he was stuck listening to sermons on the evil of the undead, lectures on the atrocities wrought by necromancers throughout history, and fabrications of evil deeds supposedly performed by Jeremiah himself.

One afternoon Allison had come home with a black eye and a split lip. She attributed it to a disagreement about "the legal ramifications of the outcome of the court case." Jeremiah deduced that only a fellow fighter could have injured Allison during a brawl. It seemed the damage to Allison's reputation for associating with him was taking its toll even within the warrior's guild. She brushed off his concern, but he went to bed with a pit of guilt in his stomach.

Determined to be useful and help make up for the time Delilah was spending looking for necromancer work, Jeremiah eventually convinced Delilah to let him help her in the lab. She ushered him through the door upstairs on the left as though they were entering a mausoleum.

Every surface of the laboratory was stacked with glassware tubing that curled around metal stands like vines, hefty beakers with swollen bottoms, and racks upon racks of tiny glass tubes filled with colorful liquids. Just looking at the equipment made Jeremiah feel overly large and clumsy, and the acrid sting of odors made his head swim. He kept careful track of his limbs as he followed Delilah between the tables.

Jeremiah tried to pay close attention while Delilah showed him around the lab, although he had no idea what she was saying most of the time. Nevertheless, her enthusiasm for her work held his attention and made everything sound either very important or very dangerous. After the introduction, she supervised him closely as he followed her instructions to distribute a viscous purple fluid from a heated container into several small jars. He breathed a sigh of relief when she declared his work satisfactory.

"What are these?" he asked as she stoppered and labeled the jars.

"Not much on their own. But when combined with a few other compounds I have cooking, it becomes that stuff I poured on the stairs at the goblin Warren. I call it blast jelly. My own recipe!" She held up a jar against the light for him to admire, beaming with pride.

"Which one is the healing potion you used on Allison?"

Delilah's face fell just a little. "Those are magic, and damn expensive. I can't make them." She looked almost guilty at the admission. "But I do have a speed-healing tonic!" She indicated a long crystal pipe that was dripping pearlescent fluid into tiny vials. "It's not useful in a combat situation, but you'll get a month's worth of natural healing overnight. You also develop an incredible fever and are weakened for a few days after, but there are lots of situations where it's worth it. The recipe is very rare."

Jeremiah took a vial and flicked it, watching tiny bubbles crawl through the viscous liquid.

"How come Allison didn't take this when her shoulder got wrecked?"

"Because it speeds up *natural* healing. Natural healing wasn't going to be kind to a shoulder ground to dust like that. But these will do the job for plenty of injuries, given enough time."

* * *

As the weeks slipped by, Jeremiah gradually earned Delilah's trust as a lab assistant. She delegated more and more complex tasks to him, even leaving him alone on occasion to run an errand or attend a meeting. Jeremiah was grateful for the opportunity to feel helpful and to distract himself from the nagging fear that his year and a day were going to pass with him remaining trapped in the house, without a single opportunity to demonstrate his capabilities. His friends would continue to suffer for defending him, and then he would be executed anyway, just another evil necromancer the world was better off without.

Jeremiah was just finishing setting up a gradual decantation when Delilah burst through the front door with a triumphant shout of his name. He called back that he'd be done in a minute. He wanted to sprint downstairs, but he forced himself to clean up as methodically as ever, not quite daring to let himself believe in the hope that bloomed in his chest.

He found Delilah vibrating in the kitchen, more animated than she had been in weeks. "We have ourselves a taker!" she said. "I don't know the details, but I was contacted by Mr. Albert Dunsimmons, one of the largest commercial farmers in the region. He's sent for us. Come on!"

Jeremiah needed only a moment to gather his things. He stepped outside for the first time in over a month to find a carriage waiting, the horses made skittish and fitful by the mob of jeering protesters. Delilah hurried him into the carriage, plopping beside him with an armful of agriculture books. "I'm not sure what he needs us to do, so we should be prepared. Read this."

Delilah forced a book upon him and dove into her own, but Jeremiah wasn't in the mood to read. He watched the city rumble by outside, craning to see the blue spring sky, hungry to soak in any sight beyond those same four walls.

They passed under the city gate. Outside Dramir, the horizon stretched on forever. Jeremiah grinned at the open fields, his heart lighter than it had been for as long as he could remember. He imagined himself running through the pastures, free to go wherever he pleased . . .

Jeremiah was brought back to earth as the carriage turned onto a narrow dirt road. They passed acres of dirt fields before arriving at the farm compound. The compound included a few houses, a row of warehouses and silos, and a truly massive barn just beside the receiving area. Workers shouted as they arrived, dropping what they were doing to assemble into formation like soldiers. An older man strode forward to meet the carriage, dressed in finery speckled with mud, polished silver buttons holding in his heaving gut.

"I will be blunt," the man said as they disembarked. Jeremiah suspected he didn't know any other way to be. "I am the richest, most landed farmer of Dramir. But a plague has befallen my entire stable of horses, and the veterinarians say there's no hope for them. Plowing season is nearly at an end, yet my fields are untouched. I risk missing out on the entire year. This would not only harm my finances and my standing, but would create a food scarcity in Dramir."

Delilah scribbled notes as he spoke. "What would you have us do, Mr. Dunsimmons?"

"Get my fields plowed. I don't know or care what kind of magic you wield, mage, but if you salvage my year, I will write whatever affidavit you need." His tone acquired a hint of menace. "And from what I hear, you can't afford to miss this chance."

Jeremiah and Delilah exchanged a look. The man was right.

Delilah gave a curt nod. "Thank you for this opportunity, sir. We will evaluate the situation and begin as soon as possible. You will not be disappointed."

Dunsimmons dismissed his assembled workers with a bark. They scattered like frightened mice, save for a gray-haired halfling. He was clad head to foot in leather apron, gloves, boots, and mask, all splotched with dark green and black. As the halfling approached the carriage, a putrid stink made Jeremiah's eyes water.

"Afternoon, sir," the halfling said. "Wish there was better news, but another six have died, and there's no sign of improvement from the others."

Dunsimmons patted the halfling on the shoulder. "Cease your worrying, Garth. The mage has agreed to help. Take us inside now. Show him what he's working with."

They followed Garth to the stables housed within the colossal barn, which turned out to be built like a labyrinth. Additions had been built over the years, seemingly at random. The stables were honeycombed with stalls, and in each and every one was a dead or dying horse.

Jeremiah's stomach swam. The stench only grew as Garth led them between the stalls. The horses were covered in weeping pustules, lying still or standing listlessly. They did not acknowledge the strangers' approach.

"You got a cure for this?" asked Garth.

Jeremiah shook his head. "No. What I do isn't in the realm of healing." At the halfling's curious look, Jeremiah knelt before a stall where a horse lay dead. He spoke the words and reached between the wooden railings to brush the horse's muzzle. At once, necromantic energy flowed through his fingers and into the corpse. A bubble formed in his head, much larger than the ones created by humanoids.

Rise.

The horse slowly rolled onto its feet and pushed itself up.

Garth gasped. "You brought her back!" He laughed and reached to stroke the mare's nose. "Hey, Daisy, you feeling better, girl?" But Garth froze as soon as he touched the creature. He looked into its eyes, then stepped away, glancing between Jeremiah and Dunsimmons. "What the hell is this thing?"

"Yes," said Dunsimmons, "what just happened here?" He kept his distance, but his gaze was fearless as he watched the animated horse.

"I've raised it as a zombie under my control," said Jeremiah. "It's still very much dead, but I might be able to use it, and the others, to do some plowing."

"Mr. Dunsimmons, may I speak with you? Privately?" asked Garth. Dunsimmons continued to watch the horse. Jeremiah imagined the gears turning in his head. "Mr. Dunsimmons?"

"Yes. Yes, of course." They departed around a corner, leaving Jeremiah and Delilah alone.

Delilah approached the horse and inspected it. "Is it . . . safe to touch?" she asked him.

"Yes. It won't do anything without me telling it to."

She reached a hand and stroked the nose as Garth had done. "It's so still." She flinched in surprise when the corpse playfully nudged at her hand.

"You're doing this?" she asked. Jeremiah nodded, letting the nudging continue. "It's strange. It's moving like a horse, but it's not the same. It seems wrong. Can you feel that I'm touching it?"

"Not exactly. I'm aware of contact with it, and the intensity of the contact. I could distinguish a touch from a blow, but that's about it. I can't use their senses, either . . . at least, I don't think I can. Flusoh never mentioned it."

There was a shout from around the corner. "You're getting what you want, so quit complaining!" Dunsimmons marched back, straight up to Jeremiah. "You've got my permission to do whatever you need to do to get my fields plowed. Garth and Randy, my head horseman, will assist you. But I need results quickly! You have a week."

Jeremiah was stunned. "A week? Sir, with the acreage you have, it must take a month to plow!"

Dunsimmons considered Jeremiah coldly. "I made my fortune doing things people said were impossible. We need to get seeds in the ground. You have a week. I trust you'll find a way."

Dunsimmons left the stables. Jeremiah worked his jaw as though chewing the enormity of the task ahead of them.

Garth's voice brought him back to the present. He was staring forlornly at another dead horse. "You can't actually save them, can you?"

"I'm sorry. I wish I could." Jeremiah brushed the flank of the still horse. It rose up to standing. Garth looked away. "Show me all the dead ones. I can't do them all today, but I can at least get started."

Garth led them through the labyrinthine stables, and Jeremiah's mind slowly filled with bubbles. He became reliant on Garth's guidance as there was less room for Jeremiah in his own head. His ability to focus and cast grew weaker, and he began to require several attempts to get the spell right.

After thirty-five horses, he just couldn't do any more. He pronounced the words correctly and his gestures were accurate as always, but he lacked the focus to exert his will. *Once you're tapped, you're tapped*, Flusoh's voice said in his ear. *Don't waste time frustrating yourself.*

"All done today," Jeremiah said. "Horses, lie down." The zombie horses silently lay down in unison. He was finally able to reduce the size of the bubbles, giving them only the barest focus needed to keep them in existence. Even so, they were larger than the bubble of a normal humanoid zombie.

Jeremiah blinked slowly and his awareness of his surroundings returned to almost normal. He was still exhausted. He and Delilah followed Garth outside, where Jeremiah gulped the fresh air with relief.

Dunsimmons was speaking with a rugged-looking half elf. "Randy," said Dunsimmons, "this is the mage."

"Pleased to meet ya," said Randy with palpable disdain. Jeremiah shook his hand, trying to hide his discomfort as Randy squeezed just a little too hard.

Jeremiah skipped right to business. "Show me what the horses have to do. How they'll be using the plows."

Randy gave a mirthless laugh. "Don't even know how to plow? This ought to be a treat."

The farm possessed a variety of plows. Most were single man, but there were a few four- and five-blade wheeled plows that ran with little effort on the part of the driver. These required a team of twelve or more horses to overcome the earth's resistance. Dunsimmons assured Jeremiah that his men were experts and would take care of their side. Jeremiah just had to worry about his magic.

And Jeremiah did worry. Commanding a few horses to walk in straight lines across the fields was simple enough, but the magnitude of the job, and the number of animals he'd need to raise to complete it in a week, sounded impossible.

Dunsimmons dismissed them for the evening and Jeremiah and Delilah bid good night to Garth and Randy, the latter still not bothering to hide his scorn. As they walked to the small cottage they'd be staying in, Delilah asked, "You think you can handle this?"

"I don't know," Jeremiah replied honestly. "The horses are a lot bigger than humans—in my head, that is—and Dunsimmons has some high expectations."

"If you can impress him, he might open a lot of doors for us. Well, he might open any other door at all."

"Huh?" Jeremiah had heard her, but he was having trouble following the conversation.

"I— Never mind, Jay. Why don't you just get some sleep? We're going to be up early."

CHAPTER SEVENTEEN

Progression

The sun hadn't quite broken the horizon when someone knocked on their door. The farm kitchens provided a massive ham and egg breakfast. Jeremiah was too nervous to be hungry, but he forced himself to eat anyway. He felt reenergized after the night's rest, but he'd need his strength to endure the mental strain of the day.

As they returned to the stables, Jeremiah could tell word had gotten around. Farmhands whispered as he passed, or openly stared. He wondered what they had heard, whether rumor overwhelmed the truth or if the truth was strange enough on its own.

Jeremiah resumed reanimating horses at once. With Garth's guidance, he focused on the largest horses that had been part of the plowing teams. This time he made the bubbles small and inactive as soon as he created them. In this manner, he managed to raise another dozen zombies under his control.

"You all right, boss?"

Jeremiah jumped, snapping back to attention. "What?" He realized Garth was standing very close to him, apparently concerned. He wondered how long he'd been staring into space. "Yes, I'm fine. Get the plows ready. We can get started today with what we have." Jeremiah wasn't even sure he could control what he had animated right now, not when they were all active.

They made their way out from the stables to find the farmhands assembled in neat rows, just like yesterday. Dozens of plows were arrayed beside the stables, from worn wooden plows with cracked handles to great iron contraptions. A small crate had been placed before the assembly. Beside it stood Dunsimmons, watching him expectantly.

Jeremiah realized with a jolt that he was expected to say something. At Delilah's prodding, he stepped onto the box and faced the crowd. No words came to mind as he looked out on sun-darkened faces, sturdy clothes, and suspicious eyes. He swallowed hard.

"Ladies and gentlemen of Dunsimmons's farm," he said, his voice squeaking. He cleared his throat. "By now you've probably heard about what I'm doing. I, uh, want to clarify a few things."

His mouth went dry again as he prepared to speak the truth that had led to broken friendships, to being run out of towns, to being put on trial for his life. "I am a necromancer."

A murmur ran through the crowd, but Dunsimmons's discipline did not break. Certain he was about to be lynched, Jeremiah continued. "I have raised some of the horses who have passed on as undead. You would know them as zombies."

Jeremiah saw hands go over mouths and anxious shuffling. He continued quickly. "Let me be clear: they are *not* dangerous! They only do exactly as I command! Think of this as . . . as a parting gift from those hardworking animals. You'll see some horses you know. They won't be at their . . . prettiest, but if you want to say goodbye, this the time to do it."

Jeremiah paused. The farmhands hadn't broken rank to seize him yet, though Dunsimmons kept a discerning eye on his workers.

"They won't get tired," Jeremiah continued. "They don't need water breaks. There won't be any bucking or biting or stubbornness. They are strong, much stronger than they were. You need only guide them and they will follow you. Are there any questions before we get to work?"

"This is evil magic!" one of the farmhands yelled, thrusting a finger toward Jeremiah. Several people nodded.

Jeremiah had anticipated this objection. "Magic is neither good nor evil. You can kill a man with an axe, or you can cut down a tree; it makes no difference to the axe. Same goes for magic."

"Still sounds like evil magic!" the man said.

Dunsimmons began walking toward the man. The line went still and silent. The man's outrage fled, and he stared at the ground as his boss approached.

Dunsimmons towered over the man. The line separated on either side of him. "Jones!" he bellowed. "If you have a problem with work, I invite you to let me know now so I can alleviate your discomforts. Do you have a problem with work, *Jones?*"

Jones wrung his hands and averted his eyes. "N-no, sir."

"Do you have a *problem* with the triple pay you're making for this endeavor? Would standard wages put you at ease? Or would you like to ask me for a favor and request *half* wages? Do you need a favor, *Jones?*"

"No, sir."

That did it. There were no more questions or objections.

"The horses will come to you!" Jeremiah shouted. "Guide them to their plows and hook them up. Once everyone is ready, they'll start pulling."

Jeremiah climbed down from the crate. He closed his eyes and, one by one, began to inflate the bubbles. Delilah steadied him as he nearly buckled under the load. His own mind was being crowded out. He had never tested himself like this before.

In the end, he had to keep several bubbles inactive. There simply wasn't enough room for all the zombies he had created. Still, they had to get started.

Rise. Come.

A rustling came from inside the stables, soft hoof clops on earthen floor. The farmhands' tension grew as they listened. For so many moving horses, it was eerily quiet.

The first of the zombies appeared in the door, and the rest followed in a long, orderly line. The farmhands were visibly shaken at the horses acting so strangely.

Randy spurred the farmhands to action. "Move your asses! Daylight's wasting! No pay for no work!"

Cautiously, the farmhands approached. Some went to particular horses, petting them and speaking softly to them. The zombies were bridled and led away from the stables.

Follow. Move.

There was so little space in Jeremiah's own mind for himself. He could see and think and move, but it was slow, as if his thoughts were trudging through mud. It was like turning around in a tunnel only big enough to crawl through—possible, but difficult and claustrophobic. Delilah whispered in his ear. "Go."

Jeremiah commanded every zombie he had.

Pull. Harder. Faster.

The plows kicked into motion, crossing slowly from one side of the field to the other and back again. The incredible strength of the zombified horses heaved giant rocks from the ground and snapped roots like twigs. But many more plows and farmhands stood uselessly to the side.

The day passed slowly. His job was simultaneously monotonous and nearly overwhelming. The remaining space in Jeremiah's head was saved for necessities, such as annoyance at his own limitations.

By the time the sun set, the field had been plowed far into the distance. Jeremiah felt exhausted as the farmhands returned the horses and plows to the stable, but he was pleased with the progress. He and Delilah retired to the guesthouse.

"That wasn't too bad, was it?" Jeremiah asked after dinner.

Delilah was scribbling on a piece of paper. "We did good," she said finally, "but not great. Based on what we plowed today, we'll be at this for a month before we finish. That's assuming it all goes just as well as it did today and there are no setbacks."

Jeremiah's satisfaction with the day's work evaporated. His face dropped into his hands. "Dunsimmons wants this done in a week! How are we supposed to make up that kind of time?"

"Is there anything you can do? Raise more horses? Make them go faster?"

"I'm doing everything I can."

Delilah patted his shoulder. "Well, keep doing your best. Maybe Dunsimmons will be happy enough with a quarter of his fields plowed to write the affidavit."

He knew she was just trying to keep him from despair. Dunsimmons had been clear about his demands, and he didn't strike Jeremiah as a man who accepted compromise. Jeremiah lay awake, pondering solutions long into the night, but when he opened his eyes at sunrise, it was without any new ideas.

The process began again, grinding away at a job that was too big for him. Jeremiah stewed in frustration at his failures as hour after hour passed.

Hard to think. Need to do more. Too many bubbles. Need space, just a bit more space. Jeremiah tried moving the bubbles around his head, pushing them together as tight as he could to free up a bit more space. They squeezed closer, allowing him a small amount of precious room to think. He used it to try to come up with ways to complete a month's task in a week. His opportunity to prove his worth was slipping away. "Good, not great" wasn't going to cut it.

He picked two bubbles and was squeezing them tighter together, hoping to salvage enough room for one more zombie, when he had a revelation thanks to the minuscule amount of spare thinking space he had created.

There's space inside bubbles! And the zombies only follow the same command . . .

With that realization, one of the bubbles suddenly existed inside the other. Quite by accident, he had nested the two bubbles neatly together, taking up the space of just one bubble. He quickly scanned the fields for any disruption in the farmhand's work, but nothing seemed to have changed.

Jeremiah chose another pair of bubbles. He wasn't sure exactly how he'd done it, but just knowing it was possible for one bubble to exist inside the other was exhilarating. He struggled for several minutes, the two bubbles remaining resolutely separate despite his efforts. He had nearly exhausted his focus when, with monumental concentration, it happened again. And again, easier this time. His elation grew as he freed more headspace and began to understand the implications of what he'd managed. He prodded Delilah's shoulder incessantly.

"Ow! Jeremiah, stop it. What's wrong?"

"I've got it! I know what to do!" Jeremiah jumped up. Delilah started at the explosion of movement. "I know how Flusoh did it, how he controlled so many!

Delilah went pale. "You can control as many as *he* could?"

"Nowhere close! But I can control many more than before. I'm going to raise the rest of the horses."

Delilah ran to find Garth, and Jeremiah went into the stables. Stall by stall, he resurrected the dead horses, making sure to double up their bubbles as soon as they were created. The process of nesting them was already becoming second nature. His heart pounded with excitement as Garth, Randy, and Delilah arrived and saw the new zombies standing and ready to work.

"Get any plow you can beg, borrow, or steal," said Jeremiah. "We've got work to do!"

The new round of reanimations had tired Jeremiah, but he was too elated to care. He had discovered a secret of necromancy all on his own. He now commanded nearly one hundred zombie horses. With experimentation, he was able to nest three, and then four bubbles within the space of one. The fourth bubble was exceedingly difficult, but he was confident it would become easier in time. Separating them out again was a chore, but as all his zombies only had to follow the same commands, he could maintain groups of them in the same stack of bubbles.

The sun was setting, but Jeremiah was too excited to rest. He gathered Delilah, Garth, and Randy. "We've got more than double the workforce as before. Let's go all night."

Delilah looked at him with concern, but Randy nodded with genuine approval. "Garth, fetch lanterns and oil for every plow. I'll set up a schedule for the men. An extra silver to anybody that goes all night!"

Jeremiah monitored the fields as the last rays of sun disappeared over the horizon. Delilah was crunching numbers beside him. "By my estimate," she said, "with the extra horses and all the men working in shifts to keep them going, we'll finish the last field in just about five days. But that's assuming the horses are going twenty-four hours a day. You'll need to sleep at some point, right?"

Jeremiah pursed his lips. "I don't know what will happen if I sleep while the zombies are working. It doesn't sound like something we can risk, though. We're going to just barely make Dunsimmons's deadline as it is. I'll just have to stay awake as much as possible."

Delilah frowned, but she rummaged through her bag and handed Jeremiah a crystal vial of clear, viscous liquid. "Use this only if you really need it to stay awake. The effects can be . . . messy."

He accepted it with thanks. Delilah wished him luck and returned to the guesthouse, leaving Jeremiah to face his vigil.

The hours of darkness crawled past. Jeremiah kept himself awake by pacing the edge of the field, watching the progress of the plows by their lanterns. The farmhands were all too eager to earn their bonus pay by working through the night. They seemed to consider it easy work, with the zombies able to continue unimpeded by the obstacles normal horses face.

Jeremiah quaffed Delilah's serum early in the morning, when the hours until sunrise seemed to stretch toward eternity. His energy surged at once, although his thoughts also became erratic. He was struck by the idea to walk the field itself, to see his minions working firsthand, and had no sooner conceived the thought than he was out there, stumbling through the freshly churned earth by dim starlight.

As he headed toward the steady lanterns in the distance, a movement caught his eye. Another group of glowing lights was approaching from the river, moving much faster than any of the plows. Galloping hoofbeats reached Jeremiah's ears. These weren't of his own contingent.

Jeremiah broke into a run as the new lights reached the slow-moving plows ahead. Suddenly, he sensed one of his zombies had sustained an injury. He separated its bubble from the stack at once. There was shouting from up ahead, and the fast group of lights once again peeled away from the plows and galloped back toward the river.

Jeremiah reached the injured zombie and its handler a few minutes later, clutching a stitch in his side. "What happened?" he gasped.

The driver glared at Jeremiah. "Some of Gifford's boys decided to pay us a visit." He pointed to a shaft buried deep in the zombie's chest, where its heart sat silent. "Guess they don't much approve of our methods. Can't say I do either." The man spat toward Jeremiah's boots.

Jeremiah wrenched the crossbow bolt from the zombie. The injury appeared superficial. He issued a few test commands and found the zombie able to respond as expected.

Randy appeared with a drawn shortsword. "Can't believe those bastards got the drop on us. Horse still work?"

"Yeah, it should be fine," said Jeremiah. "Looks like it took a cross—"

"I know that! But seeing as how it can still pull a plow, why the hell is it standing still?"

The farmhand muttered an apology and climbed back aboard the plow. Jeremiah rejoined the zombie's bubble into its stack, and it resumed its steady work, pulling the farmhand into the night.

Randy spent the rest of the night prowling the border near the river, but no further incidents arose. The sun began to rise, and the effects of Delilah's serum started to fade. Jeremiah's thoughts took on a dreamlike quality as he sat by the edge of the field, but he brightened to see Delilah bringing him a bowl of hot oatmeal.

"Keep your strength up," she said. "We're making good progress! Just get through the next few days."

That plan turned out to be easier said than done. Jeremiah became nauseated from exhaustion as the day wore on. Delilah chatted with him as a distraction, but eventually her energy began to grate on him. Jeremiah excused himself to walk the perimeter of the field, just to get his blood moving.

The day was warm for spring, and the heat of the sun didn't help Jeremiah's queasiness. He paused in the shade of a tree to catch his breath, watching his minions pull their plows relentlessly across the vast field. Despite the pressure they were under, he couldn't help but feel some pride. This was work he had made possible. Necromancy wasn't just about cults and murder; it was just as versatile and useful as other schools of magic. He'd show them, Dunsimmons and Allison, the Council, and the whole world. He'd show them what he was capable of . . .

A deep growl startled Jeremiah awake. Dunsimmons loomed over him. "Have a good nap?" Threat rumbled in his voice.

Jeremiah scrambled to his feet. "Sorry, sir."

"Sorry? While you were catching up on your beauty rest, one of the horses wandered into a river and took a plow with him. It wouldn't listen to the farm-hand. You owe me a new plow."

"Sir, I—"

"On top of that, I don't tolerate laziness. We're a hardworking farm. Don't go lounging the day away while my men are doing your job."

Jeremiah resisted the urge to protest that the men were doing nothing more than babysitting the zombies. He checked his zombies and found one was experiencing an abnormal amount of cold and wet. He separated that zombie from its stack and commanded it to return.

"I apologize, sir. I've taken care of the missing horse. You should have your plow back soon. However"—Jeremiah drew himself up to look Dunsimmons in the eye—"the fact is, I do need sleep. I can do it away from the fields, if you prefer, but if you want this work to continue at all, we're going to have to accept some risk."

Dunsimmons's eyes narrowed. He worked his jaw, like he was chewing Jeremiah's assertion to test its flavor. "Fine. But I'm holding you responsible for anything those monsters do."

The days passed like years in a rhythm that Jeremiah could just barely tolerate. Jeremiah's pride at his accomplishments was replaced by a dull desperation for the job to end. He stayed awake during the day and a good portion of the night, snatching short stretches of sleep when he thought it was safe.

Jeremiah's brief respites were interrupted occasionally by news that a zombie had wandered astray or gotten stuck somewhere. He was generally able to rectify the issue within a few moments of waking. Damage to the plows themselves was his greatest fear, but they seemed to suffer no more wear than normal on their brief sojourns.

Gifford's raiders returned on the third night, but this time Randy was prepared for them. After the skirmish, he sauntered back to the stables and dumped a body at Jeremiah's feet. It was a young man—a boy, really. Jeremiah looked away.

"Feeling squeamish, necromancer?" Randy sneered. "He wouldn't have been out here tonight if it wasn't for you!"

Jeremiah raised his gaze. "I can prepare the body for a respectful burial, if that task is beyond you."

Randy scoffed and muttered under his breath but dragged the body away. Jeremiah closed his eyes and wished he were anywhere else. At least their work continued in peace after that night.

Jeremiah sat in silence with Delilah on the last day of Dunsimmons's deadline. The plows had been operating out of sight in the far fields for some time now. One of the farmhands reappeared around the side of the barn. He stopped his plow in front of the stable and began unhooking the zombie.

"Something wrong?" Jeremiah asked. He could spot no damage to horse or plow.

"Done, boss," said the farmhand. He led his horse into the stable.

"Jeremiah, look." Delilah pointed toward the horizon.

Dozens of horses were making their way back. In a matter of minutes, the plows were being lined up and cleaned, the horses led to their pens. Jeremiah couldn't believe what he was seeing. Relief began to blossom in his chest.

As the last zombie was returned, Dunsimmons appeared, flanked by Garth and Randy.

"Gods damn, boy. You did it," said Dunsimmons. "Per our agreement, I've written a report for the courts that says you helped me out of a jam."

As he spoke, Randy produced a small, folded bundle of papers, tied and wax-sealed. He thrust it toward a beaming Delilah.

Dunsimmons clapped Jeremiah on the shoulder. "You've made me quite a bit of money already! A stable of horses that need no care, no food, and don't get tired? My profits will dwarf even my best year!"

"Actually, sir," Jeremiah said, "I'll need to cut them off soon. They'll go back to just being dead horses."

Dunsimmons's eyes narrowed as he processed what Jeremiah said. "You're telling me you're going to take my horses away. I'll have no horses again."

"Unfortunately, yes. They aren't independent, they need me to maintain them."

Dunsimmons turned to Delilah, a storm brewing in his eyes. "You lied to me, woman."

Delilah's eyes went wide as she took in a breath that was half gasp, half preparation. She thrust a finger directly into Dunsimmons's face. "How dare you! At no point did I ever say you could keep these horses. I never implied it. I never suggested it. I never even hinted at it! I told you exactly what was going to happen, and it's not my fault your greed made you hear what you wanted to hear!"

"Maybe I'll just let my counselor have that little discussion with you," Dunsimmons said.

Delilah stepped forward with her chin raised as if daring him to take a swing at her. "I. Would. *Ruin* you!"

Jeremiah popped the bubbles in his head, forever ending the possibility of the horses doing work. The sound of heavy bodies slumping to the ground reverberated throughout the stable, announcing what he had done.

Dunsimmons's voice was low and dangerous. "Mr. Thorn. Ms. Fortune. I'll trust you to see yourselves off my property."

"Thank you, Albert, we will," said Delilah, her voice dripping with acid. She stomped away, Jeremiah following closely behind.

CHAPTER EIGHTEEN

Fish Meets Hook

News of what had happened on the Dunsimmons farm spread through Dramir like wildfire. Within days, the group of protesters outside the house had swelled to double the size, chanting and yelling at passersby.

"Work is for the living!"

"Evil magic makes evil deeds!"

"No necrofood on my table!"

Jeremiah snuck a glance through the curtains. "They don't seem happy that I helped Dunsimmons."

"We don't need their approval," Delilah said, pouring over the morning mail. "We just need more opportunities, and there's always someone willing to take advantage of free labor. For example . . ." She extracted a letter from the pile and read aloud, "'If Dunsimmons can cheat, then so can I. The Limpton farm has work to do and the bodies to do it.' See? Your work with Dunsimmons is already paying off!"

A day later, Jeremiah stood beside Mr. Limpton in the middle of the Limpton family graveyard. Delilah had sent Bruno to accompany Jeremiah in her stead, and he was looking around with barely concealed mirth. The family graves had been exhumed and the old bones, several generations' worth, lay exposed beside piles of fresh dirt.

"My great-great-grandpappy worked this farm," said Mr. Limpton, punctuating each sentence by thumping the butt of his spade into the ground. "So did my great-grandpappy, my grandpappy, my pappy, all their womens, and all my uncles and aunties too. I need help harvesting, and if they worked it once, they can work it again!"

"Oh wow, that is *dark*," Bruno said, laughing.

"Are you sure?" Jeremiah asked the farmer. "They're just going to be skeletons. They're not going to—"

Mr. Limpton cut him off. "I know what skeletons are, you vile freak! I'm not looking for a family reunion; I just want my beets pulled. And if you want your letter, you'll get it done."

Jeremiah sighed. Soon an entire family tree of skeletons was wrist-bone-deep in soil, yanking beets out of the ground. Their bony fingers were perfect for sifting the soil for objects, though they frequently pulled up stones.

Mr. Limpton didn't mind; he just cackled as his new workforce toiled. "Back bothering you now, Uncle John?! That trick knee acting up again?! Not feeling too sickly now, are you?!" He had comments for several of the skeletons.

Bruno watched with a wide smile on his face. "This is so twisted. I love it." He draped an arm around Jeremiah's shoulders. "These folks might not like you, but they can't argue with the results, can they?"

Jeremiah watched as his undead clawed through the soil and fought back his sense of dread at Bruno's words. "Hopefully not."

The protesters grew more furious, but their ire could not stem the flow of jobs that had sprung up. The farmers of Dramir scrambled to figure out how to use this new resource—Jeremiah yanked out stumps using undead oxen, commanded zombie draught horses to haul many times their normal loads, and on one particularly nauseating occasion, instantly reduced dozens of hog corpses to meat slurry. The farmers spat at him or used evil warding signs, but they wrote their letters and Delilah submitted them to the Seven Judges.

The drudgery of the work began to wear on Jeremiah. The courts provided no feedback on whether he was making progress, but he had no choice besides continuing to follow the orders of people who called him evil before counting their profits.

One evening, resting in the living room after a long day of relocating an inconvenient graveyard, Jeremiah noticed Allison orbiting him. She would enter the room, then pretend to remember something and leave again. Jeremiah wondered what could make someone like Allison so hesitant but forced himself to be patient.

Finally, Allison dropped onto the couch beside him. She stared into the dark fireplace and took a deep breath. "I've got an old soldier friend. Actually old. He's dying. He always dreamed of falling in battle, sword in hand, but now he's too weak to even lift a sword. He heard about you, and he wants you to make him into a zombie so he can fight one last time."

"He won't—"

"He understands he won't be in control," she continued quickly, "but it's as close as he can get. I've agreed to be the one that fights him."

Jeremiah stared at her, mouth agape.

Allison wrung her callused hands. "I've looked up to him for a long time. He taught me to fight with a battle-axe and he's a good soldier. I . . . want to do him this honor. Will you help?"

She turned to him with such a plaintive look that Jeremiah's heart ached. "Yeah, I can do that."

Allison threw her arms around him. "Thank you, Jay! This means so much to me. I'll let you know when it's time. It won't be long."

It wasn't long at all. Two days later, Jeremiah accompanied Allison to the warriors' guild hall. Long tables had been pushed against the walls, leaving a wide-open space in the center. Dozens of men and women wearing either armor or black attire gathered at one end of the hall. At the other lay a withered man in repose, clad in ornate armor and clasping a sword at its chest. Though the face was gaunt and pale, Jeremiah could almost see the man as the corpse once was, strong-jawed and stern. Flowers and trinkets had been placed around the body, mementos from a long life among close friends.

The funeral began as usual, with a series of eulogies from his friends and family and a priest-led prayer. Then Allison, fully armored, stepped to the center of the room. "Ser Jacob was a special man to us all," she said, her voice clear and dignified. "He was patient, loyal, and an admirable soldier. His death is no tragedy—his life was long and well lived. By now, you are all aware of his last request. It's one I will have the honor of fulfilling, but he would understand if some of you would prefer not to watch. We will begin momentarily. Please take this opportunity to say your farewells if you wish to leave."

Several people left, some ushering confused children, but many more stayed. Allison drew her sword, stood at attention in the center of the hall, and nodded to Jeremiah. "Rise, Ser Jacob! Stand in battle one last time!" she said.

Jeremiah cast the spell as subtly as he could, reaching his focus toward Ser Jacob's body.

Rise.

The pale form of the spent warrior clambered from its place of rest to gasps around the room. It gripped the sword that lay on its chest in one hand and took slow, dignified steps toward Allison. Remembering Delilah's comment about the horses, Jeremiah focused hard on making the zombie's normally stiff, unnatural gait as fluid as possible. He struggled, totally focusing his will on a single bubble seemed to only give him the barest improvement in finesse. Jeremiah commanded the zombie to stop a few paces away.

Allison drew a solemn breath, then snapped a sharp salute. She and Jeremiah had planned the fight's choreography. The zombie's salute snapped just as crisp as Allison's—the muscle memory of that motion was very strong.

Allison readied her sword in a well-practiced stance. Jeremiah found that the zombie settled fluidly into the same stance with only the barest hint of a command. An alarm sounded in the back of Jeremiah's mind, but he couldn't decipher its warning as he concentrated on the next step of the ceremony.

Atta—

He hadn't even finished thinking the command before the zombie leapt forward with a thrust aimed at Allison's throat. Allison parried the blow, but just barely—even knowing what was coming, the attack came with surprising speed.

Jeremiah prepared to sever the connection upon Allison's thrust to Ser Jacob's chest. There was no need to dismember Ser Jacob in front of his friends and family. But as she performed what should have been the final blow, Ser Jacob performed his own parry, stepped toward her, and punched Allison in the mouth, sending her sprawling across the ground.

Jeremiah had not commanded the zombie to do any such thing. The extent of the old warrior's muscle memory dawned on him—these counters weren't just well practiced; they were instinct. Muscles primed from a lifetime of dedication and repetition to react to the slightest stimulus and follow complex patterns.

Allison righted herself and shook her head. Her lip was bleeding. The crowd shuffled nervously, but Allison laughed. "You always loved that counter, didn't you?" Jeremiah detected a note of excitement in her voice.

Allison swung her blade into Ser Jacob's, attempting to deflect it. There was a ring of steel against steel, and Ser Jacob followed the momentum of the blow, spinning in a smooth two-step to dodge Allison's follow up thrust, and answered with a slash at Allison's neck. Allison raised her shoulder and leaned into the blow, letting her armor take the hit. Then she whirled and thrust again from a low position, in a maneuver that Jeremiah wouldn't be able to imitate if he saw it a hundred times.

Allison's blade pierced Ser Jacob's doublet, and Jeremiah sensed a wound delivered to the zombie. He severed the connection. Ser Jacob fell to the ground and Allison extracted her sword, bloodless thanks to the work of morticians. She snapped a salute one last time, and Jeremiah caught a glimmer of tears in her eyes. Several people in the crowd saluted as well.

"Rest now, Ser Jacob," said Allison "Your fight is finished." She sheathed her sword and replaced Ser Jacob's blade on his chest. Four pall bearers collected his remains, carefully placing the body onto a stretcher to return it to its gentle repose. With the ceremony concluded, the crowd began to chat, reminisce, and comfort each other. Allison, on the other hand, grabbed Jeremiah and roughly pulled him outside.

"What the FUCK was that?" she asked in the relative privacy of the side alley. "How did you make him move like that? You don't know anything about third position's counter cut or how to roll through a deflection!"

Jeremiah explained the principle of muscle memory, and Allison's face softened as she understood what had happened. Her tension left with a sigh, and she sank to sit against the wall. Jeremiah joined her.

"I actually liked it," she said. It was an admission of guilt. "Feeling him fight the way he used to? Took me back." They sat in silence for some time. Allison eventually put her hands on her knees like she was about to stand but stopped short. "Do you think I'd make a good zombie?"

Jeremiah had already considered this question. "I think you'd make an amazing zombie."

Allison laughed. "Damn right."

The door opened again, and one of the funeral attendees stood at attention before them. He held himself with a military stiffness and wore a uniform complete with regalia.

Allison rose to her feet and raised a hand in a salute. "Colonel. How can we help you?"

The man returned her salute. "I actually think I might be able to help you, Mr. Thorn. My name is Colonel Valen of the Dramir Army. Do you have a moment to chat?"

An image of a hook and a fish popped into Jeremiah's head. "Uh, sure. What is it?" A fragment of memory told him he'd seen this man before. After a moment, he realized Colonel Valen had been in the audience at his trial.

"Mr. Thorn, I've been following your movements closely since your sentencing. I will admit I was skeptical at first about your ability to meet the court's demands. But I believe you may be honest in your endeavors, and I would like to provide you with an . . . opportunity for an opportunity. Something that would see you making significant progress toward repaying your debt to society."

"I don't think I owe society anything. You'll have to explain opportunity for an opportunity, though. That sounds flimsy." Jeremiah wondered what Vivica would say to this man and decided to keep his guard up.

"Mr. Thorn, far to the north of us is the city of Nosirin. Are you familiar with it?"

"I am." He offered no further details.

"Splendid," said Colonel Valen. "We're currently aiding Nosirin in dealing with a small incursion of savage peoples from the nearby mountain range. This is nothing new, of course, but they've become rather more troublesome lately. After your demonstration today, I believe I can offer you a permanent solution to your situation."

"Jeremiah's no soldier," said Allison, frowning.

"We have plenty of soldiers," said Colonel Valen. "Mr. Thorn, your particular talents are far more valuable than anyone in this city has realized. My proposal may lead to a chance to prove it. Of course, I cannot offer any guarantees, as it is the courts that decide whether your sentence is satisfied. But given the backing of a colonel and the gratitude of Nosirin, you'll have no better chance at success."

Jeremiah didn't love the idea of joining some military conflict, but the bait wriggling at the end of this hook was tempting. He tried not to show it, though. "We seem to have skipped over the part where you explain 'opportunity for an opportunity.'"

"Of course. To be blunt, you are still considered a rogue element in Dramir, Mr. Thorn. Many people still do not trust you. In order to provide you the chance to demonstrate your value, I would need to present evidence of your commitment to Dramir beyond plowing a few fields. Something that shows you are willing and able to put yourself in danger to protect the city's interests."

"Sounds like you have a suggestion?" asked Jeremiah.

"I do. I know of a task that fulfills that very goal. It is sensitive information, however, and I would require your commitment before divulging details."

Jeremiah gave a hollow laugh. "I don't need my counselor to tell me not to agree to things without knowing what they are. What exactly are you getting out of this, Colonel? I can't imagine you're just a fan of my work."

"He's angling for a promotion to General," said Allison, smirking. "He thinks if he can turn a political nuisance into a military asset, he can take credit."

Colonel Valen returned Allison's smirk. "You are a former captain, yes? I remember from the trial. My ambitions are now, and always will be, for the continued prosperity of Dramir. I will do what I feel is in her best interests, and I have the vision to see beyond the populace's fear. I would hope that would be appreciated."

It did feel good to be recognized by someone with power, but Jeremiah didn't need to admit that. "I'll think about it."

"Very good. Your counselor may contact me when you are ready to discuss it further. Until then, I wish you luck with your farming." Colonel Valen turned down the alley, disappearing into the night.

"You know that guy?" Jeremiah asked, once they were alone again.

"By reputation, mostly," said Allison. "Ambitious, but hardly the worst the army has to offer. Obviously, he's hoping to take advantage, but I don't think he'd double-cross us. What are you thinking?"

Jeremiah chewed his lip. "I don't know about joining the military, but it sounds like a straight shot to getting some higher ups on my side. Though there's this whole other layer of 'proving my commitment to Dramir' first. That could be anything."

Allison nodded. "Let Delilah know what he said, but hopefully what you're already doing will turn out to be enough. I don't want you getting mixed up in some officer's career plans if you don't have to."

CHAPTER NINETEEN

What You Owe

Following Ser Jacob's funeral, the jobs Jeremiah was hired for began to change. He was still asked to perform menial labor, but more and more requests came in from the dying or families of the recently deceased. The idea of performative funerals seemed to capture people's imaginations. Soon Jeremiah was helping dwarves finish projects they hadn't completed in life, guiding elves through complex religious rituals, and even raising a noble who wanted to march to his own burial site and lay himself to rest. People didn't want their loved ones to lurch like typical zombies, so Jeremiah learned to give them more natural gaits and posture. His control even became refined enough to manipulate basic facial expressions, although they retained an uncanny quality. It was hard though. Despite all his attention, one limb would sometimes go eerily still as he tried to focus on the fine movements of another, or a facial expression would have to be disassembled piece by piece.

Several people misunderstood what he was able to do, requesting immortality or the return of a loved one. Others wanted permanent servants or bodyguards, but Jeremiah refused to allow anyone ownership of space in his own mind. After the dozenth resurrection request, Delilah drafted and circulated a leaflet describing the necromantic services on offer, or rather the services not on offer, which at least reduced the number of impossible tasks. Though it seemed they could not be stamped out completely.

The protesters' numbers dwindled as Jeremiah's popularity grew. His new clientele treated him with much more dignity, as he was being trusted with a key role in important events. Accusations of his wickedness fell by the wayside as people discovered how to make his talents work for them.

"People are talking," Bruno said to Jeremiah one day. "You're putting money into pockets and creating a whole new industry among pompous rich folk. Actually, there's something I'd like you to see."

That evening, Bruno snuck Jeremiah out of the house under Delilah's nose, slipping between moments of her attention. They walked to a neighborhood Jeremiah had never seen, one awash with the stench of fish. The pockmarked earthen road coated Jeremiah's shoes in dust, and he could feel eyes on him from among the drably dressed crowds that moved up and down the street.

"Bruno, where are we?" There was a spiritual distance between these streets and Delilah's. The vibrant activity of the market square had given way to refuse, loiterers, and an undercurrent of conversation just beyond Jeremiah's perception.

"The seedy underbelly of Dramir, or as close to it as I'm willing to bring you. No better place to see the real soul of the city behind the money and the fancy wall. No matter how high the tree grows, the roots are always in the dirt."

"Bruno!" A portly half elf bellowed a greeting and swept Bruno into his stocky arms. Bruno laughed and they began speaking in what Jeremiah thought might be gnomish. The man returned to the stall he had been minding and lifted a wooden lid. Smoke billowed out and the man pulled out two splintery sticks, each with a ball of fried meat at the end. They sizzled and popped, wafting hot cherry smoke. The man handed one to Bruno and one to Jeremiah. Then he shook Jeremiah's hand in his own greasy one, saying something incomprehensible and smiling enthusiastically.

"Thank you!" said Jeremiah. Bruno and the man exchanged a few more words. Then Bruno pinched the man's cheek and swept Jeremiah onward. "Who was that?" Jeremiah asked between bites of buttery soft meat.

"That was Callus. His stall is the only place you'll find these. It's a recipe only he and his son know."

"Must like you well enough to give us free food."

"I did him a favor a while back. Helped his son out with some debts with a con man, set him on the straight."

As they ambled through the neighborhood, the greetings kept coming. People brushed Bruno's shoulder as they passed, or leaned in to whisper something in his ear before dashing off. Bruno sometimes paid them with a flick of his wrist and a flash of silver.

Jeremiah finally caught one of the conversations between Bruno and a half-orc teenager. "Morning, sir," the boy said. "Weather's looking mighty finicky today. Might be rain soon. Hope y—"

"No, screw the codes," said Bruno. "You go tell Blond Thomas that if he tries to move on Lulu's place again, I'll kill him in his sleep. Ask him what he thinks happened to the Rat Shack Gang." He glared at the boy. "If he needs a hint, you tell him he walks over their graves every day and doesn't know it."

The boy paled to an ashen green before darting away. Bruno watched him go and growled in frustration. "Okay, that was dumb of me. Not wrong, but dumb."

Jeremiah grabbed Bruno's arm and pulled him to the side. "Bruno, are you a crime boss?" Jeremiah couldn't stop himself from asking. In the exchange he saw his friend in a new light, and not one he liked. The puckish rogue he thought he knew suddenly seemed capable of overseeing murder, fraud, and extortion.

"Yes." Bruno glanced up and down the street, then overhead. "It's more complicated than you think. I have a responsibility to look after these people."

Jeremiah followed Bruno's gaze. "Then shouldn't you be preventing crimes?"

"I said it's complicated. We can talk later." He turned to leave but Jeremiah didn't budge. Bruno looked at him with frustration. "What? You want me to justify how—"

"Just tell me you're not profiting off these people," Jeremiah said. "That they're not being nice to you because they're afraid of you."

Bruno's face reddened. "No. It's a balancing act. If you do nothing, the predators tear people apart. If you try to stop everything, you take away the incomes of smugglers, grifters, gamblers, and hustlers. They get more desperate, they become predators. Most of the people down here police their own just fine, but sometimes you need an apex predator to keep the peace. That's me." He smiled grimly. "Happy?"

"Yes, actually." Jeremiah paused. "Thanks."

Bruno glanced up and down the street again. "Listen, don't say anything about being a necromancer down here, okay? It's even more important in this part of town."

"Why?" asked Jeremiah.

"You saved a lot of money for a lot of landowners by giving them free labor. Money that this lot relied on. Most are scared of you, but some are angrier than they are scared. So, while we're down here, you're just Jay. You're just a friend of mine from out of town. No more than that. Got it?"

"Got it."

"Off we go, then!"

They continued through the maze of alleys, accepting tokens of gratitude whether they came as a flower or a handshake. He was careful to stay in Bruno's wake as the walls closed in around them and surly characters watched from stoops and doorways. Jeremiah marveled at the thought of being guide and guardian to so many people, whether they asked for it or not.

They came to a door indistinct from the thousands of others in the slums. Bruno gave it a sharp knock.

A sliver of dark appeared, and a pair of suspicious eyes peered out. "Who's the other one?" a voice asked.

"A friend."

"Doesn't look like any friend of mine. Leave pets outside."

"Open the door, Choka. You're overdoing it again."

The eyes stared at Jeremiah. He felt them crawling over his body like he was a potential meal. Then the door closed, metal ground on metal, and it opened again. An orc wearing leather armor studded with metal rivets stepped to the side to create just enough space for them to squeeze by. The orc sniffed the top of Jeremiah's head as he passed.

The dim tavern they entered was a muddle of chairs and tables. Anything with four legs made the cut. The bare earth floor was packed down so tight it might as well have been smooth stone. No one spared them a glance as Bruno sat Jeremiah in a chair that somehow wobbled in every direction and took the seat across from him.

"What are we doing here?" Jeremiah whispered, trying to match the hushed volume of the room. The air was damp and noxious.

"We're getting a drink," Bruno said. He waved at a half orc who was sitting alone, taking sloppy swigs from a clay jug. The half orc stood with a grunt and plucked two cups off a pile in the corner, most still wet with their previous contents. He stumbled to their table and filled the cups from the same clay jug. The man topped himself off with another swig before returning to his isolation. Bruno swapped the positions of the two cups.

"Drink, and don't cough," Bruno said, sipping his drink.

Jeremiah peered into his cup. An oily film floated on top, along with two or three beard hairs. He reached to pick them out, but Bruno gave the slightest shake of his head. Jeremiah grimaced and raised the drink to his lips. It smelled like tar. He closed his eyes and tried to forget about the hairs.

He took the slightest taste. As the liquid washed over his unfortunate tongue, Jeremiah felt something tickle the back of his throat. He clutched the cup fiercely in his attempt not to cough. The drink didn't burn like alcohol, it just hurt, like acid brought up by vomiting. He fought back the urge to cough, gag, puke, and cry all at the same time and set the cup on the table.

"That may have been the worst moment of my life," he said without exaggeration.

"Yes," Bruno nodded. "It's significantly worse today than usual. I think Karkat might be sick."

They sat in silence for a while. Bruno nursed his drink while Jeremiah tried to keep himself from counting the remaining hairs floating in his cup. A grumble arose from the low mutter of conversation surrounding them. Jeremiah thought he felt someone staring at him.

"Why are we here?" Jeremiah asked.

"Because I don't want you to forget places like this exist."

"I know about poverty."

"Knowing *about* poverty and recognizing it firsthand are two different things. When you just know about poverty, it doesn't matter to you. It's ignorable. No different than knowing about dragons. You don't worry about dragons just like you won't worry about the poor, because it doesn't affect you."

"What's this about, Bruno? I'm happy to donate to charity."

Bruno shook his head. "It's more than just giving pocket change to beggars. I want you to remember them, remember how your actions and decisions are going to affect them."

"The people losing work on farms because of me." Jeremiah thought he heard another growl from somewhere in the room.

"Yes. I know you don't have a choice. If you rolled into town and started undercutting the local workforce for profit, then we'd be having a very different talk in a very different place. But you're just trying to keep yourself alive. I understand that."

"So, what do you want me to do?"

"You're not going to be stuck doing farm work forever. You're a disruption to the way things are done around here, a little drop of chaos. Soon the right people are going to find the right uses for you, and they'll tempt your favor with whatever sin or bauble suits your fancy. But as you step up, you need to realize that your foot will be firmly planted on the heads of people like Tennin Valamor."

"Tennin who?"

"Tennin Valamor is the man seated two tables behind me, the one who keeps stealing glances at you because he's pretty sure he knows who you are. Bald man, earrings, scar on his face. See him?"

Jeremiah tried to glance without being obvious and saw Valamor catching him glancing. Valamor looked like someone who spoke fist and not much else. A sunken red crater marred his left cheek. "I see him."

"Valamor is a stupid man, a brutal man, but also a hardworking man," said Bruno. "It's the only way he can end his days drunk. Whatever copper is left goes to his daughter to buy them food. He's been getting less work because of you, which means less money for food."

"How is it my fault he chooses to spend his money on booze instead of food?" Jeremiah whispered harshly.

"Not your fault at all. I don't want you to worry about that. He's a slob who's only now working up the courage to come and put a knife in you. He's still not sure if you're that necromancer, but he's beyond the point of caring. Hurting someone will make him feel better." Bruno kept his gaze on Jeremiah, but Valamor's glances were becoming more obvious. The drunk was grinding his teeth and clutching the table. Jeremiah could almost see him building the list of grievances to justify the impending violence.

"I think we should leave, then." Jeremiah moved to stand, but a discrete gesture from Bruno kept him seated.

"If you get up to leave, Valamor will know he's been spotted and will rush you or backstab you on your way out. You know he's going to act, but he doesn't know that you know. You have the advantage. Don't panic, observe."

"Observe what?" Jeremiah heart was starting to pound.

"I want you to remember Valamor's daughter, not him. What chance does she have, out on these streets? She doesn't learn to be a kid, or to care about people. She learns to take the beatings and survive at all costs. Is he left-handed or right-handed?"

"I don't know! What does the daughter have to do with it? Can we talk about this somewhere else?"

"Left-handed or right-handed. Stop panicking. Observe."

Jeremiah forced himself to notice the position of the man's cup. "Right-handed. He's right-handed."

"He wants to kill you. Where is he going to stand if he wants to kill you? Tell me what's going to happen."

Jeremiah tried to think. "He's going to stand to my right. He's going to try to stab me in the neck because I'm sitting down. He's going to use his left hand to grab me or expose my neck."

"Very good. You're right. Tell me more. You're running out of time. What else is going to happen?"

"I don't know. He's going to stab me."

"How? Faster."

"Overhand. He's going to stab downward with an overhand grip. He's going to do it over and over again."

"Correct on both. That little girl is in a bad place, but it only gets worse without a place to live and someone to protect her. You've just glimpsed the future. You know exactly what's about to happen. What are you going to do about it? Without killing him."

Jeremiah tried to answer, but the limitation of no killing scrambled his thoughts. Valamor stood and wavered. His face was flushed an angry red and he took an unsteady step forward. Jeremiah was out of time.

"He's up. What are you going to do when he gets here?"

Jeremiah felt his muscles tighten; only one thing to do came to mind. Valamor stood exactly where Jeremiah said he would stand, his right hand slightly behind his body, hiding the blade of a knife like a child's secret.

"You that magic man." Valamor slurred his words. The tidal stink of his breath wafted down as he loomed over Jeremiah.

"No, you got the wrong guy." Lying was all Jeremiah could think of. Maybe Valamor would be too confused or uncertain to make a move. But he knew right away it was the wrong thing to do. Valamor had already decided that Jeremiah was the source of his troubles—he wouldn't have stood up and come over here otherwise. Even if he had been wrong, he was going to kill someone.

"You callin' me a liar?"

The bar was deadly silent. The patrons watched with mild interest.

"No. Yes. No, I'm just saying you're wrong."

"Wrong?! Yeah! Maybe I'm wrong. You think you're smarter than me just 'cause I'm wrong? You some kinda—"

There was a sharp snap and Valamor's knee buckled inward as Bruno snapped a kick into it. Valamor fell with a cry of pain, dropping the blade hidden behind his back and pinning his own arm beneath him.

Bruno was on him immediately. He mounted Valamor's chest and smashed his cup against Valamor's face. Ceramic shards cut into Valamor's skin as he shielded his face with his free arm. Bruno began raining blows upon his face and jaw. His right arm still trapped, Valamor could only raise a limited defense, which Bruno weaved around with a flurry of blows. He broke Valamor's nose and knocked a spray of teeth from his mouth. Bruno's expression was utterly dispassionate. When Valamor's body finally went limp, Bruno wiped his bloody knuckles on the drunk's shirt and stood.

"You attack first, as brutally as you need to. You don't owe anyone a fair fight, Jay, not a soul. But you do owe that little girl a father. Come on, let's go home."

Jeremiah stood up to leave, but as he stepped over Valamor, he felt a hand grab his ankle. Valamor grunted as he kept the necromancer from leaving. Bruno glanced back and nodded to Jeremiah before walking out the door. Jeremiah looked down at the beaten man who gripped his leg but spoke to everybody.

"You used up everyone's second chance today. Anyone else who makes a move will serve me in death for all eternity." The hand opened. Jeremiah tried to hold his head high as he left, hoping he had sounded scary enough.

CHAPTER TWENTY

Wet Work Prep Work

All right, Jeremiah," said Delilah. "It's obvious we're not getting anywhere with farmers and funerals." She had just returned for the evening, her businesslike appearance only slightly disheveled from the day of meetings.

Jeremiah nodded. Despite all the work he'd been doing, and all of the affidavits Delilah had submitted, they had received no word of feedback from the courts, or even any indication that the Seven Judges were listening.

Delilah continued, "It's become clear that the judges have already decided the outcome of this case. They're just waiting out the clock. We need somebody who can force them to reconsider. It's past time to talk to someone with some actual influence. Listen up, you two. This concerns you as well."

Allison and Bruno joined Jeremiah and Delilah around the table. "Someone with influence, huh?" asked Allison. "Is that who I think it is?"

Delilah nodded. "I'm afraid so. I decided to hear out Colonel Valen's offer."

Jeremiah's stomach sank. "I don't want to go to war."

"You won't have to. At least, not yet. Before you can even be considered for employment by the crown, you need to be vetted on a smaller-stakes mission. That's where you two come in." She turned to Allison and Bruno. "There's a group of bandits that have been attacking small towns and caravans south of Dramir."

Bruno leaned in. "This isn't the White Light bandit group, is it?"

Delilah looked surprised. "Actually, yes. What do you know about them?"

Bruno nodded grimly. "We heard about them on the barge, remember? They've been gaining territory for months, marauding and pillaging. It's the life cycle of bandit culture: Someone big and mean enough takes over a gang, and other criminals flock to him. The group gets bigger and bolder until it eventually gets broken up by do-gooders, such as ourselves, or destroyed from within and the process starts over. White Light's been going strong for some time now. They seem better organized than most, but taking out whoever's in charge should scatter them to the winds. Do we know where they're based?"

"Not exactly. Intel has placed them somewhere in the Tarnothy Desert, at least a week's march east. But it'll be up to us to find them. If you two are willing to help, that is."

"GODS, YES!" shouted Allison. "I've been so bored! Delilah, I'll fight whatever you want, just point me at it. Oh, and yeah, I'd love to help you and Jay." She grinned.

Bruno frowned. "I don't know. This isn't squabbling goblins or kobolds or even an orc raiding party. This is a whole bandit camp. No offense, you two, but doing something that dangerous for no pay? I like you guys a lot, but . . ."

"Actually!" said Delilah, perking up. "I've negotiated salvage rights for the camp!"

"You got us right of salvage? Hell yes, I'm in!" said Bruno. At Allison and Jeremiah's confusion, he explained. "Normally if you bust up a bandit camp, everything needs to be returned to its previous owners in a drawn-out bureaucratic nightmare. But this wonderful, half-elven snake in the grass"—Bruno gave Delilah an affectionate push—"arranged it so everything in that camp belongs to us! Every silver, every gold, every gemstone, cow, sheep, shipment, writ, deed—the combined spoils of an entire organization's worth of effort—belongs to us!" His eyes gleamed.

Jeremiah didn't share his enthusiasm. "You just said yourself how dangerous this was going to be. I don't think I can ask you guys to do this, treasure or no."

Allison cocked an eyebrow at him. "We're adventurers. Going into dangerous situations for money is literally what we do. Being able to help your case at the same time just sweetens the deal."

Bruno clapped him on the back. "Jay, we want to help you. You're our friend. And you obviously don't understand just how much treasure is going to be at this camp."

Allison stood. "It's decided. This is officially an operation!" At once, the mood in the room turned serious. "We're a four-man team going after a fortified and guarded position. Not easy. Bruno, given your experience and breadth of knowledge surrounding our goals, I'm giving you command of preparation and field operations until such time as you decide to hand it back to me."

Bruno's jaw dropped. "Seriously? Are you sure?"

Allison nodded and grinned. "You're in charge. I know you'll do well."

Bruno's devil-may-care smile faded. It was as though he had been hampered by the sudden weight of responsibility, and he wasn't sure how to lift it. "Well . . . we're going to need intel," he said. "I'll do as much fact finding on White Light as I can, but the three of you will have to help pinpoint their location."

He glanced toward Allison, and she gave him an encouraging smile. Bruno continued. "If there's any gear you think could help, buy it and get proficient with it as soon as you can. We're going to need every edge we can get."

Delilah managed to gain approval for Jeremiah to travel the city the next day. Temptation tugged him in a hundred directions—for the first time he had not only gold jangling in his pocket, but the freedom to spend it. He resisted the aromatic delicacies on every corner and bought a pair of rugged traveling boots and a high-quality leather cap for protection.

Jeremiah considered the sums of gold still weighing down his pockets. There seemed few ways for him to use money to improve himself as a caster, at least in the short term. He realized, however, that helping the entire party would be just as valuable as helping himself, and he had a couple of ideas. The first would require money, enough to make him feel slightly sick to his stomach. The other was to collect on a promise made.

Jeremiah returned home well after dark, clutching a large rolled-up parchment parcel under his arm. Bruno stood in the living room, leaning over an open book. His leather armor sported seven new sheaths distributed across his torso, shoulder, and hip. Each sheath held a wicked looking dagger.

As Jeremiah watched, Bruno began an elaborate dance of attacks, circling a wooden training dummy in the center of the living room. Each swing of his shortsword was matched with a thrown dagger, flicked from his off-hand and replaced in a blur of motion. For every dagger that lodged in the dummy's chest, two more embedded in the wall or clattered off the furniture. Bruno grumbled and returned to the book on the table.

"Dominique the Blademaster," said Bruno, answering Jeremiah's unasked question without taking his eyes off the page. "His style was all about maximizing attacks of opportunity."

Jeremiah could see it now—Bruno was fluidly trying to weave ranged attacks into melee attacks. "Don't you have a bow? Why throwing knives?" asked Jeremiah. The weapons were big for throwing knives, almost short swords on their own.

"Because I lose a few seconds of 'push,' as Dominique calls it, when I switch to my bow," said Bruno. "Technically, these are called throwing swords, and they're damn expensive."

"Excuse me . . ." said Delilah from behind Jeremiah. He stepped out of the way to let her trudge past, carrying boxes full of delicate glassware and something so odorous that tears sprang to Jeremiah's eyes. Two porters followed, similarly laden. "Good to see you again, Bentley," she greeted the dummy on her way upstairs.

Allison arrived home as Delilah's porters were heading out. "Sorry, Bruno. None of my contacts were able to tell me much about the Tarnothy Desert. But at least I was able to get my name on the list to speak with an enchanter."

Bruno groaned. "They didn't know anything? They couldn't even tell you who might know more?" Allison shook her head, and Bruno sighed.

Jeremiah cleared his throat and presented his parcel. "I hope this will help." He untied the fraying string and let the vellum unroll on the table.

"A map!" Delilah said. "That might be use . . ." She trailed off as she leaned in for a closer look.

"Whooooa . . ." said Bruno and Allison together.

It was as though the landscape of the desert itself had unfurled before them. The map detailed every hill, river, elevation, underground water source, and countless other features alongside precise scale measurements.

"Jeremiah, where did you get this?" asked Allison. "This is a military intelligence map. If I were to describe this as 'highly classified,' I'd be doing it a disservice. You are not supposed to have this."

Jeremiah smiled coyly. "Oh, just a friend who owed me a favor." Allison stared at him and the truth boiled up from his stomach. "Uh, Harwick Featherfall. The man whose family I saved from the fire. He's a cartographer. He pulled every string he could to get me something we could use."

"By the pickpocket's promise, this has everything!" said Bruno. "I didn't even know they made maps like this!"

"You think it'll be useful?" asked Jeremiah, grinning.

Allison jabbed him in the chest. "Never, *ever* underestimate the power of an accurate map! Battles have been won because of good maps, and wars have been lost because of bad ones." She traced her finger along a mark indicating an underground river. "This map is a test of your creativity, intelligence, and preparation. The longer you look, and the harder you listen, the more it will reveal to you."

They all bent over the map, trying to hear its secrets. Jeremiah, Delilah, and Allison soon retired to bed, leaving Bruno still listening.

Jeremiah grew used to finding Bruno poring over the map when he came downstairs, but one day he discovered Bruno with a gnome and a halfling in the kitchen. "Hey, Jay," said Bruno. "Meet Parnoogle and Cynthia."

Parnoogle was a bulbous gnome wearing a painter's apron splattered in a dizzying array of hues. A small collection of pots was arrayed before him, full of brilliantly colored pastes, which he was mixing in precise amounts, adding the tiniest drops of reds, browns, and ochres, pausing periodically to compare with a jar of red and pebbly earth. After each new concoction was created in a tiny glass cup, Parnoogle would write out a label with a numerical code and affix it to the jar.

"I'll need to make a hue shift in case it rains," said Parnoogle in a nasally voice, "otherwise you'll stand out like a sore thumb. Can you make a reversable suit, Cynthia?"

The halfling woman had tight, curious features. Her eyes darted back and forth as she thought, and her tiny hands twitched in a staccato rhythm as though they were making invisible stitches at blinding speed. "Yes, that shouldn't be a problem, provided the paint isn't too thick. I'll send over three or four test patches for you to try."

"Good," said Parnoogle, mixing another swatch of reddish paint, browner than the others. "There we are." He continued mixing colored swatches, labeling the scraps of parchment while Cynthia took Bruno's measurements.

Once they left, Bruno turned, grinning, to Jeremiah. "Artists can make miracles for their valued patrons."

"What miracle are they making for you?"

"Camouflage suit! Parnoogle is a painter with quite an eye for color, and Cynthia is a tailor. A friend in the geological society lent me a soil sample from the Tarnothy Desert as a reference."

Bruno retrieved their new map from his room and unfurled it across the table. "I've been coming to understand this beauty. A bandit camp as large as White Light's would need access to water, a defensible position, and smooth terrain to transport stolen cargo. There's only one place that meets those criteria." He traced an area toward the south of the map, nestled in the shadow of a ridge. "But I'll need to scout it out, and cover will be sparse, hence the camo suit."

"I've got this end. Do you have your end?" asked Bruno, stepping backward onto the next step.

"Yeah, just don't go so fast!" said Jeremiah, clutching the crate of alchemical supplies Delilah had requested be brought to her lab.

"I'm not going fast! You have to push a little to tell me when you're ready to move."

"If I push, and you're not ready, you're gonna trip on the stairs!" Jeremiah could feel his grip slipping.

"I don't trip, Jay. Wait, hang on, this grip isn't working."

"So set it down or just wait so you don't trip?" asked Jeremiah.

"Just set it down, set it down!" said Bruno. They lowered the crate together and finally let it rest precariously on the stairs.

"There are really no good handholds," said Jeremiah.

"Nope, there's nothing to grab at all," said Bruno.

Allison burst through the door, grinning ear to ear, and shouted up the stair-well, "I've done it. I've ordered my first piece of magical equipment!"

"Lemme guess," said Bruno. "An enchanted sword to smite your foes!" He swung his fist and pantomimed an explosion.

"I'll admit, the magic weapon was tempting. Slicing through armor, never needing to be sharpened . . ." Allison's eyes stared wistfully into the distance. "But no! Not a sword. I'm getting my armor enchanted!"

Jeremiah nodded, using his knee to brace the crate in place. "Not as flashy, but useful in every fight. Much harder to steal as well. Very wise choice."

Allison beamed at him. "Thanks! That means a lot, coming from the party mage."

Jeremiah grinned and turned back to the crate, pretending to inspect it to hide the flush rising in his cheeks. She had called him part of the party. He didn't quite believe he was one of them, but it felt good to hear anyway.

"This thing going upstairs?" asked Allison. "Out of the way, both of you." She squeezed past Jeremiah and gripped the corners of the crate. Tilting it backward with a grunt, she slid the crate up the stairs as though it were empty.

"There's nothing to grab," Bruno said again as Allison and the crate disappeared around the corner.

Delilah had scheduled Jeremiah to meet her in the lab with three days' notice. It felt strange, given he lived with her, but she was perpetually busy, and schedules were just how she operated. She put him to work the moment he set foot in her lab.

Delilah dumped a bottle of lavender colored liquid into a great wooden basin. She held out the empty bottle and Jeremiah took it and replaced it with a bottle of orange liquid.

"Can you crush up a pair of green quartz for me?" she asked, wafting the steaming concoction toward her nose and sniffing.

"Two or three?" asked Jeremiah, he opened one of a dozen of Delilah's ingredient cabinets, went to the crystals section, and opened the small box that contained the jagged green crystals.

"Two. Three if you think they're on the small side," said Delilah. She dipped a long strip of scrap fabric into the basin and pulled it back out, inspecting it closely.

Jeremiah considered three of the crystals. It was a tough call. He brought the crystals to a set of scales and weighed the smallest. He crushed two separately, banging them between two leather sheets with a block of wood. The third he crushed and divided, returning half its dust to the cabinet in a small glass vial.

"Two and a half," he said to Delilah, bringing the crystal dust.

She glared at the small pile of crystal dust, then back at Jeremiah, eyes narrowing. She looked like she was dying to say something, but just nodded instead. Jeremiah poured the crystals into the basin.

A few minutes later Delilah used a hefty wooden paddle to fish a soaked black robe from the basin. "Once this dries, your robe will be more durable and offer you some protection, without affecting movement," she said, closely inspecting the garment.

"Like armor?" asked Jeremiah.

Delilah nodded. "It's just a single layer, so it'll be about as tough as leather armor. Don't feel compelled to test it."

A few days later, Jeremiah found himself deep in the temple of Meandris, goddess of healing. Allison was seated next to him, both across a large desk from the high priest and his war-hammer–armed bodyguard. The high priest had taken every pause in their negotiation to silently glare at Jeremiah, his bodyguard picking up the slack when the high priest and Allison exchanged pleasantries.

"Anyway, Your Worship," said Allison. "We're budgeted for four healing potions."

"Of course, Ms. Allday," said the high priest, gracing her with a gentle and disarming smile. "Will you be paying the next installment on your debt as well?"

Allison sighed, but didn't respond. Her gaze slowly sunk to the desk, eyes going glassy and unfocused.

"Allison? You okay?" asked Jeremiah.

"Yes!" She popped back to them. "Yes. I'll pay my next installment as well."

"Excellent, Ms. Allday! Now, I'm afraid the price of healing potions has gone up just a little," said the high priest. He held up his thumb and finger to show the tiny amount.

"Undoubtedly. How much?" said Allison. Her pleasant smile went rigid.

The high priest told them, and Jeremiah jumped out of his seat. "Are you serious!?" he exclaimed. The bodyguard's war hammer was drawn and poised to crush him to paste before Jeremiah had even finished his exclamation. Jeremiah dropped back into his seat with a thump.

The high priest totally ignored him, pulling four glass potions from the desk and setting them on his side of the table. Allison produced a sack of gold coins and placed it on her own side. The bodyguard reached across the table, still eyeing Jeremiah, and fetched the bag.

"Allison, are you sure we need these?" Jeremiah asked. The cost was astronomical. Even one fewer potion represented huge savings.

The high priest slid the bottles across to Allison. She slid one to Jeremiah.

"Alive," she said.

She slid it back across the table.

"Dead."

She slid it back to him again.

"Alive," she repeated.

Between books, supplies, potions, and equipment, Jeremiah was beginning to see where the money went.

One evening, Allison shoved a spear into Jeremiah's hands.

"What's this for?" Jeremiah asked. The spear felt heavy and strange. It was shorter than Delilah's, only slightly longer than Jeremiah was tall. The steel tip was leaf shaped and freshly sharpened to a razor's edge.

"Acid balls are nice, but I want everyone to be able to really defend themselves if it comes down to it."

"I can channel pure necromantic energy into someone if I get my hands on them," said Jeremiah. "It's an ugly solution and tires me out quickly, but it'll do the job."

"Sounds horrifying, but needing to physically touch someone is going to get you knifed in the lungs. A weapon gives you range and the perception of threat."

"Can I pick something different?" Jeremiah asked. His childhood fantasies had always included a fearsome axe or a shining blade. A spear seemed so . . . mundane.

"No offense, but I don't want some novice swinging anything near my head. With a spear, you poke. You're lethal in minutes, you keep your distance, and you probably won't injure any of us. Speaking of swinging . . ." She waved down Bruno, who was, once again, darting through the house. His presence had become as ephemeral as a breeze through an open window. "Can I get your approval on a primary weapon?" she asked.

Allison raised the weapon she'd settled on for the assault, a heavy flail with an ugly lead weight at the end of a thick chain. She whirled the flail in an idle circle, and a strange hole in the weight began to emit a low whistle. Then she dropped into a stance and into a series of complex arcs. The whistle heightened to a fevered scream as Allison swung the flail with increasing vigor. Jeremiah struggled to follow its movement with his eyes, the spear feeling all the more like a dead weight in his hands.

"That's perfect," said Bruno. "An exotic weapon bandits won't have encountered before, with an unpredictable movement pattern. That horrible noise is great, too. Just keep it muted for the quiet part of the plan."

To Jeremiah's relief, Allison did not insist on sparring with him, leaving Delilah to instruct him in the basics of spearsmanship while she and Bruno practiced elaborate attack sequences on Bentley. Jeremiah went to bed that night with aching shoulders and forearms, glad to have done something that at least felt productive.

* * *

It was the day before their scheduled departure, and Allison hadn't stopped glancing out the window every spare moment.

"It's here!" she shrieked and ran to the door. Allison's newly enchanted armor had arrived, delivered by an armored carriage with a cadre of guards.

They gathered around Allison as she inspected every square inch of the newly polished full plate armor. The gauntlets sported some new claws on the knuckles, but otherwise the armor looked no different. Allison flipped the pieces over to show them the fine silver lines tracing across the inside of the steel plates, spotted by tiny deposits of copper or gold. To Jeremiah, the pattern looked similar to Flusoh's ritual diagram that gave him Gus. The silver lines represented only the simplest level of enchantment, but Jeremiah knew this foundation was necessary before layering on enchantments of greater complexity.

Allison held up pieces of armor for the others to admire. "The enchanter said a blow that would have hacked through before will only get through at the joints now. And anything weaker than that won't do a damn thing." Her grin was childlike in its excitement.

"I should look into learning this stuff," said Jeremiah. "Maybe I could enchant equipment for us."

"We can discuss the ridiculous ramifications of that statement later," Bruno said. "It's time to pack up. We leave tomorrow at first light."

That night Jeremiah was too excited to sleep. He was aware of the very real possibility of death during the upcoming mission, but his mind was filled only with visions of his own heroism and glory. He imagined boasting like Allison had at the bar, with people cheering his name. He saw himself holding court with nobles and aristocrats, regaling them with stories of his victory while their young and beautiful daughters sought to capture his attention.

He imagined triumphing over evil, but his fantasies were interrupted when he remembered Flusoh's thoughts on Evil. With an uncomfortable jolt, he realized that the bandits they would be fighting were likely not Evil. He tried to weave his way back to the tone of his earlier fantasies, but they felt overly simple now, childish. Like a boat being rocked against a pier by stormy seas, he felt himself skirting up against a jarring truth, a truth about suffering and desperation, with which he did not want to fully engage.

Jeremiah tossed and turned in his bed. Gus fidgeted in his bowl on the nightstand. *They're not Evil.* He heard Flusoh's words in his mind over and over. "They're just my enemy," he muttered.

CHAPTER TWENTY-ONE

First Blood

Jeremiah awoke at the crack of dawn with a surge of adrenaline. Soon the house was bustling as everyone performed last-minute checks. Delilah served a massive breakfast of thick pound cake and milk, meant to last a full day of hard walking. Jeremiah ate as much as he could, nerves battling his appetite. Bruno's normal chattiness had disappeared, replaced by thin-lipped silence as they loaded backpacks to bursting, donned their armor, and laced their boots.

As Jeremiah pulled on his heavy pack, he felt a surge of excitement, and not just for the imminent adventure, but also for the reveal of his surprise. He couldn't remember the last time he'd experienced the special type of eagerness that comes from giving gifts to friends.

Bruno pushed open the front door and strode forward, only to freeze midstep. Allison nearly ran into him. "Oi! What's the holdup?"

Waiting outside the house was a large, ornate carriage. Jeremiah squeezed past Bruno and turned beaming, to his friends. "Ta-daaaa! What do you think?"

The others gathered around to take in the cart's craftsmanship. It was painted black with gold and crimson details and big enough for at least five passengers. While it had a slight air of funeral procession about it, that carriage was clearly a thing of prestige. "Jay, did you buy this?" asked Allison.

"Custom made!" Jeremiah laughed at the stunned expression on Bruno's face. "There's extra storage space, and you can convert the seats into beds."

"Jay," said Delilah, "while this is amazing, it looks awfully heavy. We're going to need at least a few strong . . ." She paused as Jeremiah flashed her a toothy grin, patting a large mound beside the front of the cart, covered with a sheet. "Oh no," she finished.

"Oh yes!" Jeremiah pulled the sheet with a flourish, revealing two perfectly white horse skeletons. They clambered to their feet at his command. "They're as strong as normal horses and much faster. And they are easily disguised!"

Jeremiah retrieved two massive bundles of leather from inside the cart. He unfurled one and draped the rough leather across the nearer skeleton, fussing and adjusting the fabric over the bony spine until it covered the horse's entire frame. Once he buckled the strap of the hood under its jaw, the skeleton looked decidedly horse-like, complete with faux ears and mane.

"I commissioned a couple of costume makers at the Gilded Peacock theater to do some work on the side. We also have free tickets to *The Truths of Ctharotep*. Not bad, right?" Jeremiah was suddenly nervous. Had he overstepped his bounds?

Bruno stepped in front of him. He put a hand on Jeremiah's shoulder, his face deadly serious. "Jeremiah. This is the single greatest thing anybody has ever done." Then Bruno heaved his pack onto the cart, triggering a scuffle with Delilah and Allison to claim the best seats and leaving Jeremiah flushed with happiness.

Their trip was smooth; that's what Jeremiah had paid for. Mile after mile passed each day at a brisk pace. The two skeletal horses under Jeremiah's command pulled the cart with ease. Even Bruno's stoic demeanor had faded with the unexpected comfort of the journey, giving way to his usual joviality. Jeremiah only needed to spare a bit of focus to keep the horses on the road. After all, he was an expert in making horses walk.

"What *is* magic, anyway?" Delilah asked Jeremiah one evening. They had stopped for the day, relaxing around the fire after dinner. "How is it that you say a few words and wave your hands and stuff happens?"

Jeremiah had been waiting for this topic to come up. "Simply put, we don't know. We think it's a language that, when spoken, alters the world around us. The simultaneous gestures are another aspect of the language."

"You're saying I could just repeat what you say and do the same thing? 'Cause I'll admit, I've already tried that," said Allison.

Jeremiah laughed. "Well, no. There's more to it than that. You need to know how to focus your will to actually make the words true."

Allison raised a brow. "So, you can just say things and make them true? Why the fascination with undead, then?"

The question caught Jeremiah off guard. "To be honest, I tried to do other magic for a long time, but I never really got the knack. There's something about my focus that makes me bad at other schools of casting, but necromancy is a natural fit for me. It's the only thing I've ever been good at." Jeremiah shrugged helplessly.

To his relief, Bruno shifted the subject. "Let me get this straight. I just tell the universe what I want, wiggle my fingers, want it real bad, and I can do anything?"

"Sort of?" said Jeremiah. "Except we only have a handful of words, really. So, it only works if the thing you want is something we know how to say. We find new words, rarely, inscribed on things like ancient stone tablets or the walls of forgotten dungeons. Every discovery is a major find. A fluent speaker of the language would probably be like a god."

Bruno laid back and sighed. "The only thing standing between me and god-hood is a good dictionary."

Jeremiah grinned. "Well, that and all the grammar and context it takes to say something intelligible. In that way, at least, it's like any other language."

Delilah nodded. "That makes sense. I wonder if it's any way related to Gnomish? Gnomish also relies a lot on gestures to convey meaning—head tilt, hand motion, posture, that sort of thing. A lot of context is lost without body language. It's why they tend to live really close together, since the written language is cumbersome and easily misunderstood. Meanwhile, when I was learning the different screeches in Goblin—"

"Screeches?" asked Jeremiah. "So, all those noises they make aren't just . . . screeches?"

"Nope!" said Delilah. "They live in tight, crowded spaces, so screeching is how they express themselves among the din of so many other goblins. A screech announces the emotion and intended audience for what they're about to say and alerts listeners to pay attention. So, in this magic language—"

"Can we quickly go back to you speaking Goblin?" Bruno asked. A spark of mischief danced in his eyes.

"No. So, I'm guessing mages discover these words, but with no gesture associated, it's just nonsense. You have to use words, plus gesture, plus willpower."

"Mostly right. There are plenty of words without gestures, though," said Jeremiah. "But Bruno's right, we should go back to you speaking Goblin."

"No."

"Say something in Goblin!" said Allison.

"No!" Delilah said, blushing. She crossed her arms indignantly while the others laughed.

"Come on, I need to hear this!" said Bruno.

"Do it!" said Allison, using her order-giving voice.

Delilah was trying to maintain a serious face, but the corners of her lips kept tugging upward.

"As your client, I demand you say something in Goblin!" Jeremiah said.

"Fine! Okay, fine!" She took a deep breath, then burst into a gale of laughter. "Stop it, Bruno!"

Bruno held up his hands innocently. "I don't know what you're talking about. This is just my face."

Delilah took a few hitching breaths, trying to get her giggles under control. Finally, she turned pointedly away from the group, filled her chest with air, and let out a screeching ululation into the night. The sound echoed across the plains, but Jeremiah and the others were laughing far too hard to hear it.

The landscape became sparse as they traveled, verdant vegetation giving way to the red rock of the Tarnothy Desert. Bruno grew more tense as well, remaining silent and pouring over the map for hours at a time.

"We leave the carriage here," he announced one afternoon. "We need to start trailblazing." There was a bit of grumbling, but the party dutifully hid the carriage and horses among the rocky outcroppings that grew to looming mountains in the distance. Jeremiah immediately missed the carriage as they began to hike under the heat of the desert sun, the straps of his pack digging into his shoulders.

A profound change had come over Bruno as they walked through the desert. He had become a mouse in a place that distinctly smelled of cat, constantly eyeing the horizon. Jeremiah swore he was hunching just a bit lower to the ground. It made Jeremiah feel as though there were unseen enemies in every direction.

When the sun dipped toward the horizon on the third day of walking, Bruno called a halt. He pulled a broad, hooded cloak from his pack and fastened it to his shoulders. The longer Jeremiah looked at the cloak, the more hues he was able to see. Small stones had been affixed among the dappled reds and oranges, seamlessly blended in a facsimile of the landscape.

"I should be back in three or four days," said Bruno. "If I'm away longer than six, it means I was caught but infiltrated the group and am now working from the inside. Have Allison take charge and plan an ingress and attack; I'll find you. Otherwise, wait for me here. Don't draw attention to yourselves. No open fires. I want you all on alert. We're in enemy territory now and our enemy is patient, clever, and ruthless." Bruno threw up the hood of the cloak and disappeared into the landscape.

The camp was tense and quiet while they waited. Allison re-oiled her gear, despite having done it just before leaving home. Delilah busied herself with short forays into the desert, gathering samples of the scant flora. Jeremiah hid in the shade of the rocks near their camp and tried not to think about what might be taking Bruno so long.

Bruno returned just after sunset on the fifth day. He didn't greet anyone, however, instead heading straight for the water stores. He refilled his canteen and drained it twice before indicating to the others that he was ready to share what he'd seen.

"Minor problem," Bruno said once they were gathered around him. "This isn't a bandit camp. It's a bandit fortress. Stone walls and gate, towers, parapets, the whole deal."

Allison's jaw dropped. "How the hell did they build a fortress all the way out here? Where did they get the manpower?"

"I'm more curious where they got the expertise myself," said Delilah. "A proper fortress is more than just a rock wall. Bruno, does it look engineered?"

Bruno nodded. "Very. I didn't see inside, but the walls definitely have rooms in them. Multiple exits into the courtyard from the wall interior." Bruno picked up a stick and began drawing in the sand. He sketched a large square, indicating round towers in the corners and a gate on one side. Opposite the gate, he drew a smaller square that Jeremiah recognized as a keep.

They all stared at the drawing. Jeremiah tried to stay optimistic. "If it's cramped quarters, I'll be at an advantage," he said. "Zombies won't have to travel far to reach new targets, and they fight well in hallways."

"We have to get inside first," said Delilah.

"You're in charge, Bruno," said Allison. "Do we scrap the mission or not?"

Bruno didn't hesitate. "No. Like I said, it's a minor problem. We're going to need to scale the wall and avoid detection at the same time. I have a grapple for that, but if we're spotted, we'll be brought down by numbers alone."

Flusoh's voice sounded in Jeremiah's mind. *The more the merrier!*

"Once inside, we're stuck," Bruno continued. "There won't be any way to back out until the entire group is neutralized. If we try to retreat, they'll track us through the desert. Can you all accept that?" Everyone nodded. Jeremiah's stomach cramped as the seriousness of the situation sank in.

"All right," said Bruno, and his tone darkened. He spoke to all of them, but Jeremiah felt like this was directed specifically at him. "Once we're inside, we're pure cutthroat. I'm not a fan of killing men in their sleep, but I won't hesitate either. If any of you can't stomach that, say so now." Allison and Delilah looked like they had been asked to swallow something exceptionally rancid.

"I-I'm not sure I can . . ." said Delilah.

Bruno nodded.

"I'd rather not, but it wouldn't be the first time I've had to," said Allison, "I'd sooner leave that kind of . . . work to you, Bruno, but if you need me, just say so."

Bruno nodded again and looked to Jeremiah.

"I've never killed anyone, asleep or awake," said Jeremiah, "but I assure you the zombies won't make a distinction."

"The zombies . . . won't?" Bruno sighed. "You were right. We need to have the talk, Al."

Allison nodded, and she and Bruno moved to stand together in front of Jeremiah. All at once Jeremiah felt a different kind of nervousness, like he was about to be lectured by stern parents.

Allison started. "Listen, Jay, we're going to be counting on you not to panic in there. Killing people isn't easy. I believe that you'll protect us and protect yourself, but it's not going to be cut and dry like you think."

Bruno said, "The men and women in there will do what they need to do to survive. They'll cry, they'll beg, they'll bargain, they'll lie. You might be faced with a pretty little waif of a girl that tells you, through tears, that she's a slave and begs you not to hurt her. That girl will more than likely wait for you to turn your back and then shiv you in the liver."

"You need me to just kill without mercy?" Jeremiah asked. His heart tightened at the question. He couldn't believe they were asking him to be ready to murder innocents.

"Absolutely not!" said Allison. "But you need to know what acceptable mercy is. You'll need to make a snap judgement of anybody who surrenders to you. You'll be their judge, jailor, and executioner, and you have only the span of a second for the trial."

Jeremiah imagined deciding on the death of a waif of a girl and felt cold. He silently prayed he wouldn't need to call that particular court to order. "I'll do what I have to," he said. "I won't let any of you get hurt."

Bruno held his eye for a long moment. "All right," he said at last. "We trust you." He turned to the others. "We will have a window tomorrow evening. It will be narrow, but it might be the only one we get for a long time. We head out at first light."

Jeremiah tossed and turned for hours before managing to doze off. He felt like he had barely closed his eyes before he was being shaken awake by Bruno. "Up and out, double time."

Without complaint, they began to follow Bruno through the desert. The sky was still dark but for a blue highlight that glowed over the horizon. Jeremiah admired the landscape as the sky lightened—without the heat or sun, the Tarnothy Desert was rather beautiful. Wind-worn rock formations jutted out of the ground like massive sculptures and dried up river beds wound off into the distance. He saw animals he had never seen before—horned snakes, spotted lizards, even a small owl hooting at them from atop what had once been an ambitious tree.

Their hike continued as the sun traveled the sky. The trail Bruno struck was across smooth, even terrain, and would have made for an easy journey if not for the oppressive heat. Jeremiah gripped his spear, hoping his practice would help him do what he needed to do. His healing potion was in its pouch, and Gus was safely in his reinforced pocket. He was as ready as he could be.

The fortress rose out of the dark landscape like it had been hewn from the red rock itself. Its walls rose several stories, with regular windows cutting black slits into the stone. Several windows flickered with candlelight in the growing dark, giving the impression of eyes roving the landscape, as if the fortress itself were a sentry against the dangers of the desert.

A horn sounded, crooning low into the distance. Shadowy figures patrolling atop the wall began to scurry about.

"There they are," breathed Bruno.

A few moments later, Jeremiah spotted a distant line of lights winding its way toward the fortress. As the line approached, he was able to make out torches and lanterns along a long train of wagons. Each cargo carrier was piled with goods battened down by tarps, and one sturdy wagon was carrying an entire tun that rocked dangerously with every disturbance in the makeshift road. The gate's metal-banded doors swung forward to admit them.

"Perfect," whispered Bruno. "They were headed out on a ranging when I first got here. Looks like it was successful. They'll be exhausted, dehydrated, and will break into that barrel to celebrate. With any luck, they'll be blind drunk in an hour. Until then, we wait. Quietly."

They huddled against the embankment, senses on high alert. Bruno nodded as cheers rose from the fortress. It wasn't long before a fruity scent tickled Jeremiah's nose. Cheers became songs, songs became a chaotic blend of shouts and roars, meaningless mad screams that echoed off distant mountains. Then the noise began to die down, fading slowly as the revelry gave way to sleep.

Jeremiah's pulse quickened as silence fell. Soon the bloodshed would begin.

Bruno signaled them and they peaked out over the embankment again. The lights in the windows were fewer, as were the figures on top of the wall. "Oh, Mr. Leaner, you've had yourself something to drink haven't you?" Bruno chided the lone figure that stood on top of the nearest wall. "Naughty, naughty. Mr. Swagger won't like that. And where's your buddy, Mr. Helmet?"

Jeremiah noticed that Bruno's nerves seemed to have subsided now that the moment of action was nearly upon them. For some, he supposed, waiting was the hardest part. Not for Jeremiah. His own anxiousness was increasing with each passing moment.

Jeremiah squinted in the darkness as the guard Bruno had quietly admonished leaned against his spear, sagging further and further. The figure almost toppled over, jerking awake. Then he began to lean again.

"I'm going in," said Bruno. "Eyes open. Be ready to move."

Bruno noiselessly slipped down the earthen embankment and lay flat as soon as he touched the ground. From there he began a painfully slow crawl; his painted cloak made him invisible in the darkness as he inched closer and closer to the wall. Mr. Leaner shook his head and stretched, none the wiser that his death approached. Bruno kept right on crawling until he reached the base of the wall itself. Then he stood up flat against the wall and drew his bow, nocking an arrow. He pulled the bowstring tight, then darted out several feet into no-man's-land, spun, and took a knee, aiming upward. He must have made some sort of noise, because Mr. Leaner perked up and glanced around.

Mr. Leaner looked over the edge of the wall without a care in the world. Bruno's arrow sailed straight into the man's chest, trailing a gossamer thread behind it. The man started to reel backward, but Bruno braced his feet and pulled. The man stumbled toward the wall's edge, Bruno already sprinting toward the spot he would land. Mr. Leaner's body fell like a rag doll and hit the ground with a soft thud. Bruno dragged the body into the shadow of the fortress, and crouched, cloak wrapped tight.

There was no cry of alarm, no calls, no reaction from the fortress at all. It kept staring into the desert, unconcerned about the single flea that had abandoned it.

Bruno emerged from his camouflage cocoon, assembling a grappling hook at the end of a rope. He swung the hook in a few wide circles before throwing it up and over the edge of the wall. The rope pulled taut. They all listened for a tense moment. Then Bruno began to scale the wall with fantastic speed. He disappeared over the top. Moments passed like hours as they waited for some signal.

Allison kept her eyes on the fortress. "I'll go up first, then Jay, then Delilah. I'm going to haul you both up, so don't be surprised."

Finally, a figure appeared on the wall beside where Mr. Leaner had stood. There was a tiny yellow spark like someone striking flint.

"Move!" commanded Allison in a harsh whisper. The three of them slid down the embankment and ran for the fortress. Without breaking stride, Allison seized the rope dangling from the wall and seemed to run straight up. She disappeared over the top and waved at Jeremiah.

Jeremiah then seized the rope. He started climbing, grateful for the knots that had been tied into it. His hands were slick with sweat, but he was able to use his feet to push himself from knot to knot. The rope below him went taught as Delilah grabbed on, and then he was sliding up along the wall, clinging to the rope with a death grip as he bounced and scraped along the coarse stone that had looked so smooth from a distance.

Allison hauled him over the parapet. From the wide walk atop the wall, Jeremiah got his first view of the fortress courtyard. It was lit with a ring of torches, with several tables arrayed across it. The great wine barrel had been propped up beside the entrance to the squat keep. There were a few still figures lying about the yard, drunken into a silent stupor.

Bruno was already gone. Another rope tied to a stone protrusion on the inside edge of the wall hinted as to his whereabouts. Allison sent Delilah after him first.

Jeremiah scanned the battlements. Only three other figures patrolled the fortress perimeter. One was pacing, and the other two looked like they might be asleep standing up. Allison stared at them like she was ready to kill them from here. She practically pushed Jeremiah after Delilah.

He gripped the rope and slid down very carefully, terrified of damaging his hands at a time like this. His muscles ached with the effort, but at last he reached the open space of a window. A pair of arms grabbed his legs and pulled him into the pitch-black room.

Jeremiah's feet touched solid ground with a soft splash. Water? Oh gods, he didn't step in a chamber pot, did he?

"Eyes on," whispered Bruno. Jeremiah accepted the vial Delilah handed him and let a drop of liquid fall into each of his eyes. He winced as the sting gave way to grayscale vision of the room. Then he froze. There were at least eight men asleep in here, lying in bed rolls and straw pads or piles of burlap. *One noise and we'll be surrounded!*

Allison entered the room with a splash and a thud. Jeremiah recoiled and pressed a finger to his lips. She put her own eyedrops in and looked at him shushing her. She pointed down and used her foot to tap the head of one of the sleeping men. Jeremiah recoiled. Then he saw the deep gash across the man's neck, exposing skin, fat, muscle, and the pipes of blood hidden within.

Jeremiah suddenly understood what he was standing in. He looked around with growing horror, becoming aware of the scent of blood all around them. The entire floor was layered with it.

Bruno was already moving toward one of the two doors in the room. He motioned to Jeremiah and Allison. Allison promptly took up a guard position beside Bruno's door. Jeremiah swallowed, then splashed through the shallow lagoon of blood to follow suit at the other door across the room. He held his spear at the ready, willing his hands to stop trembling.

Bruno had just raised his hand to motion them all into the next room when Jeremiah's door swung open.

A grizzled, pimply man stepped in. He was carrying a torch and stank of wine. The man saw Jeremiah brandishing a spear and paused to make sense of the scene in front of him.

Time slowed down for Jeremiah. He saw every detail of the man: the silly pointed hat, the shortsword at his belt, the generous red stains on the collar of his shirt and neck. He saw the man's eyes widen in terror at the slaughter in front of him, darting to the people in the room, then back to Jeremiah.

Jeremiah had only a moment to strike, to cut off the inevitable scream as the man took a deep breath. His spear trembled like a newborn foal as he reached out and stroked the man's chest with its point. "Shhhhh!" Jeremiah whispered, as though the man's alarm was going to be very rude.

I can't move . . . I can't . . . Oh gods, I've killed us all, Jeremiah thought. In that moment he hated himself more intensely then he had hated anything in his entire life.

The man's scream of alarm left his lungs as a wheeze as a whirling blade impacted his temple, burying itself up to the hilt, its tip protruding from the other side. The man died instantly, wobbling on his feet as though his drunkenness had outlived him, before falling.

Bruno stalked toward Jeremiah, his face a mask of fury. Jeremiah hugged his spear to his chest and tried to sputter an apology, but the words wouldn't come out. Bruno braced his foot against the man's head and wrenched the dagger out with an eruption of blood. He yanked the door shut, kicking the body out of the way, and doused the torch in the blood, which hissed and bubbled. He then turned and threw Jeremiah down so hard he spun and fell face down in the grisly lagoon.

Bruno stood over Jeremiah and bared his teeth. "Stay here," he spat. "Play dead. We'll get you when we're done." Delilah and Allison gave him pitying looks, but they stepped through the opposite door, leaving only Jeremiah and the dead.

Jeremiah felt the still-warm blood seeping into his robes and curled his knees against his chest. A voice in his head sneered at him. *What are you doing here? You're no adventurer! You're no hero! You're just a cowardly little boy who will never amount to anything. Hurry up and pretend to be dead. Maybe you can at least do that right.*

He felt lonelier than he had ever been in his life. He wanted to go home, to his real home, wherever that was. He would be safe there. Stable, unchanging, secure.

Jeremiah didn't know how long he lay curled up in blood, reliving the moment of his failure over and over again. By the hundredth time, his jaw ached from clenching. The taste of blood had seeped into his mouth.

Enough. Jeremiah stood on shaking legs and spat. Rivulets of blood streamed from his hair and robes and fingertips. He kicked his spear away with a spray of blood. He was alone in an ocean of death, surrounded by darkness and corpses. He was a necromancer.

Dead ears listened to soft incantations. He repeated them over and over again, weaving symbols with blood-soaked hands with increasing conviction.

Rise.

CHAPTER TWENTY-TWO

Butchery

Rise.

Jeremiah was unfazed by the horror of the nine bodies spasming and climbing to their feet, but he recognized it all the same. Heads lolled on flapping throats that opened like great red mouths.

Weapons.

The bodies reached in belts and under bed rolls, producing swords, daggers, and hatchets clutched in the iron grip of the dead. Jeremiah retrieved his discarded spear and thrust it into the hands of the man he had failed to kill. A body he now commanded. Jeremiah stacked the bubbles of the zombies with practiced ease. Space, there was so much space in his mind now. The months of work and toil had stretched the boundaries of his mind, creating far more room than before. He kept the spearman separate, a personal bodyguard.

March. Protect.

Nine zombies formed a circle around him, and together they marched through the door Bruno and the others had exited through. It led to a long hallway lit by guttering torches that flickered shadows over two bodies lying sprawled as if sleeping. Their throats were cut as well.

Rise.

Two rooms adjoined either side of the hallway; within them were four more corpses.

Rise.

Their bubbles joined the others. Jeremiah was vaguely aware of how easily he had come to handle this growing horde. They were fresh, as fresh as could be. They moved with a limberness he had never experienced in the long-cold corpses he'd normally worked with, their bubbles vibrant. His zombies closed ranks around him as he ordered one of them to open the door.

There was a hiss of surprise and a spear punched through the zombie's torso. The zombie proceeded into the room unabated, and Jeremiah found his friends backpedaling quickly. Jeremiah's army spread out in formation on either side of him, his spearman by his right hand.

"I'm ready," he said.

His friends' eyes darted over the zombie horde before settling on him. Bruno stepped out behind Allison's raised shield and approached Jeremiah slowly, with tentative steps, his whole body coiled like a spring.

"We okay?" he asked.

Rise.

Bruno sprang into the air like a startled cat as the bodies in the room began to tremble and twist. He landed with a *squelch* in a pile of sloughed off flesh left by two new skeletons.

"Now we are," said Jeremiah with a wicked grin. The two skeletons and four new zombies stood at the ready, fresh blood pouring from their throats. Delilah backed away, her spear tip twitching back and forth.

"All right," said Jeremiah, "you've got seventeen zombies, two skeletons, and one necromancer. What's the next move?"

Bruno was about to speak when they heard a scream of terror coming from somewhere far behind them, followed by more shouts of alarm. A bell began to clang frantically from somewhere in the fortress.

"Shit!" cursed Bruno, abandoning the whisper. "All right, it was good while it lasted. Jay, we need those things to watch our back and provide a distraction. Form up and move with us; do what you can. Allison, the sneaky side of things is over, so you're in—"

"CHAAAARGE!!!" Allison yelled and slapped down the visor of her helmet, becoming a faceless juggernaut. She began spinning her flail, her weapon's piercing scream following her as she stormed into the next room. Jeremiah, Bruno, and Delilah raced after her, Jeremiah sparing a thought to command his horde.

Spread. Kill. Quickly.

Then to his spearman:

Follow. Protect.

The horde turned and began shambling as quick as dead legs would carry them back the way they had come. The skeletons armed themselves with short swords and sprinted away, their bony feet making a staccato clattering on the stone floor.

The next room the party entered was in the process of responding to the alarm. Most of the men never got the chance to fully wake up. Allison careened into the room with her flail screaming and whipped it into the rising forms of the nearest two men, breaking necks and caving skulls without skipping a beat. The other men scrambled away from her like frightened animals.

Allison charged them as they packed against each other at the far door. She struck them down like the fist of an angry god as they raised their arms in futile efforts to block her flail. Delilah covered Allison's left flank as some men regained their wits enough to bring their weapons to bear. She drove her spear into their stomachs, driving them back against the wall. Bruno covered Allison's right, darting in and out with flashes of his blades and hammering throwing swords into those who tried to maneuver.

Jeremiah sent his spearman in to support Allison, and the zombie tore into the mass of enemies with a fearlessness that only the senseless possess. The remaining bandits' retaliation was frantic and weak. Clumsy sword chops bounced off Allison's armor and knife stabs to the zombie's chest did nothing but pierce its stagnant heart. The last bandit shielded himself behind the body of one of his comrades. Allison crushed the body, then the arm holding it, then the bandit's skull.

"PUSH!" she bellowed. Jeremiah had been busy during the fighting, and only had one body left to raise before moving on.

Rise.

Eight new zombies and two skeletons. He sent the eight zombies to reinforce the rearguard, which he sensed had finally encountered resistance. *Confusion, screaming, killing, panic.* In the drunken dark of night, men encountered familiar faces and were set upon.

Jeremiah glanced out the window and saw people scurrying about the courtyard. He sent the two skeletons leaping down to cause more havoc. Their light forms landed with ease and immediately began running down bandits and tearing at them with bony claws and steel knives.

Allison sprinted along an empty hallway, Delilah running behind her. Jeremiah and Bruno fell in step. Allison kicked open a door on the left, revealing an empty room. She turned and kicked the opposite door open and, seeing nobody, continued her charge down the hall. Delilah followed closely.

Jeremiah and Bruno both saw what happened next but were too far behind to help. The door on the right had rebounded far too quickly. As Delilah passed, hands jumped out and seized her. Bandits hauled her into the room and slammed the door.

"Allison!" shouted Bruno.

Allison was already skidding to a stop. She shoved Bruno and Jeremiah away from the door and began ramming it with her shoulder.

"Hurry up and kill the bitch!" came a voice from inside the room. There was a strained reply. "Stop trying and cut her damn throat!" They heard Delilah's piercing scream.

"FIGHT HIM, DELILAH! WE'RE COMING!" Allison screamed as she slammed against the door.

Jeremiah ordered his spearman against the door as a crack of light appeared in the jamb from Allison's efforts. The zombie shoved its arm into the narrow space even as the door was shoved closed from the other side. The zombie's arm was crushed, but each subsequent ram from Allison allowed it to force more of its body inside.

The zombie's shoulder and chest widened the gap, and Jeremiah could sense and see someone stabbing relentlessly at its flesh. The man behind the door shouted triumphantly as he impaled the body over and over again, only to scream as the sword embedded in its chest did nothing to impede the zombie from clawing his arm, leaving red bleeding furrows and whole fingernails behind. The man was forced to release the blade that had become stuck in the zombie's sucking chest.

Allison's next blow forced the door open, and she rushed inside. A mace blow to her helmet immediately sent her stumbling. The door guard retreated to block the rest of the narrow room. He was a brute of a man, braced behind a tower shield and raising a mace high above his head. The zombie lurched at him, and he swung the mace downward. The zombie's shoulders splintered as it was driven to the floor. With its remaining strength, the zombie dragged itself toward the man and bit into his ankle. The man roared in pain and swung his mace again, crushing the zombie's skull to pulp. The bubble in Jeremiah's head popped.

A bellow of pain drew their attention. A second man had Delilah pinned against the far wall, his forearm across her throat and a curved knife raised over his head. She was gripping him by the wrist with both hands, trying desperately to redirect the knife. One of her cheeks was a bloody flap, her hands and forearms were covered in tremendous cuts. But the cry of pain hadn't been hers—the man's face was a mess of blood, with shards of glass embedded in his flesh and eyes.

As Jeremiah watched in horror, the enraged man forced the knife down toward Delilah. The blade pierced her throat right above her collarbone and drove deep.

Jeremiah screamed as Delilah's blood squirted outward in a geyser. Bruno darted at the shielded man blocking their way, but was forced to dodge backward to avoid being crushed by the mace. Allison caught the head of the mace with her flail and pulled with all her might. The brute lost his footing, and Bruno took the opening to slip past him and thrust a dagger up into the base of the man's skull. He dropped like a puppet with its strings cut.

Delilah's captor had enough vision left to see what happened. He spun, knife to Delilah's throat, ready to finish the job. Delilah was hemorrhaging blood and weakly clawing at the man's hand.

"Now, let's not go crazy!" he said, his eyes manic. "Maybe this little sweetie can still live yet, eh?" He sidled his way over to a window. "Oi! I got 'em up here!" he called down to the courtyard.

Jeremiah, Bruno, and Allison spread out and advanced on him.

"Let her go now, and you'll just be 'overpowered' and live to see tomorrow," said Bruno. "You don't want to end up like your friend, do you?" He gestured toward the crushed zombie.

"Pitch that!" the man spat. "I got time on my side!"

Come.

"Your girl is fixing to bleed out any second—"

Kill.

"—and you want to have a little chat?! Put your weapons down and maybe, just mayb—"

Skeletal hands, the rigid fingertips blunted from climbing the walls, reached through the window and seized the man's face. Fingers sunk into his mouth, eyes, and nose and wrenched him backward, flensing and tearing his flesh. He cried out as they pulled him backward through the window, his hostage forgotten as he flailed for the window's edges. He screamed all the way down.

Allison caught Delilah before she could hit the ground. "PRESSURE!"

Jeremiah rushed forward to press his hands hard over the spurting wound. He could feel Delilah's blood pulsing between his fingers.

"You're gonna be okay, hon. Drink this now." Allison poured the crimson potion down Delilah's throat.

The slashes in her face and scalp began to close, but Jeremiah could still feel the pump of blood against his hand. "Another!" he yelled.

Bruno crouched next to Delilah, pale and fumbling through his pockets. "I can't—I forgot which—she's bleeding so much . . ." He finally produced the vial, and Allison snatched it from his hands. Moments later, the gashes across Delilah's face and arms were healing. Jeremiah pulled away briefly; the geyser of blood had slowed to a gush. Delilah's eyes were starting to brighten again.

"One more!" said Allison. Bruno had backed away and was staring at the scene with his hand over his mouth. Jeremiah removed his hands from Delilah's wound to retrieve his own potion. Upon pouring it into Delilah's mouth, the gushing finally ceased.

Color slowly began to return to Delilah's cheeks. She started trembling, which Jeremiah decided to take as a good sign, then she summoned the strength to pull bottles of her own. A sizzling white powder that foamed on the remains of her wounds, a golden vial that she downed in a gulp, and a terrifyingly large syringe filled with a clear liquid that she jabbed dispassionately into her leg.

"Okay," she croaked. "Okay." She suddenly sobbed and held her face in her hands. Allison hugged her hard.

"We can't wait," said Bruno, and they knew he was right. They'd be swarmed soon. Jeremiah realized his hoard contained fewer bubbles than before, but even now the feedback from his remaining undead was pure carnage.

Allison helped Delilah to her feet. She still looked unsteady, but she fixed the others with a stern gaze. "Come on, we need to finish this." She flipped up Allison's visor and put her hands on Allison's face. "I'm okay. Al, we need you in berserker mode right now. Can you do that for me?"

Allison took a breath and nodded. She flipped her visor down. "No more dying, any of you. That's an order. Move out!"

Before following the others out of the room, Jeremiah peered out the window at the man who had nearly killed Delilah. His broken body lay far below, flat in the dirt.

Rise.

The extra distance made his head swim a little, but the effort was worth it. He sent the zombie off to kill.

Allison rampaged through room after room. Her screaming flail struck like a viper as the bandit resistance grew stronger. Delilah defended her flank, keeping her from being overwhelmed, and Bruno's arrows and throwing swords covered any other openings.

More bubbles popped among Jeremiah's rearguard of zombies. The bandits were rallying and beginning to overcome their confusion, but with each room Allison and the others cleared, he sent more undead back as reinforcement. He also changed up his commands.

Spread. Scatter. Kill.

Now the zombies would break off from the main group to attack previously safe areas. It wouldn't take them long to find new prey.

Jeremiah's head was finally starting to feel crowded. He sensed countless confrontations. He paused to look down at the bodies strewn across the courtyard. A skeleton heaved someone off the top of the wall. The body bounced lifelessly off the ground.

Bruno joined Jeremiah at the window as a bandit sprinted across the courtyard. "Come on," Bruno muttered. "Come on, do it, you scared little rabbit." The man reached the fortress gate and, in an impressive terror-fueled feat of strength, heaved the massive wooden locking beam out of place. He shoved the doors with all his might until they opened just enough to allow him to escape into the desert night.

"Yes! We're on a roll now!" said Bruno. As he said it, Jeremiah watched two more bandits break for the exit.

"PUSH!" ordered Allison, and the others fell in with her perpetual charge. She powered into the next room where a group of men were struggling to fend off some zombies and made short work of them. Her skill and speed were startling next to the sluggish, clobbering undead. They came to a rough stone staircase, and she raced downward, smashing the neck of another man as she ran.

Rise.

Allison kicked in the door at the bottom of the stairs and they streamed into the room just as a bear of a man charged through the opposite door. He collided with Allison, toppling her backward, then continued his charge over Jeremiah, then Delilah, then Bruno. A swarm of bandits streamed in after him, leaping on Allison as she swung wildly from the ground, breaking a shin in half before they pinned her down.

Jeremiah tried to climb to his feet, but a bandit bashed him upside the head with a truncheon. His vision flashed red and swam. He curled up and covered his head with his arms as smashing blows rained down on him.

A weight settled on top of him. A man was sitting on Jeremiah's chest, pinning him on his back. The bandit was screaming in rage, his mouth opened wide. Drool dripped onto Jeremiah's face as the man wrapped his hands around Jeremiah's throat and squeezed. Blackness and panic immediately set in. Jeremiah kicked his legs and clawed at the hands choking the life from him, but they were solid and strong. His eyes bulged and the man started to laugh and lick his teeth, lustful with murder.

A furious croak came from Jeremiah's robes as blackness crept in the edges of his vision. A moment later, the pressure on his throat lessened. Jeremiah gasped for air and blinked. His vision cleared enough to see his attacker seizing Gus, a line of puncture wounds seeping blood from his wrists. The man hurled the toad across the room, then returned his attention to Jeremiah. But his fingers didn't respond when he tried to wrap them around Jeremiah's throat. His hands were inert lumps of meat.

The man stared at his limp hands. Jeremiah could almost see Gus's venom coursing through the man's system as his body slowly stiffened, his face frozen in horror, then toppled sideways off of Jeremiah's chest.

The bear man was pummeling Bruno in a corner. A skilled pugilist by the looks of it, he stayed right on top of Bruno and bashed him in the guts with a gauntleted fist before lifting him clear off the ground and body slamming him. Delilah was just getting to her feet; the man who had tackled her was clutching his eyes and screaming, white smoke wafting off a pale yellow liquid that was smeared across his face. Allison was fully pinned by a group of bandits, her arms outstretched as a dwarf woman repeatedly smashed her chest plate with an axe, which bounced off harmlessly.

"Lift her visor! I'll pith her fucking brains out!" the dwarf screeched, switching the axe for a metal awl. She laughed and slammed the awl into the joint at Allison's hip. She licked the weapon clean and then stabbed it into her shoulder, gleefully sampling the blood again.

Jeremiah charged the bandit pinning Allison's weapon arm, ramming him with all his might. It was only enough to roll the man back, and he threw a wild elbow into Jeremiah's jaw as they fell. But the respite was enough. In a flick of the wrist, Allison stole the dwarf's awl and planted it between the ribs of the man pinning her shield. He died with a gasp. She was free.

Allison took out her rage on the dwarf. She tore the bandit's face to ribbons with her clawed gauntlets before raking her throat open. Jeremiah turned away from the gruesome display only to watch Delilah charge her spear into the fleshy belly of the man grappling Bruno. It pierced all the way through him. The man gurgled a pitiful moan and went limp. The room was quiet.

Bruno clutched his ribs and winced. Delilah produced a tiny paper parcel and held it under his nose. "Sniff hard."

Bruno inhaled through his nose and stumbled back, face drawn in silent agony. His eyes squeezed shut, then suddenly opened wide. "Holy shit!"

Jeremiah comforted a grumpy but uninjured Gus. Allison retrieved her weapons, growling to herself, "Careless. Stupid. Weak. Bandit bastards." She noticed the man who had attacked Jeremiah, still frozen in the same position. "Yours?" she asked Jeremiah.

"Gus's," he replied. He glanced around the room at the new cache of bodies. *Rise.*

The room opened onto the courtyard, where chaos was in full swing. Jeremiah sensed his minions all around him, in every hall and room, tearing people apart and being destroyed in turn. Screams and the sounds of battle permeated the desert air.

Rise.

More bandits were sprinting for the gate, but not enough. The party moved out into the center, and Jeremiah took a moment to spur his undead on. His minions were pulling him in countless different directions, but instead of being overwhelmed, he felt strong. His focus was unified despite being fractured into so many pieces, and he found he could impart his will in every direction it was needed without diluting it.

His minions spread through the fortress like a wave of death. For the first time in his life, Jeremiah felt truly powerful.

CHAPTER TWENTY-THREE

Boss Fight

Let's finish this," Allison said. They stood with her in the courtyard, the eye of a hurricane of chaos.

They had barely stepped forward when the doors of the keep exploded outward, tearing free of their metal hinges. From the dark emerged a huge humanoid on cloven hooves, ten feet tall and clad in plate armor shaped to show off its colossal musculature. The beast had the head of a bull, horns capped in steel points and corded muscles as thick as a man's forearms bulging outward. Two enormous double-bladed axes hung from clips on his belt. Jeremiah and his friends froze.

The creature gazed around the courtyard, lingering on zombies and fleeing bandits. He threw back his head and boomed a raucous laugh, deep and barking. "This is incredible!" he said, sweeping his arms wide. "Just the four of you did all this? What a disaster!"

"Is that him?" Allison asked.

"Gotta be," Bruno said, taking a step back.

"A minotaur," said Delilah with a touch of awe. Jeremiah had never seen a minotaur before, but they were as huge and frightening as the stories described them to be. And to top it all off, this one was wearing plate armor. The minotaur's bovine mouth showed flat teeth in a strange but jovial smile.

"My name is Narooka of the Ironhorn Tribe, and I want to sincerely thank you for relieving what has been an incredibly boring few months. I mean it—I've been going stir crazy here! In thanks, I'm going to give you some special options I don't normally offer. There are three roads to choose from and you're the ones driving the cart, so just let me know where we're headed.

"First, obviously, we can scrap it out. I tear all four of you to pieces, heads on pikes, that old chestnut. Or! As thanks for wiping out some of the worthless filler around here . . ." He flicked a stone the size of Jeremiah's fist toward a bandit making a break for the exit. The bandit's skull exploded. "I'll let three of you turn around right now and walk out that door. You can pick who stays."

"What's the third option?" asked Bruno.

"Now, this one's special!" One of Narooka's cloven hooves pawed the ground in excitement. "Would you four be interested in work? You in the armor, I could use a second-in-command, someone to whip these thugs into shape. For you, Bruno—yes, I know who you are—I'd like you in charge of operations. Have you ever run a bandit camp like this? You'll be great if even half the rumors are true. Now you, little lady. I'm guessing you're an alchemist?"

"Among other things. Legal counselor for instance."

"That's good! We could really use both of those skill sets. Hells, the legal side might be even more useful." The minotaur turned his formidable gaze toward Jeremiah. "Now, as for you, who I'm guessing is the mage responsible for all these undead, I can't really tell you about the job I have for you. It's not mine to give, you see, but my boss would kill me stone dead if I didn't at least offer you something. Consider it an open invitation."

The minotaur stepped toward them, smiling, arms spread in a welcoming gesture. "What do you say? It's late and you all look tired. Come on in, we'll get you something to eat. I've got a butternut squash soup simmering. We've got extra rooms, especially now, so you'll be comfy-cozy inside an hour. I only ask that you keep the undead going; these guys need some practice."

The party exchanged glances. "Are we saying no?" asked Jeremiah under his breath.

"What kind of question is that? Of course we're saying no!" said Delilah.

"He makes an attractive offer is all," Bruno said.

"We're saying no regardless of how attractive his offer is," said Allison. She lifted her visor to address the minotaur. "With all due respect, Narooka of the Ironhorn Tribe, we can only counter-offer you fair treatment and the lives of your men if you surrender to us immediately." Allison readied her flail and shield. "Now, unless you're going to surprise me . . . ?"

Narooka put his hands on his hips and shook his head. "No surprises here, I'm afraid. You and I are just gonna have to be boring ol' warriors. But, hey, necromancer, offer stands open to you. If at any point during this bloodbath you decide to take the deal, just let me know." He drew the two enormous axes and gave them a cavalier spin.

"He'll charge. Head first," said Allison.

"How do you know?" asked Jeremiah, planning which direction he would run.

"Oh, he will. We killed a Matriarch. We can kill him. Focus." She took two long steps forward, stomped her foot on the ground, and swiped it backward in a deliberate motion.

Narooka tilted his massive head, eyes narrowed. Allison repeated the motion. After a split second's hesitation, Narooka mirrored the movement with one of his massive hooves. Delilah inched behind Allison and tapped Allison's pauldron twice with the tip of her spear. Then she braced the butt of the spear into the earth and lowered her stance, tightening her grip and gritting her teeth.

Allison swiped her foot one more time, and Narooka let out a roar of challenge that reverberated over the sounds of battle in the courtyard. He lowered his head nearly to the ground. Then he pounded his axe-wielding fists into the dirt and charged toward Allison, churning up great dusty clouds. Allison roared in kind, tossed the flail aside to draw her sword, and charged the minotaur. Bruno and Jeremiah fled the impact zone.

She's mad! thought Jeremiah. There was no way Allison's armor could possibly stand up to such an impact, magic or not. But as the distance closed and Jeremiah fought the urge to look away from his friend's impending death, she dropped into a feet-first slide, lying as flat against the dirt as she could. The minotaur's head passed over her, and she thrust her sword up into the great beast's jaw.

The thrust lifted the Narooka's head upward, his neck outstretched. His momentum carried him into Delilah's waiting spear, braced with the earth itself, which slid like a lethal splinter into the gap between his throat and his armor. The spear pierced his torso, a guttural scream escaping the Narooka's muzzle as his weight forced the spear deeper and deeper. The spear shaft bent and buckled, but the hardened wood held as the spearhead burrowed into its victim. The force of his charge carried Narooka off his feet as the spearhead erupted out his lower back and barely punctured his armor. Delilah was lifted along with the spear before the minotaur crashed to the ground in a flat heap.

Allison stood from her slide with a leaping, victorious whoop. Jeremiah, Delilah, and Bruno ran to join her. Any bandits that had watched the spectacle abandoned all pretense of resistance and bolted for the door.

"Legendary!" Jeremiah said as Delilah and Allison wrapped each other up in a delirious embrace. "That was legendary!"

Then Bruno stopped. "Guys," he said. His tone made Jeremiah's skin crawl. He turned to see what Bruno was looking at.

The minotaur's huge bulk twitched, shifted, then clambered to its feet. Narooka turned to face them, Delilah's longspear protruding from his throat. He grabbed the end of the spear and yanked upward with a pained bovine howl. He pulled the spear out of his body, one length at a time, then glared at them, eyes blazing. The fist-sized wound stitched together before their eyes, like the effects of a healing potion. The flow of blood from his punctured armor slowed to a drip.

"Jay, what the *fuck* am I looking at?" asked Allison.

"Healing magic!" said Jeremiah, looking around wildly. "Where's it coming from?" He had seen no spells, no potions.

"Minotaurs don't regenerate. They don't," said Delilah, sounding more curious than horrified.

Narooka stood upright, gripping the weapon that should have killed him—the weapon that he had removed from his own organs. "Never bail out of a challenge like that. Very bad form. However, I'm willing to overlook it because that move was brilliant! This might be more fun than I thought."

Narooka hurled the spear like a javelin at Allison. Allison casually angled her shield and deflected the longspear into the ground beside her. "I'm going in close," she said. "Bruno, get that armor off. Delilah, keep him off balance. Jay, get us whatever backup you can spare." She slammed her visor down and stepped forward to face her opponent again.

Narooka and Allison hefted their weapons, eyeing the other with more wariness than before. Bruno and Jeremiah flanked out to surround the upcoming confrontation while Delilah raced to retrieve her spear. Jeremiah began mentally sifting through his bubbles, finding those undead that weren't involved in combat and calling them to the courtyard.

He almost missed Narooka's glance and shift in weight. His brain cried out in alarm only an instant before the minotaur leapt toward him. Jeremiah tried to dodge, but tripped over his own feet and toppled. The axe blade cleaved the air where his neck had been, the rush of air billowing his robes.

Narooka raised the second axe overhead. Jeremiah's adrenaline surged, and he rolled desperately to the side as the axe caused the ground beside him to erupt. He tried to roll onto his feet, but he was stuck—the axe had pinned his sleeve.

Jeremiah yanked to free his arm, but it was held fast. The minotaur raised one great hoof to stomp his head in. "Offer's closing fast!" laughed Narooka. But as his hoof dropped toward Jeremiah's skull, Allison charged into his leg with all her might.

Narooka twisted and fell awkwardly to his knee, nearly crushing Jeremiah anyway. Allison was on the beast at once, swinging her blade at the minotaur's corded neck. He deflected her blows on his horns.

Bruno rushed to the minotaur's side and thrust a shortsword into a seam under his breastplate. He twisted the blade, forcing the armor plates apart. The minotaur tucked his head and rolled over his own horns with surprising agility, tossing both Bruno and Allison aside. On his feet again, he swung a hewing chop behind him and caught Allison on her interposed shield. He spun to press the attack against her with a steady drumbeat of blows.

Allison parried and countered each strike, landing superficial hits on Narooka's exposed lower legs, which healed instantly. Narooka caught Allison with a kick, lifting her into the air where his axe slammed into her chest. Sparks showered from her armor as she spun to the ground. She was on her feet in an instant, her breastplate sporting a narrow gash along its side.

"Magic armor? Incredible! I've never seen that before," Narooka said.

"Banger!" called Delilah. A clay ball arced toward the minotaur's head. Jeremiah and Bruno covered their ears as the banger impacted the minotaur's horn and exploded. There was no fire or shrapnel, but the bang was so loud it distorted the air around the point of impact. Narooka shouted in pain and lurched sideways, his bovine ears folding back. Allison took the opportunity to slash at the joints of his greaves, to little effect.

Narooka was regaining his footing when a second banger struck the other side of his head. This time Jeremiah also launched a ball of acid into the minotaur's face, causing him to roar in anger and pain. The acid only burned away at the surface of the beast's tough hide. The scorched flesh healed more slowly than the minotaur's other wounds, but Allison's proximity as she searched for an opening in Narooka's defense made Jeremiah hesitate—an errant splash could maim her.

Narooka's wounds closed as he adjusted his stance to Allison's fighting style. He held one axe close to the head and the other low on the haft. The variation would allow him to attack her at arm's reach and defend himself when she darted in close.

Bruno reappeared, leaping from the minotaur's blind spot, and sliced into the armor covering the beast's upper legs. His blade caught something important to the armor's integrity, and a tasset slid down the minotaur's leg with a crash, forcing him to step out of it like a shoe with loosened laces. "Gotcha!" said Narooka and his hoof caught Bruno in the chest. Bruno flew across the courtyard like a rag doll and bounced off the ground, where he curled up, clutching his ribs and gasping in pain.

Jeremiah sensed his undead before he saw them. They emerged from doorways or dropped from low windows and began ambling toward the minotaur, many holding weapons but some just reaching with eager hands. Narooka eyed them without losing a step in his melee with Allison. He began backpedaling as he fought, his long strides easily outpacing the accumulating zombie horde as well as forcing Allison to run just to keep up.

She put on a burst of speed in an attempt to circle Narooka and position him between herself and the undead. As she was mid-dash, though, Narooka sprang to cut her off, swinging his axe in a wide arc toward her feet. She leapt to avoid it, but too slowly, the blade caught her ankle and sent her to her knees.

He was on her in an instant, air whistling as a heavy axe arced toward her.

Allison scrambled to raise her shield just in time, but the blow knocked her onto her back. Without missing a beat, Narooka seized her legs and whipped her over his head. He body slammed her into the packed earth with a deadened thud.

Jeremiah strained to spot some movement from Allison, any sign of her magic armor having protected her from the impact. Before he could comprehend her terrible stillness, though, Narooka had straightened up with a broad grin, brushing aside half the zombie horde in a casual sweep with one axe. "That's one!" he said.

Jeremiah scrambled to the edge of the battlefield to regroup with Delilah and Bruno, who was on his feet, though his face was drawn and pale. Delilah's expression was grim, her lips a thin, determined line. "I need you two to keep him busy," she said. She hefted her spear and hooked several flasks to her belt for easy access.

"We're going to need more help," said Bruno. He hissed with pain as he drew his bow.

Jeremiah summoned every undead under his command to the courtyard. "They're coming, but they'll need time."

The small horde already there hacked and clawed at Narooka's ankles, drawing minor wounds that closed as soon as they appeared. The minotaur paid them no mind. He pointed an axe at the trio. "I hope the rest of you together can give me as enjoyable a fight as she did!" He gave a snort of laughter and charged toward them.

Bruno hurled himself to the side and began loosing arrows at the beast as he bore down on them, seeking a vulnerable spot. Delilah circled the other direction and lobbed a flask. A cloud of white mist exploded around Narooka's unarmored leg, drawing a snarl of pain and slowing his approach for a precious moment. Jeremiah launched an acid ball toward him, which he batted out of the air with an axe, sending acid splattering over his armor and the few undead still on his heels.

"Boring!" shouted Narooka. "Predictable! Please tell me you have more than that."

As if on cue, more zombies began shambling into the courtyard, lurching with what passed for haste for the undead. Only a few at first, but they kept coming, crawling over each other with monotonous groans to reach their target.

The minotaur paused to consider the situation. "Shame, necromancer. With us, you could have been formidable." Then he lowered his head and rushed Jeremiah.

Jeremiah turned and fled, managing a scant few steps before something slammed into him from behind and he was thrown into the air. His stomach swooped as land and sky melded into one, then the ground reasserted itself, rushing up to meet him with solid finality. The breath left Jeremiah's lungs in a whoosh.

His limbs were numb. His head rang. Jeremiah considered never moving again. He could hear Narooka laughing. "That's two!" the minotaur said.

What was two? Jeremiah sat up and realized something felt wrong. Loose. His hands went to his gut and came back slick with blood. He pulled the fabric of his robes away.

Fleshy worms spilled from his abdomen in all directions. His own intestines. His vision swam at the sight. The world dimmed in a final sunset before blackness. Jeremiah felt no pain. An odd peace settled over him as he reinforced his last command to every undead under his control.

Kill him.

His minions would fight unabated until he died, then most would collapse. A few may gain autonomy and continue on after his death, joining the ranks of undead roaming the world. Jeremiah wondered with dreamlike curiosity what determined whether an undead would persist. Flusoh probably knew, but he'd never thought to ask.

A motion in the center of the courtyard drew his fading attention. Right, there was a fight going on. Narooka was wading through a legion of zombies to reach Bruno, who was vanishing and reappearing within the horde of undead to strike from unexpected angles. Color began to run out of the scene, and Jeremiah knew he was feeling death's introduction. He let himself fall back and gazed at the pinpoints of light in the desert sky as they blurred into velvety black.

A burst of color, and Jeremiah's world exploded back into light and sound. His every sense was alive and working overtime. Overwhelming pain bloomed in his guts alongside a viscous, almost slimy heat. Jeremiah inhaled a tremulous breath and began to scream.

Delilah withdrew an empty vial from his lips and began applying alchemical agents to his back and abdomen. Jeremiah's skin crawled across his wound, flesh knitting back together. His scream faded as the pain receded, leaving him breathless and disoriented.

"That was the last potion. Now get up and help!" Delilah stared into his eyes, pleading as well as ordering.

"Wha—why me? Why not Allison?"

"If you die, we all die." Delilah disappeared from his side, leaving Jeremiah to blink and try to make sense of her words. The undead horde attacking Narooka had swelled to nearly a hundred, and now they were not so easily brushed aside. Skeletons climbed his legs, tearing at his unarmored thigh. Zombies hacked at every inch they could reach, impeding his movement even as he kicked them aside. Meanwhile, Bruno peppered him with arrows, sneaking shots under armor plates and sending them spinning like flipped coins.

Far from seeming distressed, however, Narooka was laughing. He spun in a whirlwind of axe blades, cutting a swath through the horde. Others shambled in to fill the ranks, but not enough. He cut down a dozen more in a rapid flurry. "I know you're one of these, little man!" he crowed. "Can't hide forever!"

We need more, Jeremiah realized. *Many more.*

He forced himself to move. Delilah had given him their last potion, had chosen him as their best chance to survive. He wouldn't freeze again. He wouldn't let his friends down.

Jeremiah staggered toward a door into the keep and threw it open. His night eyes were still working well enough for him to see where men had died, lumped together in corners or strewn across the floor. His zombies had done their work here. Jeremiah barely registered the carnage and merely reached toward those bodies intact enough to contain his will.

Rise. Fight.

He returned to the courtyard and continued onto the next door, where he was greeted by a similarly grisly scene. A dozen men crushed into a corner, torn nearly to pieces. He performed his magic without pity, turning death to his purpose.

Rise.

Onto the next. He glanced back at the battle, saw Delilah by Allison's side as Bruno and the zombies did their best to distract the minotaur. The freshly raised undead were doing their job, forcing Narooka to fight them to avoid being overwhelmed. Jeremiah tore his eyes from his friends to concentrate on the task at hand.

Jeremiah continued around the courtyard. From every door and window, the undead spilled out to reinforce their brethren. He had no idea how many he had raised; his mind's organization was haphazard—he crammed bubbles wherever there was space. His focus was fraying from the strain, his willpower was beginning to fatigue, but the magic continued to flow and he didn't dare allow himself to stop. He fought distractions—urges to check on Gus, to reorganize his undead, to watch the battle, to observe a bloodied man hiding in a corner and crying hysterically, but he gritted his teeth and kept raising.

Jeremiah found a room that contained no bodies, then another, and another. He realized he had completed a loop of the courtyard. He turned to see if it had been enough.

Allison was fighting again, but she was much slower. She weaved among the horde, using the shifting mass as cover as she struck blow after blow. Jeremiah heard the musical sound of Bruno's bow string nearby and spotted him shooting from the cover of the door. Narooka's exposed flesh was a pincushion of arrows, which the minotaur had no time to remove. Delilah hurled flask after flask, which exploded in a variety of effects—sonic blasts, shrapnel showers, a bloodred mist that drew a roar of pain from Narooka when it shattered against his horns.

Jeremiah found a group of skeletons in his head, and ordered them to climb upward. At once, the skeletons scrambled up the walls of the fortress and leapt onto Narooka's arms and shoulders, digging their claws in as he spun to dislodge them. Allison darted in and carved into his exposed leg, hewing off a chunk of flesh. Narooka howled as he dropped to a knee and the zombies began to swarm, tearing and hacking at his body as his wounds regenerated.

"BRING HIM DOWN!" Allison screamed. She jumped, her steel boot ringing out against his breastplate, and slashed at his head with her sword. He turned his horns to deflect her, only to receive a flask of burning fluid to his face. Bruno seized the opening to spring toward the beast, daggers flashing in his hands before flying toward gaps in his armor. Blades sunk into flesh like needles, and Bruno kicked them deeper into Narooka's body.

Climb.

The zombies began crawling up the minotaur's body as Narooka stood, his leg healed. Allison stabbed without finesse at the places on his torso where armor had been stripped away. A barbed arrow trailing a rope leapt from Bruno's bow and buried itself in Narooka's corded neck. Bruno heaved against the rope, but was dragged several feet as Narooka whirled, hacking at the zombies crawling over his body.

Jeremiah ran to help, adding his own strength to the rope. At this, Narooka noticed the danger, but it was too late.

Pull.

Dozens of hands suddenly grasped and heaved against the rope. Narooka grunted with the effort to resist falling, leaning against the pull at his neck. Then, with a flick of her sword, Allison sliced across one of his ankles. The minotaur staggered as the joint gave way. Allison next thrust into his other knee, turning his stagger into a stumble and then a fall.

She scrambled onto Narooka's chest before he could protect himself. As zombies tore indiscriminately with blades and teeth, Allison slashed the beast's throat, releasing a geyser of blood that healed over in the next moment. She roared in frustration as she slashed again and again. "WHY! WON'T! YOU! DIE!"

Narooka gargled blood and snapped his jaws at her. He fought to free his arms from the hordes weighing them down. Slowly but surely, he was escaping.

"Come on! We need to take this thing apart!" said Bruno.

Jeremiah drew his dagger, letting bloodlust fill his heart. They descended upon Narooka like mad butchers, piercing and slicing at him as desperately as the undead. But his wounds sealed themselves even as they withdrew their blades. Jeremiah realized they were exhausting themselves with nothing to show for it.

"You can't kill me!" came Narooka's rasping voice. "I. Am. Immortal!"

Jeremiah dropped his knife and pressed his hands against the minotaur's blood-soaked flesh. He summoned an outpouring of necromantic magic, brought forth by a powerful ancient word with a primal meaning: *DIE.*

Energy flowed from his palms into the beast. All at once, Jeremiah sensed within Narooka a vast ocean of healing magic, circulating throughout his body, reaching tendrils to instantly treat every wound. It felt foreign, as though it had been placed there, and immense. Even with the wounds Narooka was receiving every moment, the magic drained as slow as the sea through a pinhole. With great effort, Jeremiah focused his remaining will. In the face of his necromantic magic, the great sea of healing began to boil off.

"What are you—" Narooka's head lolled as the agony of his wounds flared. "No! Get off!" He lashed out in desperation and bit Delilah's leg. She screamed as the bone snapped. He swung his horns into Bruno, catching him in the chest with the blunt curves and crushing his injured ribs. He threw his head back toward Allison, forcing her to block the point of his horn with her shield and driving her from her post.

Jeremiah rushed to where Allison had stood. Already the gash at Narooka's throat was closing. He pressed his palms into the hot, slimy wound.

DIE.

His spell rushed through the minotaur. The reservoir of healing dwindled steadily as Narooka's wounds began to accumulate. The flesh at Narooka's throat blackened and rotted while the beast bellowed. Jeremiah gave everything he had and more than he never knew was his to give. Darkness was encroaching on his vision, but he knew he only needed to keep it up a little longer . . .

Narooka spasmed in agony. He croaked, voice filled with fear, "Don't . . . don't make me into one of those . . ." He slowed, retched, contorted, and finally died under Jeremiah's hands just as the darkness finally closed.

CHAPTER TWENTY-FOUR

Death and Dying

Jeremiah's head throbbed. Only incapacitated for a moment, he awoke sticky with warm blood. But the stillness of Narooka's body, the lack of pulse coming from his neck, was the world's sweetest silence.

Narooka's body shifted as Allison, battered and bloody, climbed on top of his chest. She panted in heaving breaths and growled with effort as she raised her sword overhead. "WHO ELSE WANTS SOME?"

Her challenge echoed around the courtyard, which was blessedly silent save for a few fleeing footsteps.

"Look alive," said Bruno. "The fortress is routed, but it's not safe. Some will try to raid the place, establish themselves as leader, or just kill us."

Delilah leaned against the minotaur's body. One of her legs was grossly deformed, the flesh reduced to a bloody mess. "Bruno, I've got a few precious chemicals left in my blood that are staving off shock. Your ribs are beyond broken, and I think your collar bone is too. Allison's hurt, Jay's hurt, and we're out of potions. If you think we're still not done . . ."

Bruno shook his head. "We bunker up. If Jay can get the rest of these undead patrolling and wiping out pockets of resistance, we'll be okay."

Allison jumped to the ground, landing with her hands on her knees. "Into the keep. Jay, give us an escort and help Delilah. Bruno, shoot anyone that even looks at us."

Jeremiah clung to Delilah and Delilah clung to Jeremiah. Together they formed one person that could barely hobble. With a ring of zombies surrounding them, the party sought refuge within the walls of the keep.

They found an unoccupied bedroom, an underboss's quarters judging by the single larger bed, rug, and collection of keepsakes. Jeremiah helped Delilah onto the bed, and Bruno carefully lay down beside her.

"Allison, can you and Jay handle watch?" asked Delilah. "Bruno and I need to take Quick Heals, and we'll be out of commission while it works."

Allison turned a lock on the door. "We'll stand guard. You two do whatever you need."

"I've set the zombies to patrol," said Jeremiah. "And I left a few on the walls in case anyone wonders what happened here."

Delilah produced two vials of pearlescent liquid and handed one to Bruno. They *tink*ed the vials together.

"To waking up feeling better," said Bruno.

"To waking up at all," said Delilah.

They quaffed the admixture. Delilah stripped her armor, though she needed to cut away the boot on her broken leg. Allison helped Bruno remove his own armor. Bruno and Delilah were already becoming drowsy and flushed. They soon drifted between fever dreams and utter stillness, twitching and groaning as their bones mended with meaty cracks, foreheads sheened with sweat.

Allison handed Jeremiah one of Bruno's short swords. "I'm hurt," she said. "If anything happens, you'll need to cover my back. If someone tries to get through that door, bring every zombie you have to stop them. If they get through, I need you to at least pretend you're going to use that. Do you understand?"

"Yeah," said Jeremiah. He felt a pang of shame. Despite everything he'd done, he had still revealed himself to be a coward.

Perhaps Allison sensed his hurt because her tone softened. "You did good, Jay. You did really good. I don't think we could have done it without you."

She set aside her helmet and Jeremiah was shocked to see her face. The blood vessels in her eyes had burst, her nose was broken, and a deep purple mask was rising around her eyes. She grinned at his reaction, her teeth standing out white and unblemished like a lighthouse amid a dark sea. "I must look almost as good as I feel. Now help me barricade this door."

They dragged a heavy desk across the door, then Jeremiah helped remove Allison's damaged armor. She applied salve and bandages to her wounds before donning her armor once again.

As the night passed into early morning without disturbance, Allison permitted them each a few hours' doze while the other kept watch. Desperate as he was for more sleep, Jeremiah took his vigil with pride. His friends rested, trusting him with their lives. His zombies roamed the fortress, dispatching the diminishing resistance without difficulty. Jeremiah kept watch, the quiet hours bearing witness to his new responsibility.

Just after noon the next day, Bruno sat upright with a start. He wiped sweat from his face, eyes darting around the room. "Food."

Delilah stirred beside him. "Hush. Look at me." She pulled herself into a sitting position and palpated Bruno's ribs. "Deep breath. Good." She felt her own leg, moving her toes and rolling her ankle. "Also good. Allison, let me take a look at you."

She crawled over Bruno, who rubbed his palms into his eyes. "How does your head not feel like it's about to explode?" he groaned.

"It does," Delilah said. She unbuckled Allison's armor and inspected her wounds. "Not bad, actually. That's some impressive armor."

"I gotta eat something," said Bruno, rolling gingerly out of bed. "I'm feeling well enough to find it myself, I think."

Allison's mouth twisted with worry, but Delilah laid a hand on her arm. "He's right. We all need plenty of energy to recover. Water too." Allison's worry persisted, but she nodded, and Bruno slipped through the barricaded door.

He was quick and quiet, returning with several loaves of bread, a roasted chicken that had gone cold, and a barrel of water. Jeremiah hadn't realized how hungry he was, but the food rejuvenated him like a full night's rest.

"Ahh, that's so much better," said Bruno. "Let's get out of here and see what we've salvaged!"

"Hold it," said Allison. "We're going over every square inch of this place ourselves until we're sure it's clear. I'm not getting jumped by some clever bandit pretending to be a zombie."

They reapplied bandages and armor and crept from the safety of the room. Most of the fortress halls were empty of anything living at least. Groups of zombies on patrol shuffled past without sparing the party a glance. Jeremiah reanimated the corpses they came across to bolster his ranks.

Allison seemed to relax slightly after they had completed their first perimeter of the fortress without meeting any challenge. Jeremiah ventured a question that had been on his mind. "Allison, how did you know about that challenge ritual, the one that made Narooka charge?"

"The Montello campaign, about six years back. Wasn't anything special, but we stayed with a minotaur tribe for almost a month, and I got to know them," Allison said. "But I can tell you, Narooka wasn't a normal minotaur. He had combat experience, *very* expensive armor, even some kind of education. Plus, they don't usually stray too far from their tribes."

"He had that healing magic, too," said Delilah. "I've never met a minotaur, but I know that's abnormal."

"That was all stored inside him," said Jeremiah. "I felt it when I used my magic on him. At some point, someone filled his body with an enormous amount of latent healing energy. It was like having a million healing potions ready and waiting."

"That sounds incredibly useful," said Bruno. "How do we get some?"

"I have no idea," said Jeremiah. "I didn't even know it was possible before last night. But the implications . . ." He drifted off, lost in thought about the possible applications of latent necromancy.

Allison shuddered. "Imagine if every bandit here had been charged with the same magic as Narooka. They'd be able to fight a group a hundred times their size."

Jeremiah pondered the idea. "I'm willing to bet a large creature is able to contain more latent magic. So regular-size bandits would be able to heal a few times but probably wouldn't be as invincible as Narooka."

"I'd still like to know who put that magic in Narooka in the first place," said Delilah. "To invent a brand-new method of healing, and at such a scale, they must be immensely powerful."

"Hell, who built all this?" Bruno asked. "This fortress is way too advanced to be built by common thieves, especially all the way out here."

"It would take a lot of people and expertise," Allison agreed. She had pulled up short, and she and Bruno were exchanging a hard look, pushing each other to the same conclusion.

"People, expertise, and leadership," said Bruno. "Narooka kept this place in line pretty good, better than any bandit gang I ever saw. And he wanted you to train them."

"Me, not you," said Allison. "Narooka wanted soldiers, not thieves."

"He wanted a necromancer, no questions asked," said Bruno. "But he didn't have a specific reason, said it was up to his boss."

"Hidden fortress, disruptive fighting force, leadership, recruitment, and advanced magic," said Delilah, ticking the items off on her fingers.

"Drawn from the underbelly of the city," said Bruno. "These bandits were locals, with active knowledge of routes and passages. With training, those are the best spies and saboteurs you can ask for."

"A hidden fighting force disrupting trade lines, under the guise of a bandit camp." Allison gestured to the fortress around them. "This was military, an advance placement. Whoever orchestrated this is preparing an invasion."

They continued their sweep in silence, contemplating their revelation. Jeremiah was awed by the thought of an army backed by latent healing magic. Then he realized that, until the conclusion of his sentence at least, he would be right in their path, and shivered. The walls of Dramir that had once been so formidable now seemed merely a token defense.

He paused as Allison declared another room clear. There was a closet in the room, the upper half of its door reduced to splinters. Something about the closet tugged at him, a dark curiosity that drew him closer. He peered over the jagged wood.

Curled on the floor of the closet was another body staring up at him, eyes wide and frozen in fear. Jeremiah saw the thick red gash where a sword had been plunged into the man's shoulder, saw deep furrows across his hands and forearms. His throat was a red ruin, his face smeared red with blood but for twin streaks that tears had cleansed as he died.

Jeremiah staggered back from the closet, his mind's eye awash with the man's last moments. Terrified, trapped, crying, helpless. Jeremiah hadn't been aware of this moment when it happened, would have only been aware of another violent encounter, and not one that threatened his undead. Irrelevant.

The wave of emotion left Jeremiah breathless. He had waded through blood only a day ago, but this scene was so personal, the details so telling that it tightened his chest and set his teeth on edge.

Bruno appeared by Jeremiah's side. "Gods, that's awful," he said.

Jeremiah felt a hand on his shoulder, pulling him away from the scene. It was Allison. "Jay, listen. Everyone in our line of work goes through this. I live through it over and over and I remember my first, clear as the day it happened."

The words tumbled out before Jeremiah could stop them. "He didn't want to fight. How many didn't want to fight? How many died this way?" He remembered the bodies he had reanimated the night before. They had been piled in bloody corners, no chance of escape.

"Don't give him a story," said Bruno. "It doesn't help anything if you give them a story."

"But this *is* his story!" said Jeremiah, alarmed at his own words. "I didn't make it up. It happened to him!"

Delilah laid a hand on his arm. Jeremiah realized he was shaking. "I have a lot of nightmares about people I've . . . about people I've killed," she said. "I know seeing this makes it real, too real, but it's a fact of life. We don't need you to be okay with it, just keep it together till we're home. Then you can sort it out and we can talk about it. It helps to talk."

Allison squeezed his shoulder. The physical contact softened him, let him catch his breath. "Okay," he said. "Okay, I can keep it together for now." He looked up at Allison, pleading. "This happens to everyone? To all adventurers?"

Allison shook her head. "No. Just the good ones. 'Walk with me, soldier. Sleep in earth, live in my dreams. Be my silent scar.' Paladin Eagon."

She squeezed his shoulder one more time, then turned to Bruno. "You, on the other hand, are so selectively squeamish! There are dead people everywhere, and you still haven't puked like when I got my fingernails torn off!"

"Oh gods!" Bruno gagged at the memory.

Jeremiah followed the others out of the room, letting their banter wash over him like a cleansing rain. Still, as they continued their sweep, a tiny piece of his mind dwelled on tear tracks running down a dead man's face.

CHAPTER TWENTY-FIVE

Treasure Vault

It took hours, but finally Allison declared the fortress safe. Jeremiah breathed a sigh of relief, his muscles finally releasing the tension they'd held since the previous night.

Bruno led them out to the courtyard. "We're not wasting time pilfering pockets for coins. The shipment that came in went somewhere, and it was too big to be stashed away in someone's room. I'm betting it never left this courtyard. Everyone, fan out and start probing the ground. We're looking for a hatch of some kind. Let me know if you find it—*do not* attempt to open it."

The entrance to the underground storage turned out to be a massive trap door hidden in the dirt in front of the keep. Bruno brushed dirt away from its entire perimeter, scrutinizing every seam and hinge. With Bruno's go-ahead, Jeremiah summoned a half dozen zombies to lift the hatch, revealing a ramp descending into the earth.

The air was cooler as they lit a torch and descended the ramp. Jeremiah's anticipation grew with each passing step. Bruno clearly expected a wealth of treasure with this camp—Jeremiah had no idea what they'd find.

A pair of large steel doors blocked the bottom of the ramp. The doors were sealed by a complex mechanism, featuring six keyholes in the center of raised interlocking gears. Jeremiah thought the lock looked valuable all on its own.

"What do we have, Bruno?" asked Allison. She lit a few more torches around the room, the doors glowing orange with reflected firelight.

Bruno cracked his knuckles and shook out his hands, strutting toward the lock like it was a beautiful woman and he was about to risk it all. "We have here a leadership caste lock. Six keys held by the six most trusted members of the organization. The six interconnected gears are an insightful piece of design—a thief only has two hands, of course, so turning all six requires three prideful, impatient thieves working in close proximity, blaming each other when it doesn't turn." He caressed the lock's surface, leaning close to absorb the smallest details.

"You were built by Atesh Fellspring, or one of her students. So, one of you"—he gently traced each of the keyholes—"is actually a cylinder key with a wonderfully sensitive pressure trigger that injects poison if tickled in just the right way." He teased each of the keyholes with the tip of a finger. "Ah! You're the one."

Bruno pulled a small brass device from his belt. He opened it with a flick of his wrist, revealing a wick held before a convex mirror. When he lit the wick, the mirror reflected the light to a single point, which Bruno shined into the trapped keyhole.

"Poor Atesh, your students never have your forethought." Bruno next withdrew a long, folded wire. Tiny joints connected each segment like the legs of a bug. He slipped the end of the wire into the trapped keyhole and slowly slid it deeper, unfolding new segments as the wire traveled further inside the mechanism. "Now, I'm not certain which student it was, as I've only met three. But I'm seventy-five percent sure it was Marietta, an elf. Something you learn in this business is that different cultures have certain ways of approaching problems, especially when it comes to mechanics."

The wire caught on something. Bruno worked the wire, easing it carefully past the snag, and continued. "Now, take a dwarven lock for example. They love their practicality—heavy bolts, pins under so much pressure they could take a finger off. Blocky, uncuttable, mechanisms rugged as all hell. But finesse isn't their strong suit. You can tempt and tickle those locks open with enough careful maneuvering. Elven, on the other hand, is the exact opposite . . ."

Bruno fit a narrow copper sleeve around the wire and began sliding it along the wire into the lock. "Far too exacting, far too delicate. You're as likely to break the damn thing as you are to unlock it." He braced a foot against the door and strained, pulling the wire as hard as he could. Jeremiah was sure the thin filament would snap.

"What an elven locksmith doesn't expect," he grunted, "is for you to gum up the primary bolt on purpose"—metal ground against metal inside the mechanism— "and just yank the damn thing till it turns!" There was a loud dull thud from inside the lock and the doors parted just a little. Bruno waved his hand in a flourish. "Ta-daaa!"

They pulled the metal doors open, revealing a long storeroom stretching back into darkness. Allison lowered her torch to a pair of narrow oil troughs that ran along both walls, filling the room with flickering firelight.

They were standing in a thoroughfare that stretched to the far wall. Piled high to either side were stacks of crates, blanketed goods, and wooden chests.

"Now don't get excited," said Delilah. "Odds are most of this is food and trade materials."

But her caution was far too late. Bruno skipped down the center aisle. He selected a tarp and tugged, revealing a life-size marble statue of an elven woman in a fluttering dress. Her upward gaze led to her slender, reaching arms. The statue was a moment frozen in time, like she could spring back into motion at any second.

"Ha!" laughed Bruno. He popped up on one foot and kissed the statue on the lips. "That's a funny-lookin' barrel of apples!"

Jeremiah, Allison, and Delilah gave into Bruno's enthusiasm and began investigating the piles. Jeremiah buried his arms in a wide chest filled to the brim with silver coins, scooping them up and letting them rain from his hands with a tinkling clatter. They opened chests and drew back covers, exclaiming at each new discovery. There were very few trade goods.

Bruno whooped as he opened a tiny steel chest to reveal three sizable diamonds seated on a plush purple cushion. The gems glinted brilliantly. "These guys pulled the Poselthwait job? This operation was even more organized than I thought."

"Ooh!" said Delilah, looking over his shoulder. "Let me take those. I can return them for a favor!"

"I thought we got to keep whatever we found!" said Bruno, holding up one of the gems against the light.

"Trust me, a favor from Alistair Poselthwait is worth *far* more than any precious gem." Delilah closed the chest and tucked it inside her robes.

"I have no idea what I'm looking at," Allison said, examining a bolt of green fabric. "Cloth? Is it special?"

Bruno joined her and ran his hands over it. "Cotton, decent quality. But that dye job is incredible! Are they all like that?"

"We're taking everything of value," announced Delilah. "I bought extra space at the warehouse for us to store our findings until we can get a broker to sell it. But, of course, we get first dibs." She looked to Jeremiah and swept her arms out in front of her, like she was revealing it to him for the first time. "If you see something you like, it's yours!"

Jeremiah dug through art objects, jewels, riches he'd never imagined possessing himself. In fact, he could hardly imagine claiming any now—surely they belonged to someone else, someone far more important. He browsed the wares, admiring and appreciating, but nothing more.

"This looks pretty," said Delilah. She was examining a half-unsheathed silver longsword in the firelight.

Allison took it from her to inspect more closely. "Plated. Weight's all wrong, cross guard is too short"—she shook it a little—"and either the tine is loose or there is none. Shiny but hardly a real weapon."

"Someone probably paid for it, so don't throw it against a wall just yet," said Delilah, in the nick of time.

Bruno held up a thin leather case. "Allison, can you come take a look at these? They look like military blueprints for siege weapons of some kind."

Allison peered at the drawings. Then she snapped the case shut, stood ramrod straight, and announced, "By the order of King and Queen Thorisis, in accordance with the Kingdom Securities Act, I, Captain Allison Allday, take possession of this item as a matter of Kingdom Security!"

From across the room, Delilah also stood at attention. "I, Counselor Delilah Fortune, acknowledge the recipient Allison Allday as custodian of said item. Let all who hear this announcement be aware that tampering with said item is a violation of the Kingdom Securities Act, Section Twelve, Article Fifteen, and is punishable by law."

Bruno and Jeremiah exchanged a look.

"Sorry about that," said Allison "but they clearly had no idea what this was. There's a weird protocol about handling documents of this sort."

"I didn't know you were versed in the Kingdom Securities Act!" said Delilah. She looked positively smitten with Allison.

"It all came back at once. That's training for you."

Jeremiah cleared his throat. "Paperwork is *very* interesting! So interesting, in fact, that I guess no one would want to bother with the enchanted weapon I found."

The others rushed over, knocking over boxes in their scramble to reach him first, only to find Jeremiah empty handed. He gave a rakish grin and gestured to the piles beside him. Bruno, Allison, and Delilah began dismantling the pile, inspecting every object for signs of magic while Jeremiah was doubled over with laughter at their franticness.

He finally relented when Allison beseeched him, her eyes so pathetically pleading they made him want to give her a hundred magic weapons. He reached up to a pedestal supporting a statue of a grizzled hermit, and plucked the walking stick from his silver hands. The rod was four feet long, its ends tapered to sharp points.

None of the others seemed to understand what they were looking at. "A javelin?" Allison guessed.

In response, Jeremiah separated a thin wire that rested invisibly against the metal rod. He gripped the rod and pulled the wire, and the rod bent in a curve.

"A bow?" said Bruno. "That thing is a bow? I've never seen anything like it!"

Jeremiah grinned. "From what I can tell, the bow itself is solid steel." He demonstrated that he was unable to bend the rod with his hands, then swung the weapon into the lid of a nearby chest. The wood splintered with a resounding crack. "See the magic etchings? From what I can tell, the enchantment allows you to use the wire to bend the bow and for it to return to its shape afterward."

Bruno was holding the bow before Jeremiah had even realized he'd taken it. He nocked an arrow to the wire and drew it. The rod bent into a graceful curve. Bruno released the wire and the rod snapped back to its original shape, hurtling the arrow against the back wall where it exploded into dozens of wooden splinters.

"Oooooh!" said four voices in unison.

"Dibs," said Bruno, spinning the bow between his fingers like a baton.

"What? You're not the only one that knows how to use a bow!" Allison stamped her foot in outrage.

In response Bruno drew a second and third arrow. He loosed the first into a silver plate that lay atop a chest, sending it flipping end over end into the air. The second he shot straight through the flipping plate. The arrow penetrated clean through the center and shattered against the wall. The plate spun on the floor, its metallic hum growing louder and higher until it settled with a cymbal crash. Bruno gave Allison a smug smile. She glowered back.

"Allison, you already have a suit of magic armor, and you're a frontline fighter," said Jeremiah.

"Shoulda got the magic sword," Allison grumbled.

As exciting as it was, at the end of the day the plundering of the vault was a logistical chore. Treasures, trinkets, and trade goods (the few that there were) were arranged into piles of piles of "sell," "leave," and "maybe." Delilah suggested that all but the most valuable of these would need to be left behind, as the profit from reselling them needed to be worth the effort to transport them and store them in Dramir.

"Oho, I am definitely keeping this," said Allison. She withdrew a weapon from a chest she had been sorting through—but it was unlike any weapon Jeremiah had ever seen. About the length of Allison's forearm, the weapon was a flat plane of blades jutting out at strange angles, as though a blacksmith had been inspired by a bolt of lightning while forging a knife. She grasped the one safe appendage and hefted it. "Aw yeah, this is definitely going on my wall!"

"What is it?" asked Delilah as she and Bruno shoved a block of gold-veined marble across the storeroom from "maybe" to "leave."

"No idea!" said Allison. She spun the weapon in her palm. "I'll ask around the guild, but I've never seen anything like it."

Jeremiah flipped the clasp on a lacquered box and gave an involuntary gasp. Three gold rings set with gemstones were inside.

"What?" asked Delilah. "Are these magic too?"

"No!" Jeremiah laughed. "No, I just recognize these. My father made them a long time ago. I'm surprised they're still in circulation." He picked up a ring and held it up to his eye. The gold of the ring flowed around the onyx gem in a firm yet elegant embrace. Sure enough, a capital *T* and a sharp arc were inscribed on the band. Thomas Thorn.

"May I?" Bruno asked. Jeremiah offered the ring to him. Bruno inspected it with a discerning eye, turning it over in his hands. He frowned. "It feels . . . wrong. The weight is off. It's too light."

"Ah." Jeremiah took the ring back. His now-grown fingers still remembered the particular movement the ring expected. The onyx popped away from its setting to reveal a hollow cavity.

Bruno laughed. "Your father made poison rings?"

"He made whatever people ordered. Sometimes he would have me mess with them to make sure they held up. I just recognize this design."

Bruno slapped his forehead. "Thomas Thorn! Of course! I feel so dumb. I didn't realize you were his son."

"You know him?"

"Not personally, but I know his reputation. I once requested one of his ring mechanisms to study. My coin may have graced your table at one point! Funny how that happens."

Jeremiah slipped the onyx ring onto his right hand and closed the other two in their box to add to the "sell" pile. The ring jostled on his finger as they continued to work through the storeroom.

CHAPTER TWENTY-SIX

Temptation

Jeremiah summoned his undead horses the next morning. They were miles away and still harnessed to the carriage. It would take them most of the day to arrive. The party spent the wait finishing their organization of the treasure vault and preparing one of the bandits' own horse-drawn carts to help haul the plunder.

Dark thoughts began incubating in Jeremiah's mind as he helped his friends organize. He fiddled with the onyx ring as the day progressed. Listening to the others' joviality only soured his mood further. They were celebrating their discovery, newfound wealth, a hard-fought victory—all of which they owed to him. And what was awaiting him back in the city, his reward for ridding Dramir of its problem, uncovering a threat, defeating a great enemy? As Bruno and Allison loaded chests onto a hand wagon, Jeremiah made his decision. Jeremiah left the vault and headed up the ramp to the courtyard without saying a word.

Outside, standing in the bloodstained dirt, he breathed in the smells of dust and death. He called to his undead.

Come to me.

Patrols halted their rounds, guards abandoned their posts. From every corner of the fortress, they came. Jeremiah observed them as they formed ranks before him, awaiting his next order. Some could pass for human, some were barely mobile, but they all kept coming, lining up in neat rows to fill nearly the entire area of the courtyard.

"Jay!" Delilah's voice called from behind him, breathless. "Is everything okay?" She stopped short at the top of the ramp, her eyes falling on the horde of undead arrayed before her.

"I've been thinking," said Jeremiah. "I won't be returning to Dramir with you."

"What?" Delilah asked. "Of course you will."

"No, I won't." Jeremiah gestured toward his minions. "How many do you see here? One hundred fifty? Two hundred? All men that were alive just yesterday. Most died gruesome deaths. Most died because of me. If I return to Dramir, they'll force me to participate in whatever military skirmish is brewing. They'll make me kill more people, and I'll be good at it. Delilah, they're never going to let me go."

"Jeremiah," said Delilah, with an edge of threat to her voice, "I know we've had a stressful couple of days. But think for a second. You'll be breaking the law if you stay. The court handed down a decision, and this is the way you're meant to prove your innocence. If you just hide, you'll be proving them right."

"I know who I am. They're the ones that don't know. You said it yourself— they've already decided. It's time to free myself. This is a fortress in an isolated location. Here, I have food, water, and an undead army. You guys are free to take all the treasures, of course, but I'm staying here."

He turned toward Delilah for the first time and felt his skin crawl. She wore the same expression of steely determination she'd had in court. "You ungrateful child!" she spat. Jeremiah was stunned. "All the work I did to save your ass, pulling every string I have to get you a fair trial, putting everything I've worked for on the line to perform the miracle of saving your life, and you're just going to yank the rug out from under me?"

Jeremiah's own anger helped him recover. "Forgive me if I'm not grateful to be a slave of the state! To spend every day performing tricks like a trained rat, and all the while whether I live or die is decided by some bureaucrats who are just looking to advance their own careers! Just go back and tell them I was killed in the raid and I'll be left alone. Your precious reputation will be safe then."

"Ha!" Delilah barked. "Of course, a necromancer in his fortress that left dozens of witnesses isn't going to raise any suspicion at all. We were doing well, Jeremiah. This whole thing was to prove your potential and get you that much closer to freedom, but I guess you'd rather follow in Flusoh's footsteps. Isolated with your undead, is that just the natural order of necromancers? I give it two months before some band of adventurers comes to plunder the evil wizard's fortress."

"I can take care of myself." Narooka's last request rang in his ears, but Jeremiah gestured toward the hulking form that still polluted the center of the courtyard. *The dead want for nothing*, he reminded himself.

Rise.

The body of Narooka clambered to its feet, towering over the other zombies.

His blood-matted fur was a dusty red, his throat and face a ruin, but these details only added to the savagery of the colossal zombie. A huge bubble appeared in Jeremiah's mind, but there was more than enough room for it.

Delilah took a step backward, a glimmer of fear in her eyes. "What exactly do you plan to do here all by yourself?"

"Practice. I can improve my magic. I've already come farther than I ever thought I could."

"Mm-hmm. You're going to practice necromancy. See, here's the problem I have with that: what does necromancy require to function?"

"Usually, it—"

"Death! Things need to die. And there's not much in the way of life out here, so you'll need to find your share of death somewhere else."

"You know I'm not going to just start killing people, but—" Jeremiah clenched his fists in frustration. "I'll be able to do whatever I want! That's what I'm getting at. I won't have to be under house arrest. I won't have a set execution date. I could go anywhere in the world if I wanted to. I could have my life back!"

"You're not the only one—"

"I swear to every god, don't you dare compare what's at stake for you with what's at stake for me." Jeremiah's voice was a dangerous growl. The nearest zombies shuffled. "Tell me I'm wrong, Delilah. Tell me my life is not a piece on some game board."

"I . . ." Delilah sighed. "I can't tell you that. It is. They gave themselves a year to figure out how best to use you. But they will *not* kill you. I won't let that happen. I'd use everything I have and everything I'm owed to prevent it."

"Can you tell me that I'm not going to continue living in bondage? That there'd be no legal argument for me to become some sort of property of the state?"

Jeremiah watched Delilah wrestle with the question, referencing years of legal education and practice in a moment. She rubbed the heels of her hands into her eyes. "Okay, fine! Yes, there's a case to be made for keeping you under legal jurisdiction. I can't promise you'll ever actually be legally free. I can't promise you anything! I can just . . . I can promise I'm never going to stop!"

"I appreciate that, Delilah. I really do. But you can't fight the system, not really." The zombies nearest him knelt and reached out with dozens of hands. Jeremiah stepped into them and the hands raised him up, lifting him until he stood atop a sea of undead. He began to walk away across the horde, the zombies' hands automatically creating platforms for his feet.

Delilah spluttered behind him. "There's nothing for you out here! The zombies don't care about you. You'll be alone, with no one to hold you to a higher standard or worry about what happens to you or give a damn if you had a bad day!"

Jeremiah continued to stride across the courtyard, leaving behind the futile argument.

"Jeremiah Thorn! If you receive anything less than a full pardon, I swear, I-I'll smuggle you out of the city myself! I'll find you a place in a caravan, or put you in an empty cask of wine, or bribe a guard and give you a fake identity!"

Jeremiah stopped. "Delilah, that's illegal."

"You're gods-damned right it is."

Jeremiah felt a heat creeping up the back of his neck. Something drew him back toward her, the zombies handing him from one to the next, then lowering him to solid ground in front of her. "Delilah, I can't bear being a slave anymore."

"I know. I'm doing everything I can to put an end to it. But . . . you live in my home. I will not leave you all alone out in the desert."

Jeremiah wished he could summon the energy to yell at her, to make her comprehend the enormity of what she demanded of him, but the heat of his anger had dissipated. Something told him she already understood, anyway. "You can't protect me."

"Not from everything, no. I'm sorry." Delilah looked at her feet as she said it. Jeremiah had never seen this version of her before. "I can't imagine the pressure you've been under and how scary every day must be. The ticking of the clock like a headsman's axe swinging closer and closer. Toiling to serve silent, capricious gods that you don't understand in the hopes that they spare your life."

"Um, yeah. That was . . . well put? Very well put."

"Jay, can you trust that I'll do everything to keep you safe? That I won't allow you to be harmed or held in perpetual bondage?"

"I can do that. I'm . . . I'm sorry."

Delilah nodded. "I'm only one woman, trying to guide you through a labyrinthine machine and promising you it somehow doesn't end in your death. I get why you'd be afraid and why you'd want to run away."

"Thanks." Jeremiah studied the dust on his own shoes for a moment. Then Delilah embraced him, squeezing him tightly. After a second's hesitation, he returned the hug. She felt surprisingly small in his arms.

Delilah rubbed her eyes when she pulled away. Jeremiah felt the urge to do the same. "Don't give up," she said. "We're going to get through this together."

Jeremiah nodded. He felt the onyx ring on his finger again and pulled it off. It slipped free easily. He hefted it once in his hand, then hurled it among the sea of undead. With a few commands, he ordered the zombies back to their patrols. They began shuffling around at once, their activity soon burying the ring in the dirt.

Delilah and Jeremiah started back down the ramp. "You're so much better at apologizing than me," Jeremiah said.

"I've had a lot of practice."

CHAPTER TWENTY-SEVEN

Magical Ethics

Take your last looks and mount up!" Allison said. After two days of preparation, they were eager to escape the charnel house the fortress had become. The continuous patrol of zombies atop the walls had kept at bay any bandits with dreams of glory.

The remains of Narooka were invaluable in moving the heaviest of the treasures. However, Jeremiah couldn't bring himself to look at the enormous creature, nor could he reduce Narooka to a nondescript pronoun as he had with so many other zombies.

Jeremiah also avoided Delilah whenever he could. She had witnessed his moment of weakness, and it was only her concern for him that had rescued him from becoming the type of necromancer he swore he'd never be. He felt exposed before her. Part of him wondered if she had told Bruno or Allison. He had a feeling she hadn't. The sympathetic smiles she flashed whenever he hurried past reassured him that the incident would stay between them, but he still felt a pang of shame each time.

Jeremiah jumped as Allison clapped a hand on his shoulder. He had been lost in thought as he watched Bruno check the attachments of one of the bandits' carts. They had decided to appropriate several carts to help haul treasure back to Dramir, with the aid of some of the bandits' horses that had been killed during the battle. "What are we doing with these?" Allison asked, gesturing toward the zombies and skeletons milling idly around the courtyard.

"I'm guessing I can't keep them?" said Jeremiah.

"No chance."

"Can I request something akin to a proper burial?" asked Bruno, coming up behind them. His eyes traveled across the haggard faces of the undead. "They didn't choose this."

The undead shifted at once in response, and Jeremiah's friends jumped. The zombies began spacing themselves evenly around the courtyard, filling in the ranks as they descended the walls and streamed in from around the fortress. Narooka took up his position in the center.

Dig.

As one, the undead horde stooped and clawed at the hard-packed earth, weapons and fingernails clawing through the crust to scoop out the softer soil beneath. They dug straight downward with ferocious speed, descending deeper into the earth. Soon the courtyard became a tilled field, sown with bodies that continued to dig. When just the tops of their heads protruded from the deep but narrow holes, Jeremiah ordered them to stop.

"Shouldn't we say something?" Allison asked. She cast a wary glance at the spontaneous burial site, unconsciously edging her shield side toward it.

"Umm." Jeremiah racked his brain for something appropriate to say, but his necromancer training hadn't exactly covered this. Seconds ticked by. Finally, he thought back to the many funerals he had attended in Dramir. "A moment of silence," he said, "for the passing of hard lives, at last, into rest."

They bowed their heads. Jeremiah released his hold, his mind stretching the fill the space left as hundreds of bubbles popped and bodies collapsed. All that remained was Narooka, who moved among the piles, using his huge hands to push loose dirt back into the holes, covering his former comrades. Finally, Narooka climbed into his own massive grave and scooped the earth over himself. At last, he too was still.

"We done here?" Bruno asked.

"I think so," said Jeremiah. He turned to go, but Bruno stopped him.

"Allison, you and Delilah go on ahead for a minute," said Bruno. After a moment's hesitation, Allison returned to where Delilah waited by the carts. Bruno turned to Jeremiah to face him. "All right, tell me."

"Narooka begged me not to reanimate him. Right before he died." The words came forth like bile, poisoning the air as he spoke them. Jeremiah watched Bruno work the confession over in his mind.

"I'm guessing you told me that just now because you feel bad about ignoring his last request?" asked Bruno.

"Yeah, I think I do. He was noble, courteous. Even though he was trying to kill us and lead some sort of army."

"Jay, what you do is beyond me. I'm just a thief, I pick locks and pockets. I don't know anything about magical ethics. If you're looking for me to tell you that it's okay, well, I don't know. I think that's something you need to decide for yourself."

"Well . . . I'm a necromancer. That means I have dominion over death. And If I had to respect every enemy's dying wishes, I'd probably never raise another undead. So, I guess even though it feels bad to turn them down, being a necromancer means accepting the responsibility of these decisions. I have to be okay with that."

Bruno nodded along with him. "If that's what you believe, I can go along with that. I trust you, and while I never want to hear you say 'dominion over death' again, you're not wrong."

"Could I raise you?"

"What?"

"If you died in combat, could I raise you? As a zombie or a skeleton or whatever else I need?" Jeremiah suppressed a smile as Bruno's face paled.

"Um. Zombie only. I can't handle that liquid-flesh thing. But you know what? I'd be happy to continue to be of service. Just, you know, please don't make me a pet? Proper burial eventually?"

"Deal."

Being in their own carriage, finally about to leave the fortress behind, was a relief. Allison winced as she rested her head against the wall. They were all still injured to varying degrees, consequences taking root in their joints and scars. "Take us home, Jay," she said.

The carts began to roll as the caravan pulled by undead horses strained against their load. They passed into the sun-bleached desert, adrenaline finally ebbing.

"Everyone okay?" Allison asked. Everyone nodded or grunted their affirmation.

"You okay, hon? With everything?" Delilah asked Allison. She placed a reassuring hand on Allison's knee.

Allison's gaze flicked to Jeremiah and away again. Jeremiah recognized that there must have been a prior discussion between Allison and Delilah concerning him, but he was too exhausted to wonder as he waited for her answer.

"Yeah," said Allison, "I think I'm okay. It was a bit . . . well, nightmarish."

Bruno snorted. "A bit."

"But I'm good," Allison finished firmly.

The carriage crawled across the desert. Jeremiah, his mind finally free of the burdens of the last several days, thought of something. "Delilah, we had right of salvage, right? Anything we found was ours?"

Delilah stirred from her fatigued stupor. "Huh? Oh, well, there are a few clauses that muddy things when you really drill down, but not many. Why?"

"We went out there expecting to find a bunch of tents and such. But we found a fortress. Can we salvage a fortress?"

Delilah froze. Her eyes widened, her pupils dilated, and Jeremiah though he detected a high-pitched whine just beyond his range of hearing. "I guess we'll see," she managed eventually, her voice strained.

The rest of the journey passed peacefully, seeming much faster than the journey forth despite their load. At the outskirts of Dramir, Delilah hired several couriers to transport the bulk of the goods into the city proper so the undead horses could be left behind. Only the disguised skeletal horses remained under Jeremiah's control as he directed their carriage back to Delilah's house.

The house waited for them as though no time had passed at all, although Jeremiah was sure he had aged several years in the intervening weeks. He trudged to his room, shrugged off his gear, refreshed Gus's water, and collapsed onto the bed. It was over. Well and truly over.

Jeremiah was tidying up in the lab a few days later when a distinct wail made his blood run cold. Delilah had been busy since their return, so he was trying to help keep the laboratory productive in her absence. She had disappeared in a flurry of errands, returning the map, filing reports with dozens of official bodies, and meeting with Colonel Valen. She was tight-lipped about the latter—"I'll tell you when there's something to tell" was all she'd said when Jeremiah had pried. She had also arranged for their treasure to be stored in a warehouse as it was brokered piece by piece. None of them dared estimate its value for fear of jinxing it.

The wail came again. Jeremiah abandoned his work and rushed downstairs.

Delilah was at the table, her face buried in her arms. She was bawling uncontrollably, her shoulders shaking with each sob. Allison rubbed her back soothingly.

"What happened?" Jeremiah was suddenly incensed, preemptively enraged at whoever had traumatized Delilah.

"You want to tell him, girl?" Allison asked.

Delilah looked up, her eyes red and puffy, face streaked with tears.

"I—I—I asked—I asked if the fortress counted for salvage rights!" She sniffed. "And they said it does, but instead—instead of . . ." She broke into sobs again.

Jeremiah sat beside Delilah and took one of her hands, stroking his thumb across the back of it. He had guessed something as critical as a military fortress would be one of the caveats to salvage rights that Delilah had mentioned, and it appeared he had been correct. "Go on, it's okay," he said.

Delilah managed to continue. "Instead of—of selling it, or returning it, they said that I get to own it and all the land around it!" She wailed and collapsed back onto the table.

"Oh! Well, that's good, right? Owning land and a fort? I mean, it's not the best land, but—"

"No! You don't understand!" Delilah wiped away fresh tears. "You can't own land unless you're a noble! So, in recognition of what we did and of my role as the party's chief administrator, I get to be . . . I'm . . . I'm gonna be . . . they're going to make me a Lady!"

Jeremiah stood. "That is indeed a vital step toward your goal of becoming queen. Let me be the first to congratulate you, Lady Fortune." He gave a deep bow, hoping it was the proper way to address a noblewoman.

Delilah's sobs stopped abruptly. She stared up at Jeremiah with wide, shocked eyes, her mouth hanging open. Suddenly her features scrunched and she extended a shaking hand as regally as she could. "A pleasure to make your acquaintance!" The nicety morphed into the loudest bout of wailing yet.

"There, there, come on." Allison patted Delilah's shoulder and grinned at Jeremiah. "She's a good-news crier. And this is the best news she's had in a long time."

Jeremiah returned the grin. "Good news for all of us! An actual noblewoman in the party could give us some real clout."

It took a few weeks for Jeremiah's prediction to come to fruition. He started accepting odd necromancy jobs again just as an excuse to get out of the house, but without any real expectations. Until Colonel Valen came through on his promise to provide a real opportunity, he was just killing time.

Jeremiah staggered home one evening in a dull stupor. He had endured a dreary day of reanimating a group of ancient monks to participate in a ritual of solemn prayer—that was, to kneel in the monastery alongside the living monks, motionless and silent, for fifteen straight hours.

"*There* you are. Finally!" Delilah materialized at his side and seized his arm. "Gather round, everyone, and listen closely!"

Jeremiah blinked as he was ushered to the table. Delilah buzzed with unmistakable vibrancy. "What's going on?"

Delilah cleared her throat impatiently as Bruno and Allison joined them in the kitchen. "We've been invited to a royal ball in recognition of our service to the city of Dramir! It's going to be held at the palace in a fortnight and more importantly, we'll be meeting with Colonel Valen about Jay joining the military operations up north."

A rush of excitement and fear broke Jeremiah's fugue. "Are you sure this is a good idea? Going into a war zone?"

"It's the best chance to get you off the hook. Likely the only chance. Even after everything we were able to report from the bandit camp, Valen had to pull a lot of strings just to get you this opportunity. You're doing this, and we're going to help you."

Delilah looked to each face around the table, inviting objections. Finding none, she continued. "I want everyone to get new clothes for the ball and briefing. This isn't like dropping by Corbyn's. This is the real deal. Jay, do you know how to dance?"

"Yes."

"Then we'll need—wait, really?" Delilah eyed him closely.

"Yes, really! A girl in my town was obsessed with dancing and always wanted a partner, so I obliged her. I'm sure I'm a bit rusty, but I know the steps of any of the classic courtly dances." Jeremiah was suddenly aware all three were staring at him.

"Well, that's adorable," said Bruno.

"Excellent, that's one less thing to worry about," said Delilah, pointedly ignoring Bruno. "Now, we're all going to learn about how to properly address different noble, military, and religious rankings!"

"Oh . . . good."

CHAPTER TWENTY-EIGHT

The Bloodlust

The following weeks consisted of preparation reminiscent of, but altogether distinct from, the exercises they undertook to prepare to raid the White Light camp. Delilah drilled them relentlessly on proper decorum, responding to Bruno's cheek with stern lectures underlaid with such fierce desperation that teasing her soon lost its charm.

Perhaps to reassure Delilah of his commitment to the cause, Bruno volunteered to help Jeremiah procure appropriate clothes for the ball. Jeremiah found himself standing on a wooden platform, a dozen versions of his reflection looking back at him from jigsawed mirror fragments. Bruno had stepped out on a different errand, leaving Jeremiah alone with Bab, the young gnomish seamstress who flitted about, taking Jeremiah's measurements, and gossiping about the goings-on of the dock slums.

"So Grodo drops to his knees in front of Seelia's house and just starts hollering drunken love declarations. Tears his shirt off right in the middle of it! Seelia starts throwing rocks at him from her window, says she's going to kill him. Gordo starts yelling that *he's* going to kill *her*! Next thing you know, their donkey Christopher is trying to kill them *both*! What colors were you thinking, love?"

It took Jeremiah a long moment to realize she had asked him a question. "Oh! Actually, I was thinking something a bit brighter. I've had enough of black, to be honest."

"Really!" Bab shrieked with delight. "Wonderful! And here I thought I was going to have to drab you down to match the whole 'necromancer' aesthetic. No, we'll find the perfect shades for you." She began to dig through a chest of fabric swatches, holding them up and rejecting them in the same breath. "No, far too serious. Looks funny with your hair. No . . . no . . . no . . . How about this?" She considered a silvery swatch just a bit longer before declaring it "too on the nose" and diving back into the chest. The discarded swatches accumulated around Jeremiah's ankles like a flamboyant snowfall.

Finally, she brandished a blue silk that had just a whisper of purple. "Yes, yes! It's perfect! Do you love it?"

Jeremiah grinned at her enthusiasm as the swatch vibrated in front of him. "Yeah, actually. I think that'll do just fine."

Bab bounced and giggled like a trill of chimes. "Perfect! This is so exciting. I can't believe actual nobility, maybe even *royalty*, will be seeing my designs!"

Jeremiah glanced around the shop again. It was well-kept but tiny, crammed with textiles and sewing equipment. Each piece of furniture looked as though it had been reclaimed from the gutter. "Bab, do you need help with anything? Like . . . money?"

Bab froze, the first time he'd seen her still. "Obviously I need money. Everyone down here needs money. That's why I'm working. We're not looking for handouts, Mr. Necromancer, we just want the opportunity to craft the life we want to live."

"Sorry," said Jeremiah, shifting on the platform. He wasn't sure what else to say.

"Don't you worry," said Bab, clapping her hands together. "You're all set! I'll work out payment for the outfit with Bruno and send it over just the moment it's done." She ushered Jeremiah off the platform. "Now shoo. I have work to do. A royal ball! Don't forget to tell Bruno how great I was!"

Bruno met Jeremiah just outside the shop, eyes scanning the dilapidated roofs. "Have fun?"

"Yeah," said Jeremiah. "Can I ask something, though? How come we came to this shop?"

"Because Bab's the best in the city, that's why," said Bruno. They began to wind their way home. "I could have taken you to Matelli's in the south end. They're not bad, but everyone knows their work, and your job is just another drop in the bucket for them. But you wear Bab's work to a royal ball, people get to talking. Maybe Bab gets a little more of the business she deserves. Maybe she gets the chance to buy some real mirrors. Hell, maybe even a damn rug."

Jeremiah thought back to the small pyramid of gold bars. He could have retired off it if he chose, but instead he'd gone on to spend more money than most of these people would ever see in their lives. "Bruno, how much are we going to make off the bandits' stuff?"

"Don't worry about it."

"I'm serious. Are we talking as much as last time? More?"

Bruno sighed. He glanced around and ran a hand through his hair. "Enough that you're not actually going to see it. There's not going to be a division of gold like last time. It's theoretical money now. At least, that's how Delilah described it to me."

"Theoretical?"

"Yeah, like it's numbers, not coins. And it's held by a bank. A real one, not just a safe under the floor. Please don't ask me to explain more because that's all I understand."

Jeremiah stayed silent as he followed Bruno through the slums, shadowed by a vague guilt he couldn't quite explain.

The palace of Dramir stood as a monument to indulgent architecture. As their hired carriage passed through the outer palace gates, Jeremiah had to stop himself from gawking at the scale of the building—countless rooms, halls, and barracks stretched across the main estate. Gargoyles larger than men loomed over doorways, each one a work of artistic mastery. Painted reliefs and mosaics of historical victories adorned the palace's white stone construction like gilded coats of arms.

The carriage rattled through a gate in the secondary defense wall, the only entry point to the palace proper. Allison tugged on the high collar of her parade uniform. Her hair had been straightened and rolled up into a tight, professional bun, and her eyes were still slightly puffy and red from the endeavor. Otherwise, she was every bit the heroic soldier.

Jeremiah admired the way they all looked. Delilah had chosen to effect a regal elegance with a scarlet fur-trimmed gown. Golden accents glittered across her eyes and a complex braidwork framed her face. She embodied the essence of a noblewoman as though she'd enjoyed the title from birth.

Bruno was sulking next to Jeremiah, his ego bruised after a long fight with Delilah. She had forced him into clothes that completely concealed his tattoos, had vetoed his shoes adorned with tinkling bells (Jeremiah hadn't realized before that footwear could be sarcastic), and had confiscated a set of lockpicks that Bruno swore he'd only brought by force of habit. In the end she had practically dressed him herself. He wore a simple charcoal gray hooded tunic over black trousers, along with a pair of white gloves that Jeremiah suspected were intended to keep Bruno's hands easily visible and were likely to be misplaced quickly.

Jeremiah was even proud of his own appearance tonight. The outfit Bab had delivered was resplendent—a vibrant blue doublet that caught the light with flashes of violet and glinting golden fasteners, complemented by simple cream-colored trousers. She had even included a jaunty yellow cap to complete the look. Allison had said he looked like a foppish poet, but Delilah had praised the way the outfit would subvert everyone's expectations of a necromancer. More importantly, Jeremiah loved the way he looked. He couldn't remember ever feeling so confident while out in public.

They joined a procession of carriages approaching the main entrance. Footmen strode up and down the cobblestones, providing refreshments. Delilah fidgeted as their turn approached, reaching over to fuss with increasingly minute details of everyone's outfits. "Everyone needs to be on their best behavior. You are to make no promises, offer no unsolicited advice, no bawdy stories, no jokes—"

"No rants about hypocritical disparity!" said Allison directly to Bruno, who cocked a half smile.

"Yes, none of those either!" said Delilah. "And no nicknames. If someone has a title, you use it every. Single. Time. Most importantly, if the king shows up, you are not to speak unless spoken to, approach him at all, or even move."

"How do we know if the king shows up?" asked Jeremiah.

"Oh, you'll know," said Allison. "King Hector is HUGE! When he stayed with our unit in Jalberta, we all had to eat outside because he didn't fit in the dining tents."

"I . . . Really? You never . . . Anyway, there will also be an announcement," said Delilah, eyeing Allison oddly. "Just, *please* nobody ruin this for us."

"I'll be on my best behavior," said Jeremiah. "No promises, no jokes, no nicknames."

"Neither will I do none of the things you said not to do," Bruno said.

"Don't insult me with double negatives," said Delilah. "I mean it, you guys! The way you compose yourselves tonight could mean the difference between a lot of doors opening or locking. Which for Jay also means life or death!"

Bruno held his hands up in surrender. "All right, I'll be good. I know there's a lot riding on this."

"Delilah, try to relax." Jeremiah worried her nerves would become contagious.

"This has to be perfect! Does everyone know what foot they're going to lead with to step off the carriage? I was thinking my left foot, but is that too expected?"

"Lady Fortune! This is just another royal function. I can't see why you're so excited for yet another night of dancing and mingling. Surely you're used to them by now?" Jeremiah said with a wink.

Delilah froze at the use of her new title, but then melted into a cool, merely amused affectation. "I suppose you're right. Just another day for a Lady of the realm." Delilah forced her attention out the window to other goings on. Allison tapped Jeremiah's foot with her own, giving him a surreptitious thumbs-up.

Finally, their carriage pulled alongside the plush river of red leading to the festivities. A footman presented a hand to help Delilah down the step. She managed the transition with poise.

Inside the manse, they followed the red carpet toward the melodies of vibrating strings and the rumble of chatter. They were stopped at a set of doors by a herald who took their names. Delilah's nerves returned all at once, and she smoothed her dress and hair over and over. Jeremiah squinted through the masterwork stained glass door at a shadowed sea of movement beyond. The music and talking had grown into a dull roar. They were only a few steps away from another world.

The herald positioned Delilah at the threshold and gave a smart rap against the frame. The door swung open and a wave of perfume scents and rhapsodist music washed over them.

"Presenting for the first time!" announced the herald. "Lady Fortune and entourage!"

Delilah's knees went weak just for a moment, but she composed herself and stepped into the ballroom with grace. Heads turned to take the measure of the newest addition to their ranks. There was polite applause, which Delilah acknowledged with a gentle nod, and they made their way into the party.

Jeremiah was out of his depth almost immediately. He lived within the trappings of wealth; he owned gold bars that represented more money than his family had ever seen. But these people had mastered their fortunes and dealt in the currencies of influence and power. He felt like a stray dog who had snuck into the house.

They followed Delilah's lead at first, greeting lords, ladies, archbishops, and commanders, learning so many names, ranks, and titles that Jeremiah forgot them immediately. Fortunately everyone was far more interested in speaking with Delilah, asking her what she'd be doing with her new lands and the fortress that she would be overseeing. Jeremiah detected some subtle jabs at the quality of her holdings, implications that the land was useless due to being in the middle of nowhere, but Delilah navigated these veiled criticisms with an unflappable ease born of the courtroom.

The group split apart when Allison recognized a general she had served under and broke off to speak with him, Jeremiah spotted a waiter carrying a tray of tarts that he had to chase down, and Bruno simply disappeared into the crowd.

Jeremiah knew that taking three tarts was perfectly acceptable. He was pondering the exact cutoff of good taste when he was approached by a slim man with hard angular features. Liver spots were just beginning to appear on the man's balding head, and the friendly smile he gave Jeremiah didn't even brush against his calculating eyes. "Mr. Thorn." The man's voice was as soft and rich as caviar. "I'm glad to see you in attendance tonight."

Jeremiah, suddenly aware that Delilah was nowhere nearby, gave the man a courteous nod. "I don't believe I've made your acquaintance, sir."

"My name is Gordus Wren. I hope the name is familiar to you?" Jeremiah shook his head. Gordus's smile didn't falter, but his eyes twitched just a bit. "No matter. I am a prominent businessman of Dramir, and a man of great influence and wealth. My reach is broad, my fortunes vast, and my patience limited. I will not dally with pleasantries or flattery, Mr. Thorn. I have sought you out for a singular purpose." His eyes burned into Jeremiah's as he spoke.

Jeremiah placed a tart into his mouth and mustered what he hoped was an expression of suitable concern as he chewed.

Gordus continued. "I am man of mastery, Mr. Thorn. Once I have set myself on the path to perfection of an art, I am relentless. Unstoppable. You have a skill set I wish to master. Accept me as your pupil in necromancy, and I will elevate you far beyond your station. Together we will reshape the economics, the politics, the very soul of Dramir. You will find yourself rich beyond your wildest dreams. There is no vice I cannot access on your behalf, no wish beyond my reach. You need only agree, and your life will change. No need to ans—"

"Oh wow. No." Jeremiah had found the first tart quite enjoyable and began on the second.

Gordus's smile crashed into a solid sneer. His eyes bulged. "Please understand that I have many boons to offer you, but the banes that are at my disposal are as wick—"

Jeremiah laughed in his face. "In what world would I give up my only bargaining chip? Not to mention you don't exactly give the impression of a man that would use such powers responsibly." It was easy to imagine Gordus Wren clad in hooded robes, leading an undead cult. Jeremiah saw a man drawn to power for its own sake, saw how he himself might look on a slightly different path. It was a glimpse into another timeline and it was painfully banal.

"Do *not* take my ire with triviality, Mr. Thorn! You are only a single piece of a larger game. With but a word I could bring a great deal of misery on you . . . or your friends." He stepped forward, now uncomfortably close, and spoke with a venomous hiss. "The reputation of a new Lady is oh so fragile, and the military record of many a decorated soldier has tarnished after service."

"Now you're trying to threaten me into teaching you?" A flush crawled up Jeremiah's neck. He was aware of a few people near them tilting ears in his direction. "I have an alternative proposal for you, Gordus. You are now responsible for those particular friends' reputations. I now hold you personally responsible for any downturns that might befall them, regardless of circumstance!"

Gordus Wren was taken aback by the change in Jeremiah's tone and volume, which had departed conspiratorial whispers and was heading toward shouting. "Mr. Thorn, be mindful of how—"

"No! No! Here's what you've signed on to. Any misfortune, any rumor, any snide remark about my friends that reaches my ears, it's *your* fault now. I am not a man that dabbles in games of intrigue, so if I hear something that requires my attention, I will deal with you in the only way I know how."

Gordus Wren fixed Jeremiah with a threatening glare. "Violence is well within my—"

"*Violence?*" Jeremiah leaned close to Gordus, fists clutched tight. "What I do isn't violence, Gordus. It's human butchery! I won't tarnish your reputation or damage your business prospects. I'll have you eaten alive by blunt-toothed monsters. If I need to make an example of you and dress your ruined corpse in motley to prance behind me forever, I will!"

His anger was blooming out of control. He didn't see Gordus's veneer splinter into fear or the other guests staring openly at the confrontation. He saw gore strewn hallways and faces streaked with tears as people died, desperate and terrified.

An iron grip closed on his arm. He was being pulled, the crowd parting for him. Allison guided him to a far corner of the room. She put a warm hand on the back of his neck and pulled him against her. "You're okay. You're okay. Calm down. You're okay." She repeated the mantra, holding him close, and her secure grip and soothing words began to smother the rage that burned in him.

Jeremiah took a shaky breath. "I'm sorry, I don't know what happened. He threatened us. I'm sorry." He returned her embrace, fighting a sob that had appeared in his chest.

"It's okay. It's called bloodlust. It happens to adventurers and warriors sometimes—anger that comes out of nowhere and you can't control it." It wasn't a question, but he still nodded against her.

Bruno appeared at their side. "That was awesome. I want your autograph. Delilah's publicly raking the guy across the coals; the feeling in the room turned against him hard. Apparently, threatening the necromancer is considered poor taste. Or just stupid."

"Is there going to be a problem?" asked Allison. "Delilah okay?" Jeremiah found comfort in her voice vibrating through his body when she spoke.

"I think she's having her debut moment right now siphoning clout off this guy. But I'm going to make tonight worse for him, just for fun. You okay, Jay?"

Jeremiah pulled away from Allison. "Yes, I'm okay. I think I'll just hang back for a while, though. Tell Delilah I'm sorry."

"I will. Two gold says I can break this guy's ankle by the end of the night and make it look like an accident." Bruno left.

"If you need to go home, we can. There's no shame in it." Allison kept a comforting hand on his neck.

"No, I'm fine. Just going to avoid that guy. I saw someone with a plate of shrimp, and I need to find out where he got it."

"You have a problem with food, but okay. Be safe." She gave him another squeeze and returned to the crowd.

Nobody else bothered Jeremiah. In fact, the other guests turned away when he looked in their direction and stepped out of his path. He was all right with that. Delilah found him again after some time, her cheeks gently flushed from wine.

"We've been summoned to an audience with Colonel Valen and a few other military leaders. This is what we were waiting for. Are you good to do this now?"

"Let's do it. I'm sorry about—"

"Hush. That man is a creep and he got humiliated. Don't expect any more trouble from him."

Allison and Bruno were waiting at the back of the ballroom. A servant let them into a narrow hallway. The door closed, and the party behind them faded to a murmur. Jeremiah heard a distant crash followed by a cry of pain. Bruno nudged him with an elbow.

CHAPTER TWENTY-NINE

Your Mission

Their footfalls echoed in the quiet as they made their way down the hall. Another servant hurried them through another series of passages, Delilah hiking her dress to keep up.

They arrived at a small room. The servant announced their arrival and disappeared. The room was as somber as the party had been lively. The only sounds were pops from the roaring fireplace that spanned most of the wall. A man and a dwarf gazed into the flames, speaking inaudibly. Colonel Valen leaned over a map with three other men. They glanced up at the newcomers.

"Captain Allday, Mr. Thorn," Colonel Valen said. "Thank you for joining us. Please make yourselves comfortable. The rest of you can wait outside, as this meeting will contain privileged information."

"I'll vouch for them," Allison said. "Their presence is nonnegotiable." She stood in the doorway, prepared to leave if necessary.

The men at the table shared looks of impatience, but didn't protest when Colonel Valen said, "Fine. Counselor Fortune and Mr. . . . I don't believe we've met. Please understand this meeting will include information that would prove valuable to our enemies. I ask for your utmost discretion."

"How have things fared since our last meeting, Colonel?" asked Allison.

"Terribly." Colonel Valen invited them to approach the map. The map was nearly as detailed as the one of Tarnothy Desert, but showed a much larger area of Nosirin and the surrounding area. Jeremiah recognized some of the iconography, illustrating trails, roads, and elevations.

"Nosirin overcommitted themselves to burning the barbarians out of the mountains," said Colonel Valen, indicating a cluster of military markers lined up on the map. "We sent troops and mercenaries to support them, but no one was ready for the guerrilla-style combat they encountered. Besides their terrain familiarity, the tribes triggered an avalanche that cost us three divisions. Now Nosirin's forces are depleted, mercs refuse to take the job, and Barad Celegald and Shabad are hesitant to commit forces."

"Didn't you say these are just a small group of savage people?" Jeremiah asked, earning a reproachful look from Colonel Valen.

"I'll remind you, Mr. Thorn, you're here as a potential military asset. Leave the speculation to the professionals."

"I don't think it's speculation that 'depleted' is shorthand for 'dead,'" Jeremiah said. "I'm willing to bet you've got more corpses than soldiers, and you need me to fix that."

Colonel Valen gave Jeremiah a hard stare, but Allison spoke before he could respond. "Tribal attacks from the mountains aren't new. What's different this time?"

"You've encountered what's different," said Colonel Valen. "Your report on the regenerating minotaur mirrors what we've heard from the front: warriors healing from lethal wounds, unbreakable morale, and suicidal attacks that prove effective. Intelligence has seen them training against each other in mock battles with no restraint and no casualties."

"What, the whole army?" asked Allison. "They can't *all* be mages, can they?" Allison asked. More than one officer shivered at the thought.

A half elf next to Colonel Valen answered, "We don't think so. The warriors themselves aren't casting spells, but we've observed what we believe to be a network of lieutenants that seem to know some form of magic. They cast spells on the warriors on a regular basis."

"Narooka had healing magic stored inside of him. Are these lieutenants imbuing the warriors with healing?" Jeremiah asked.

"Something like that," said the half elf. "The lieutenants appear to be tribal leaders who have sworn to an alliance. But we've also caught glimpses of a single leader who we suspect is the actual provider of magic. The lieutenants seem to need to return to this leader regularly in order to continue to distribute healing."

"So only the leader is a mage, and a healer at that?" Allison stared at the map, deep in thought.

"We surmise as much," said Colonel Valen, "though we've spoken with a number of healers and none of them are aware of a way to impart magic to followers like this. Especially at this magnitude. She's an exceptionally powerful mage to say the least."

Delilah whistled. "A woman leading a bunch of barbaric tribes? That is rare, isn't it? Is she a giantess or something? How is she keeping them in line?"

Colonel Valen bristled. "Again, I would ask that nonmilitary personnel please remain silent unless questioned directly. She's providing them with near immortality, and we believe she's the sole source of this power. She has also demonstrated considerable leadership and tactical skills, as evidenced by the unity of the barbarian tribes and the way they defeated Nosirin's forces."

The dwarf handed around packets of paper. "This is what we have on the leader."

"An elf?" Bruno laughed. "An elf in charge of a bunch of barbarians?" Colonel Valen ignored him.

Jeremiah skimmed the precious little information contained in the pages. Some of it was repeated, seemingly to pad out the report. He flipped to the last page and came to an artist's rendering of a familiar copper-haired elven woman. Recognition hit him like a slap in the face. "Oh shit, Vivica?"

The room stared at him. Allison's head dropped into her hands. She sighed all the air from her lungs. "Jay, are you about to tell us that you know her?"

"I do! I mean, I did. I saw her do it herself, or something similar. She escaped her cell and—"

Delilah suddenly spoke over him. "My client has nothing more to say on this matter!"

"Shut the hell up, Counselor!" Valen shouted. He was gripping the edge of the table so hard the wood creaked. "Thorn, you're going to tell us everything, and if I think for even a moment you're holding out on us, I'll behead you on this very table."

Jeremiah recounted his experience in prison, being extra careful not to leave anything out. They winced when he described how Vivica squeezed herself between the bars of the cell. The room was quiet for a long time after he finished.

Colonel Valen broke the silence. "I want all information regarding her arrest and imprisonment. I want her jailers interrogated. I want to know *why* she was in this city!" One of the men hurried from the room.

Jeremiah gazed at the portrait. Even through ink and charcoal, he could feel the rage smoldering within her.

The door to the room swung open and a liveried footman entered with a stomp of his black heeled boot. "Presenting His Royal Majesty, King Hector of Dramir!"

There was a mad scramble. The woman on paper was forgotten. Jeremiah spun, unsure of where he should go or what he should do, then Delilah yanked him down to a knee.

The wooden planks of the floor groaned. His head bowed, Jeremiah watched them bend under their load. He flinched as a pair of boots as long as his forearm stepped in front of him, one after the other. He resisted the urge to look up. Instead, he glanced to his left and right to see everyone arrayed in a line, all having taken a knee. He was surprised to see even Bruno in the same position.

"You may look upon the royal person!" the footman shouted.

"Calm down, Sylvester." The voice rumbled like an earthquake. Jeremiah had never heard a king speak before, but the casual authority of the voice perfectly fit his idea of royalty.

He looked up and discovered that Allison had not been exaggerating. King Hector was massive! Jeremiah guessed that even standing he'd only come up to the man's elbows. The king's arms and shoulders were gigantic muscled slabs on top of a heavy gut that hung in front of him. His golden crown gave him the appearance of being even taller, and thick robes, billowed pants, and a bejeweled war-maul hanging from his belt helped him seem to take up every spare inch of space in the room. A thick black beard hid his mouth, and his keen eyes swept the room . . . but then fixed on a particular person. "Allison?"

Allison's eyes flicked to the king's face and away again before answering. "Yes, Your Highness. Captain Allison Allday."

The king's face broke into a jovial smile. "Allison! It's me, Hector. From the halfling peacekeeping campaign. I was the one with the crown?"

Jeremiah saw Allison struggle to maintain a straight face. "Oh, you're *that* King Hector? Now I remember!"

Hector grinned and Allison stopped trying to look away. Bruno leaned out from the line and locked eyes with Jeremiah. *Oh my gods!* he mouthed. Jeremiah felt his own lips trying to screw up into a smile, but it was nailed down when he turned and saw Delilah, glaring at Allison so fiercely he was sure she was trying to commit murder with her thoughts.

Colonel Valen cleared his throat. "Your Highness? To what do we owe the pleasure?"

"Hm? Ah yes. I wanted to check on this meeting. Has everyone been briefed?"

"Yes, Your Highness."

"Very good. Now, which one of you is Jeremiah Thorn?"

Jeremiah's breath hitched. "I am, my highness." The footman who accompanied the king tutted. "I mean, your liege." Faster, furious tutting.

"Calm down, boy, I get it," said the king. "You can stand, by the way. You're all small enough as it is."

Everyone rose to their feet. Jeremiah still had to crane his neck to see the king's face.

"Your name has been in my ear more times then I care to count lately." The king was inspecting him like a particularly interesting specimen. "Younger than I thought you'd be, less scary-looking as well. But I'm sure you get that quite a bit."

"Yes, sir." Jeremiah wasn't sure what to say. He'd never met someone so effortlessly imposing that wasn't trying to kill him.

He is *trying to kill you. It's the king that will sign your death warrant,* said a voice in his head that sounded equal parts Bruno and Vivica.

"Your kingdom needs you, Jeremiah. I intend to send you north as soon as possible. Serve us well, and I'll personally see to it that you're taken care of. Can we count on you?"

"Yes, sir," said Jeremiah automatically. A mixed feeling of relief and dread settled in his chest. He finally had a promise to be free from his deadly burden, but it was as a weapon for the people who had hung the weight on him in the first place.

"Good. I look forward to the results. Colonel Valen, High Marshall Esteed, I hope I don't need to stress that you are not to underestimate this threat. Arrogance has cost many soldiers their lives, and our enemy has enough allies already without recruiting our own egos."

"Yes, my liege," said Colonel Valen and the dwarf together.

"Good." The threat rumbled in the king's words. "Now then, Captain Allday. I would like to speak with you about the mission and get your perspective on . . . on a number of issues. Will you join me in the ballroom?" The floor beneath the king protested as he shifted from one foot to the other.

"Of course, Your Highness," Allison said. Jeremiah thought he saw a smile threatening to break her solemn expression. Bruno's grin, on the other hand, was ear to ear.

"You heard the king, Mr. Thorn," said Colonel Valen. "We have a fresh batch of troops departing in a week's time. We'll add you to the caravan."

Jeremiah's stomach dropped as he realized what he'd agreed to. His mouth felt dry. "I request that the rest of my party be included. If they want to come, of course." He hoped they would. There was no way he could do this without them.

"I'll give you Captain Allday. You'll have no need for a counselor and a . . . friend on this trip." Colonel Valen returned to studying the map.

Jeremiah raised an eyebrow. "Colonel Valen, with all due respect, I'd be happy to let the bodies continue to pile up until you have no choice. Two extra people for the hundreds of soldiers I can make for you—that seems fair, doesn't it? Or would you like me to get the king's permission? I'm sure Allison can—"

Colonel Valen slammed his fist into the map. "This is not a negotiation, necromancer!"

"You are correct," Jeremiah said.

Colonel Valen closed his eyes and took a deep breath, letting it out slowly. "Fine. Get out."

Delilah and Bruno followed Jeremiah out into the hallway. As soon as the door swung shut, Bruno clapped him on the back. "Now that's how you throw your big—"

"Dance with me! Now!" Delilah grabbed Jeremiah's arm and yanked him down the hall back toward the party. Jeremiah hadn't realized a person could dance angrily, but he soon learned as Delilah whirled him in tight circles, glaring daggers at Allison and King Hector dancing and chatting on the floor.

CHAPTER THIRTY

Betrayal?

Several hours later, a nobleman announced his retirement for the evening, apparently signaling the festivities to begin winding down. Allison had spent the evening in the company of the king, and Delilah's mood had smoldered all night.

"I'll be in the carriage," she told Jeremiah and Bruno, who were entertaining a pair of women with light tales of adventure and humorous exploits. Jeremiah knew they were only interested in him because of his semi-celebrity status, but their attention was still enjoyable, especially when Bruno set him up to deliver a punch line to genuine laughter. Despite his encounter with Gordus Wren, learning of the impending military mission, and Delilah's temper, he'd had a surprisingly good time rubbing elbows with the social elite of Dramir.

"My dear ladies," said Bruno with an elaborate bow. "I'm afraid I must retire to the shadows of the evening once again. Though the hour is late, the night is still young, and I must attend to matters that might offend your delicate sensibilities." He gave them a wink. They returned curtsies and coquettish smiles.

"Since when is going home a matter that needs attending?" Jeremiah asked as they made their way toward the palace entrance.

"It's more fun to say than 'I'm cranky because it's past my bedtime.' More fun for them to hear, too."

They heard a familiar voice behind them and squeezed aside to allow Allison and King Hector to occupy almost all the space the hallway had to offer. The king was roaring with laughter that rattled Jeremiah's teeth.

"The ballista fires and the beehive just explodes on the rail!" said Allison. "Everyone starts running and screaming, and wouldn't you know, it's the general himself they swarm around. He had to run all the way back to camp and jump in the lake before they'd leave him alone!" It took a moment for her to notice Jeremiah and Bruno standing beside her. "Oh! Hey, guys."

King Hector nodded toward them. "Gentlemen, I hope you enjoyed the festivities. I was unaware you were so close with Alli—Captain Allday."

To Jeremiah's relief, no one tutted when they didn't kneel before their king.

"Oh yes, Your Highness," said Bruno, grinning like the cat that caught the canary. "We'll be talking about this night for *quite* a while."

"I'm sure you will! Now I must be away. Captain Allday, it was a delight to see you again. I sincerely hope it won't be as long next time?"

"Thank you, Your Highness" was all she said, her face reddening before the mischievous smiles of her friends. They walked toward their carriage, which was waiting at the end of the red carpet. Delilah's profile was visible in the window, motionless and staring straight ahead.

Allison paused at the step into the carriage and looked back at Jeremiah and Bruno.

"After you, Captain Allday," said Jeremiah.

Allison took a deep breath and entered the carriage. As Jeremiah started to follow, Delilah's hand shot out and slammed the door closed. "Walk," came her voice, brimming with fury.

Bruno threw an arm around Jeremiah's shoulders as the carriage pulled away. "Wonderful night for a stroll!"

A few miles' walk brought them home. Bruno's explanation of the pros and cons of rondel daggers died on his lips at the muffled shouting emanating from the house.

"We're small," said Jeremiah. "We're invisible. We're unimportant. We go straight to bed."

"Don't make eye contact, especially with Delilah," Bruno said. They made their way to the front door like men approaching the gallows.

"You don't need to apologize to me!" Delilah was shouting.

Jeremiah pushed open the door.

"You need to apologize to *him!*" She thrust a finger toward Jeremiah, frozen at the threshold, as if she had revealed him herself.

Bruno slipped past Jeremiah and crossed the kitchen unnoticed. He moved like a man late for a meeting that didn't concern you.

"Don't pretend to be mad for some noble reason," Allison shot back. "This isn't about Jay at all. This is about *you* feeling left out, *you* missing out on some big career connection!"

"How . . . how *dare* you!" Delilah trembled with anger. She looked on the verge of leaping across the sofa that separated her and Allison in an ill-advised attack. "This is about you having the power to save Jay's life, to end this whole debacle before it even started, and you couldn't even be bothered to try!"

"Fine!" Allison turned to Jeremiah, who had made it to the bottom of the stairs. "Jay, I'm sorry I didn't think to ask *the king himself*, whom I had met once, *years ago*, to step in and pardon a guy I barely knew. I'm sorry I didn't assume he'd be on speaking terms with me, instead of the far more likely scenario that he'd have no idea who I was!"

"Aha!" Delilah's eyes flashed triumphantly. "You didn't ask because you were afraid of being disappointed! You didn't want to put yourself out there and risk proving to yourself that you weren't important enough to remember. Ergo, you didn't ask for selfish reasons! You didn't tell me for selfish reasons! You! Were being! Selfish!"

"That! Makes! No! Sense!" Allison shouted back. "With the information I had at the time, how would it even occur to me to try and fight through all of red tape it takes to get a meeting with the fucking *king*?"

Against his better judgment, Jeremiah spoke up. "Allison, it's all right. Things are turning out okay. I'm glad King Hector remembered you."

"Thank you, Jay. I'm grateful you understand and accept my apology. Tell me, do you give lessons? Cause I've got a friend who could use some!"

Jeremiah cringed as Delilah turned bright red and seethed at him. "You're taking her side? You do realize it's turning out 'okay' because I busted my ass moving heaven and earth to make it okay? You could be dead right now, could have been dead months ago! *I* pulled out all the stops to keep you alive, *I've* been doing everything possible to get you through this sentence, and what has she been doing besides tagging along for the ride? She said *in court* that you were a good man for risking your lives to save others, and she couldn't even risk her own ego! Tell me, Allison, what kind of person does that make *you*?"

Allison set her jaw. "Is that it? Hmm? You think I'm a bad person now?"

The question hung in the air as the women glared at each other. Jeremiah was too afraid to move from his spot on the bottom stair. He watched a hundred retorts run through Delilah's mind. Then, to his surprise, she broke off her stare. Delilah rubbed her fingers behind her ears as she struggled to formulate a response; it was the first time Jeremiah had ever seen her at a loss for words. Finally, she said, "No, I don't think that. Of course I don't think that."

Allison shoulders dropped with genuine relief. "I'm glad."

The heat seeped from the room. Jeremiah remained perfectly still, as though any motion might escalate the situation again.

Delilah sighed. "It's just . . . It feels like such an important thing, you had to be keeping it a secret on purpose."

"I know it seems that way, but I'm honestly just as surprised as you," Allison said. "I never thought he'd remember who I was. Apparently, I was . . . wrong. I made a mistake. You know I'd never hold out intentionally, right?"

"Yeah, I know." Delilah collapsed onto the sofa, rumpling her elegant dress.

Allison perched on the edge of the cushion at the other end of the sofa and stared into the empty fireplace. "I'm sorry I didn't tell you. I should have been offering any help I could, even if it was a long shot."

Delilah nodded. "I understand why you didn't think you'd be memorable; you've got the humble soldier thing when it comes to military matters." Delilah raised her gaze, then extended her hand toward Allison, palm upturned and fingers soft. "I'm sorry I blew up on you. And for saying you were selfish."

Allison clasped her hand. "It's okay. I guess it must've been quite a shock."

They stayed quiet for a long moment. Then Delilah asked with a half smile, "Any other royal hookups we should know about?"

"What? No! We didn't—it was just a—"

"No, it wasn't!" Bruno yelled from his room.

"He doesn't even—"

"Clearly he does," Jeremiah said.

"Ugh!" Allison's face flushed as she fled to her room.

CHAPTER THIRTY-ONE

To Raise an Army

Dramir's troops traveled to Nosirin in a long and winding train of infantry and wagons. Jeremiah, Delilah, and Bruno rolled through the fields and forests in their comfortable carriage. Allison rode among the soldiers on horseback, having taken up her former role as captain for the mission. The troops were young and carried their spears awkwardly.

Allison guided her horse alongside the party's carriage. "Almost all fresh recruits, from what I've been able to tell. I don't know what Valen's expecting from you, Jay, but Dramir didn't exactly send a seasoned force to help deal with this problem."

Jeremiah swallowed as Allison rode away. Delilah patted his knee. "Maybe it's a good thing," she said. "You're here to prove your value, after all. After a mission this high profile, they'll have to release you from your sentence!"

"Yeah," Jeremiah said. *Unless I'm killed first.*

The city of Nosirin appeared on the horizon after the tenth day. It was squat and gray, a utilitarian city where decoration was seen as snobbery and the quality of food was measured in amount. Blending in with the foothills of the mountains, Nosirin was utterly bland after the grandeur of Dramir. Its wall stood just three men high and, despite the ballistae bristling between the crenellations, looked like an afterthought.

Jeremiah expected to feel some sense of homecoming upon passing through the city gates—after all, Nosirin had been the nearest city for most of his life. But all he felt was trepidation, a sense that the noose around his neck was tightening even as he struggled to free himself.

Horns echoed off the mountains, announcing their arrival. The city was quiet as they rolled through cobbled streets, watched only by a few women and children.

"Where is everyone?" Jeremiah asked.

"Mostly dead," Bruno said as casually as if they had all gone to the tavern. "In times of war, bodies are currency to be spent, and Nosirin has been generous. Wait till we get to the wealthier neighborhoods, then you'll see more people."

He was right. As they neared Nosirin's central fortress (in no way could it be called a palace), there were more gentry about, speaking on corners or walking with their families as if the fighting that threatened their very walls were nothing but a distant rumor. It would be handled by others, said their casual manner.

The fortress itself was surrounded by an echo of the four-sided city wall. This inner wall stood ten feet high and was inset with a metal gate in each cardinal direction, just like its larger counterpart. Their carriage followed the officers' wagons through the gate south and into a whirlwind of chaos.

A single Nosirin soldier stood at attention among the background scramble. Colonel Valen jumped out of his carriage. "Cadet! Report!"

The dwarf, dressed in the charcoal gray of Nosirin's soldiers, snapped a salute and shouted back, "Sir! The tribes are making their move!" His breath caught a little. "By gods, they're almost right on top of us. The whole damn army was hidden just out of sight!"

"Attacking? Now?" Delilah spluttered. "But—but—we've been marching for days, we have thousands of men that need rest and, more importantly, to be reorganized!" She sounded indignant, as though some protocol of war had been disregarded.

"Clever bastards," agreed Allison. "We have to hold them at the walls."

"Why didn't they attack us earlier, in the open?" Jeremiah asked, trying to focus on anything besides the fear rising in his chest.

"They would've been stuck between us and Nosirin, and we'd have seen them coming. They're making the best of the hand they've been dealt." She turned her horse back toward the gate.

"Hang on, where are you going?" Jeremiah asked.

"I'm a field commander. I'm going to help command the field. Be safe!"

"Always the soldier with you!" Bruno called.

"Allday, every day!" Allison said with a wink. She reared her horse and rode to rejoin the troops still streaming into the city.

Jeremiah stared after her, suddenly certain he'd never see her again. Colonel Valen's rough voice brought him back to the moment. "Mr. Thorn! Please focus. You and your people need to come with me."

They hurried down austere corridors, dodging as men and women rushed past from either direction, shouting orders and information like hawkers at the market and every deal was critical. Twice Jeremiah was nearly taken off his feet by a body in armor, appearing and disappearing in the blink of an eye.

Colonel Valen led them to the next floor, where the chaos ebbed and the rank insignias of those passing grew more complex. They entered a war room, a high-ceilinged circular chamber bustling with constant yet precise activity, like well-maintained clockwork. The main wheel at its center was an exacting diorama of the city of Nosirin. Every alley and street was meticulously catalogued, the four gates of the city walls crafted with tiny mobile portcullises and drawbridges. A dwarf wearing steel armor and a thin crown of silver moved tiny figurines around the model, representing archers, cavalry, and more. With each movement, a messenger sprinted from the room to relay the information. As Jeremiah watched, a Nosirin cadet deposited a large group of figures in Dramir's colors beside the model city's wall. The dwarf gripped them by the handful and dropped them unceremoniously at the north gate.

"King Growlack," said Colonel Valen, raising his voice over the din of activity. "I have brought the necromancer. With your permission, he will begin at once."

King Growlack glanced at Jeremiah. His eyes were flinty chips, sharp and almost colorless. His neatly combed beard was grayed and frayed at the ends like a worn broom. King Growlack waved to a servant, who produced a box containing more figurines—tiny skeletons on circular stands. The king seized a fistful and began placing them across the tops of the city wall. Half wound up on the north wall, most of the rest were divided between the west and east. A scant few stood to the south.

"Your Majesty," Jeremiah said, "if this battle is really as imminent as it seems to be, I need to begin resurrections as quickly as possible. It will take time to raise as many as we need."

The king only stared at his map and waved a dismissive hand as he repositioned some of the figurines. With each adjustment, a messenger ran from the room.

"This way, Mr. Thorn." Colonel Valen waved for him to follow, but Delilah lingered.

"Your Majesty," she said to King Growlack with a bow, "my name is Lady Fortune. I am a master alchemist and physician. I would be honored to serve in defense of your kingdom."

The king regarded her coldly. "Can you fight?" His voice grated like gravel.

"Yes, sir."

The king glanced at a gnome standing so still at the king's side that Jeremiah hadn't noticed him. Withered and ancient, the gnome took a peg of wood and small knife and began to carve. In just a few turns of the blade he produced a small figurine approximating Delilah. The king set the figure among a group of medics near the south gate's corridor into the city.

"Right this way, my lady!" said a messenger.

"Delilah, what are you doing?" Bruno asked.

"The best I can. Keep Jay safe."

Jeremiah felt another flash of fear as Delilah disappeared. He swallowed and followed Bruno and Colonel Valen into the hall.

Colonel Valen led them through less traveled corridors to a narrow spiral staircase. They hurried downward, the air growing chilly as torches replaced sunlight. Soon the hubbub of the fortress faded, replaced only by their footsteps echoing on stone.

"They're attacking sooner then we'd expected," said Colonel Valen as they descended. "Our scouts had them farther in the mountains, but apparently, they've covered ground much faster than we thought possible. Inconvenient, but it doesn't change much. We've got a hardened defensive position."

"How weird that they'd just throw themselves against a wall with no reason or plan," Bruno said.

"Savage tribes have a history of misunderstanding the objectives of siege warfare," Colonel Valen said, either not hearing Bruno's sarcasm or choosing to ignore it.

Jeremiah and Bruno exchanged a look. Clearly King Hector's warning had faded from Colonel Valen's concerns.

The staircase delivered them to a long hallway ending in a set of splintering double doors. Jeremiah recalled the tunnels they had explored in the goblin Warren. He thought he already knew what was behind those doors.

Colonel Valen turned to Jeremiah with a proud smile. "I think you'll be most impressed with our preparations." He pushed open the doors.

The smell hit them all at once. Decay.

Bruno recoiled and Colonel Valen covered his mouth with a sleeve, but the scent was nostalgic to Jeremiah. The space was enormous, rivaling the footprint of the entire fortress, and was filled with bodies stacked in rows like cordwood. Hundreds, maybe thousands of bodies. There were dusty skeletons exhumed from ancient graves, delicate husks of the elderly, young soldiers whose uniforms were still sticky with blood. Jeremiah saw men and women of all ages and races in varying states of decay. He doubted there was an interred body anywhere else in the city.

"You . . . certainly have quite the collection," Bruno said as they walked one of the rows. "Can't help but notice a few rope burns." He tapped Jeremiah's shoulder and pointed out a body wearing a collar of bruised skin like black lace. The body's tongue protruded, also swollen and black.

Colonel Valen's face remained neutral. "Gentlemen, Nosirin is not a city that suffers criminals lightly. When they heard a necromancer needed bodies to defend the city, King Growlack made it his business to obtain as many as possible. The idea that men could serve the city in death better than they had in life appealed to him so much his aides say he was damn near delighted."

"You're telling me he killed his own people to make more bodies for me to raise?" Jeremiah wanted to feel horrified, but after seeing King Growlack tossing figurines by the fistful, the revelation was not truly surprising.

"I am telling you that very thing. It wasn't long ago that exile into the mountains was the punishment of choice in Nosirin, which is considered a death sentence in its own right."

Bruno rolled his eyes. "I wonder how that will factor into the impending attack."

"We have accounted for the potential for enemy familiarity with Nosirin! They won't get past the walls, so it doesn't matter." He stiffened with this last accusation but didn't quite meet Jeremiah's gaze. "Now, in case you missed the happenings upstairs, we're in a hurry. Mr. Thorn, do you need anything else?"

"Just time."

"There is little to be spared. At the far end of this chamber is a flight of stairs that leads to the main boulevard of the city. Weapons have been placed alongside the door for the undead to use. There are men waiting to direct them. That will work, yes?"

"If the men just prod and push them along, yes."

"Good. Return upstairs when you've finished."

Colonel Valen left. Jeremiah began casting while Bruno paced around the gruesome display. "Think you'll be able to animate all of these?" Bruno asked, looking into the face of an old woman, her head sticking out between a larger half orc and a bloated gnome.

"There's way more than I can raise all at once, but with enough time I can rest and raise more. As for keeping track of them all . . ." He looked out over the rows of bodies and felt his excitement building. "I think I've got this."

Jeremiah raised corpse after corpse. Seeing the soldiers marching in formation from Dramir had inspired him. He grouped the skeletons and zombies separately and maintained four distinct areas of his mind to represent the four city walls. The south wall would be mostly skeletons, as they might need to redeploy quickly as reinforcements. The north wall was mostly zombies, and the east and west walls would be evenly split.

He finished the first hundred bodies in the time it took Bruno to patrol the room twice. He sighed in frustration, already feeling a bit crowded. He had stacked the bubbles four deep, his previous limit.

"If I can fit just one more . . ." mumbled Jeremiah. No sooner had he thought it then a fifth bubble snapped inside a stack. It was easy. It was very easy. "Whoa," Jeremiah breathed. A sixth, a seventh, an eighth. The bubble resisted now; try as he might Jeremiah couldn't force any more into the stack. He rubbed the bridge of his nose and pulled Gus from his pocket. "Now's not the time for 'good enough,' is it, buddy?" Gus let out a low croak and protruded his spines.

With a monumental effort, Jeremiah added a ninth bubble to the stack. Then, elated and inspired, he added a tenth. "Good job, buddy," he said to Gus. There was no more room for effort—the bubbles could not be budged—but Jeremiah's pride in his improvement swelled.

The newly animate forms stood in three-by-three squares, with a tenth "leader" at the front. Jeremiah paused and considered the number of bodies remaining.

"More than you thought?" Bruno asked.

"Yes, but . . . but it's okay." It was true. It was as though the space in his mind had expanded since the bandit camp. He wondered how many he'd be able to command now. Then he thought of Flusoh's endless field of wheat and realized that, although he was still orders of magnitude away from that display, he was closer today than he had ever been.

He ordered the first group to arm themselves and sent them out in formation. They pulled from the nearly endless supply of spears that had been haphazardly stacked like cheap firewood.

March.

They trudged into the dark corridor, and Jeremiah set about creating more.

Jeremiah was finishing up the two hundredth undead and he felt . . . fine. His attention was wandering a bit between castings, but nothing like back in Dunsimmons's stable. He was eager to test his limits.

Three hundred undead. Bruno was watching him with some concern.

Four hundred. Jeremiah's focus was finally wavering.

Five hundred. His mind was starting to feel crowded.

After six hundred undead, he sat cross-legged on the floor and held his head in his hands. He was nearing the limits of his capacity and endurance. But he had created more undead than he had ever dreamed of raising himself.

"You, uh, seem to have improved a bit," said Bruno, his eyebrow raised. About half of the bodies in the massive room had been depleted.

"Yeah. Made a bunch. I can feel them walking. First ones are where they need to be. I can feel the wind on them; they're up high. On the walls, I think. Others are still walking. No trouble, though. People know they're coming."

Bruno helped him to his feet. "Well, I think you've done more than enough. Let's get you upstairs and let those kindly gentlemen know you're done."

CHAPTER THIRTY-TWO

Siege Warfare

Jeremiah was absolutely lost in his spent state, but Bruno guided him back through the fortress proper. The pace upstairs had increased. Orders reverberated even louder than before, and messengers scrambled to and fro.

Colonel Valen found them before they reached the war room, strutting and smiling broadly. "You fielded a battalion on your own! Our expectations may have sold you short. Come this way. We're heading to an observation tower."

"What's a battalion?" Jeremiah asked. He knew Valen had said something after that, but he couldn't quite remember what. Colonel Valen furrowed his brow with concern.

"He gets a little flaky after a lot of casting," Bruno explained, patting Jeremiah on the head. "The worst of it will fade soon, but don't expect any cognitive miracles for a while."

They followed Colonel Valen outside where a wagon waited. A group of Nosirin soldiers rode with them, just as young-faced and nervous as Dramir's infantry.

"Did you see those monsters coming out of the sewer?" a soldier asked in a low voice as the wagon set off.

Others nodded. "Yeah! Zombies and skeletons!"

"Sergeant Fasso said we were lent a necromancer from Dramir."

"Thank the gods for that. We got shit from Barad Celegald."

"They're holding back in case they get attacked next."

Jeremiah's heart quickened with elation at his creations being regarded not with disgust and terror, but as saviors. Bruno gave him a nudge and pointed out Allison in the distance. She was still on horseback and riding alongside a squad of spearmen, spurring them faster and shouting words of encouragement. Jeremiah missed the sense of security when she was by his side, but he had his own troops to command.

The wagon rolled through a city steeped in dread. Soldiers stood atop the walls, their expressions ranging from grim stoicism to abject fear. When they arrived at the north observation tower, the infantry sprinted to their assignments. Colonel Valen led Jeremiah and Bruno up the tower, twice as tall as the wall itself and roofed with a cone of metal plates. A collection of spyglasses sat at the ready, affixed to pivoting brass stands.

They ascended to the very top through a winding narrow staircase. Several heavily armored soldiers snapped to attention as they entered. "Gentlemen!" Colonel Valen said. "My name is Colonel Valen. I will be the commanding officer of this tower, designated Tower One. Tower Two is our neighbor commanded by Colonel Gwiddop." Valen pointed to an identical tower built into the northern gatehouse. "This man here"—he pointed to Jeremiah—"is the VIP you were informed of. You are to protect him at all costs. He's the necromancer responsible for the undead squads you see on the walls."

The men saluted, which Jeremiah did his best to return. Jeremiah felt something was wrong, but couldn't put his finger on what. "Why . . . Wait, why am I up here?" he mumbled. Wasn't he going to watch the battle from King Growlack's table? Hang on, what was he thinking about? He couldn't remember, and the concern fluttered away.

Bruno was already peering through one of the spyglasses pointing toward the foothills. He let out a low whistle and beckoned Jeremiah to look.

Jeremiah peered into the eyepiece. Out from the rocky foothills snaked a long black serpent: a dark column of foot soldiers marching toward Nosirin. Among them lumbered dozens of massive gray-skinned giants. They were shaggy and lanky, and each carried what appeared to be a pine tree stripped of bark and branches.

"Wow, I've never seen a giant!" Jeremiah said. "They're really tall." Bruno snorted a laugh behind him.

"Giants are a known factor." Valen waved a hand dismissively. "They plague Nosirin frequently; that's what the ballistae are for. They're big, but they're dumb as rocks."

There was a long, low horn blast from the mountains. The long serpent split down the middle, opening up like a mouth to engulf the city. Orders were shouted, and the soldiers on the walls began to scramble, redistributing their concentration from the north gate. Jeremiah wondered if he should move his undead as well. The fog over his thoughts was dense and stagnant.

The serpent had become a ring, surrounding Nosirin. The attacking army didn't look nearly as threatening, dispersed as it was.

"Spreading themselves too thin. No concentration strong enough to take the wall," said Colonel Valen, furrowing his brow.

"You don't sound convinced," said Bruno.

"It's just . . . strange." Colonel Valen swept his spyglass across the horizon.

A cold silence settled over the city. Soldiers stood frozen in combat readiness. After the stream of shouted orders and military scramble since their arrival, the stillness chilled Jeremiah. He swept his spyglass across the line of barbarians outside the north wall.

"She's out there somewhere, isn't she?" Jeremiah asked.

"Assuming she's not hiding in the mountains, which I doubt she would," Colonel Valen said.

Jeremiah inspected the battle line. An array of races in ragged leathers stood at the ready. Despite their light armor and the imminence of the attack, Jeremiah saw no fear on their faces, no nervous shuffling. They were hardened veterans, one and all.

Another blast of the horn echoed off the mountains, and the noose around Nosirin began to tighten.

"They'll be in range of the ballistae soon enough," said Valen. "Then we'll see ladders and grapples to scale the wall while their siege equipment tries to punch a hole."

"What siege equipment?" Jeremiah asked. He heard the rapid squeak of Colonel Valen's spyglass pivoting.

"Sir!" One of the guards, a halfling, peered through his own spyglass, bracing his feet against the pole that supported the brass instrument.

"Yes?" Colonel Valen said.

"Look at the giants. Do you see the canvas attached to the trees they're carrying?"

Colonel Valen's spyglass squeaked. "I see it. What about it?"

"Looks like a sling-staff, sir. Halfling kids use them to hunt. Stone-throwers."

"Ah! There's the siege," Colonel Valen said with relief.

"Don't see no stones, chief," Bruno said. The guards shifted on their feet. Some drew weapons. Bruno checked his weapons and tightened his leather armor.

A pit formed in Jeremiah's stomach, shifting some of the fog. A half-formed thought drifted across his mind. *We're not safe here.*

"In range!" called a voice from Tower Two. All the ballistae on the north wall swiveled to life at once.

"Loose!" ordered the voice.

The *thrum* from so many ballistae shooting at once vibrated in Jeremiah's chest. Hundreds of arcing bolts sailed into the distance. The barbarian line sprang to life, coalescing around the nearest giant, who raised a warding hand to protect the fighters against the incoming fire.

Bolts impacted gnarled giant bodies, shafts driving deep or even punching straight through. The giants staggered, then strode toward the wall as their smaller comrades followed on their heels. Jeremiah watched them yank the bolts free from their bodies and cast them aside, the wounds rapidly closing.

"Oh wow, they can heal. Who could have foreseen," Bruno said.

"Instead of making insolent comments, Mr. . . . I actually don't remember your name," said Colonel Valen, "I ask you to note the poison barrels."

Jeremiah turned to see a Nosirin soldier dunk a ballista bolt into a barrel of noxious purple ooze before loading it. "Will that work?" he asked.

"The healing magic, while strong, can be overtaxed. It's our belief that concentrated poison, in addition to the wounds themselves, will be too much for the healing factor to cope with. Please see the giant at eleven o'clock, for example."

Jeremiah turned his spyglass and saw one of the giants had fallen to his hands and knees, his torso riddled with bolts. Barbarians yanked the bolts out as even more impacted his exposed back. The giant's head hung limp.

But where are the stones? Jeremiah wondered. *Those staves must have a purpose . . .*

They soon learned.

Another giant, mostly untouched by ballista bolts, took a knee. He unknotted the long tarp at the end of his tree. It billowed out onto the ground and a group of barbarians pulled it out flat. Another group of barbarians clustered tightly together in the center of the tarp and waved to the giant. The giant tied off the loose end of the tarp, forming a large canvas bag that dangled down from the tree. He cocked his arm back, took a hopping step forward, and whipped the tree over his head in a wide arc.

"Trebuchet . . ." Colonel Valen murmured.

The canvas bag broke open mid-arc, and the cluster of barbarians sailed through the air and high over the wall. Jeremiah watched them fly past, at roughly the same height as their tower. The barbarians crashed through the roofs of buildings or bounced lifelessly down cobbled streets.

"What the hell are they—" an armored guard began. But he was struck dumb as one of the barbarians whose body had smashed into the street began to move again. His broken, twisted form writhed, one arm bent in an *S* straightened itself, and he climbed to his feet. The man unsheathed a sword and heaved a ceramic canister into a nearby stone building.

The other barbarians from the flight were now joining him, hobbling on broken legs and pushing jags of flesh-piercing bone back into place. The barbarians let out a war cry as tongues of flame began to emerge from the stone building. Then the men scattered, disappearing down alleyways. Smoke soon rose from dozens of spots around the city.

"Enemies in the city! Enemies in the city!" Colonel Valen's face had gone chalk white. He leaned over the parapet to yell at a group of soldiers headed for the wall. "Counter attack! Kill them now!" The soldiers rushed to obey.

Jeremiah raised his gaze in time to see more barbarians flying through the air from all sides of the city. The giants launched groups of five to eight barbarians with every throw, and they kept throwing. Some part of Jeremiah was screaming at him to shake off the fog, but it sounded like a voice from across a great distance.

Bruno ran to the edge of the tower, grabbed the edge of the roof, and swung himself up onto it. They heard the rapid thuds of Bruno's boots overhead, then a hard metallic *twang*. His magically propelled arrow struck a flying half orc, sending blood in a great spiral as the barbarian spun in midair from the impact. The force of the arrow disrupted his fight path, and he landed on the wide walkway of the wall. He struggled to stand but was cut down by soldiers before he could heal. His body lay mangled beyond any magic's ability to save him.

"Bows! Bows! Shoot them down!" Colonel Valen screamed. Their guards began firing wildly at the incoming soldiers. Only one in a dozen shots connected. Some of the ballistae started targeting the flying men, lessening the pressure on the giants, who began flinging faster. Invaders filled the sky like a cloud of flies, and great plumes of smoke began rising across the city.

"Incoming!" Bruno called from above them. A flight of barbarians slammed into Tower One. Jeremiah's world spun as a body crashed into him, the smack of the cold stone floor cutting through the fog in his brain. He gasped as he suddenly grasped the danger of his situation.

Two of the barbarians in their tower had already been set upon by the armored guards and beheaded. The roof rang out in another crash and Bruno shouted in fear and pain. Jeremiah heard metal scraping down the angled roof. He sprang to his feet and rushed to the side of the tower.

"Bruno!" Jeremiah reached out into the empty air. A second later, Bruno fell. He twisted and managed to grasp Jeremiah's wrist as he hurtled past. Jeremiah grunted in pain as his arm was wrenched downward. His shoulder strained to remain in its socket. Another body fell past Bruno, its skull exploding on impact with the stone road below. That one stayed dead.

Colonel Valen grabbed Jeremiah and hauled him and Bruno back into the tower. "Any new orders, fearless leader?" Bruno shouted. Rage supplanted any mirth in his voice.

Colonel Valen was staring over the city, jaw slack and eyes wide. "This can't be happening. Tower Two! Tower Two, we need new orders!"

But no new orders came—the second tower was consumed by battle. They stood atop a tiny boat in a churning sea of chaos.

CHAPTER THIRTY-THREE

The Mistakes of Powerful Men

Sir! The stairs!" shouted a guard. The armored men arrayed themselves in front of the entrance as war whoops and roars of triumph rose from the twisting steps.

"Move!" Jeremiah forced his way between the guards. He brought his will to bear and began bellowing out great breaths of poison gas down the stairway. He recast as fast as he could, his focus fraying rapidly. The victorious cries became coughs and strangled gasps of pain. The first of the attackers reached the door, his face pale, black veins standing out from his skin. Jeremiah was yanked back to safety as the guards struck down the attacker.

To me.

Jeremiah commanded several undead units from the walls, who until now had been standing idle as barbarians flew overhead. They broke rank, drawing fearful looks from the men positioned alongside them, and made their way to the tower.

"We need to get to safety," said Colonel Valen. "If they're in the gatehouse, they'll try to raise the portcullis. Soldiers, we're taking the VIP to the fortress!" The soldiers' acknowledgment was drowned out by three clangs of a bell from the southern wall.

"No . . . no, no, no!" Colonel Valen ran to a spyglass pointing south. Jeremiah jumped to another and swiveled wildly, searching for the cause of distress. He found the two towers that mirrored their own. As he watched, long leather banners adorned with dozens of symbols unfurled from them. The portcullis of the southern gate lurched upward.

Attack!

Jeremiah commanded his undead on the southern wall to the gatehouse. But it wasn't enough. The narrow confines within the gatehouse kept them from bringing their numbers to bear. The portcullis continued to rise. He ordered all undead to move toward the nearest gatehouse and protect it from the invaders.

Reinforce! Protect! Defend!

Jeremiah was yanked away from the spyglass. "C'mon, looky-loo, we're getting out of here!" Bruno said. Jeremiah, Bruno, and Colonel Valen hurried down the stairs, the guards bringing up the rear. They stepped over destroyed bodies, and Jeremiah heard gasps from his comrades. Any corpses that had stayed dead were in no condition to be raised.

The scene at ground level was utter chaos. Fires burned out of control. Nosirin soldiers clustered together, trying to engage small groups of enemies, who simply scattered deeper into the city. One trio of barbarians taunted a loose phalanx of Dramir soldiers. The young soldiers charged, funneling toward their enemy like sand running down an hourglass. Out of formation, they were flanked by another group of enemies and routed.

Bruno yanked arrows from the quivers of fallen soldiers to feed his insatiable magic bow. His shots found their marks with relentless precision, damaging targets enough to overcome their already depleted healing stores. He shot continuously, but his shots merely picked individual insects out of the swarm of attackers descending upon the city.

"Brace!" screamed one of their guards. A group of barbarians charged into the guards' locked shields. Blades and maces rose and fell like windmill arms. One guard was yanked to the ground, his armor protecting him only momentarily before his head was yanked back and his throat split open. The remaining guards kept up their defense with confident, expert blows, delivering wounds that healed more and more slowly, until they didn't heal at all. Then Jeremiah's undead arrived, crashing into the attackers' flank, spears driving deep. The barbarians broke and retreated toward the center of the city. Bruno claimed another two while their backs were turned.

"Move!" Colonel Valen commanded, and the group broke into a run toward the fortress. Jeremiah marveled at how quickly the plan had fallen to pieces. Where were the ordered formations? This wasn't a war, it was a drunken melee, no more disciplined than the White Light's defense of the bandit camp. Only this time it was Jeremiah's side that was falling apart. Soldiers fled through the streets, their objective of "hold the city" devolving to "survive."

Three panicked bell clangs from the west drew a litany of curses from Colonel Valen.

Bodies littered the streets. Cobblestones shone, slick with blood.

A small tight wedge of armored cavalry scattered a horde of barbarians like pins.

A Nosirin soldier stripped off his uniform jacket, kicking open the door of a home. Jeremiah heard him shouting, "Melissa! Melissa, where are you?! We gotta go!"

A barbarian laughed maniacally as he pulled a longspear deeper into his guts, working his way closer to the Dramir soldier holding the other end, paralyzed with fear.

"Fall back to the fortress!" Colonel Valen shouted to any soldiers they saw. Jeremiah sensed his undead engaging the enemy in the gatehouses, a few bubbles popping as they were destroyed, but many were inert, simply waiting their turn to attack.

The enemy presence lessened as they neared the fortress, a core of safety with rapidly crumbling edges. The gates of the fortress wall were sealed now, the guardsmen opening them briefly for soldiers seeking refuge.

Jeremiah's group dashed through the gate, all gasping for breath. The fortress courtyard harbored nearly as much chaos as the city streets, and its interior had become a hive of panic. Messengers dashed this way and that, delivering reports and arguing over updated orders. The wounded wandered in search of aid. Displaced soldiers either rushed to regroup or lurked in corners, trying to go unnoticed.

Colonel Valen led them upstairs to the war room—or rather the cyclone of pandemonium that it had become, whirling around King Growlack and his map. King Growlack's keen eyes darted over the model, his hands snapping out like vipers to pluck pieces off and redistribute them as he took in the frantically shouted updates. Jeremiah could see the skeleton figurines clustered around gatehouses, a growing pile of enemies in the southern thoroughfare, and five giants heaped off to the side.

"Your Majesty!" shouted Colonel Valen over the din. "I've brought the necromancer. The northern tower and gate were under heavy attack, and we couldn't risk losing him." The king didn't reply, but snapped up a black hooded figurine at the north observation tower and deposited it in the center of the map.

"Colonel, what do you want me to do?" asked Jeremiah. "The undead aren't very effective right now, at least at the breached gate." For all his supposed power, he felt helpless to affect the situation.

Colonel Valen motioned for him to wait as he watched the king's hands move. Enemy figures all over the map coalesced into larger and larger groups. One group inside the southern gate began shifting, piece by piece, toward the medical station Delilah had joined. Bruno casually reached across the table and moved Delilah's figure to the fortress. King Growlack replaced her among the medics without looking up. Bruno held up his hands. "Just a suggestion."

More messengers poured in, shouting updates, contradicting each other, struggling to convey the tactical information of so many groups in motion. The king's hands began to falter as he updated the board. Pieces were dropped and needed to be retrieved. Those mistakes created a backlog. Messengers had to repeat themselves as more bodies and noise built up in the room. The temperature climbed. Sweat poured down King Growlack's face. He wiped his forehead on his sleeve and a single soldier slipped from his fingers, bouncing off the table with light wooden plinks and disappearing under the feet of the surrounding crowd. The nearest messengers dropped immediately to look for it. The king held one hand out, waiting, while the other tried to maintain the pace. The figurine remained elusive. King Growlack's empty hand curled into a fist and then slammed into the table, an earthquake that toppled hundreds of tiny men. The room went silent.

Nobody spoke. The messengers remained quiet. The only sound was the labored panting of the king.

"M-my lord?" said a uniformed man by King Growlack's side.

The king answered in a stilted, rasping voice. "Retreat to the fortress. We concentrate our forces here and counterattack. Necromancer?" He searched for Jeremiah in the crowd.

"Huh?" Jeremiah had been nearly hypnotized by the movements on the board, the fog of his mind leaving him susceptible to distraction.

"Cover the retreat. Hit them from behind if they try to pursue."

"Yes, sir."

Come to me. Kill them all.

Jeremiah felt the undead already obeying his command, abandoning their fruitless positions.

The king's hands sprang back to life, pulling allied pieces to the center of the map. "Move." He spoke, and there was a gust of wind as dozens of messengers ran out the door. Colonel Valen pulled Jeremiah to the side while Bruno hovered near the table, his eyes never leaving Delilah's figure.

"Will you need more undead for the counterattack?" asked Valen.

Jeremiah shook his head. "I'll be a zombie myself if I try to raise any more." His undead encountered enemies at every turn. They fought continuously even as they made their way inward. Jeremiah sorted through the avalanche of sensory inputs.

Violence. Attack. Screams. A voice.

A voice? He'd never sensed that before, a singular voice cutting through the onslaught of information.

Bubbles popped as undead were struck down. The cyclone of messengers had resumed, but the king moved carefully now, making only macro adjustments to the board.

Jeremiah's hands went to his ears as a tremendous clang shook the room. It felt like his eyes were going to rattle out of his head. He saw Bruno jump and a few people cover their ears, but no one else seemed surprised.

"What the hell was that?" Jeremiah shouted over the ringing in his head.

"The Great Bell of King Montgustus," said Colonel Valen, looking toward the vaulted ceiling. "It's signaling the retreat for the entire city. They may have tricked us with their wall gambit, but once we've regrouped, we'll march out and crush them against those very walls."

A voice.

"Shit!" Bruno shouted. The enemy line had overtaken Delilah's position. The king picked up the entire assembly of medics and removed them from the board. Bruno made for the door, his face livid. "Stay here!" he ordered Jeremiah, then he was gone.

Jeremiah was suddenly alone. Alone with the king who used people as pieces and a colonel who treated him like a weapon.

A voice!

Louder this time. *How is one voice cutting through all that noise?* Jeremiah thought. He focused, searching for it.

"Stop!" He heard the voice speak a single word. It was faint but somehow familiar. He hadn't known any details could be gleaned from the dull shared senses of the undead. He concentrated, trying to separate the voice from the countless other sensations.

"JAY, STOP! YOU—! FRIENDLIES!"

It was Allison. She was screaming for all she was worth in the face of a particularly damaged zombie. The others in its unit were currently engaged very close by.

"That means . . ." Jeremiah whispered out loud, piecing the situation together like a nightmarish puzzle.

The bell meant retreat. I told them to attack . . . I told them to attack before the bell! The soldiers hadn't begun their retreat!

With dawning horror at his mistake, Jeremiah severed every single undead under his control. The dreadful clarity of his actions filled the void in his mind. Every moment that had passed since his last order, his undead had been attacking indiscriminately, barbarians and unsuspecting allies alike. Jeremiah ran to the map and swept the skeletons off, sending them onto the floor as if it would undo what he had just done. The king paid no mind.

Jeremiah stumbled backward, hands gripping around his skull as nightmarish images flooded his mind. The man in the closet wore the faces of his friends and the soldiers he had traveled with. His heart pounded in his chest. His throat began to close, and his body felt cold as ice. Colonel Valen grabbed him and spun him around.

"What did you just do? What just happened?"

"I made a mistake . . ." Jeremiah sputtered as he tried to explain.

Valen slapped him, numbing his jaw. "Tell me! What did you do?"

Jeremiah haltingly explained. Colonel Valen's shoulders sagged in relief when he explained he had attacked their own people, but the tension returned when he said he had destroyed the undead.

"Mistakes happen, Mr. Thorn. It's war. We all make them, and the mistakes of powerful men are all the greater." Jeremiah got the sense the "mistake" in question was wiping out the undead, according to Colonel Valen. "But I need you to focus. Your mistakes will be even greater if you submit to battle shock."

Jeremiah had never heard of "battle shock," but it made sense. He didn't know for certain he had killed his allies, so he would allow himself to assume the best for now, if only to offer himself a brief respite from knowledge he was sure would break him.

He felt numb as he watched the figurines clatter. The messengers were coming more slowly now; there was less to report as groups entered the relative safety of the fortress grounds. The news that was worth bringing was only dire.

"The west and north gates have fallen."

"The giants are approaching the gates."

"The field hospital has been taken."

Every eye in the room was fixed upon the map. Enemy figurines amassed outside the fortress wall. A figurine of a giant appeared at the fortress gate. A tremor rolled through the stone under Jeremiah's feet. The giant was moved inside the fortress wall. The figures on the map rattled. Across the courtyard. Flecks of stone and mortar rained down from the ceiling. As King Growlack placed the giant beside the fortress itself, the window darkened. The king let out a growl like rocks rolling down a hill.

King Growlack stomped to the large window. He grabbed the ringed handles and threw them open. The glow of the setting sun was blocked by a hulking figure. Jeremiah's attention, however, was commanded instead by Vivica, standing upon a massive, outstretched hand. The city smoldered behind her.

"Good evening, King Growlack. I'm here for your surrender."

CHAPTER THIRTY-FOUR

Negotiations

Vivica wore simple leather plates, no different from any light infantrymen, and a metal gorget around her neck. Her copper hair was pulled back into a ponytail that shimmered in the light breeze.

"Good evening, King Growlack. I'm here for your surrender."

"No," Growlack said. Jeremiah drew closer to the window. Steel sang as guards drew swords and moved to protect their king.

Vivica smiled. "I expected nothing less!" She gestured, and the giant stepped to the side, revealing the northern thoroughfare. Her barbarians lined the streets, jeering at a parade of nearly one hundred captured soldiers trudging toward the fortress. Even from a distance, Allison's gleaming armor stood out at the head of the column. Jeremiah's breath caught in his throat.

The captives were stopped outside the wall. The barbarians forced them to their knees.

"Surrender. For the sake of your men," Vivica said, a dark edge to her voice.

"No."

Vivica raised a hand and paused, her eyes traveling over the king's men assembled in the war room. Her eyes widened when they met Jeremiah's, but she continued without comment. Jeremiah held his breath, waiting for somebody to do something, for someone with authority to save the soldiers.

Vivica threw her hand down. Barbarians swarmed around the kneeling soldiers. Red mist sprayed into the evening air as their throats were summarily cut. Allison slumped in the street along with the others.

"No!" cried Jeremiah. His voice was not alone in the war room, nor the courtyard below. King Growlack did not so much as flinch. His eyes never left Vivica's face.

Vivica held her hand up again. "I can save them if I act quickly. You know I can. All I need is for King Growlack to offer me something. Come on, Growlack, what will you give me to save them? Tell me what your men are worth."

The room was silent. Jeremiah felt numb. He stared at the motionless silver figure below. *This can't be happening. Not to Allison.* He looked to King Growlack, willing him to do something, anything, to save the captives. Save his friend.

King Growlack turned away from the window. He scooped up a handful of figures from the map. His eyes locked with Vivica's, then the king stretched out his hand and emptied it. The figures clung briefly to his palm, then clattered to the floor.

"I expected nothing less," said Vivica softly.

"Wait!" Jeremiah screamed and barreled forward to the window, shoving the dwarf king aside. "Vivica, wait! Please save them, please!"

"Hey, Thorn, how you been?" Vivica smiled at him like an old friend.

"Save them, please! I'll give you anything you want!"

Vivica's calculating eyes twinkled and flicked to something over Jeremiah's shoulder. He heard movement in the room behind him halted by her gaze. "Oh look, someone with a heart," Vivica said. "All right, Thorn, you're twice the man the king is anyway. What do I want from you? Let me think."

Jeremiah was aware of every passing second bringing Allison closer to death. He struggled to contain the scream in his chest as Vivica continued.

"Let's see, what do I want from you? Oh, I know!" She grinned wickedly. "While I appreciated that little assist you gave us with the surprise undead attack, I don't need your talents complicating my plans. What I want from you is your hands. You let me chop them off, and—"

"Deal!" Jeremiah thrust his arms toward her, and Vivica recoiled like he had brandished a weapon.

"I—what?" Vivica's gaze became clouded by doubt. One hand slowly unsheathed a shortsword from behind her back. Its bloodred blade was etched in runes, and Jeremiah sensed the magic emanating from it. The giant lowered Vivica to be face-to-face with Jeremiah. Vivica took Jeremiah's hands with surprising gentleness and held them together at the wrists. She raised a brow. "Pretty stupid of you to do this with no leverage, considering I can take them and still let those people die."

"My friend is down there, the one in silver armor! Please save her! Hurry!" He tried not to think about how much blood Allison had lost already, or how much this was going to hurt.

"You don't even—"

"I trust you. You'll do the right thing! I have to trust you! Hurry, please!"

The blade swung down. A burning wind singed his face, as hot as flame. The heat connected with one wrist, then the other, lancing white hot pain up his arms. Every muscle in Jeremiah's body seized in agony. He rose on his toes and let out a strangled scream. For several horrific moments, everything was pain. Then he felt a hand firmly gripping his forearms. The pain blissfully subsided. He forced his watering eyes open and found Vivica's, soft and pitying.

"You're too good for them, Thorn. They'll use you till there's nothing left. They'd feed every man, woman, and child into the meat grinder to preserve their status quo, their power, their money. You'll see that soon, if you don't already. When you do, come to me. We'll be great together." Vivica straightened up and traced her fingers along his arm. When she reached his hands, the echoes of agony fell silent.

The giant pulled her away. Jeremiah glanced down with surprise to find his hands still attached to his wrists. The back of each hand bore a blistering sear that healed over even as he watched, leaving a circular pattern of glyphs etched in his skin.

Vivica's giant stepped back over the short wall, still holding Vivica aloft. She spoke to the defeated soldiers below, her melodious voice carrying in the silence. "I don't come seeking your lives. I don't come seeking your treasures. I come to free you from those men in high towers that hoard wealth beyond your wildest imaginings. Those that even now are imagining how best to feed you to my army!"

The giant lowered her toward the slain captives. Some still twitched even as a river of blood flowed through the streets.

"Know that I am merciful! Know that I am the key to a life free of disparity! All who stand against me shall fall, but none who value their lives need perish!"

She spoke words that Jeremiah didn't recognize and raised her hands to the sky, and as the sun kissed the horizon, she lit up with a golden glow. A mist of liquid light flowed from her, expanding to a glimmering golden nimbus that enveloped everything beneath her. The bodies of the soldiers stirred and began to move. Tears of elation sprang to Jeremiah's eyes as Allison struggled to her feet. The soldiers looked at each other in confusion, then to the golden figure above that had both doomed and saved them.

The giant gripped the gate in the fortress wall with his free hand, the metal roaring under his grasp. He crumpled the gate as though it were made of paper and tossed it aside. The captive soldiers looked dazed, unsure about this turn of events. Then Allison barked a command, and they streamed into the courtyard.

The flinty eyes of King Growlack sparked in barely suppressed rage. A jab of his finger opened a hidden drawer in the map table, revealing a glass bottle set in purple velvet. He pulled the cork with his teeth, took a swig of clear liquid, then poured the rest over the map table.

"Prepare for counterattack. Evacuate leadership." He smashed the bottle into the wooden city, pointed at it, and spoke a single word. A flash of red came from his outstretched finger, and the miniature Nosirin burst into flames.

"Come on!" Jeremiah dragged Colonel Valen out of the war room.

Colonel Valen yelled at Jeremiah's back as they descended to the courtyard. "Do you have any idea what could happen to you for laying hands on the king!? For bargaining in his stead!? Besides the fact that you, a military asset, willingly subjected yourself to—"

Jeremiah whirled on the colonel. "Shut the hell up, Valen! This battle is over, and you know it. We're going to find Captain Allday, and you're going to order her to evacuate."

"Mr. Thorn! Captain Allday will stay here as part of the counterattack and you will be evacuated. This is not a suggestion! Besides, Captain Allday would never leave her soldiers behind."

"That's why you're going to *order* her to do it!"

Colonel Valen's voice was low and dangerous. "You don't get to make demands, Mr. Thorn."

Jeremiah was sick of being helpless. Being dragged places, being ordered around, being told what was important to him and what wasn't. At this moment, his interest in obeying orders was precisely nil. He looked Colonel Valen hard in the eye. "With all due respect, Colonel"—wisps of poisonous green gas began to seep from Jeremiah's sneer—"I will kill you, the king, and anyone else that thinks they get to decide what I want anymore. I'm willing to bet Vivica would listen to what I have to say. I suggest you listen to me. Consider this your final warning."

Colonel Valen shook his head in disgust. "I should've known you were only a hair's breadth from treason, necromancer."

Jeremiah couldn't care less. "Get Allison out of here and there won't be a problem."

They found Allison in the courtyard preparing to mount up, looking for all the world like she hadn't been murdered moments earlier.

"Captain Allday!" Colonel Valen strode toward her. "You are to report to the war room for evacuation immediately."

"I'm fine," said Allison, adjusting her horse's tack.

"That's an order, Captain. Immediately!"

Allison made no effort to hide her disgust, but Jeremiah's relief was impervious to the scowl she wore as she followed them inside.

The miniature Nosirin was now black and smoldering, a forecast for the city itself. People dashed about piling chests and boxes together.

"Bruno!" Allison said. She and Jeremiah hurried toward a badly wounded Bruno propped up against a wall. Delilah and another medic were trying to stem the blood flowing from his back and chest.

"I found him during the retreat," said Delilah, without looking up from her work.

Bruno wheezed. "So embarrassing . . . Took a javelin . . . right in the back." He cracked a half smile at Delilah, blood smeared across his teeth and lips. "I was coming . . . to save you . . . you know."

"My hero," Delilah said dryly. "He'll be okay for now, but he'll need a potion or a healer soon. What's going on?"

"We're evacuating," said Allison. "First the brass, then the infantry behind us." An assumption that Jeremiah did not intend to correct.

"Ready for evac!" shouted an officer. A final few people rushed into the war room and the doors slammed shut. Jeremiah had a moment to wonder for the first time how they were planning to escape the occupied city, then, with a horrendous screech, the floor lurched downward. The walls of the war room climbed higher around them before giving way to a smooth stone shaft. The last rays of sunlight faded farther upward until the moving room was cast into darkness.

They descended for several minutes, grinding down the bare stone walls. Finally, a doorway appeared, growing from below, and the room came to a shuddering halt. The king led the way, raising a torch as he shoved open the stone door to cast an orange glow along a long stone corridor.

The others grabbed what torches were available along the walls and followed the king into the darkness.

"How far . . . do these tunnels . . . go?" Bruno wheezed as he limped along, supported between Allison and Delilah.

"Nosirin was built on top of an ancient dwarven iron mine," Delilah said. "From what I understand, it goes deeper than anyone has explored. There are still miles of tunnels that have never been cataloged." Allison shivered.

They walked for so long that Jeremiah began to feel claustrophobic. Their entire world had been reduced to the same few feet of solid rock, rediscovered over and over out of the darkness. Jeremiah knew they must have traveled far enough to escape the city limits, but they continued to plod along the endless corridor.

The stone steps were such an abrupt change they startled several people. At the top of the long staircase was a wooden trapdoor, heavy with the dust of centuries. King Growlack hefted a thick iron bar from the trapdoor and tossed it down the steps behind him, his followers sidestepping just in time. Almost as an afterthought, he snatched the silver crown from his head and tossed it back down the stairs before throwing open the trapdoor to reveal the brilliant night sky.

They emerged in the middle of a wood. As he breathed deep with relief, Jeremiah detected the distinct scent of manure. King Growlack soon led them to its source—a dilapidated stable, leaning comically as though every board was either too long or too short. Thick green lichens growing on the structure gave the impression that the forest had built the stable itself from its own fallen soldiers.

They heard shuffling snorts from the stable as they approached. From inside, two dozen tacked up horses craned their necks to see who had disturbed their sleep. The travelers wasted no time in choosing mounts.

Allison mounted up with Bruno, who groaned as he was lifted into the saddle. "Where are . . . we . . . going?" he asked.

"South to Dramir," said Valen. "We ride hard through the night. We need to put as much distance as possible between us and Nosirin."

"Are the troops rendezvousing with us at some point?" Allison asked. No one answered.

CHAPTER THIRTY-FIVE

Responsibility

Move out," King Growlack ordered. He set off on a great black warhorse. They followed a dark path in the woods, one the horses seemed familiar with. They rode for hours, taking short breaks only when the horses absolutely needed it. Bruno's breathing became more labored as he bounced in his saddle, relying on Allison to hold him upright.

"He needs something soon," Delilah said, pulling her horse alongside Jeremiah's. "I'm sure one of these people has a potion. You're the VIP; could you ask around?"

"I can do that." Jeremiah eyed the other travelers, weighing who would be best to ask and how. He settled on a woman who looked like some sort of administrative magistrate. She wore a number of bottles strapped to her, and Jeremiah guessed one of them had to be a potion. But there was no way something so precious would be wasted on an unknown tagalong like Bruno.

He rode alongside Bruno and Allison. "Bruno, I need a favor."

Bruno slowly turned to look at Jeremiah. His face was sallow, his eyelids drooping. His leather armor was sodden with blood in front and back.

Jeremiah asked, "Can you injure me in a way that isn't serious, but looks—"

Bruno moved in a flash. Jeremiah lurched in pain and bit down on his fist to keep from screaming as something punctured his side. He glanced down to see the backward facing barbs of an arrow protruding just slightly from his skin. Bruno removed the arrow with shaking hands, causing Jeremiah to bite down harder, then snapped the arrow shaft in two and inserted the back end into the wound. The arrow now appeared to be lodged deep in Jeremiah's flank.

"Could've at least warned me," Jeremiah hissed through clenched teeth. Bruno patted Jeremiah's cheek like an affectionate drunk.

While the pain was still fresh, Jeremiah rode up to the magistrate. He introduced himself and struck up a conversation about the battle before revealing his mortal wound with a grimace.

The woman was aghast. She thanked him for his service, commended his bravery in concealing his wound until they had escaped and, despite Jeremiah's objection, forced the crimson potion into his hand.

Bruno downed it in a gulp. His back spasmed, then his breathing deepened and he stretched in the saddle. Delilah rode beside him and applied a medicinal paste to the barest wounds that remained. "Potion took care of the worst of the internal damage. You'll be okay, but it'll be sore for a while. Thanks, Jeremiah." She smiled at him.

They continued to ride past daybreak and finally took their rest at noon in a peaceful glade. The horses were spent, as were their riders. They pitched camp in silence. Each horse was equipped with a personal tent and several days' rations. As night fell most of the travelers gathered around the king's fire, but Jeremiah and his party settled farther away.

"I hope the soldiers got out all right," said Allison. Jeremiah's heart sank at the way she was looking at him. It was expectant, pleading. She knew.

"I don't think they're coming," he admitted. "Their job was to counterattack and try to retake the city."

Allison didn't respond. Just gazed into the fire.

"There's something else . . ." Jeremiah told them about negotiating with Vivica and showed them the raised scars on his hands. The pain was already a distant memory; he had forgotten the wounds during their escape. But looking at them now, he knew that anytime he cast a spell, he would be reminded of her.

"Girl after my own heart," said Bruno. "She knows how power works."

"Why does she care so much about you?" Delilah asked Jeremiah. "There's the power aspect, sure. Imagine soldiers that regenerate and then keep fighting after death. But still . . ."

"I don't know. She seems . . . curious? Like when you've got a particularly interesting bug in a jar."

"Intrigued," Allison said to the fire.

"Yeah, intrigued. She seems intrigued by me."

"Think you could kill her?" Allison asked.

Jeremiah paused, taken aback. He hadn't considered the possibility. "I don't know. I was able to burn the healing magic out of Narooka, but Vivica is the source of it. I doubt I have the stamina to get through all that. She has got a gorget, though. Maybe she doesn't want her head cut off."

They heard footsteps and Colonel Valen appeared out of the darkness, smothering conversation.

"Gentlemen, ladies. We'll be continuing to Dramir at first light. It'll be at least a few days before those brutes gain full control of the city, and by then they'll have found themselves in a highly precarious position."

"Precariously in control of a major city?" asked Bruno.

"Precisely. Flanked by Shabad and Barad Celegald, with Dramir just south. A three-kingdom assault on a city with frankly uninspiring defenses will see them broken."

"Sir," said Allison, finally looking up, "with all due respect, that makes no sense."

"Explain, Captain." Valen crossed his arms.

"Simply put, sir, she must know all that. She might send out diplomats to negotiate from a position of strength or attack Shabad or Barad Celegald to capitalize on her momentum. She might do any number of things, but I can't imagine she's going to just sit on her laurels."

"You may be right, Captain, but we shan't speculate on unknowns. Whatever her plan, it'll be weeks before she's able to organize another maneuver like that one. By then we'll have our own plans in motion and have the initiative advantage."

Colonel Valen squatted down in a collegial manner, wearing a winning smile. "I know we got a black eye today, but don't worry. A couple of months from now it'll be like this never happened. We've lost cities before, and it's always spelled disaster for the attackers." He rose to leave. "Oh, and Mr. Thorn, I forgive you for the indiscretion back in the fortress. I realize we were both on edge, but I still consider you a steadfast ally. Your loyalty to your friends is admirable."

"Thanks," Jeremiah said. Colonel Valen nodded to him, filling in Jeremiah's own apology and accepting it in the same gesture, and returned to the royal campfire.

They traveled for four more days, their pace relaxing as they gained distance from Nosirin. They had received no word from the allies they left behind, but they had little hope of that anyway.

On the fifth day, before their final ride to Dramir, Jeremiah was torn from a familiar nightmare by footsteps outside his tent. The sun wasn't up yet, but he got up anyway.

They had camped on top of a small, bald-topped hill. Jeremiah spotted Allison in the predawn light, sitting on a large rock and looking toward the dark horizon. He joined her. They sat in silence for a while, enjoying the peace of each other's company.

After some time, Jeremiah asked the question that had been on his mind. "What was it like?"

"What was what like?"

"Dying."

Allison considered. "I didn't die. But I don't think I've ever been that close to it, and I've come damn close."

"Was it scary?"

"Never is."

Jeremiah couldn't fathom the sentiment.

"Allison?"

"Yeah, Jay?"

"I don't want to be a necromancer anymore."

They sat in silence for a few moments longer before Allison spoke. "You studied for years to be a necromancer."

"I know."

"You're important now, like you wanted. You've earned respect and responsibility and probably a royal pardon."

"I know all that."

"So why quit?"

Jeremiah drew shapes in the dirt with his foot. "I can't handle it. I have the power to hurt or kill so easily. It's too much. The other day I made a mistake and innocent people died. My allies." The knowledge of having attacked his own forces was catching up to him. He found himself revisiting the bloody closet night after restless night.

Allison frowned. "Accidents happen. It wasn't your fault. It's important that you realize that."

"I appreciate you saying that, but it was still my responsibility. I don't want anyone else to die just so I can go on feeling important and special. It's not worth it."

Allison regarded him in the wan light. "Stepping away from this kind of power isn't always easy."

Jeremiah chuckled. "Honestly, I don't think I'll miss it. It sounds like a relief." He doodled a line of stick figures in the dirt. "Do you think they'll still let me go when we get back if I refuse to do more necromancy?"

"They damn well better," came Delilah's voice behind them. She yawned and sat with them as the first glow of the sun broke over the horizon. "Bruno, you might as well join us. I know you're awake."

Bruno emerged from his tent and sat beside Allison. "Whatever you decide to do, Jay, you've got my full support. I'll see you free if it's the last thing I do." He put a hand on Jeremiah's shoulder.

"Same here." Allison put her hand on top of Bruno's. Delilah placed hers on his other shoulder. Jeremiah's guilt melted away, and for a precious moment he was glad to be himself.

"You'll still want to help me? Even if I'm not useful anymore?" He was pretty sure he knew the answer, but he needed to hear it.

Bruno flicked his ear and Jeremiah yelped. "Obviously. Quit milking it."

"Well, I'll go wake everyone up so we can start running," said Delilah. She gave Jeremiah one last clap on the shoulder before hopping off the rock and jogging toward the main camp. It took a moment to register what she had said. Jeremiah, Bruno, and Allison exchanged confused looks.

"Why are we running?" Jeremiah called after her.

"Because that"—she pointed toward the glowing horizon—"is north."

CHAPTER THIRTY-SIX

The Crown

Camp was broken in a panic. Tents were abandoned, armor haphazardly donned, and horses harnessed with desperate speed. The light cresting the horizon had turned from the promise of a bright tomorrow to a harbinger of doom as the familiar nebulous golden glow crawled toward them.

"Impossible!" said one of the generals. "It must be miles across! They must have been sprinting flat out day and night to catch up to us!"

King Growlack set a steady pace for the group, but a few panicked riders charged ahead, relentlessly spurring their horses toward the safety of Dramir. However, they soon found themselves overtaken by the king's group, their horses lathered and rebelling against the brutal tempo.

The true sun began to rise as they pressed onward. "Will we make it?" Jeremiah asked Allison, glancing over his shoulder toward their pursuers.

"If we do, it will be just barely. Don't waste time wondering."

As the sun passed over their heads, Jeremiah began to recognize the landscape. The travelers shouted to anyone they passed to seek shelter or make haste to Dramir.

Shortly past noon, they heard the faint echo of a war horn far behind them. Jeremiah glanced back again to see that golden radiance arcing up into the sky as though the sun were about to crash into the world.

"They're at the hill!" someone shouted. "By the gods, they're going to catch us!"

Jeremiah could see the tops of Dramir's walls in the distance, their finish line. But the group was exhausted, and some of the weaker horses had fallen far behind the pack. The king commanded them to take a brief, tense break to water their horses and let them stretch. The animals bucked and stomped in frustration when they were remounted all too soon.

The wall grew, and the golden haze rushed closer and closer, flowing through the forest like an avalanche. One of the king's entourage produced a wooden tube and launched a smoke-billowing rocket that bloomed like a scarlet flower above their heads. A green bloom answered from the wall.

The ground trembled and tree trunks behind them snapped with wooden explosions. "The giants!" Jeremiah cried. The towering monsters glared at the fleeing travelers through the canopy of the forest, wading through the trees like tall grass.

Jeremiah dug his heels into his mount, but the tremors had given the horses all the inspiration they needed. They were close now—Jeremiah could make out figures atop the wall. The portcullis was open.

Horns sounded behind them. Jeremiah risked a look back. The golden cloud reached toward them, emanating whoops and war cries. A man-sized stone dropped out of the sky, crushing one of King Growlack's men and raining clods of earth on the rest of the group. The figures on the wall waved at them frantically.

The ground shook in rhythmic seizures as the group reached the wall and passed through the tunnel toward the portcullis. A roar of rage filled Jeremiah's eardrums to bursting, but his horse carried him into the city with the others. Metal screeched as the portcullis crashed down behind them, the slowest of their group crushed between the massive hands of the diving giant and the metal crosshatching that stopped them both. Jeremiah turned in his saddle to see the giant writhing as oceans of burning liquid poured from murder holes. With new flesh slowly crawling over charred, exposed bone, the giant crawled out from the gatehouse and escaped.

"Loose!" Trumpets blasted alongside the order. A resounding chorus of *twangs* sounded as the wall archers shot at targets beyond the wall.

The travelers followed King Growlack as he wheeled his horse along a series of stone switchbacks leading to the top of the wall as wide as the city's thoroughfare and packed with archers shooting an eclipse of arrows. A dozen giants retreated below them, their backs black with arrow shafts. At the edge of the archers' range, the giants turned and jeered but did not advance past the new siege line.

Delilah gasped. "Gods, look at them all!"

The narrow stream from the mountains of Nosirin had transformed into a flood, charging through the countryside. Men, horses, chariots, and giants raced with everything they had, never slowing, bolstered by golden magic. At the center of the advancing force was Vivica, gripping a podium atop a broad platform mounted on an armored giant's back. As her army reached the range of engagement, the golden cloud began to evaporate. Vivica's giant knelt down, and she collapsed. The giant tenderly handed her to the barbarians, where she disappeared into the crowd.

Good to know it wasn't easy, thought Jeremiah.

The remaining giants sprang into action at once, lowering their trebuchet staves to the ground. Halflings and gnomes swarmed into the tarps.

"Shoot them down!" Bruno said. The archers on the wall had only seconds to make sense of this command before dozens of small-race barbarians were hurtling toward them. The walls of Dramir weren't as easily surpassed as Nosirin's had been, and the giants roared with the effort of giving their ammunition the height and distance they needed. Not all of them made it.

The archers were late, shooting at the bodies that landed in the city, crashing through roofs or stalls or down to the streets below. Despite the height of the fall and the rain of arrows, Jeremiah spotted survivors darting away.

"We've got saboteurs," said Bruno.

"And rabble-rousers, assuming she didn't already have people on the inside," said Delilah.

"She did," said Bruno.

"Come on, we need to report to King Hector," said Valen, turning his horse. "Your Majesty, we'll see you to the palace."

King Growlack spat over the wall.

Dramir's throne room was as resplendent as the palace itself—a marble-clad hall bedecked with banners and trophies of Dramir's military victories, positioned to remind the visitor as they approached the gilded throne of the power and influence of Dramir and its royalty. Today, the decor seemed a satire, with the uncrowned King Growlack standing beside King Hector the final punchline.

Colonel Valen finished his report to King Hector. The king sat on his throne in silence, surveying the dozens of worried faces that crowded his court. He glanced at the missive in his hand. Vivica had given the king one week to surrender the city before she would commence the attack in earnest.

"What's the state of our army?" King Hector asked.

"Not strong," said one of the officers. "We had committed a significant force to support Nosirin even before the last reinforcement. And this latest advance set upon us too quickly to summon the peasantry within the safety of the walls, which would normally constitute a significant portion of our defensive force. Even if we assume each of our heavy cavalry is worth fifty barbarians, they're still grossly outnumbered. And that's not counting the giants or the regeneration."

"Reinforcements?"

"One week isn't enough time for anyone to marshal enough manpower and move it into position. Barad Celegald and Shabad wouldn't even commit troops to Nosirin. Besides, approaching Dramir now would be a suicide mission." The officer sighed. "If this witch takes the city, she will be a mighty foe to dislodge."

The king slammed his fist on the arm of his throne. "Give me solutions! Options!"

Jeremiah stepped forward. "Surrender."

A rumble ran through the assembly. "Excuse me?" King Hector stood from his throne and descended the steps. He towered over Jeremiah. "Did you just suggest we open our doors and surrender Dramir?"

"Yes. Give her the city without bloodshed. Make terms for a peaceful transition. If she's going to win anyway, you might as well limit the damage. Regroup and strategize with more time, resources, and allies." Jeremiah glanced at his friends. Bruno gave him a quick nod, but Allison and Delilah looked stricken.

The king looked at Jeremiah thoughtfully. "Necromancer . . . I wonder if we can't use you to turn this around."

Jeremiah braced himself. "Your Highness, with all due respect, you said my obligation ended at Nosirin. I would ask you to honor your word."

"In our moment of need. What's to stop you from allying with her once she attacks? Based on your suggestion, it even seems likely," said King Hector, looming over Jeremiah. His hand fell precariously close to his war hammer.

"Your Highness, I have spent the better part of a year serving the gentry and military of this city. I have worked to fulfill the stipulations of an unprecedented sentence as an effective slave of the city, I have acted as honorably as I could in the good faith that the city authorities would honor their agreement, and now I ask that you extend that same faith to me."

The king was silent. Colonel Valen stepped forward, pushing Jeremiah aside. "Your Highness, if I may. Dramir is facing its most dire threat of the last century. Mr. Thorn is simply too valuable an asset to be released."

Jeremiah glared at the back of Colonel Valen's head. *Vivica can stop being right anytime now.* "Your Highness, if you renege on your promise, I will have no reason to continue to be a valuable asset. The truth is, I have no desire to continue to be a necromancer. I have already killed far too many people, made far too many mistakes. If you demonstrate that fulfilling my end of the deal is no guarantee that you will fulfill yours, then frankly I have no reason to continue to shoulder that burden."

This time it was Colonel Valen's turn to glare at Jeremiah. The king collapsed onto his throne. He pressed a finger to his temple, closing his eyes. "Necromancer Thorn." The king sat up. "I desire for you to remain in the employ of Dramir's armed forces and to defend this city with every mote of power you can gather."

Jeremiah had expected this, yet he was still disgusted.

King Hector sighed, stood tall, and recomposed himself, speaking with his utmost authority, "However, the honor of the crown does not care for my desires.

I promised your freedom for involving yourself in Nosirin, and the crown must honor its promises." He stood again. "Jeremiah Thorn, I, King Hector, hereby absolve you of all crimes and punishments that have been charged against you. I declare you a free man. I declare Counselor Fortune to be absolved of all penalties and leverages resulting from her defense. You are free to reenter the service of the crown should you so wish, and I hope that you will. But until then, I dismiss you and your associates from my court."

And just like that, it was over. The noose Jeremiah had lived with for so long was lifted away. He was stunned.

Delilah appeared by his side. "Thank you, King Hector. You are wise and just." She curtsied and elbowed Jeremiah. He bowed.

A guard ushered Jeremiah, Bruno, and Delilah from the throne room. Allison was permitted to remain. The door whispered shut behind them, and Delilah exploded. "We did it!" she cried, wrapping Jeremiah up in a hug.

"You're a free man!" said Bruno, clapping him on the back.

Jeremiah pulled out a kicking and croaking Gus to share in the excitement. "Delilah, I can't thank you enough for this. I couldn't have done it without you. You too, Bruno."

Delilah waved her hand dismissively. "You earned this. You worked your ass off to prove you're a good man."

"Can we go get drunk now? Please?" Jeremiah asked.

"Jay, we're under siege, shouldn't we—"

"Yes!" Bruno said. "Before anyone figures out they can jack up the prices!" He sprinted back and yanked open the door to the throne room. "Allison! We're going to Corbyn's!" He slammed it shut, and soon all three were running into the night.

CHAPTER THIRTY-SEVEN

Rabble-Rousers and Saboteurs

The siege had apparently dried up everyone's thirst. Corbyn's was quiet, save for the die-hard drunkards, Jeremiah, Bruno, and Delilah. They ordered the fanciest wines and liquors and scoffed at the prices. Jeremiah felt muscles relaxing that had been tense for months. He howled with laughter at nothing at all and felt nothing but joy in doing so. They cheered when Allison showed up. Her drink orders were few and her participation in revelry was limited, but they were glad to have her.

They departed with a drunken racket, singing bawdy songs to darkened streets. Their voices echoed in stark contrast to the subdued atmosphere of the city, but Jeremiah didn't care. He carried Delilah on his back in a stumbling two-step while she crowed in his ear. But another voice split the night.

"If you look upon their faces, you'll see not foreigners, not soldiers, but men and women who seek a better world! They're willing to fight, to die for a better life for you. The snobs in those towers want to keep you in your place, because that's where they can best exploit you!"

A gnome stood on a barrel, proselytizing to a small crowd. "How many of you have heard tales of the mountains of wealth hidden in the banks? How would your lives be changed, your problems solved, with even a single gold coin from their endless supply?" There were nods and grumbles of agreement among the crowd.

"Ah, shit," said Bruno.

Delilah hopped down. "What's going on?"

"They're building support for their cause," said Jeremiah. "Making allies out of enemies." His heady lightness had been snatched away all at once.

"Support?" asked Allison, glaring at the gnome. "Why would anyone support the people who are sieging the city?"

"They see a chance at a better life," said Bruno.

"That's treason. I'll put a stop to this." Allison moved toward the gnome, but Bruno blocked her.

"No. Nothing will legitimize him more. Let this one go. Tomorrow I'll see about hunting down the people she sent over the wall. Delilah, can you get the courts to agree to a bounty for these guys?"

"I'll see to it first thing. Any spy captured will bring a small fortune, assuming they can prove it."

They continued home, the bounce gone from their step.

"What'd the king decide?" Jeremiah asked, adding his boots and cloak to the pile at the door.

"Nothing." Allison's boot bounced off the wall.

Within two days, the siege had changed every aspect of life in Dramir. Giants patrolled outside every gate. No supplies came in or out. On the second night, a massive inferno destroyed a warehouse full of grain, flour, and oats, causing the price of basic necessities to skyrocket. Law enforcement didn't share Bruno's belief that forcibly silencing the preachers would only strengthen their message, but the gnomes and halflings were particularly evasive. In fact, gnomes and halflings became something of a rarity on the streets, as guards began stopping them for lengthy interrogations.

Now that he was a free man, Jeremiah had no idea what he should do with himself. The siege bought him some time, as he was trapped along with everyone else, but he couldn't stay in Delilah's house forever, especially without contributing his necromancy. For now, he was a glorified errand boy, accompanying Delilah as she drew up bounties on the invaders and restocked her lab.

He and Delilah stopped on the way home to listen to a human speaking before a crowd, condemning the wickedness and greed of Dramir's elite. "You remember seeing any humans get thrown over?" asked Jeremiah.

"Nope."

"Me neither."

On the third day, the draft began. Every able-bodied man and woman was to enlist in the city's defense. They were equipped with cheap spears and only enough training to know which end was dangerous. The too old or too young were put to work stitching together cloth armor or helping to fletch arrows.

Allison came home late that night and dropped into her seat as the others were finishing up dinner. "I was putting conscripts on the wall, you know, showing them where they needed to be? One of them fucking waves at the siege line, they wave back, and he stares me dead in the eye and drops his spear over the edge."

"What'd you do with him?" asked Jeremiah.

"Sent him over the wall to go get it." The table went quiet for a long moment; there was an uncomfortable shifting of gazes. "It's a war. We can't tolerate open treachery in the ranks," said Allison.

"Morale isn't high," said Delilah.

"How? How did she gain so much traction so fast?" asked Allison.

Jeremiah ventured a guess. "Not sure if you took a close look, but there are some Nosirin uniforms out in that siege line. If she really is able to speak to the downtrodden, really offer them a better life, well . . ." He remembered Valamor's rage in the slum tavern, a man eager for bloodshed if it meant revenge on the necromancer who stole his livelihood.

Bruno nodded. "Yeah, she got traction quick. Not enough to mount an insurrection quite yet, but enough to fizzle out that patriotism you're looking for." He was reading over his notes from contacts within the city, tracking leads onto the location of saboteurs.

"What's the fight going to look like?" Delilah asked Allison.

Allison bit into a roll. "They can't breach the walls, even with giants. We'll be ready if they throw more people over. It won't be like Nosirin."

"So, what *can* they do?" Jeremiah asked.

"My guess is they're hoping the saboteurs get a gate open, but . . . if *I* were leading her army, with her powers? I'd commit all my magic to a single giant and have him bash the portcullis down while I keep him alive. Now, I don't *know* she's that powerful, but I suspect she is."

"How do you counter that?" Bruno asked.

"If I were in charge? I'd mount our defense right there, keep them trapped in that slaughterhouse as long as possible. But then, if I were her, I'd be looking for such a trap . . . Well, I can go back and forth like that for a while." Allison rubbed her eyes. When she left for her room, she left behind a void of uncertainty around the table. Outside, alarm bells accompanied the orange glow of another fire.

CHAPTER THIRTY-EIGHT

Visitor

Vivica was sitting beside his bed when Jeremiah woke up. His window was pale with predawn light. He blinked to dispel the obvious dream, but instead the dream grinned and asked, "How you doin', Thorn?"

Jeremiah's heart thudded in his chest. Had he slept through an attack? Was a grisly scene awaiting him downstairs? Vivica held no weapons. She was wearing a simple dun hooded tunic. Where were his weapons? Did he have any? He struggled to remember. He could splash her with acid, or maybe he could scream and roll between the bed and the wall, and then—

"Relax. I'm not here to hurt you."

Jeremiah considered that. She could have ended him while he slept, but he was still alive. Adrenaline still burned in his veins, but he decided to believe her.

"Is this your familiar?" She stroked Gus in his water bowl. "He's cute." Gus wiggled with approval.

"Traitorous toad," Jeremiah said. He saw the glimmer of her gorget peaking up around the collar of her tunic as she leaned over Gus. Could he throttle her? If he could stop her from speaking, maybe he could prevent her from healing herself, call for Allison, and end this war in one fell swoop.

Her eyes flicked back to him. "Go ahead."

"What?"

She pulled a knife from her boot and handed it to him. "Go on, if it'll satisfy your ambitions." She unclasped the gorget and presented her naked throat.

He raised the knife to her neck, anticipating she would leap into action to break his hand, but she didn't move. He pressed the point to where he knew an artery lay but he couldn't bring himself to push. "I can't. I've never . . ."

She raised an eyebrow. "You've never . . . ?"

"Killed someone."

She broke into a tinkling laugh of genuine amusement. "You're joking. You must be. I have it on very good authority that you have killed a *lot* of people!"

"Well, I have. But not, like, with my own hands."

She squinted at him. "Thorn, you've got a weird sense of accountability. But I'll spoil the surprise for you. You're not going to kill me."

He bit his lip, then pushed the knife into her neck and, remembering a conversation with Bruno, twisted it. The blade turned in her flesh without spilling so much as a drop of blood. It was as though he had sunk the blade into soft clay. She didn't even flinch, just looked on with amusement. Jeremiah pulled the knife out. The steel was slick with blood, but the spot he had stabbed was unmarred.

"Now no one can say you didn't try." She took the knife and wiped it clean on his bedsheet.

"Why are you here?" Jeremiah asked. "How did you find me?"

"Those glyphs on your hands aren't just for show," she said. He waited for her to answer his other question. She toyed with her knife, the blade glinting as she twirled it and danced it across her knuckles, seemingly lost in thought. "You told me people want to do the right thing," she said finally. "But here you are on the opposite side of what I believe is right. You're fighting to uphold a corrupt regime, one that has long profited off those it should serve, including yourself. Yet you believe you're fighting for good."

"One of us must be wrong," Jeremiah concluded for her.

"Must be. Which one?" She inched a little closer, like she was eager for him to reveal the secret.

"I guess I can't say for sure. I only know what I believe, same as you."

Vivica looked surprised. Jeremiah supposed she had expected him to try and convince her. Instead he asked, "What exactly are you planning to do here? If you win, that is."

Vivica smiled and passed her flat hand through the air, slow and even. "I'm going to knock down every tower taller than the smallest hovel. The people of this city need me. They need someone to free them from the cycle of poverty and violence, fettered by desperation to the greed of heartless men."

"You're going to kill a lot of those people in order to free them."

"No, I'm not. You've seen what I can do. I recognize that some will likely perish, but my quarrel isn't with Dramir's slaves. The wealthy, on the other hand, those in love with the city as it is . . . some of them will need to die."

"Say they die. Then what? You crown yourself queen and throw coins to the poor?"

Vivica looked stung by the venom in his words. "I have no idea what comes next."

"You don't . . . have a plan?" Now he wondered whether she was just insane.

"It's not up to me. I can't build the new Dramir. That's for greater minds than mine. I can only tear down the old one."

"Isn't that just anarchy?"

"Only in the beginning. From chaos rises order, an opportunity for a new world. But unlike other revolutions, I have the power to make it as painless as possible for those who need it most. That's why they follow me for the chance at a new world. One life to give is a steep price, but my people can die over and over in pursuit of our dream."

A thought occurred to Jeremiah. "What'd you promise the giants? They can't have a serious interest in this new world."

"Heh. Clever boy. No, they're strictly mercenary. The power I provide keeps them safe from predators."

"Predators? Predators of giants?" Jeremiah shuddered.

"Those mountains are older than you think, and ancient things walk between those peaks." She looked away from him, focused on the middle distance of memory.

Neither spoke for a moment. Then Jeremiah asked, "Why can't we fix the system we have? You've got their attention, you have leverage, you can make demands! Why not create change without the destruction and bloodshed?"

Vivica sighed and pet Gus again, scratching the space between his bulging eyes. He leaned into her affections. "I was born Viviana Aliwyn. The archives of this city go back further than anyone's memory. Follow my name and maybe then you'll understand."

She made to rise, but Jeremiah grabbed her wrist. The scars on his hands tingled when his skin touched hers. "Vivica, stay. We can work together, change things for the better without anyone having to die. I hear what you're saying, I know the system is broken, but—"

"Then come with me. It's not too late."

"Stay with *me*! We can figure it out together." He squeezed her hand.

Vivica leaned forward and put her forehead against his. Jeremiah was suddenly back in the prison with a fleeting worry, or was it hope, that she was going to kiss him. "You make a tempting offer, Jeremiah Thorn. You really do. But power corrupts and I won't let them get to you."

Jeremiah woke up again, this time sprawled on top of the bed. His jaw throbbed and his head rang. Vivica was gone. A morning breeze came through his window. He threw on his robes and made his way downstairs, where the rest of his party was sitting around a table eating ham and eggs on bread. Allison gave him a beaming smile; Bruno and Delilah were eyeing him suspiciously.

"Good morning, Jay!" Allison greeted him without turning her attention from the skillet. "There's plenty to go around, including for any guests."

"Yeah, tell the little harlot she can join us," said Delilah, poking at her eggs. Allison hushed her.

"But we *are* gonna have a talk about how you got a girl into this house without me knowing about it." There wasn't an ounce of humor in Bruno's voice.

"It was Vivica," said Jeremiah, rubbing his bruised jaw. "She snuck into my room and—"

Bruno was out of his seat and up the stairs in a flash. The front door banged open and Allison was gone, Delilah on her heels. Jeremiah sat alone in the kitchen as a plate spun on the floor.

Jeremiah made his way to the center of the city, taking a long and meandering route. The conversation with Vivica kept playing in his head. Was she right? Did Dramir need to be destroyed to make way for a new, undefined society? Was the potential for thousands to have a better life worth the devastation? Or was Vivica naive to offer no solutions alongside the violence, no guarantee that something better would rise from the ashes?

With fresh eyes, he took in the great buildings of the city, the gentry that walked the street, and the solemn stone banks that kept his own riches safe. He passed beggar children pleading for mercies, men in alleys hatching conspiracies, and brutes that glowered down at passersby. Countless guardsmen marched new conscripts in formations, the recruits clad in armor that would buckle against dinner cutlery, much less a true blade. They marched to preserve the darkness that festered within the city walls.

But he also saw a robed official reprimand a food merchant for price gouging during the siege. A group of soldiers carried an injured civilian to a healer. Guards oversaw the distribution of emergency stores of grain to the poorest and most vulnerable.

Vivica was right, but she was also wrong. The city wasn't without its cruelties, but neither was it a hopeless pit of slaves and despots.

He reached the palace. A cadre of guards patrolled the perimeter, watchful for violence or unrest. Jeremiah had planned what he would say to gain access to the palace, but as he approached, the guards parted and waved him through. He entered the lofty halls and found the staff just as helpful in guiding him, as a footman asked his destination.

"I'm here to see Colonel Valen. Do you know where he is?"

"Right this way, Mr. Thorn." Jeremiah started at the use of his name, then followed the footman.

Colonel Valen's office was a gallery of bureaucracy. Papers, forms, and missives of every conceivable type crept toward the ceiling in balanced piles on any surface flat enough to hold them. Colonel Valen was scribbling furiously, cross referencing with lightning speed between countless papers.

"Can I help you, Mr. Thorn?"

"I need to know how to find information on a specific person from a long time ago. A city resident."

"If this isn't in some way related to the current siege, I'll have to ask you to leave."

"It is. How are things going? Is there a plan yet?"

"Not that it's any of your concern, but we intend to run out the clock. She's got an uphill battle ahead of her and we're spending what time we have to turn that hill into a mountain. The addition of a necromancer would go a *great* distance toward making that happen, if I can persuade you." Colonel Valen didn't even look at him to pitch the halfhearted request.

"Sorry, Colonel Valen, but no. I'm done with necromancy. Where can I find that information?"

"Well, at least that's one less necromancer in the world. Go to the archives in the basement. One of the creeps down there can help you."

"Thank you, Colonel." Jeremiah turned to leave, then paused. "Colonel, what are you doing exactly? All this paperwork—is it related to the siege?"

"This"—Colonel Valen patted a stack of papers—"is war, Mr. Thorn. You're a civilian. You think of war as marching troops and battle lines. But this mess is the lifeblood at the heart of war. This tells the troops where to march, when to march, in what numbers, with what equipment, and how supplied."

The banality of it struck Jeremiah as odd. Sheets of paper that determined the fates of men.

"Here I was thinking it was all tactics and strategy."

"Tactics are for amateurs, Mr. Thorn. Logistics are for professionals. Now, if there's nothing else . . ."

Jeremiah took his leave, happy if he would never see Colonel Valen again.

CHAPTER THIRTY-NINE

Archives

Jeremiah descended the dusty stairs to the darkened basement of the palace, too deep for the gilding of the halls to penetrate. The city archives were stored in a single cavernous chamber. The room was lined with shelves, stacked with crates, filled with boxes, and packed with parchments. The dusty scent of paper reminded him of (somehow) simpler times in Flusoh's library.

Something skittered in the dark, the scattered torches creating more shadows than illumination.

"Hello?" Jeremiah called.

"Hello," came a tiny voice behind him. Jeremiah shouted in surprise and whirled. A sallow-skinned halfling smiled up at him. His expression was perhaps a touch manic.

"Yes, hello," said Jeremiah, regaining his composure. "I'm looking for information on a citizen of Dramir from a long time ago. I was told to come here."

"You were told right, sir! Please, allow me to assist you. May I have the name?" The halfling's voice was scratchy, as if seldom used.

"Viviana Aliwyn. She lived here a long time ago."

The halfling's face brightened in delight. "Ah! The Aliwyn family, but of course. Quite the tragedy. Nearly two hundred years ago, few remember now. Right this way, come along. Yes, they were a name of note at the time, quite wealthy, quite influential. Entire family murdered by the father!"

"Murdered . . . ?" Jeremiah hurried after the archivist. The halfling led him down into the shadows, row after row, striding confidently as Jeremiah stooped to squint at barely legible brass labels.

"Yes, yes! Very much so. Though I recall there was some dispute on the verdict. Ah! Here we are! Strong lad, please pull down that box there—yes, that one! Let me see. Ah! Here's the ticket!"

Laden with dusty and yellowing parchments, Jeremiah followed the archivist back toward the flickering torchlight. He set them into the thick layer of dust covering a table as the halfling lit a candle for him and then disappeared back into darkness.

Jeremiah started to sort through the files. The disjointed pile included crime scene reports, witness depositions, mortician's analysis, census data, newspaper articles, bills of sale, and court records, all jumbled together and faded with time. Jeremiah read and reread each page, scrutinizing each detail, and began piecing together the story.

"Family murdered by father . . . but he was also found dead? No motive . . . House burned to the ground. One survivor, grievously injured. The daughter, Viviana."

"Yes, yes!" The halfling reappeared at Jeremiah's elbow, making him jump. "That's the rub right there! Daughter claims the father killed her sister and tried to kill her, but the father was found slain in his bed alongside the wife. Some blamed the daughter. I have my doubts."

Jeremiah kept reading. The family's fortune was claimed by creditors. The investigator's disgust was evident in choice words used to describe the people who had taken everything from a child who had just lost her family. The girl was sent to a public orphanage. Jeremiah read the words of one reporter with a ghastly chill: *If even half the things I've heard about that place are true, may the gods keep her close.*

"I need more," said Jeremiah. "Is there anything more than this?"

The archivist tilted his head. "You need something specific, hmm? If you tell me, perhaps I can help you faster."

"This woman is the leader of the army sieging the city. I need to learn everything I can about her. Track every moment of her life, if possible."

The archivist practically danced in excitement. "A challenge! A puzzle! Most just look for names and dates, but you want more! Oh yes, oh, this will be *most* exciting! Necromancer Thorn, I ask you to fetch a hearty lunch for us. We will unearth a story never yet told!"

Hours later, Jeremiah was poring over more disjointed documents, choosing them at random from the slipshod stack that the archivist had compiled. He continued to flit to and fro, his energetic movements ceasing only long enough to devour a few bites of the smoked fish Jeremiah had procured, before dashing off again with a new jolt of inspiration.

The history the documents told was bleak. Viviana Aliwyn was sold from one orphanage to another. To another. To a work house. Adopted by a man with an unsavory record of violence, drinking, and debt. Removed from his custody when he was yet again arrested on vague charges. She reappeared months later in another shady orphanage.

"I'm afraid it only gets darker from there, sir . . ." The archivist presented a new stack of parchments. His joviality seemed undaunted by the subject matter of his research.

Jeremiah read the new pages. "The orphanage was shut down, the owners charged with prostitution and enslavement."

"Part of a conspiracy. The legal side becomes harder to follow, but"—the halfling traced a slender finger down one line of a court record—"we know that those who were truly responsible for this 'network' escaped punishment. As we can see in these reports, a number of children were taken up by a company formed the same day the orphanage was shut down." He pointed at another legal ledger. "Several years later, this same company was dissolved when investigated for similar crimes."

"Was there no one to protect her? Not one soul who tried to keep a child safe?" Jeremiah felt sick. He tried to imagine the girl whose life was emerging from these parchments as the same woman who sieged Dramir's walls at that very moment.

The halfling shook his head. "Justice is lumbering, ponderous, and often powerless. Those that seek to avoid it need only hide themselves between parsed words of the law. There are countless examples among these records. I believe our trail may be coming to an end, Necromancer Thorn. I hope you have found whatever answers you sought."

Bruno, Allison, and Delilah sat around the kitchen table, frustrated and exhausted from a day of chasing fruitless leads through the city, listening to Jeremiah's account of Viviana Aliwyn's life. The breakfast Allison prepared was still on the table, cold hours since. Nobody was hungry.

"Disgusting," said Bruno. "All the worst things that can happen to a girl in this city happened to her, and I bet we don't know the half of it."

There was a grumble of agreement around the table.

"I remember studying this case," said Delilah. "The legal backing behind the asset seizure was valid, but it was the dirtiest kind of law interpretation. A first-year law student could have seen this girl protected, but seems like no one was interested in that."

"Well, we're paying the piper now. That poor girl got herself an army of zealots." Bruno leaned back in his chair.

Allison shook her head. "She believes her people follow her out of loyalty, but I don't think that's true. I think all she is to them is invincibility while they seek vengeance against people who've made them feel powerless."

"What is it about you?" Delilah asked Jeremiah. "Why does she keep coming back to you? Beyond the necromancy, what does she want with you?"

"I honestly don't know." Jeremiah spread his hands on the table, as though his scars could tell him the answer. "Maybe she's looking for someone to tell her what she's doing is okay. Another caster, one who was pushed to the fringes of society. She keeps expecting me to be angry, to side with her. And I do agree with her a little. I mean, if it weren't for you guys standing up for me and taking me in, maybe I would have ended up part of her army. Willing to start a war for the chance to change things."

"Our system is flawed; it always has been," Delilah said. "The farther from the top you are, the less you can look to the law to protect you. But she wants to remove the rule of law completely. I can't imagine what that would look like."

"I can," said Bruno. "I see it every day, in the darkest holes of Dramir. Where the strong possess the weak like coin and barter them in kind. If you want to glimpse the savagery people are capable of, just visit those streets you usually avoid. The 'rule of law' just keeps that world conveniently tucked away."

"It's not perfect, but it's what we've got," said Allison. "And change can happen without bloodshed, without killing innocents."

"Vivica believes that those with power will go to any lengths to protect it," said Jeremiah.

"Not every rich person is corrupt," said Allison. "Not every noble is ruled by greed. King Hector could have kept you under his thumb, could have had you executed just by pointing at you, but instead he honored his word. And there are others like him"—she nodded toward Delilah—"who use their affluence to help people."

"Yeah, but I never did anything wrong," Jeremiah said. "I shouldn't have been under the crown's thumb to begin with."

Allison sighed. "What do you want me to say, Jay? We're all just out here, trying our best. I agree, it's not fair. Some people suffer more than their share. But I don't buy that the only solution is to raze the whole thing to the ground and start over."

"No. Me neither," said Jeremiah, his heart heavy. "We need to kill her, don't we?" He squeezed his eyes shut. Vivica knew the truth of Dramir better than anybody and had every right to her fury against it. Yet Jeremiah had to oppose her. In the end, he would be yet another enemy in her tortured life.

"Easier said than done," said Allison. "We can't reach her. Even if we could, I don't know if we could finish the job. I don't know that anyone could."

Jeremiah studied the backs of his hands, "I have an idea," Jeremiah said. "But I need you all to trust me, without any doubt or reservation."

Delilah, Bruno, and Allison looked at one another. "Of course we trust you, Jay," said Delilah. "You wouldn't be here if we didn't."

"I'll also need to convince more than just you three. The military, for one, and I can't imagine Valen and the generals think of me as fondly as you do."

Delilah held up a finger to silence him. "The *king* is the only person you need to convince."

"I'll take point on that one," said Allison. "Just fill me in."

"All right, I only need two things: corpses and money."

"We can find corpses, and we've got money," said Bruno.

"No, I mean a *lot* of money."

CHAPTER FORTY

Old Friends

Hands over your head," said the guard.

Jeremiah and Delilah raised their arms, allowing two other members of Duke Majig's security team to run their hands along their sides. Jeremiah wondered whether the duke always required visitors to his home to be searched, or if this treatment was a product of the ongoing siege.

"What's this?" the guard asked Jeremiah, probing Gus through his robes. Gus froze at the disturbance.

"A toad. He's my familiar," said Jeremiah.

"Take it out slowly," said the guard. All three guards stepped back and leveled crossbows at Jeremiah. Delilah held perfectly still.

With careful measure, Jeremiah removed Gus from his pocket. The toad was curled up into a tight little ball, trying to remain tiny and inconspicuous.

"Is it dangerous?" asked the guard, leaning to inspect the creature as if he might spy a tiny knife.

"Does he look dangerous?" asked Jeremiah, dodging the question. Leaving Gus with Delilah was one thing, but the idea of leaving him in the hands of a guard on some noble's payroll was intolerable.

The guard grunted and waved off the toad. Satisfied that Jeremiah possessed no weaponry, he turned his attention to Delilah. From beneath her professional attire, the search had revealed a small bandolier of vials. "What are these?" he asked.

"From left to right: anti-toxin, anti-toxin, anti-toxin, expectorate, anesthetic gel, anesthetic gel, eye wash, analgesic, ametic—"

"Anything dangerous?" asked the guard. He had popped open one of the vials and sniffed, his face screwing up at the smell.

"Waft, please," said Delilah. "And, technically, yes, but only—"

"It'll have to wait out here," said the guard, tossing the bandolier to his subordinate. Delilah grumbled but accepted the confiscation.

"You're clear," said the guard, stepping back and waving them through.

"I had no idea houses like this even existed," Jeremiah said to Delilah as they made their way into the atrium. Duke Majig's home reminded him of the palace in opulence if not quite in scope. But he had been expecting to be awed by the palace of Dramir—to see similar riches displayed in a single man's living space felt very different indeed. Every square inch of the spacious atrium had been graced by the labor of a master craftsman. Each marble slab of purest white or darkest black beneath their feet was etched with exquisitely detailed battle scenes. The brass dragons that served as bannisters of the grand staircase seemed nearly alive, and the chandelier was vast enough to be its own constellation.

"How many portraits does any one person really need?" asked Jeremiah as Delilah hurried him up the staircase. After days of Vivica's story echoing around his head, the amount of wealth on display here was enough to make him feel ill.

"Duke Majig is known for his extravagances, yes," said Delilah. "But remember to be polite. The duke was kind enough to host a special meeting at our request—"

"Only because the king ordered him to," grumbled Jay.

"—and we're going to need buy in from him and the other nobles for your plan to have even a chance of succeeding. So please stop making that face and try to remember we're all on the same side here."

Jeremiah muttered a few more phrases that Delilah chose to ignore, but he tried to arrange his features into an expression of pleasant camaraderie as they reached a set of heavy double doors at the landing. Delilah tugged at his clothes, smoothed his hair, and got her hand swatted when she licked a finger to try to fix one of his eyebrows.

"Do you know what you're going to say?" she asked. "There's still time to go over my outline if you want." Her fingers twitched toward her pocket, which Jeremiah had no doubt contained that very document.

"I think I'm ready," he said, wishing it felt truer. Every speech he had attempted to plan had sounded awful, even in his head. "Let's just get in there."

Jeremiah shoved the double doors apart. A cloud of cigar and pipe smoke rushed out to wrap him in an unctuous fog of heady scents as he and Delilah entered the room.

For a brief but telling moment, conversations stopped. They were neither announced nor greeted. Clustered into conspiring little cliques around the room were the greatest elites of Dramir. Financial and mercantile overlords, influential landowners, and magnates of industry paused in their gossip to regard Jeremiah the necromancer.

It's your fault she's here, Jeremiah thought as he stared back unflinchingly. *Greedy, selfish lives built on the blood of others.* In that moment he knew it didn't matter what he said to them. They had lived their whole lives uncaring, unwilling to use their resources to help others. Why would that change now?

A touch of pressure at his elbow. Delilah steered him farther into the room. Slowly, the murmur of discussion rose again, now accompanied by sidelong glances at the new arrivals.

Jeremiah took in their surroundings as he followed Delilah. An ornate study with vaulted ceilings, no less extravagant than the atrium outside, had been appointed for the meeting. Two dozen empty chairs were arranged in a circle in the center of the room, around which servants tended to the gathered aristocrats. Each servant held a silver tray balanced with crystal decanters, delicacies, tins of pipe weed, and other various indulgences. Jeremiah noticed that none of the servants so much as glanced in his direction.

"There's Majig," said Delilah, indicating a group across the study. "I need to officially thank him for having us. *Please* try not to get in trouble while I'm gone."

Jeremiah glowered while Delilah floated across the room, dipping in and out of cliques she passed with ease to share a word and a laugh, turning cold shoulders into soft smiles in her wake. *This is the dance, isn't it?* he thought. People talking to people, politics in action. *She's willing to burn down everything good about this city just to get to you.* He briefly imagined bringing the entire siege to an end with a single bout of violence. But it was a fleeting thought—even if he could stomach such a thing, he knew these people were products of the system, not the system itself.

A large man split off from his group to approach Jeremiah. Albert Dunsimmons, having eschewed the durability of field clothes in favor of a businessman's finery, placed himself directly in front of the necromancer. His cigar glowed brightly as he took a hefty drag. "Thorn! I remem—"

"Fuck off, Albert," said Jeremiah, maneuvering around the big man to make for an empty corner where he could despise the meeting attendees in peace.

Out of the corner of his eye, he spotted another political vagrant, a gnomish man bouncing from group to group. People cheered and laughed and raised their glasses as he spoke with them. Jeremiah watched as the gnome finished speaking to Dunsimmons's cluster, earning himself a slap on the back.

"Jeremiah!" The gnome stopped in his tracks upon meeting Jeremiah's gaze, shocked and delighted to see him. Jeremiah shuffled uncomfortably and tried to remember Delilah's tutelage as the gnome approached. Was he supposed to know him?

"It's me, Magnus!" The gnome reached Jeremiah and grabbed his hand, shaking it vigorously.

Jeremiah's tension dissolved into relief. "Thank the gods, a friendly face!" he said. He pulled Magnus into a hug that the gnome returned with gusto. Gus wriggled in his pocket.

Delilah returned at that moment, her smile strained. "Jay, why don't you introduce me to—"

Magnus beamed up at her and mumbled something.

"Oh. Oh my gods!" Delilah practically shrieked in delight when she saw Magnus.

"Delilah, you know Magnus too?" asked Jeremiah.

"Hm? Yes, of course. I've always known Magnus!"

Jeremiah laughed at the revelation, finally feeling at ease. "Me too. Isn't that funny! I—Hang on. Gus, calm down."

Gus was hopping madly inside his pocket. Jeremiah reached in to reposition him when the heavy double doors burst open.

"All kneel in the presence of the king!"

King Hector strode into the room alongside his aide, Sylvester. Around the room, grumbles and sighs accompanied painfully slow descents. Sylvester practically vibrated in fury.

"Let's get this started," said King Hector. His voice boomed, banishing any thoughts of continued pleasantries or conversation.

"Excuse me a moment," said Magnus, slipping away in King Hector's direction.

A pit formed in Jeremiah's stomach as he realized he was about to address the crowd. He and Delilah took their seats around the circle. King Hector, finding no seat large enough to suit him, had a pair of chairs removed and stood in their place.

The king spoke with practiced ease. "My esteemed nobles and leaders of commerce, I thank you for joining us in this most pressing time. Ruin lurks just beyond our walls, and we are ill equipped to repel it. The host arrayed has given us precious little time to offer an unconditional surrender"—there was a smattering of chuckles and scoffs—"which of course we do not find acceptable." King Hector spared Jeremiah the briefest of glares.

The king took a breath to continue, but Magnus had moved to the center of the circle. "Apologies, I just need to set this up. Ignore me," the gnome whispered. "Please continue, Your Highness." He placed a tiny cauldron in the center of the room and gave a quick wave to a trio of orbiting servants.

King Hector smiled at Magnus and continued. "Our own Jeremiah Thorn has had contact with the leader of this assault on multiple occasions and knows of her ambitions. He has developed a proposal to be presented here today. Mr. Thorn, if you would."

Jeremiah stood, painfully aware of the optics of being the second tallest in the room even when the floor was his. He surveyed the skeptical faces, trying to steady his shaking breath. The first word he wanted to speak, whatever it was, remained trapped in his throat. He glanced at Delilah, who nodded encouragingly at him, then at Magnus who was dumping a bag of white powder into the cauldron. The gnome gave him a reassuring smile, and Jeremiah felt braver.

"G-gentleman. Ladies. Thank you for coming. I would like to start by sharing with you what I have learned about the motivations behind this siege."

As quickly as he could, Jeremiah spoke of Vivica's visit to his room only days before, and what he had learned of her history. The nobles made an inattentive audience, continuing to sample treats carried by the servants and to chat with their neighbors. Jeremiah's nerves turned to annoyance as he finished describing the atrocities hinted at in the archives. He glanced toward Magnus again, but the trio of servants had returned bearing small sachets and the gnome was busy emptying their contents into the cauldron.

"Sounds to me like she's a mad woman," said a dwarf draped in a thick golden chain necklace. "Perhaps some kind of anarchist?"

Jeremiah shook his head. "No, she's not against order as a concept, from what I can tell. It's just this system she wants to destroy, and she doesn't care what comes next. She said the creation of something new isn't up to her."

More scoffs and chuckles. "Why are you telling us this, boy?" asked Dunsimmons. "What's any of this got to do with us?"

With great effort, Jeremiah resisted the urge to curse their callousness. "An unkillable enemy is at your gate. She sacked Nosirin in a matter of hours, made an impossible march, and now stands poised to destroy this city. With your help, I believe we can put an end to the siege without any further bloodshed."

Now at least he had their interest. The nobles were finally silent, perhaps curious what grotesque solution the famed necromancer had come up with.

Jeremiah took a deep breath and steeled himself. "We pay her off."

The assembly erupted in jeers and laughter. "A simple bribe?" said a human noble. "What sort of offering would such a lunatic even consider?"

Jeremiah spoke over the peals of mirth from the gathered nobles. "I am advising you to—and I'm not exaggerating—relinquish the platinum reserve ingots held by the greater banks of Dramir, as many land holdings as can be found, and as many artifacts and magical treasures as you have in your possession."

"You can't be serious, boy," a dwarf guffawed. "The city would be insolvent!"

"I know it sounds excessive!" Jeremiah said. "But if you don't give it to her, she's just going to take it, and your lives too. At least this way there's a chance she'll spare the city."

Jeremiah was surprised to see a few nodding heads, "This city is our home, and its people are our neighbors. We must do anything we can to protect both," said a robed elf.

"Why should we bother?" asked a silken-clad halfling, fanning herself. "In fact, it sounds like you're just conveying her demands! Are you her messenger boy? A lackey?" The woman fanned faster as she hurled accusations. "I say we let the walls do their work and hang the necromancer for a traitor!"

To Jeremiah's relief, King Hector spoke. "The walls will not hold her indefinitely. In fact, my lateness here was due to a development of that matter. Less than an hour ago, the western portcullis was destroyed. Her giants used a massive chain and hook to yank it down."

There was an uproar as several nobles stood in alarm. Jeremiah exchanged a startled look with Delilah. Was Nosirin about to happen all over again?

"Everyone is safe here, don't worry," announced Magnus. He was adding several vials of liquid to the cauldron and holding a cloth over his nose and mouth. A thin smoke was beginning to rise, and Magnus was sweating. Jeremiah wondered if he was okay. He looked exhausted.

King Hector nodded. "They have made no move to attack. It appears they want to repeat the maneuver on the other gates as well."

Delilah stood at Jeremiah's side. "We cannot sit idly by while our city is taken. Whatever means we have to end this conflict must be considered!"

"You won't be safe here forever," said Jeremiah. "She is relentless, and I promise she is coming for you!"

This time there was no laughter after Jeremiah spoke. "Do you really think she'd take it?" one noble asked.

"She'd be stupid not to!" said another before Jeremiah could respond.

"What does it matter? It all comes back to us sooner or later," another reminded everyone.

"Why can't we just kill the bitch and be done with it?"

"You haven't heard? She's damn near immortal."

Jeremiah sat as the discussion roiled around him. He had said everything he'd meant to say; what decision they came to was no longer in his hands. He blinked away a stinging in his eyes as the nobles debated. The air had grown rather acrid. Was someone smoking bad leaf?

"This is good," Delilah whispered to him. She cleared her throat before continuing. "You've got them talking, and they're scared."

Jeremiah nodded. He was trying to follow the conversation and control Gus at the same time, who was threatening to escape again. He coughed from the burning in his throat. Maybe a servant would bring him a glass of water.

Magnus appeared at his side. "Jeremiah, we need to go now. Come with me, okay?"

"But, Magnus, I need to . . ." Jeremiah broke off into a coughing fit. The debate had devolved into a full-blown argument. Gus was frantic in his pocket.

"You already did it. Come. Now." Magnus lifted him by the elbow and ushered him toward the door. "Two seconds," he whispered back to Delilah as they left her behind, bewildered.

They passed through the double doors. Jeremiah took a grateful breath of fresh air. The trio of servants were waiting.

"S-seal it," Magnus gasped.

The servants wrapped a length of chain around the door handles and snapped a sturdy lock onto it. Magnus let out his breath. "Gods, that was a lot of minds to hold on to."

"Magnus, are you okay? What's going on?" asked Jeremiah. He kept one hand on Gus as the toad continued to struggle.

"I'm fine, Jeremiah. Don't worry. It's just that mesmerizing that many people at once can be a bit of a task." Magnus stood a bit straighter, the strain and weariness gone. "And thank you for this meeting. It was very useful!"

Magnus started hurrying down the stairs, and Jeremiah followed automatically. "You're . . . welcome? It was useful?"

"Oh yes, very useful getting all those people in one place like that. Now, if I were you, I'd be getting out of here right quick. That stuff is *nasty*."

"Shouldn't we—hey!" Gus had finally wriggled free and fallen out of Jeremiah's robes, landing with a plop. He began hopping back up the stairs, and Jeremiah hurried to retrieve him.

Jeremiah had taken just a few steps when comprehension broke over him like a bucket of ice water. The cauldron. The locked doors. Delilah!

He sprinted back up the stairs to the sealed double doors. Yanking on the chain did nothing against the heavy padlock. He could hear shouting and retching coughs from the other side. Whisps of white gas escaped from cracks in the great wooden doors like tiny ghosts.

"Delilah!" Jeremiah bellowed. Focusing his will, he directed his acid spell against the chain and doors. It hissed as the acid began eating away at the wood. Slow, much too slow. He heaved at the chain again, and sent spell after spell against the ornate doors, ignoring the acid splashing back over his hands, his ears filled with the screams from inside the room.

He had only a second's notice to avoid being crushed. The great doors jumped once, slammed by something from inside. Jeremiah scrambled out of the way just in time as the once-resplendent doors exploded outward. Face nearly purple with fury, King Hector plowed through the opening, a collection of servants and nobles tucked under each arm, accompanied by a billowing cloud of gas.

Guests and servants fell over themselves to escape, stumbling and falling down the stairs as they retched and gagged. Delilah came soon after, dragging a particularly venerable noble. "Out—outside!" she rasped. "All the way outside!"

Jeremiah helped Delilah out of the house with the rest of the beleaguered nobles. They sprawled in the street in the shadow of the great mansion, looking like sickly beggars on their last nights. Magnus and his accomplices were nowhere to be seen.

"You can't run from her," Jeremiah said as the nobles gasped for breath. "You can't hide from her. It's too late for that." A soot-stained man stepped dispassionately over a prone nobleman, spitting as he passed. "She's already here. She's all around you. She always has been."

CHAPTER FORTY-ONE

It was high noon on the day before Vivica would begin her attack. Jeremiah stood outside the gates of Dramir, struggling to drag a wheeled chest across open ground. He had sent an official message requesting to meet with Vivica in the no-man's-land between the walls of Dramir and the siege line. Now she watched with her arms crossed as he struggled to roll the chest over the uneven ground.

Behind her, the barbarian army looked on with interest.

The chest caught on a root, forcing Jeremiah to push it backward a few inches before pulling it again. He was drenched in sweat. The chest was impossibly heavy, even after the lightness enchantment had been placed on it. After scoffing at his request, even calling him traitorous, the noblesse of Dramir had come around to providing him with what he'd asked for and more. Magnus's attack had turned the tide very much in his favor—coming so close to a grisly death, with their inner sanctum breached and betrayed by their own servants, the nobles found a great deal of generosity. Contributions from a reluctant few were procured through emergency royal seizure, dubious and convoluted legal argument, or outright theft by a rather gleeful Bruno.

Even as Jeremiah struggled, a quick mental check showed everything to be progressing as planned. The timing would need to be perfect, and that meant he had to get the chest moving again. Feeling Vivica's keen eyes on him made him question everything he thought he knew. He doubted his entire plan, wondering if he'd misjudged something about her. A part of him wished she would surprise him and the day would end without bloodshed. But it was a desire with no real hope behind it, so he kept pulling.

"That's close enough," she called. He was still about fifteen feet away but glad for the opportunity to rest. The chest was as long as he was tall, but also broad and deep, made of solid steel, and wrapped in reinforcing iron bands. "Let me guess, you've decided to join me and that's your wardrobe?" She flashed a half smile.

"No, I haven't. I've come to resolve this conflict. To make things right."

"That implies you understand what's wrong."

"Yes. I read about the murders. And about after. Gods, Vivica, I'm so sorry. It was a gross miscarriage of justice and decency. I have the king's apology as well. He felt immense shame for his city upon hearing what happened."

"Doesn't change anything, but nice to hear nonetheless." Vivica gestured to the chest. "And that is?"

"An amends," said Jeremiah, fighting to keep his tone even. He threw open the heavy lid.

The contents of the chest were blinding in the midday sun. Vivica instinctively shielded her eyes. Jeremiah reached inside and lifted out a heavy gleaming brick.

"Solid platinum," he said. "There are a ton of these in here. Each is worth tens of thousands of gold. They're meant for trading between banks and royalty." He returned it to the chest with a metallic thud and held a gleaming red gem aloft. "This is the Heart of the Crown, the largest cut ruby in the world. I've got a grain sack full of diamonds in here too. We've got the Mace of Argong the Unrelenting, an artifact that can cause earthquakes. The Glass Dagger, supposedly so sharp it can cut steel as easily as paper. The Black Envelope, which contains a secret so profound, it can only be read once. This here is a . . . a vial of star-something; I can't remember."

Vivica cut him off as he reached for the next priceless artifact. "Thorn, you must be joking. Why do you think any of this would interest me?"

"This chest is Dramir's power. It's being offered to you to show how serious the kingdom is about making this right. This is the wealth of nobles, merchant lords, the secret chambers of the palace itself. We pilfered Dramir's banks dry, save for minor coinage that didn't make the cut. At this moment, there is more money outside the walls than within them."

"Wow. All that effort for a bribe."

"Not a bribe. A means to fix things. With this chest, you could be the most powerful noble in the kingdom. In all the kingdoms. There's a royal pardon for you and everyone in your army, writs of ownership for several keeps and castles, and land deeds. You can influence policy, stick up for the little guy. They're giving you the power to change Dramir however you want."

Vivica stepped toward him, glowering. "I told you, I don't want power. Did you really think I'd give up everything I've achieved for the chance to become a player in their little game? To become exactly what I've set out to destroy?"

"Then redistribute the wealth as you see fit," Jeremiah said. "Vivica, please just consider that there's another path!"

"And how convenient that those who benefited from the system for generations would escape punishment yet again," said Vivica. "How fitting that their wealth would once more buy their exemption from justice. I thought you better than this, Thorn. I thought perhaps you would understand."

"But I do understand!" Jeremiah said. "You're angry, and I'm angry too. I hate what they did to you. I hate what they did to me. There's a few people with a death grip on the system, but they're not worth the total destruction of the city."

"Yes, they are! " Vivica said, angry and frustrated. "They built this monstrosity from the ground up. It *exists* to serve them." She smiled piteously at him, but her body was still tense with anger. "It's okay if you don't want to join me, Thorn. That's okay. I don't think you're cut out for what's about to happen. All I need you to do is stand aside. I'll take care of everything."

Jeremiah shook his head. "I can't do that. There's a sickness behind those walls—I know that. But don't throw out the good with the bad. The city can—"

"The city is beyond saving! I sent you to the archives so you could see for yourself how deep the rot goes. The only cure is to cut it out, and that's what I intend to do."

"Vivica, please!" Desperation tinged his voice. If only he could figure out the right thing to say, he could stop the violence about to occur. "You've seen the worst this city has to offer, and you're right to despise it. Just . . . just please believe that it can be better! We can change it together!"

"I'm going to change it. And everything and everyone that stands between me and Dramir is just as guilty."

Her eyes flashed as she advanced on him, her anger carrying her more than half the distance between them. Jeremiah heard a distant *twang*, and then an arrow plunged into Vivica's right eye. Her head whipped backward as the arrow punched out the back of her skull.

Far behind Jeremiah, Bruno threw aside a grass-covered cloak. Magic bow in hand, he fled toward Dramir as fast as his legs could carry him. Vivica's army cried out and loosed their own arrows, but few shots even neared their mark.

Vivica's good eye glared at Jeremiah. She raised a fist and stilled the army behind her. Snapping the end of arrow shaft where it penetrated her eye, she drew the rest of the arrow through the hole in her skull. Just like the knife, it left no evidence of injury.

"An assassination attempt. Your backup plan, maybe your plan all along, was to shoot me with an *arrow*." She unsheathed the magic blade at her back.

The hatred and betrayal on her face broke Jeremiah's heart as he was sure he was breaking hers. But she had left him no choice. "Not just any arrow," he said.

"It was tipped with a particularly powerful poison. Poison from a particularly powerful toad. Poison that, right now, is probably freezing you solid."

"Not a chance." She started toward him again, blade in hand. A mere five feet away now.

"Except maybe it is," Jeremiah begged. "Vivica, please listen. Maybe it is working. Maybe if you just stop now and hold still, you'll find that you can't continue. I can bring you back to the palace. You won't betray your men. I know Dramir's not perfect, but what is? Maybe you can just be paralyzed and come with me." Almost there. Please, Vivica, don't make me do this.

He hesitated a moment too long. Vivica closed the last of the distance between them in an instant and thrust her blade deep into Jeremiah's stomach. There was no pain, but Jeremiah lurched forward, clutching her armor. The lid of the chest fell shut with finality, its treasures locked within. He became aware of a quivering sensation in his stomach, an intense spreading heat. Some small part of his rapidly diminishing mind knew his guts were cooking in the magic heat of the sword.

Come.

"You blind, stupid man," she hissed. "They finally broke you. You're not just an enslaved weapon in their arsenal, you're a willing servant to their hypocrisy and tyranny." She lifted his drooping chin. Jeremiah gagged up blood, splattering her face.

Closer. Faster.

He mouthed the words but no sound came out, only flecks of blood. Black spots danced in front of him, obscuring her demonic glare. He willed her to understand anyway. He needed her to understand.

"I trusted you," she said. "I believed in you. Nothing ever made me doubt myself before you. Thank you, Jeremiah Thorn, for finally showing me what you really are, what you have been this entire time." Jeremiah's grip tightened as pain started to follow the fire inside him.

Then Vivica's eyes widened. She whispered, "But . . . that's not what happened, is it? You're not really their lap dog, are you?" She looked to the chest of treasures, sighed, and closed her eyes. She pressed her forehead to Jeremiah's.

He couldn't speak. He was barely there.

"Is it too late?"

The ground at their feet quivered, buckled. Jeremiah nodded a fraction of an inch.

They felt the earth sag beneath them.

"We could have done great things together . . ." They were falling. The ground dropped away beneath them, revealing a deep tunnel filled with grasping, clawing undead. Hunks of dirt fell into the bony vortex of limbs beneath them.

Pull.

They seized Vivica's legs and pulled her downward. She was ripped away from him and Jeremiah fell to the ground, clinging to the edge of earth that remained. Then he reached for her. He didn't know why. She grasped his hand. Time stood still as she stared at him, grudging admiration in her eyes.

More decayed hands seized her now, pulling hard. She gripped Jeremiah's arm. *She's trying to take me with her,* Jeremiah thought. *So be it. I deserve at least that much.*

But Vivica was pulling herself higher, kicking viciously at the creatures grabbing at her. In one final burst of effort she surged upward, above the lip of the pit. She released Jeremiah and grabbed the handle of the wheeled chest that balanced on the pit's edge. The fragile earth gave way, and the huge chest fell, narrowly missing Jeremiah where he clung to the edge with the little strength he had left. The chest followed Vivica down into the depths of reaching, writhing undead, where both disappeared from view.

Bury.

The deepest undead dug deeper, and the undead above began pulling earth down around them. Then a spear of golden light arced upward from the mass of bodies and earth. It splashed against Jeremiah, and his stomach instantly began to twist and knot, his flesh knitting itself back together. The pain in his guts receded as he entombed his enemy.

Dig.

The mass of undead continued downward. The earth beneath Jeremiah stopped shifting. He rested face down in the dirt and willed his undead to keep digging, to never stop dragging her deeper and deeper into the earth. Then footsteps, hundreds of them. He looked up, expecting to see Vivica's army bearing down, prepared to kill him and dig for their commander. But they were scrambling backward, reforming a defensive line.

The first of the cavalry leapt over Jeremiah's head. A massive armored steed bearing a massive armored rider. Fifty more horsemen streamed past Jeremiah toward the barbarian line, forming a charging wall of muscle and steel, their lances coated with viscous purple poison.

The cavalry smashed into the barbarian army. Lances ripped into a giant, who howled and collapsed as his legs were split by poisoned steel. He swatted at the horsemen in rage until a single rider thrust a lance through the roof of the giant's mouth and into his brain. The giant spasmed and fell still. Jeremiah recognized the rider's magic armor.

The armored cavalry broke through the line. Allison wheeled her horse around to lead the charge through them again. With a heavy heart, Jeremiah witnessed Dramir's triumphant victory and the death of Vivica's dream.

CHAPTER FORTY-TWO

Meetings

Allison and Jeremiah were nodding off, Bruno was drooling, and Delilah sat with rapt attention. It was the sixth hour of meetings with the public that day and the fourth day of an endless stream of bureaucracy that had begun the moment the cavalry returned from their charge.

An official at the other end of the long table addressed the gathered crowd. "With the last of the giants returning north, we believe the most critical threat to our security has departed."

A citizen spoke up. "Aren't you worried the army is just going to reform and come back?"

Another official responded, "The loss of their leader and source of healing has left the army no more than a loose association of tribes. Several chieftains have surrendered to us already and the others are splintering off. The reclamation of Nosirin is already underway, and we expect little serious resistance."

Jeremiah's stomach rumbled. The meeting felt interminable.

"I have a question for Mr. Thorn," someone asked.

Jeremiah forced his eyes open and looked for the source of the voice. "Um, yes. Go ahead."

"Mr. Thorn, first let me thank you for what you've done. You're a hero of the realm and an inspiration to us all." A smattering of applause.

"Thank you," Jeremiah said mechanically. "Your question?"

"Is it possible that someone might attempt to unearth Viviana Aliwyn? Are we sure she's both deceased *and* inaccessible?"

"She . . . umm. Well. The undead are still digging at this very moment, always downward when possible. If they can't travel downward, they go horizontally, looking for a way down. So, they're already quite far from Dramir. It's been requested I maintain the undead for at least a month, after which we'll review the situation again."

"Is she still alive?"

Jeremiah always hated this question. "No, I don't believe so." The truth was he couldn't bring himself to check. The undead were getting so much sensory information from each other and the environment that it would be hard to scan for signs of life. He was terrified he would discover her still struggling, still fighting—trapped but alive.

A portly man stood. He looked rich and angry.

"Necromancer! My family's private vault was pilfered by you and the other cronies in this thieving government! The gauntlets you stole were a family heirloom, crafted from the bones of—"

"Do you have a question?" Jeremiah asked.

The man huffed indignantly. "When can I expect the return of—"

"Gone forever."

"What?"

"Gone forever. Everything that went out there is gone forever. Next question."

Bruno hiccupped a sleepy laugh.

Jeremiah didn't feel like laughing. He didn't feel anything these days. He went where he was told and answered the ceaseless needling questions. All the congratulations and promises of titles and favors held no sweetness for him, the criticisms no sting.

At long last, the meeting adjourned.

"*Must* you antagonize the aristocrats?" Delilah asked Jeremiah.

"Not my fault they're antagonized. Are we done here yet?"

"No, we have one more hearing with . . ." She checked her program. "The Urban Development Guild and Builder's Hall." As she spoke, more people began filtering into the plain hall that housed the endless bureaucratic chores.

"Can I leave? Just me?" asked Allison.

"No! None of you are allowed to leave!" Delilah reached over and pinched Bruno's shoulder.

"Ow!"

"Or sleep! We're here to support Jay and help get things back to normal. Rumors are the bane of favorable reputation."

"Aren't I supposed to be a hero now? Can't I claim heroic immunity?" Jeremiah asked.

"Jay, you *literally* lost most of the money in Dramir!" said Delilah.

"Oops," said Jeremiah.

"There are some very broke nobles out there right now who are itching to see you punished for that. We need widespread public support to keep you safe," continued Delilah.

"Broke, huh?" Bruno grinned.

"Well, close to it! The economy is in shambles right now!"

"Funny, the people on the street don't seem any worse for wear."

Jeremiah leaned on his elbow while Delilah and Bruno bickered about the economic repercussions. It was as interesting as the preceding meeting.

Just before he could slip fully into a stupor, something snapped Jeremiah awake. His forehead broke out in sweat. His pulse quickened. He took a deep, cleansing breath, but a prickle of fear raced down his spine. He was cold. He was afraid.

"Jay? You all right?" Allison interrupted Delilah and Bruno's debate.

"He looks sick," said Bruno.

Delilah felt his forehead. "What's wrong?"

"He's here," said Jeremiah, scanning the hall as the last of the meeting attendees walked in.

There. Flusoh entered from the back of the room. As Jeremiah stared, he made his way toward the front row. "'Scuse me. Pardon." He stepped around the knees of seated attendees. They twisted to allow him to pass. Flusoh took a seat right in front of the table, checked his program, then glanced around, waiting for the meeting to start.

"Who's here?" Delilah whispered, eyes sweeping the crowd.

"Flusoh. Can't you see him?" Jeremiah's heart was in his throat. Allison and Bruno scrutinized the faces before them.

"Which one? Where?"

"Him, there." Jeremiah gestured with the barest of movements.

Delilah furrowed her brow. "Jay, that's Councilman Riggado of the Urban Development Guild."

"It's him."

She looked at Allison and Bruno to confirm her eyes weren't deceiving her.

"If Jay says its him . . ." Allison's eyes bore into the councilman.

"What does he want?" Delilah whispered.

"Maybe he has questions about our plans for urban development?" Jeremiah chuckled. The intensity of his fear was subsiding, whether because he was growing accustomed to it or Flusoh was consciously controlling it, he didn't know. But it was being replaced by a sense of fondness at seeing his old teacher.

"Good morning, everyone." The official in charge started the meeting. If it weren't for Flusoh, it would have been the most boring one yet, but Jeremiah could sense his friends' tension. The discussion on rebuilding warehouses and grain store supplies washed over Jeremiah as he watched the lich nod thoughtfully along with whoever was speaking.

Flusoh raised his hand. Allison and Bruno gripped the table.

"Yes, sir?" the official said.

"Thank you," said Flusoh, standing. "While I recognize that pilfering the crypts and cemeteries was necessary for Mr. Thorn's plans, my colleagues and I are wondering if the newly vacated burial grounds will be put back into use."

"Thank you for your question, Councilman Riggado. We are grateful to those who served the city in its most dire moment. The graves will be repaired and remain unfilled, and the families will receive minor remunerations."

"Thank you." Flusoh sat.

A handful more questions finally concluded the day's meetings. As people filed out, Flusoh approached Jeremiah, his horrible cord-pierced eyeballs boring into Jeremiah's.

"Mr. Thorn," Flusoh asked, "do you have the time for a quick private discussion about cobblestones or something?"

"I do, but I'll have to insist my associates join us for the discussion."

"Couldn't care less! Meet me in the back room."

Flusoh exited into the small waiting room used to corral speakers before their time.

Allison leapt up, her hand on her sword. "What does he want?"

"I have no idea," said Jeremiah. "Easiest just to ask."

"I don't like you talking with that . . . *thing!*"

Delilah shushed Allison's outburst and waved away the few people who had paused to see what the commotion was about.

"Just relax, all of you," said Jeremiah. "I don't think he's going to do anything bad." Jeremiah could see his friends were still frightened. He didn't blame them.

Jeremiah bade his friends follow. The doorknob of the speaker's room was ice-cold. He took a deep breath and opened the door.

Flusoh was leaning back in a chair, idly folding his program. "Kid!" he cried as they entered. "Come on in! Bring your friends. You'll all fit."

"Hey, Flusoh!" Jeremiah said. Now that the shock had worn off, he was actually excited to see Flusoh again.

Flusoh must have dropped his glamour, for Delilah gasped when she entered the room. Allison only pursed her lips, but Bruno wavered on his feet and went deathly pale. "Oh, gross . . ." he whispered.

"Rude but true!" Flusoh laughed and snapped his teeth together. "You know, Jay, when I saw you leaving my castle I thought to myself, 'He'll be dead in a week.' Thought I must have been right, too, when I felt your graduation gift pop. What the hell did that?"

"Goblin Matriarch."

"Ah, that'll do it. Ugh, not even the worst part of the goblin life cycle." Flusoh stood and extended a hand toward Jeremiah's friends. "Hello there, folks, my name is Flusoh. As I'm sure you know, I was Jeremiah's teacher."

Bruno and Allison stood stock still, but Delilah reached out a quivering hand and shook Flusoh's bony one. "Delilah Fortune. A pleasure, Mr. Flusoh."

"Aaah, the counselor. Takes guts to stick up for a necromancer. Jeremiah owes you a big one for that."

"No, no! We're straight, I promise." Delilah's smile wasn't reaching her eyes, despite how wide she was stretching it.

"Nonsense! The world needs more people willing to defend necromancers. Here . . ." Flush reached into a pocket and fished out a blackened fingerbone. A scrap of parchment was tied to it with a sinewy cord. He dropped it in Delilah's hand. "You ever need me, whether you're in a scrap or need information or just need someone to chat with, snap that bone in half, and I'll come a-runnin'!" Flusoh moved his arms in a pantomime of running.

"Thank you. That's very thoughtful." Delilah's smile was still all teeth, but Jeremiah watched her carefully stow it in a secure pocket.

"So, to what do I owe the pleasure?" Jeremiah asked.

"Kid, you've done so remarkably well that I've decided it's time to further your education. Oh, I've got all sorts of great things to teach you, but first is gonna be Abominations. They are just *so* fun!"

At Flusoh's offer, Jeremiah's old ambitions bubbled to the surface. He had come so far, perhaps he really could become that great and powerful mage. Then he remembered the man in the closet and his enthusiasm ran cold. He didn't want power in a dank castle anymore, didn't want the responsibility that he had failed to keep. He wasn't sure what it was that he did want, but he knew becoming a greater necromancer wasn't it.

"Flusoh, I'm sorry to have to tell you this, but I won't be joining you."

Flusoh's skull tilted. "Really."

Jeremiah heard a low rasp behind him as Allison began to draw her sword. "Really. I greatly appreciate what you've done for me. I wouldn't be where I am today without you, but . . . I'm giving up necromancy."

"Well, okay!" Flusoh said. "Fine by me."

"Wait, Really?"

"Kid, I'm not worried. Power justifies its own use, and you've got a lot of it. I know you've got some moral hang-ups right now—believe me, we all go through it. But when you're ready to get back on the horse, you just come on home!"

There were footsteps outside the door. It flew open with a slam, revealing the portly aristocrat who had yelled at Jeremiah earlier.

"There you are, necromancer! You can't hide from me, traitorous coward! You owe me my fortune, and I'll see you strung up by your thumbs if—"

The color drained from the man all at once. He dropped like a rag doll.

"Oh no! He died!" said Flusoh.

Delilah leapt to the man and rolled him over. "He's ice-cold." She shuddered. "It's like he's been dead for days."

"Well, I'm gonna head out," said Flusoh. "You be good, kid. Don't let the naysayers get you down. Delilah, Bruno, Allison, pleasure to meet you all. I'm just gonna squeeeeeze by you there, thank you. Come on, buddy, you're coming with me." The aristocrat's corpse dutifully clambered to its feet. "All right, then! You take care, you crazy kids." And just like that, Jeremiah's teacher was gone.

CHAPTER FORTY-THREE

The End

Jeremiah was procrastinating. He was supposed to be packing up his bedroom in preparation for leaving in the morning. After all, there was nothing keeping him in Dramir—no outstanding payments, no court mandates, no siege of the city. In fact there were more reasons to leave than to stay; he had become public enemy number one in the eyes of the highest levels of Dramir's nobility. But most of his things were still strewn around the room. The thirst to prove himself that had once driven him to the open road had been more than sated.

"Hey, Jay?" Delilah called from downstairs. "Are you still packing?"

Jeremiah cringed. They'd been talking about taking him out for some sort of last hurrah, but he didn't feel much like celebrating his newfound freedom. He got up anyway. He would finish in the morning.

Delilah, Bruno, and Allison were waiting for him downstairs, but Jeremiah immediately sensed something off about the scene. He paused. "What is it?"

"Well, we've been thinking," started Delilah. She looked to Bruno and Allison for confirmation. Bruno gave a hardy nod and Allison gestured for her to continue. "We know you've been talking about leaving Dramir tomorrow, and we definitely don't want to get in the way of any plans you have, but we would be remiss to let you go without asking—would you be interested in becoming an equal signed partner in the Delilah, Bruno, and Allison Adventuring Corporation on a non–per diem basis?"

Delilah's words came faster and faster as she spoke so that Jeremiah wasn't certain he'd heard the last part correctly. Had she really said what he thought she said?

Allison sighed and rolled her eyes. "Jay, do you want to officially join us? Stay here and be a member of the party?"

Jeremiah's heart leapt, but he resisted the rush of excitement. "I'm not a necromancer anymore, remember? The thing with Vivica was a one-off."

"We know that," said Bruno. "We were all there when you told the king you were quitting, remember?"

Jeremiah shook his head. "You're famous now. I'm sure you can find a mage to join you who can actually be useful on missions."

"We're not asking because we want you to cast spells, Jay," said Delilah. "We're asking because we want you to be part of the family."

Delilah's words hung in the air while Jeremiah struggled to process them. He had caused his friends no end of trouble, stress, and grief. Six months ago, they were ready to kill him. Now they were talking about family. Tears welled up in his eyes, but he tried to keep his voice even. "Yeah. Okay, yeah. I'd really like that."

There was a long pause. The others stared at him expectantly. He wondered if they were waiting for some sort of speech until he blinked and a single tear escaped down his cheek. The room erupted in an uproar, with groans of dismay from Bruno and Delilah and shouts of jubilation from Allison.

"That counts!" shouted Allison. "I told you he'd cry when we asked him. I knew it! You both owe me a drink!"

"Yeah, yeah," grumbled Delilah, though she was smiling. "Welcome aboard, Jay. I have some paperwork for you to sign."

Delilah hugged him and Bruno dabbed at Jeremiah's eyes with a handkerchief. Jeremiah laughed. Despite having gone nowhere, he had arrived home.

It was a typical evening in the Fortune household. A potato stew on the stove filled the room with an enticing fragrance. Jeremiah was reading on the couch in front of the fireplace, enjoying its warmth in contrast with the dismal rain falling outside. He became dimly aware of the rapid scribbling from where Delilah and Bruno conspired behind a stack of papers. Delilah occasionally paused to consult Gus, who sat on the table.

"What are you two working on now?" he asked.

"Contracts for land sales," said Delilah. "A lot of nobles are having to sell off plots of their land to laborers." Delilah had been spearheading multiple public initiatives in Dramir in the wake of the economic crisis. The foundations of many great and powerful houses had crumbled, and the city was ripe for change.

"Land for laborers?" Jeremiah asked. "How can the laborers afford that?"

Delilah waved the paper she was working on. "We've been doing some community organizing to give people the chance to purchase these plots as a conglomerate."

"Oh. Well, that's nice." Jeremiah didn't fully follow what she had said, but more people owning land sounded like a good thing. The public education initiative had been more straightforward.

"This girl's doing good work," said Bruno. "Getting the downtrodden organized isn't easy, but she's making it worth the effort."

"Speaking of which," said Allison, "do we have any new leads for work? We're practically downtrodden ourselves." She was curled up on the other end of Jeremiah's couch with a book about technical fighting.

"No leads yet," Bruno said. "Well, I guess there was the one about a dragon. Reward is pretty good. Anyone interested in hunting a dragon?"

"Hell no," said Delilah at the same time Allison asked, "What's it pay?"

"Okay, I'll put that one in the 'maybe' pile."

Allison reached a foot to tap the book Jeremiah was reading. "What's that?"

"*Fundamental Principles of Enchanting*. If I'm not going to be a necromancer, I should learn to help in some other way."

"Cool," said Allison. "Always wanted a glowing sword. What can enchantments do?"

"Anything, apparently."

"Do we have any new hearings tomorrow?" asked Bruno.

"Nope," said Delilah. "We should be done with mandatory meetings for a while. That said, I could always use Jeremiah at some of these events. Your name brings a lot of people around."

"I can do that." Jeremiah liked the idea of being able to be useful again. He looked up from his book, taking in the moment. The tattoo of rain against the windows made the fire feel even warmer.

Necromancy had started as his escape from a dull provincial existence. It had brought him to the headsman's block, to infamy and bondage, and eventually to the adoration he'd craved. Maybe Flusoh had been right, maybe one day Jeremiah would take up the mantle of necromancer again—one day, after his nightmares turned back into dreams. But whether or not that day came to pass, he knew family would be beside him.

About the Author

Jack Pembroke is the author of the Necromancer's End series, originally released on Royal Road. He brings his twenty-five years as a Dungeon Master to the page in stories of adventure and kinship featuring strong characters. He believes in struggle as a primary source of drama and that weaknesses make characters (like humans) more believable. Pembroke also has a dog; he's a good boy.